OFF THE RAILS

Sìne Peril

Printed in the United States of America

First October 2018
This edition August 2024

ISBN: 979-8-3303-0807-1

For my mom, who inspired my interest in history and
historical fiction. You are always my number one
audience.
Also for the "residents" of the Ohio Village, both past
and present. You have each inspired and educated me
in your own unique ways.

And in loving memory of the real Mary Lou Hurst.

chapter one

November 1865

Moonlight cast my bedchamber in an eerie blue glow. Shadows softened the corners of the furniture, turning them into ominous creatures lurking in the darkness. Somewhere in those shadows, *something* watched me with an intensity that pulled me from restless slumber.

I'd been consumed with a lingering dread since dinner, but it sharpened suddenly when I spied the figure on the other side of my bedchamber. Was it merely a trick of the light? Or something else entirely?

Cold sweat dripped down the back of my neck. I pressed myself back against pillows, my breath coming in ragged gasps as I gave the figure a name.

"James."

A small smile traced its way across his pale, shadowed face. He was thinner, but so handsome in his blue army uniform. It was not as crisp as when I'd waved farewell at the train station three years earlier, but I didn't think I could ever grow tired of seeing my husband in the gold officer's braid.

My chest tightened at the blood staining the front of it. It dripped down the side of his face, and welled from a wound in his chest. I fought the urge to recoil, even as I wanted to run to him. I lay frozen in bed, unable to move either way. I closed my eyes, willing the image away. He wasn't supposed to be here. He was hundreds of miles away. This wasn't right, it wasn't time—

He was by my side in an instant, a cold hand on my forehead. "Be easy, my darling. You've nothing to fear. I'm right here."

"But—"

"Shh. Rest. There will be time enough for worries in the morning."

My eyes squeezed shut in a vain attempt to keep tears at bay. "You've come to say good-bye, haven't you?"

"I'm sorry I couldn't do it in person."

"I'm sorry you have to do it at all."

"Give Olivia my love."

"I will." A single tear escaped from the corner of my eye. I brushed it away.

When I opened my eyes, I was alone, save for the icy depression in the bedclothes at my side.

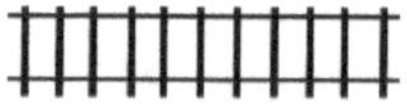

The telegram came the next day. Black script on yellowish paper. *Dear Mrs. Andrews, Regret to inform you Capt. J. Andrews killed last night.* It was signed by his aide de camp, Private Hamilton.

I'd hoped—prayed—it was a mistake. That the vision was the result of an anxious mind given to too little sleep. But I knew in my heart that was the last conversation I would ever have with my husband.

Two days after the telegram, I was on a train to Washington City to collect his belongings, and, if I could manage it, his body. I watched the countryside flash past, first New York, then Pennsylvania and Maryland. Bare branches stabbed skyward like the pitchforks of an angry mob, protesting the churned earth still bearing scars of battles and mass graves.

With more than forty-eight sleepless hours to contemplate the vision, one question nagged at me through the packing and preparations: How could my husband have been killed when the war had been over for six months?

I turned this question over and over in my mind during the long hours in the sitting room of my private car. Once, it had been *our* car. We always traveled together. It was one of the rewards of owning a rail road company.

I hadn't used it since his departure, however, preferring to travel first class when it was only myself to worry about. Why waste the resources with a war on?

But the company insisted it was my right to use it, that under the circumstances, it was my due. Still, it felt like a betrayal to have another man in James's seat—his business partner, Gunther Richardson. I was thankful, at least, for the wall of newsprint between us. While I may have required a male escort for such a long journey, I was hardly in the mood to play gracious hostess. Despite our long acquaintance, we'd never really gotten along.

At least he is easily distracted, I thought, consulting the watch around my neck, a gift from my husband—my *late* husband, I reminded myself—and addressed my maid. "Colleen, would you please check on our luggage? We should be arriving soon."

Colleen vanished into the adjoining car. I stared down at the Celtic knot work on the back of the watch. "A true railroad man always needs a good watch," James had said, draping it gently around my neck. "Punctuality is the key."

"That must go double for me, then, since I'm usually the reason you're on time, watch or no," I laughed. He had kissed the tip of my nose, the way he always did when he was teasing me.

The memory made tears spring to my eyes. I blinked them back before Mr. Richardson could see.

He folded up his newspaper, leaving it on the side table. "We should be nearly at our destination," he said, consulting his own timepiece. "Ten minutes."

I set aside the knitting I'd been ignoring and the book I hadn't been reading, tucking them both back into my valise. Ahead, the tracks curved to the right and I caught my first glimpse of Washington since before the war. The entire city was surrounded by fortifications now, though nearly all of them were abandoned these past few months. I wondered how long it would be until they were removed—or even if they would be removed.

My companion's voice pulled me from my contemplation of the horizon. "We shall see you settled into a hotel straight away. While you are resting, I'll go to headquarters and—"

"No, Mr. Richardson. Please. I understand your urge to help, but I would prefer to handle my own affairs."

His eyes widened in shock. "My dear, I wish only to make this trying time easier for you to bear. James was my dearest friend, nearly a brother to me. There will be many more trials once we return home. At least allow me to share this burden with you while I can."

I offered him an apologetic smile and accepted the offer of his hand as the train began to slow. "I'm sorry. I have spoken sharply and it was not my intent. I am overwrought. But my husband has always treated me as his right hand; I will not fail him in death. I will handle his affairs personally. It's the least I can do." Mr. Richardson might have been my husband's business partner, but the man was a snake. I didn't want him anywhere near our personal affairs.

Our truce reached, I allowed Mr. Richardson to escort me from the train, pulling my hated veil of black crepe down over my face.

It was strange, after nearly ten years, how some parts of the city seemed untouched while others were so different. Entire swaths of land had been developed, or their contents torn down and rebuilt to house the burgeoning population. As the train slowed, it passed clusters of tents, housing the poor or displaced. Every inch of the city bore the signs of the recent conflict, but there was something else there, too. The sun was out, the air crisp but not cold; a far cry from Buffalo, where winter was already in full swing. The war was over. Our beloved president was dead. But despite the black bunting still draped in some doorways, rebuilding had begun.

We disembarked, leaving Colleen to direct the porters with the luggage. Mr. Richardson summoned a cab and in short order we were jostling though packed streets toward our hotel.

"Have you been to this city before, Mrs. Andrews?" Mr. Richardson asked.

"Once. Several years ago. I've not been back since the war started. Washington was a different city, then."

"Piece of advice, ma'am," said the driver, looking over his shoulder to fix me with one weary blue eye. "Don't go out at night, and don't go nowhere alone."

"The war is over, my good man. Surely the streets cannot be as dangerous as all that," laughed my escort, but he looked uneasily at a group of negro workmen passing by.

"War is over, but hardship's not. Lotsa folk lost everything they had, and a lot of 'em is tryin' to get it back. A fine lady like yourself, there, ma'am, you might see how a desperate man might take an opportunity anywhere he sees it." The cabbie nodded to me, and my gloved hand went reflexively to the watch around my neck. He turned back to the road.

Mr. Richardson glowered at the man. "See here, sir! You have distressed the poor woman. Can you not see she is a widow? Newly made, even, here to collect what remains of her husband—"

"Mr. Richardson!" I said sharply.

The cabbie looked back at me, pity in the blue eye. He tipped his hand with his free hand. "My apologies, Missus. No harm meant. Opposite, in fact. I sees you from out of town, and wanted to offer a bit of friendly advice."

"Your advice has been noted, thank you," I said tersely. I turned my gaze back to my companion. He gave a sharp little nod, which I assumed was meant to be taken as an apology.

At long last, we reached our hotel. The Willard Hotel was the finest in the area, only a few blocks from the White House. Though the street out front showed some wear, the building itself was in fine form, as though war had never touched it. I took Mr. Richardson's elbow and allowed him to lead me up the front steps to the registration desk, and did not object as he arranged for our rooms and hot baths.

"You must be exhausted, Mrs. Andrews. Please, allow me to take care of the remainder of the arrangements," he said as we moved towards the stairs.

"No. I'm all right. I'll rest tonight. It's already almost time for dinner, too late to be making calls. I'll sleep tonight and we will begin first thing in the morning. I need to speak with the officer in charge. I'll send Colleen around with my card. Is that the way things are done when one calls on military personnel? I am not certain..." Suddenly, I was certain of nothing except that I wanted out of my corset and into bed. The journey had been long, made longer by the pell-mell fashion in which it was arranged.

"I'll see to it he is expecting you after breakfast," Mr. Richardson said with a nod.

He left me at my door with a kiss on the hand. As soon as he was gone, I wiped my glove off on my skirt.

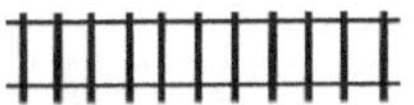

True to his promise, Colonel Seagraves was waiting for us the next morning, bright and early. He greeted us warmly, and after perfunctory introductions, ushered us into his commandeered office in one of the finer homes in the area. There was an abused piano pushed into a corner and the walls were lined with books of literature, music, and nature that clearly held more appeal for the previous occupant. Only the broad mahogany desk appeared to be as well loved and cared for as it deserved, though it, too, bore the battle scars of hard use.

The man himself was stout and mustached with dark hair fading quickly to gray. "Mrs. Andrews. Such a pleasure to meet you, despite the circumstances. Captain Andrews always said such wonderful things about you."

I opened my mouth to thank him, but for some reason the words would not come.

"Excuse me," I said quickly, retrieving a handkerchief from my reticule. I had been calm and collected since the telegram came, but suddenly the sound of my husband's name on a stranger's lips undid me.

The men allowed me several self-conscious moments to regain my composure before I continued. "I—thank you, sir. My apologies. I don't know what came over me just now."

"Nothing to worry about, Mrs. Andrews," the colonel said, his brown eyes softening. "I understand completely. Please, allow me to offer my condolences." Though he must have been very busy, his eyes were patient and kind.

I nodded, not trusting to my voice.

My companion cleared his throat. "Perhaps, in light of Mrs. Andrews' distress, we might dispense with some of the formalities...?"

"Certainly." The colonel removed a box from his lower desk drawer. "The Captain's secretary has seen to his belongings. I've already arranged to have his trunk and the coffin delivered to the R&A depot. We've followed the instructions from your telegram.

He should…that is…everything should be in order for your journey home." He'd been embalmed then, and placed a finer casket than the simple pine boxes the military ordered *en masse*.

I closed my eyes to will back the tears, and regretted removing my veil upon entering the office. Why did my emotions choose that moment to betray me?

"These are his effects, those items in his possession at the time of his death." He offered the box to us, and Mr. Richardson took it, swallowing audibly as he laid it in his lap. It was hard to tell through my own misty eyes, but he seemed near to tears himself.

With great difficulty, I forced myself to ask, "How…the telegram did not say what happened. How did James…?"

Mr. Richardson put a hand out, as if to stop me. "Now, Mrs. Andrews. You are over set. I'm certain details are not necessary."

"I did not ask for details. Only the reason I am now a widow. In case you haven't noticed, the war ended in April. It's November." My voice was harsher than intended. Dabbing once again at my eyes, I took as deep a breath as my corset—and my grief—would allow.

The colonel nodded. "Washington is a city still in turmoil, Mrs. Andrews. The war is over, but many Southerners are still fighting. Jim—that is, Captain Andrews—was off duty. He'd gone out with some of the boys in his company. He did that from time to time, especially during the war. Helped to keep moral up."

I smiled. "That sounds like him. He was always thinking about his men, even at the railroad. He could have just stayed in his office, but he would always go down to the yard, talking to the conductors and the engineers, even the boys who shovel coal. He started out working with them, and even after we made our fortune, he never forgot how it felt to come home covered in dust." Good god, I would miss that man.

Across the desk, the colonel smiled warmly. "Yes. Jim was a great man. Always looking out for those around him. He was coming back a little early from the gathering. At any rate, he was walking back with Private Hamilton, his aide, when they were attacked.

"We've done a lot in the last few months to make Washington a more peaceful city, but there are still some...*unsavory* elements. Bad feelings lingering since those Rebs have been defeated. Sometimes they form a gang, and take out their aggressions on those they see responsible for their hardships. Private Hamilton was lucky to survive. As it was, he was badly injured, and will likely not return to duty.

"I'm sorry, Mrs. Andrews. I wish I'd been with him that night. Then maybe you wouldn't be sitting here today."

I nodded, my throat so tight I could barely breathe. I twisted my handkerchief between my fingers, so tight I thought it would tear.

The colonel's face crumpled with pity. "We're perpetually short on supplies here, but I think I can rustle up some coffee if you'd care for some?"

"Thank you for your hospitality, but we won't take up any more of your time," I managed. I held out a hand but instead of giving me the box, Mr.

Richardson linked my fingers through the crook of his arm and began walking back towards the door.

I bit the inside of my cheek to keep from saying something unladylike. Long training in social graces could only do so much when confronted with grief and too little sleep.

"You were very quiet on the drive. You must be tired. Perhaps you should go upstairs and rest," Mr. Richardson said as we alighted at the hotel. "I have a few matters to look into, but I will join you for dinner later."

"I feel quite well actually," I said firmly, holding out my hand. "But I would like my husband's effects."

He looked at me in surprise, as though shocked a widow might want her husband's belongings. "This? Oh, of course. I was merely holding on to it for you."

"Yes, I see that. But I would like to be the one to hold on to it now." He was still holding the box. I wiggled my waiting fingers.

"I only wanted to clean things up. Make sure there was nothing to disturb your delicate sensibilities. The items may not be…clean."

"I appreciate your concern, but I assure you I am not stranger to blood."

"Yes, but—"

"Mr. Richardson, I would like that box!" My voice rose ever so slightly in frustration. Damnable man! Why wouldn't he just hand it over?

A burst of anger flashed across his face, but was gone suddenly, replaced with a hearty laugh. "Of course. Here you are then." He practically threw it into my hands. I nearly dropped it. "I was merely trying to be helpful, but obviously my concern is not needed. I'll see you this evening, Sophia."

Always pale, I felt the remaining blood drain from my face. "That is very forward of you Mr. Richardson."

"What? We have known each other quite some time now. Over fifteen years. Certainly I should be able to call you by your Christian name by this point?" He smiled, but I saw the serpent in his eyes. I'd watched him charm other men's wives at dinner parties, but those women seldom saw him more than a few times a year. I saw him several times a week.

"I think it is quite inappropriate for you to be so familiar with me when I am in mourning. Now if you will excuse me, I think I shall take advantage of that rest you mentioned. Good day." I turned and walked quickly away.

Once back in the safety of my own room, I locked the door and set the box down on the coverlet and kneeling beside it with my fingers resting on the lid.

Hands shaking, I opened it.

When I woke some hours later I was still kneeling on the floor and as stiff as old wood. I felt like my face had been stuffed with cotton. My eyes ached from crying, and my feet had fallen asleep. There was a kink in my neck like a railroad spike, and I thought someone might have taken the sledgehammer to the side of my head.

Scattered on the quilt were the remains of my husband's last night: His marks of rank and his sidearm. A tintype of the three of us, taken when

Olivia was ten years old, just a few years before the war. His wallet. A pencil stub and a scrap of paper with a hastily drawn sketch illustrating the best way to win at darts, mathematically speaking.

I traced each item with a fingertip. The mother-of-pearl handle on his revolver and the tooled leather holster; the edges of his medals and the much-abused case protecting the photograph. His handwriting.

Someone knocked. I jumped, dropping the photograph.

"Mrs. Andrews? It's nearly time for dinner. I've come to help you dress, if you've a mind to go down," Colleen said through the door joining our rooms.

Gathering myself, I smoothed my hair and got awkwardly to my feet. "Yes. Yes, Colleen, come in." The photo case was still on the floor. I bent to pick it up, smiling at James in his finest suit, pocket watch in hand, with Olivia at his side. His free hand rested on her shoulder affectionately.

I snapped it shut as the maid bustled into the room. "I saw you were asleep earlier, and thought you must need your rest. Mr. Richardson has gone out for the afternoon to attend to some business, he said, but he should be back in time for dinner."

"Business?" What on earth could he be working on now, when he had come to claim his friend's body?

"For the railroad, ma'am. He didn't say what. I expect he's arranging for the return journey." She helped me put away the things on the bed, then went to the wardrobe and produced another black dress for me to wear to dinner.

More black. I would have to get used to it, I

supposed.

"Do you want the jet earrings tonight, or the enamel?"

"Jet, Colleen. And for tomorrow, the smaller bonnet. I feel as if I can't see anything with blinders and veil on." I'd nearly walked into at least three soldiers during our earlier outing, simply because the long sides of my bonnet prevented me from seeing anything not directly in front—and that view was obscured by the veil. I likely would have broken my neck on the stairs, if I'd not be holding Mr. Richardson's arm.

"Of course, ma'am. I'll set it out now, if you like."

An hour later I had been cleaned up and made presentable enough for the hotel dining room. As I left my room, Mr. Richardson was just leaving his. He cleared his throat, glancing at me up and down in surprise. "You plan to eat in the dinning room tonight? I thought you would take your meals in your room. As you are in mourning."

"The rules of etiquette state that I may withdraw from society, Mr. Richardson. Not that I must. Tonight I feel inclined to eat among company." *Though now I am starting to regret it*, I thought. Maybe a tray in my room with Colleen for company wouldn't be so bad, if the alternative was dinning with my current companion. I'd been hoping to slip down and eat alone before his return.

Those hopes were dashed, however, when he offered his arm. With an inward sigh I took it and once again allowed him to lead me to our destination.

"Is everything well?" I asked. Jesus, Mary, and Joseph. The man had the conversational skills of an end table when he wasn't inclined to be charming.

"What? Of course. Why shouldn't it be?"

"Colleen mentioned you had some business to take care of this afternoon. I hope everything is well with the railroad. I understand business is a little...uncertain, now that James is gone."

"Don't worry yourself, my dear. Things will continue on just as smoothly as they ever did. James has hardly even been involved with the company these three years, except in name."

I raised an eyebrow. James was first approached by the government in '62, as a civilian contractor. He could have sat out the war in comfort and luxury, as many of our class had, but he wasn't that sort of man. Instead he volunteered, and due to his knowledge and experience was given a place of leadership with the engineers stationed in the capital. Before he left, he'd placed everything in my name, as his custodian, should the worst happen. It was an unusual arrangement, as businesses went. At least the law was finally beginning to recognize that families could not stay afloat when their women did not legally exist or have any means of providing for themselves.

"My husband hardly left the business to wither on the vine, Mr. Richardson. If you remember correctly, I myself brokered the compromise with Mr. Rochester and Mr. Blackburn when we acquired their lines in Pennsylvania last year." Mr. Blackburn in particular insisted he would not deal with us, until I convinced him over one of my famous dinner parties that it really was in his best interest to sell.

Mr. Richardson waved a dismissive hand. "Of course, of course. But it hardly matters now that he's gone. Speaking of…did he, by chance, write to you concerning the business?"

"What do you mean?"

"Oh, he just mentioned some projects he wanted to implement once he got back home, but was rather vague on the details. I thought he might have said something to you."

What exactly was he getting at? "He mentioned his eagerness to work on the western expansion."

"Is that all? Well, that's all anyone is talking about these days." The government wanted to put a line all the way through to California and the Pacific Ocean. R&A was already working on a bid for the project, but competition was stiff.

We were shown to a table by the window. Looking around at the crystal chandeliers, the crisp white linen, and the well-dressed people at the tables, it was hard to imagine cannon fire and rifle shot just a few miles away. The darkness outside reflected the dinning room back at us, showing off the opulence that hadn't been diminished by years of fighting, disease, and short supplies, while outside the poor lived in tents and the city was littered with hospitals only just returning to the original functions as churches, schools, or private houses.

"The privileged always come out on top," I muttered, examining the carved trim around the ceiling.

"Here, here," Mr. Richardson said, gesturing to the waiter. I tried not to roll my eyes at his clear misunderstanding of my point.

Our meal came shortly thereafter. The bill of fare had listed long strings of French words that roughly boiled down into cold soup, fish, seasoned mashed potatoes, steak, wine, and a plate of cheese for desert. It was delicious, but being surrounded by such a showy display of wealth suddenly had me homesick for the boarding house we lived in, before Gunther Richardson, before R&A. Back when James came home covered in grease and coal dust, and a side of gristly beef was cause for celebration. It hadn't been warm, but it had been cozy.

It had been hard—so hard—but in a way, I did miss it. That boarding house had been our testing ground, where we proved ourselves, and our marriage, strong enough to take on the world.

Though I certainly didn't miss hauling buckets of water up two flights of stairs every day, especially not at seven or eight months with child.

I could still picture that kitchen table, covered in drawings and bits of metal and tools. James was convinced he could create a stabilizing force, something to provide a smoother ride that would make rail travel, then still in its infancy, not only more comfortable for passengers, but safer for cargo and more efficient to fuel in the long run.

He was right. A year later, I nearly despaired of our situation—Olivia was due to be born any day, the harsh Buffalo winter covered the entire city in a layer of ice an inch thick. But once the tracks were cleared he presented his idea to Garfield Richardson. The senior Mr. Richardson hadn't been overly impressed but his son, Gunther, had been—sufficiently so that he left his father's company to start his own with James. The R&A Railworks began by manufacturing cars for all the major lines, before laying tracks of its own—eventually connecting Buffalo to more than two hundred cities from New York to Mississippi.

With so many holdings in the south, we could have lost everything, but James was clever and charming. By the time the first round of three-month soldiers were coming to the end of their tour, he secured contracts with the Union Army, leaving his partner to concentrate on expanding the lines westward, instead of south. James's advice to the military on the movement of supplies and the infrastructure necessary to deliver them resulted in the commission with the Engineer Corps.

He could have declined. He could have even hired someone to take his place in the draft.

But not my James.

Lost in memory, I took several bites before I realized Mr. Richardson was addressing me. "...checked the timetables. We can be on our way home by nine o'clock tomorrow morning."

"I would like to stay for a few days, actually."

He froze with his spoon halfway to his open mouth. "Stay? I thought you would want to get home to Olivia as soon as possible. And there is the funeral to plan, after all."

"Certainly. But there are some things I would like to do."

Mr. Richardson put down his spoon. "Such as?"

"Calls to family friends. It seems appropriate, under the circumstances."

"Under the circumstances, they should be coming to you."

"Nonsense. If I stay in my room waiting for callers, I shall go mad. I need an occupation, even if it is only taking a carriage from one end of town to the other.”

When he looked ready to object, I favored him with the same indulgent look I gave my daughter when her temper was up. “Two days, that's all. Besides, I imagine you will have business to take care of yourself. Now would be the perfect time to woo congressmen about that westward expansion contract. Colleen can join me for my calls; you needn't be taken from your work.”

It was so infallibly practical he could hardly argue. James always said that was my greatest strength—and my secret weapon. No one could argue when I presented the facts plainly.

“Very well—”

“I checked earlier. There's a train at eight o’clock in the evening the day after tomorrow, and it's on a more direct route than the one tomorrow. We'll be back in Buffalo in time for lunch the next day.”

With a heavy sigh, he resigned himself to the new plan and went back to his dinner. “Well. I suppose we are staying then. I'll make the arrangements.”

chapter two

The next day, veiled and accompanied by Colleen, I set off to make my calls. The maid followed at a respectable distance as I strode through the streets, the swath of black crepe covering me from the top of my head to my knees.

"I'm sorry ma'am, but this is a military establishment. You can't enter without a pass or an appointment," said the uniformed young man guarding the front door of the house we had visited the day before.

I produced my card. "I understand. I wonder if you might help me then, or perhaps ask Colonel Seagraves if he could spare a few moments for Mrs. Andrews? I am trying to find Private First Class Joshua Hamilton."

While he went to make the inquiry, Colleen and I waited on the steps while the young man went into the foyer and spoke to someone inside.

"Ma'am, I thought we were going to see your relations?" she whispered.

"Colleen, I don't have any relatives. You know that. But we are doing the next best thing. Now, please do be quiet. And whatever happens, you saw and heard nothing, do you understand? Particularly if someone asks about it."

She looked even more confused, but eventually nodded. "Yes, Mrs. Andrews." She lowered her head as if her black lace gloves held the secrets of the universe. I nodded approval and turned as the young guard reemerged.

"Ma'am? Private Hamilton is on medical leave. But I found out where he's staying." He handed me a slip of paper with an address on it.

"Can you tell me how far this is?" I asked, holding up the paper.

After gaining directions, we set off again. Ten minutes later, we arrived outside another commandeered home, this one three stories of red brick with white Grecian columns and a veranda.

There were uniformed men everywhere—smoking on the porch, talking in the yard.

"Can I help you there, ma'am?" called a bearded man with a cigar dangling from his mouth. He was playing checkers with another soldier, a little slenderer and less long in the tooth. The one with the beard seemed too startled by our appearance to remember a gentleman would have put out his cigar in a lady's presence.

I wrinkled my nose and tried to ignore the slight, if not the smell. "I am looking for a Private Hamilton. I was told he could he found here."

The bearded man got slowly to his feet. "You family?"

"He was my late husband's secretary. I should like to speak with him, if it is at all possible."

He removed the cigar quickly, stubbing it out on a china plate already overflowing with ash. "Mrs. Andrews."

"Yes, Colonel."

He bowed. "Jim's wife?"

"Yes."

"I'm sorry for your loss. Captain Andrews was a

real good man."

My voice came out flimsy and strained. "Yes."

"I'm afraid Private Hamilton is in no shape to come down just now. His injuries, while not life threatening—for the moment, anyway—do limit his mobility somethin' considerable."

"For the moment? What happened to him?"

The Colonel's opponent saw fit to jump in at this point. "Why, the same thing that happened to Captain Andrews, ma'am. The same band of ruffians that killed your husband shot Hamilton in the knee and gave him a crack on the head. The doctors wanted to keep him in the hospital, but when he found out what happened to your husband, he insisted on coming back here to pack up his things personally. Nearly did him in. He's been bedridden since."

"Then I really must see him. Can you show me to his room?"

With some reluctance, the Lieutenant nodded. "Mind, you'll have to excuse the mess. We're just rough soldiers here, and there's no lady's touch to keep things tidy."

"I shall walk as if with blinders." It was not a hard promise to keep, as my bonnet served much the same purpose.

Colleen and I followed the Colonel up to the second floor to a lovely but feminine room with blue paper on the walls and a feather bed. The dressing table had been converted into a writing desk, and books of science and engineering lined the top of a chest of drawers, but any other personal effects had been tidily packed up, as though the occupant was about to take a journey. The only familiar thing was the battered trunk at the foot of the bed, much more beaten and abused than when I'd packed it three years earlier.

I clutched the timepiece at my neck like a ward against distress and tried to keep the sudden prick of tears at bay.

"Private Hamilton's room is just through there," he said, pointing to a small room that would have belonged to a lady's maid. "I'll see if he's awake."

Colleen put a light hand on my arm. "Are you well, Mrs. Andrews?" she whispered with concern.

I nodded and tried to smile. "I'm fine. It comes in waves, is all."

Straightening my spine, I took a deep, steadying breath as he returned.

"He's awake. Just a few minutes, though. Poor man's worn himself out."

I agreed and entered the tiny room, little more than a closet. There was a desk and trunk, a narrow bed, nightstand, and not much else. I squeezed my wide skirts between the bed and the desk to take the chair. They bumped a pair of crutches, sending them sliding sideways toward the oil lamp on the night stand. I caught them before they could do any damage.

"Colleen, would you mind waiting in the other room. I'm afraid it's a bit tight in here."

There was only one small window, looking out on an alley, which did not let in much light and had evidently been painted shut at some point. The air was hot and damp, thick with the smell of the invalid. I leaned the crutches against the wall and removed veil before giving Private Hamilton my best smile.

He was of average height, medium brown hair and complexion. Convalescing in his undergarments, a quilt had been pulled up for modesty. Wood shavings sprinkled over the bedding and on the floor. On the night stand was a knife and a lumpy piece of wood that had not yet resolved itself into the desired shape. Several days growth of honey-brown beard covered his face. Above it, his skin was damp and flushed.

There was a pitcher and water on the nightstand. I poured him a glass.

"I'm sorry I could not send my card to give you some advanced warning," I said, offering him the drink. He took it, gulping it down gratefully from his half-reclined position. "My name is Sophia Andrews."

"I know who you are, ma'am. Your husband kept your portrait on him, always."

I smiled, my heart fluttering slightly against my corset. I couldn't tell if it was in fondness for my husband, or from pain at the loss. Both, perhaps. "I understand you were with him when...when this unfortunate..."

"Yes, ma'am. I was." His voice was very soft and almost as regret-filled as my own.

"I wanted to ask you what happened, if you wouldn't mind."

He shook his head. "I hardly know myself, other than what they told me. I took a pretty good hit on the head. We were walking back from a tavern near the river, and turned onto a dark street. There were men walking the other way."

"How many?"

"Three, I think. It's all a bit muddled, still. The ruffians set on us. I tried to help the Captain, but the big one pulled me back. When I fought him, one of the others shot me in the knee, and then I think he hit me over the head with his gun. I woke up in the infirmary, and they told me the Captain was dead."

"Do you think you would recognize the men again if you saw them?"

"I don't know. I got a fair look at one of them, but it was too dark to see the others under their hats. Could you hand me that book?"

I picked up the black leather-bound notebook on the nightstand and handed it to him. "I've been trying to get it down as clearly as I can, but it's difficult. I only got a look at one, the one doing most of the beating. He had a false tooth. Gold, probably. This one here." He pointed to an incisor on his upper jaw. "I remember because every time he kicked me, it would catch the light. It was the last thing I saw before I lost consciousness. Ah, here it is." He turned the book towards me to showcase a sketch done in the simple, straight-lined style of one more used to drawing schematics of machinery than capturing the curves and shadows of the natural form. It showed a square-jawed man with a close beard broken by an ugly scar, a fleshy sort of nose that appeared to have been broken once or twice, and a hat which obscured his eyes with shadow.

I was not expecting the wave of anger that came over me when I saw the face of the man who had killed my husband, but it hit me with such force that had I been standing, I'm sure I would have swayed on my feet. I laced my fingers together tightly and fought to keep my expression neutral.

"I'm trying to get it down, but it's hard to remember. But all the boys in our unit are looking for him. They won't let him get away with what he's done to Captain Andrews." He said the last gently, as if to offer some measure of comfort.

"I appreciate it." Looking at his bruised, pain-creased face only made the anger worse, but for a different reason.

"The war is over. It's over, and you boys are still dying. Captain Andrews made it through all the fighting and the illness and the long marches. He was supposed to come home. I always knew he might not, but I thought he would die in battle or of some terrible camp disease. Not in the streets of a fine city after the fighting was all over."

Private Hamilton allowed the book to fall closed in his lap, and sat there staring at it for several moments. "It isn't right, ma'am, that's for sure. Pointless violence. They were just doing it for sport."

"What do you mean?"

"They weren't robbers, ma'am. That much I know. I still had all of my money when I woke up, and they didn't touch my gun."

I nodded slowly and rose to leave, but at the door, I stopped. "The men downstairs said you insisted on packing up my husband's things."

"Yes ma'am. I couldn't do anything when we were attacked, but as his aide—his *friend*—I felt it was my duty to make sure all his books and everything went back to you. He had quite a lot of drawings he's done over the past few months, and he was always real protective of those. I didn't want anyone throwing them out by mistake. Some of this notes could be…cryptic. I just wish I could have done more." He hung his head, ashamed. I touched his shoulder lightly, for just a moment, and for an instant the shared pain was a little less.

I cleared my throat. "And the drawings are all in the trunk?"

"Yes, ma'am." He reached for the night stand again, rummaging through the little drawer until he found a small brass key, dropping it into my outstretched hand. "I locked it up myself last night."

"And my husband's watch? Is it in the trunk as well?"

"No, ma'am. He always carried it on him. Said he was a railroad man at heart, no matter what his uniform said, and railroad men live by their timetables. It's a shame he couldn't die by his, too."

I touched my pendant again. The trio of watches had been a celebratory Christmas gift when R&A Railworks broke ground on our first new line. Mr. Richardson had the third, of course.

"You're certain the watch was nowhere in his possessions?"

Private Hamilton's brows knit in confusion. "No ma'am. Wasn't it returned to you with his effects?"

"No. No, it wasn't."

Hamilton knew no more of the flask and ring than he did of the watch. I wanted to speak with him further, but it was clear he was exhausted. At last, I took my leave, giving him one of my cards as a parting gift. "If ever you are in need of anything, please don't hesitate to ask. And…thank you. From the bottom of my heart, for everything you've done."

He seemed surprised at the gesture, but I only smiled in return. "You may not think so, but you have done a great service to my family. We are in your debt." I departed before he could object.

I could feel Colleen's eyes on me as we walked back towards the hotel. I moved slowly, allowing the new information gleaned to percolate through my mind. With each drop of knowledge, I felt my chest grow tighter, constricting as if to contain the ever-increasing bubble of suspicion. Something about the situation wasn't right.

"Colleen," I said at last. She came to stand next to me, awaiting her next orders.

"We have one more stop to make before we return to the hotel, which I hope will not be redundant. This afternoon, please see to it a basket is sent around to Private Hamilton—fresh fruit, medicine. Anything that might help with his recovery. And make sure there is a physician attending him regularly. I have the impression he has mostly been left alone in that little closet. Then I will have another errand for you, and you mustn't tell anyone of it."

Her lips twitched up in a small smile. "Especially if they ask?"

"Especially then, for I do not know who we can trust just now."

"You think...You think Mr. Andrews' death was intentional, ma'am?" she whispered.

"It is beginning to appear so." I sighed, rubbing my forehead. "I really must talk to Colonel Seagraves again now that I have this new information."

My attempts were thwarted, however. A return to the colonel's office proved he was out for the remainder of the day.

"Do you know when he will return?" I asked the lieutenant who came out to greet us.

"I'm afraid I don't. I can leave your card for him, though, if you'd like to leave a message?"

I shook my head. "No, I'm afraid...I'm afraid the matter is somewhat delicate. I'd rather speak to him in person, to avoid any confusion."

He glanced me over, brows furrowing. "You're Captain Andrews' wife? I suppose...You're certain it won't take long?"

"I'm very succinct. Five minutes. Three, if we dispense with the pleasantries and get to business. I'm certain I no more want to take him away from his work than he cares to be interrupted by the concerns of an old widow."

"Hardly." His lips twitched under his bushy gray mustache. He was easily twenty years my senior. "Come by at eight-thirty tomorrow morning. He'll be at breakfast. I'll see if I can get you in then, or just after."

I thanked him profusely and we were on our way again. "Now for your task, Colleen. You have my purse?" She nodded, holding up the reticule. A lady didn't carry money; that was a job for servants. "I want you to check at any place they might sell old jewelry or used goods. See if you can find the watch. You remember his watch, and the ring he used to wear?"

"Of course, ma'am."

"Exactly. Find it, and remember the place, then come back here to me. I can't go to the lower end of town, now without drawing attention, but you can.

Don't put yourself in any danger. Hire a cab if you must, or send a local boy to look. There should be enough here for both. Get a list of local places from the front desk. And whatever you do, don't be out after dark."

"I'll be back in time to dress you for dinner, ma'am."

"Very good." I handed her the bills. "And Colleen, do be careful."

"Yes, ma'am."

With the afternoon left ahead of me, I retired to my room to think, feeling as though I had just awakened from a long, hazy dream. Until my meeting with Private Hamilton, I had been wading mostly by force of will through an expansive sea of grief. For three years my husband and I communicated mostly by letter, aside from the one time we were able to meet in Baltimore, to sign the papers giving me custodianship of the company. Never seeing each other face to face in all that time alternately turned that sea from the shallow depth of a tide pool to raging ocean with waves tall enough to swallow a ship.

Returning to the box from Colonel Seagraves, I sifted once again through the contents, mentally assigning a value to each one. The watch was valuable, but hardly worth killing over unless one was truly desperate. Still, I supposed men killed for less, and with a blue uniform to paint a target on his back, the killers could have just rifled through his pockets after the fact, taking what they could get. If the flask had been full, it might have been of more personal value to the thief than even the watch.

But then, why not take his money, as well? And why take nothing from the unconscious, bleeding Hamilton? Clearly an officer would provide a better target than a simple soldier, but it seemed unlikely thieves would not even search him, and then pass over the obvious valuables of cash and sidearm to take two much smaller items from an interior pocket. Perhaps someone interrupted their task? It would make sense. Someone had to call for assistance. But who?

I picked up the portrait case and opened it, staring at James's handsome face until my eyes began to cloud, searching his expression for the answer to the riddle.

By the time Colleen returned, I had already gotten myself dressed for dinner, and was merely waiting for her help with my hair and the buttons I could not reach on the back of my dress. She finished the job swiftly while relating her progress.

"I'm sorry, ma'am, but I couldn't find it. I did round up a small band of boys however, who will keep an eye out. I gave them each a penny and told them if one of them saw it, to come find me and he'd receive a quarter. I'm not sure how much progress they'll make in an evening, though."

"Generous of you," I smiled.

"I thought you would approve, Madam."

"I do. Anything else of note?"

"I'm afraid not. But Mr. Richardson wanted me to tell you he has returned, and will be waiting for you in the parlor."

I sighed. I'd almost forgotten I had to dine with

him again. Without James or business subjects to act as a buffer, we had very little in common, and I was in no mood to play hostess. If only it wasn't necessary for a lady to travel with an escort. It would have been so much simpler if I could have set off on my own with Colleen. We could have left the very day the telegram arrived, rather than waiting for Mr. Richardson to tie up pressing business matters. Widows had more freedom in such matters than married women, but my companion had impressed upon me the importance of an escort, and my in-laws were hardly willing to let me travel alone, as none of them could accompany me.

I pondered the irony of the situation as I walked down to the parlor. A woman was expected to travel with a man so she could be protected from men, while the same men who would supposedly harm her could roam far and wide without attracting a second glance. It was utterly infuriating.

Mr. Richardson was smoking a cigar and playing cards with a gentleman who had a great, thick, gray mustache, not unlike the fur of some beast. I found myself imagining it was a ferret or rat from the way it quivered as he spoke and seemed to take on a life of its own. The image made it possible for me to smile almost cheerfully as I greeted the men.

"Ah, there you are, Mrs. Andrews," Mr. Richardson said as the pair of them rose from their seats and put out their cigars. "Mr. Burton, may I present the ever-lovely Mrs. Sophia Andrews. Mrs. Andrews, this is Mr. Howard Burton. He has been keeping me company this afternoon."

I offered a slight curtsy. "How do you do?"

"Verra well, thank you. Gunther here has told me about your husband. I would like to offer my condolences," he said, a slight Scottish burr coloring his words.

I thanked him. Over the mustache, sea-green eyes studied me with kindness and a hint of buried humor—not as though he were laughing at me, but as though he was waiting for the solemn moment to pass so we could laugh together. I felt it tugging at my own smile. Now that I was free of bonnet and veil, I felt much more at ease.

"I should hate to break up your conversation, since it appears to have been so enjoyable. Mr. Burton, would you care to join our table for dinner?"

His eyes lit up, like clouds parting and sunlight reflecting on the ocean. "I would love to, my dear." He offered me his arm, which I accepted happily, and the three of us moved into the dining room, where we took up a small round table, with a floral centerpiece almost covering a stain on the abused table cloth.

Mr. Burton regaled us with stories of his travels through the first part of dinner. He had lived abroad through most of the war, and was now moving westward.

"I'm a photographer, you see. I go where the interest lies, and now it is turning west."

"I am rather surprised you did not stay through the war, then. I've read there were many photographers making names for themselves with pictures of the battlefields," I said. Two years earlier, one such exhibition in New York City drew my curiosity, but Olivia was reluctant so we went to the theater instead.

"At first, that was my intention. But I couldna do it. I came here thirty years ago, and I made this country my home. I traveled all over, from Louisiana to Pennsylvania, Virginia to Maine. I love every part of this country, and I couldna bear to see it being torn apart. So I went back to Scotland a while, and then the continent, and even saw a little of Africa while I waited for the fighting to stop. Tonight is only my third night back on American soil, and I can't tell you how happy, and how sad, it has made me."

"Well, we've trounced those Rebs good, so now all that's left is cleaning up the mess they've made." Mr. Richardson did not bother to moderate his volume or his tone as he took another swig from his brandy glass, garnering several filthy looks from surrounding tables. A few men nodded and raised their glasses. Though our capital, the citizens of Washington clearly still held divided loyalties, straddling both North and South.

I tried to smooth over the awkward moment by changing the subject. "Mr. Burton, how did you find Europe? I have always longed to go."

And so he expounded on his travels, elaborating on the landscape of the Alps, the crisp air of his native Scotland, and the rich food of France. Of Irish descent myself, he was more than happy to describe Dublin for me. I found his description of the libraries at Oxford and Trinity College most intriguing, and promised myself an overseas trip at the first opportunity. It would do Olivia good to see more of the world as well, I thought.

It was late in the evening by the time we finished. When he took his leave, Mr. Burton bowed over my hand, sweeping it with his thick mustache. "Mrs. Andrews, I can't tell you what a delight it has been to dine with you tonight. You have reminded me the sweeter nature of our country still exists, even if it has been through hell. Ah—pardon my language."

"The pleasure is mine, I assure you," I said. "How long will you be in Washington?"

"My train leaves first thing in the morning. First Cincinnati and then Chicago, and then west from there—Kansas, Wyoming, maybe even California."

"Well, if you ever make your way to Buffalo, you simply must call on my daughter and me. I know Olivia would be most interested to hear you speak, and I would very much like to see your work."

"I'd be very pleased, Mrs. Andrews. And one day I hope to photograph you—but I'd like to save it for a happier occasion," he said, nodding at my mourning dress.

He finally departed with a smile and one of my cards. Feeling much more relaxed and pleasant than I had in days, I turned toward the staircase.

"Well, that was interesting. Never expected a cold fish like you to be fawning over an old chap like that," Mr. Richardson said as we reached our floor, his words slurring slightly.

I whirled on him with barely restrained anger. "Mr. Richardson, you are drunk. In the future, I would advise you to consider your words more carefully when in public, and when addressing a lady. Good night!"

If he had a retort, the only one who heard it was my chamber door.

chapter three

I was halfway through my breakfast the following morning before Mr. Richardson showed his face in the dining room, looking somewhat the worse for wear. He paused when he saw me, waiting for me to acknowledge him. I ignored him for several moments, keeping him in awkward limbo in the middle of the dining room before setting down my tea cup and nodding at him.

"Mrs. Andrews—*Sophia*—I must apologize for my behavior last night," he said, standing behind the chair opposite me. He rested his hands on the carved back, but did not pull it out, as he had not been invited.

I kept my face expressionless as I sipped my tea. Much as I wanted to give him a proper dressing down, it would only make working together more difficult. Much as I enjoyed working at the railroad, I was almost willing to give it up if it meant not spending time in close quarters with Gunther Richardson any longer. Really, I never could understand how he and James had such a strong working relationship.

I pressed my lips together. "Very well. We've all been out of sorts lately." It was the most delicate thing I could think to say. If I'd been a Southern belle, or a touch closer to my Irish roots, I would have thrown in a "bless your heart," but decided it would be too much.

His expression suddenly relaxed. I started to

correct his use of my given name, but he cut me off. "Good. Good. Now that is out of the way. I presume you have more calls to make today?"

"Yes. But don't worry, I shall be finished in plenty of time for our departure. Colleen is finishing with my luggage as we speak."

"Very good. I've already spoken to the front desk and made the arrangements for our luggage."

Once again, I started to object. I'd already handled the arrangements myself when I came down for breakfast and ordered the carriage.

"Well, I should be off then. I want to speak to Senator Morgan about our bid for the overland route."

"Senator Morgan? Perhaps I should come with you then. We've dinned with him many times, and—"

"No, no. Don't trouble yourself, Sophia. I know the senator quite well and I assure you this is nothing you need worry about. Business is no place for a lady, particularly one in your state. Cooler heads must preside in matters of business."

He turned and walked away before I could object—or even correct his use of my name again.

Fuming, I threw down my napkin and started to go after him, only to be stopped by Colleen in the lobby. She was carrying my veil, bonnet, and wrap. "Oh, Mrs. Andrews. Are you ready—" I stormed past her, searching for Mr. Richardson, only to catch a glimpse of him climbing into a cab just outside the front door.

"Mrs. Andrews?"

I let out a little huff of frustration and held my hand out for my things. "Let's go, Colleen. We have quite a lot to do today."

"Is something the matter?" she asked, pulling on her gloves and adjusting her wrap. It was much cooler today than when we first arrived.

"No, it's nothing. I've only had a very strange and infuriating conversation with Mr. Richardson. Would you believe he just addressed me by my Christian name for the first time in seventeen years?"

Colleen blinked several times in surprise, forgetting herself just enough for her accent to slip. "Whyever'd he do that, ma'am?"

"I assure you, I have no idea."

The brisk morning air put a spring in our step as we traversed the several blocks between the Willard and the home where Colonel Segraves had established his command post.

I'd hardly given the man at the door my card when the Colonel himself appeared, with his secretary and several other officers in tow.

"Mrs. Andrews. What a surprise. I was just on my way down to the rail yard to inspect some incoming cargo. I'm afraid I don't have time for a meeting this morning," he said.

"What I have to say won't take long, sir. In fact, the rail station was one of the errands I myself intended to make today before we depart this evening. If you would be so kind to allow me to accompany you, I believe we can clear up a few things."

"Indeed. Well, then, allow me." He offered his hand to help me into the carriage. Colleen climbed in beside me, followed by the Colonel, and we set off.

The Colonel settled back on the bench across from me, tilting his hat to better block the sun. "Now, what can I do for you?"

"In the interest of time, please forgive me for disposing with pleasantries so I may cut to the point: Several of my husband's personal effects are missing."

He scratched his chin. "Missing, you say? What items?"

"His watch, gold, with a Celtic knot on the lid. Like this." I held up my pendant. James himself never set foot on Irish soil, but was proud of his heritage all the same.

"He also had a garnet ring, also gold, which he always wore on his little finger. And there was a silver flask, engraved with his initials."

"Yes, that's right. I remember those."

"All three are missing. I wondered if perhaps they had been laid aside somewhere. I spoke with Private Hamilton yesterday. He assured me he packed all of my husband's belongings that were at his lodging, and they were not among them. Nor were they in the box you gave me yesterday."

He shrugged, leaning back and turning to watch the city pass, unconcerned. "No doubt they were taken by the assailants."

"But neither man was robbed. They both still had cash. Why would their attackers pass over obvious ready money for a flask and watch? The ring is hardly a great treasure." True, it was gold and an heirloom, but it had more sentimental value than monetary.

The Colonel scratched his chin again, as though the act was in some way connected to stimulating the brain. "I assure you, ma'am, everything in that box was just as it was when I received it from the hospital."

"Which hospital?"

The colonel pursed his lips, clearly growing annoyed with my questions. "It's my last question, sir. Answer it, and you shall enjoy the rest of your journey in perfect silence," I said with my best smile.

He narrowed his eyes, as though he didn't believe me, then sighed. "Pearl Street, just north of the bridge. And before you ask, no, I don't know who it was that found him or which doctor treated him."

Still smiling, I sat back on my side of the bench, mimicking the Colonel's satisfied relaxation.

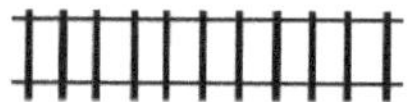

At the railway station, I found a porter who showed me to the baggage car Mr. Richardson and I would be using.

When he opened the door, I froze. Tied down to one side was an ebony casket trimmed with silver paint and hardware.

James.

"Are you well, ma'am?" asked the porter.

"I—Yes, I'm fine. Could you leave me alone for a moment?"

He nodded, and I listened to the crunch of gravel as he walked away.

With great effort, I dragged my eyes away from the casket and towards the trunk brought over that morning from the officer's lodging house. I noted with satisfaction that our trunks and larger items had already been loaded and secured.

I left Colleen at the door and went to the trunk. About to insert the key, I noticed several heavy scratches on the metal, though the lock itself appeared intact. Were those there the day before?

I ran my fingers over the gouges. No, I did not think they were.

Producing the key, I unlocked it and sifted quickly through the contents, trying not to look too closely at James's personal belongings.

Clothing, a blanket. Books. Papers. But no watch, ring, or flask.

Releasing the hidden catch in the lid, I allowed the cardboard lining to drop down. Out slid a leather folio and several loose sheets of paper covered in charcoal and ink scribbles. Stuffing all the papers into the folio, I secured the lock and tucked the leather envelope into my shawl.

Halfway to the door, I paused, staring once again at the casket.

Colleen's face appeared at the opening. "Mrs. Andrews?"

"I should check, shouldn't I? To make certain it is him, and not a mistake. There were so many stories during the war of the wrong men being pronounced dead, and then arriving home again. Do you think...?"

She put a hand on my sleeve. "You don't trust them, do you? Those Army men?"

"No, that's not it. I don't think they would intentionally deceive me. Not about this. But if I do look, and it is him, then I don't want that to be face I remember."

I had seen dead men before. Newly dead, lying in gutters, back when we lived in the Buffalo slums. But this was my husband, and his corpse had been laid out for five days now in the balmy southern autumn. There was a distinct lack of decay in the luggage car, which implied he had at least been well preserved by the undertaker in preparation for the journey back to New York and the casket was well sealed, but I did not know how a lack of smell would translate to his visage. Would I even recognize him?

Colleen took my arm, placing one hand at my waist to steer me back towards the door.

"Come along, Mrs. Andrews. I believe you wanted to visit the hospital as well? The doctor there will be able to tell you one way or another. There's no need to distress yourself further."

"I should look though. I should make sure. It's my duty as his wife." I broke free of her grasp and went to the casket. With every heartbeat, I became more sure. It wasn't him. There had had been some mistake, and they were trying to send me back with the wrong body while my real husband lay injured somewhere. Someone had robbed him, and—

"Mrs. Andrews—"

I threw back the lid.

Fifteen minutes later, on the narrow strip of grass beside the track, I wiped my mouth and gratefully accepted the tin cup of water one of the railroad employees brought me.

Colleen received one as well, and we quickly rinsed our mouths.

"Ye alright there, missus?" asked the filthy man who brought the water. He was covered in dirt and coal dust, but heard us emptying our stomachs and offered his assistance.

"I'm much better now, thank you," I said.

He refilled the cup from his canteen. "Is there anyone ya want me to fetch for ya?"

"No, that's alright. I think we will be fine now. I just need a place to sit down."

On unsteady legs, I was led over to another car, where I sat on the lowest step. My stomach rolled, and though I had managed to stop sobbing there were still wet tracks running down my cheeks my sodden handkerchief did little to wipe away. For once, I was grateful my face could be covered.

"Thank you for your help, sir, but I can take over now," Colleen said quietly, handing back the tin cup. He took it, as though unsure of the dismissal, but the maid made it clear I needed a moment alone.

Once he was gone, I began to cry again in earnest, though much quieter now. Colleen knelt beside me, patting my hand, and offered her handkerchief.

"I'm sorry," I said when I could speak again, dabbing at my eyes. "I'm afraid that was not one of my better ideas."

Colleen smiled gently "Not to worry, ma'am. I promise I won't tell. Shall we return to the hotel now?"

I took a deep breath to steady myself. "No. Not just yet. I still want to speak to the doctor."

We hired a driver to take us across town to the hospital, passing the open dome of the Capital building, and the abandoned construction on the Washington Monument. The half-finished spire mocked the people of the city, who had been trying unsuccessfully for years to raise the funds necessary to finish the monument.

The streets were crowded, slowing our progress.

I'd never seen so many freedmen in my life; they flocked to Washington City at the beginning of the war, their numbers only increasing as it wore on. The city could hardly tolerate the sudden influx of soldiers and civilians. The streets stank of sewage, and I covered my nose with my handkerchief.

During the war, Washington became home to dozens of field hospitals. With the war more than six months over, most of them were closed now or returned to their original function of shops, schools, hotels and churches. The Pearl Street location was still in use, though not as busy as it would have been a year earlier.

A nurse with a register sat just inside the front door when we arrived.

"I'm looking for information on my husband, Captain James Andrews. I'm told he was brought here, late Friday night or early on Saturday morning."

"Let me look." She checked her book, skimming the long list of names. "Ah, here we are. Captain James Andrews."

She looked up at me with a steely kind of regret; the sort that says no matter how sorry the bearer of the unfortunate news is, there is no time for condolences or platitudes. Work must go on, and death is to be expected.

"I know...I know he is... he did not survive," I managed before she could say it. The words were difficult and stuck in my throat, but I forced myself to say them. I shook my head against the image from the casket as my empty stomach clenched. "I would like to know what happened to him."

"He was killed."

"He was murdered. I want to know what happened."

The nurse studied me for a moment. I met her businesslike gaze with one of my own, straightening my shoulders. A new widow I might be, but I would not be a wilting flower who flew into hysterics.

She looked back down at her ledger, following the line with my husband's name to its termination with her finger. "He was brought in just before midnight on Friday. It says here he was attended by Dr. Wood, and pronounced dead a little after one in the morning. That's all the information I have here."

"Can you tell me anything about his wounds?"

"Mrs. Andrews, this is a military hospital. We treat wounded men day in and day out. We don't have the luxury of detailed records or—"

"Yes, I know. But please understand, my husband was not killed in battle. He was assaulted while off duty, by persons unknown and brought down in the street. I need to know what happened to him."

The nurse sighed, leaning back in her chair and folding her arms over her chest. Like all the nurses recruited during the war, she was plain, hair tied back in a simple bun. Her dress was dark blue, with no ornamentation, and covered by a white apron. She wore no jewelry. She stared at me as though by the force of her gaze she could make me turn around without the information I had come for.

Then she abruptly closed the ledger, stood, and marched away.

"Ma'am?"

"Just wait, Colleen. If I must sit here until our train departs, I will do so," I said, taking a straight-backed chair against the wall and settling in.

Five minutes passed. At last the nurse returned, followed by a man in shirtsleeves wearing a bloody apron and an exhausted expression. His rumpled black hair was threaded with gray and appeared to have been pulled by force out of his skull, where it stood on end in every direction.

"You're Mrs. Andrews?" he asked with a thick New England accent.

"I am. And you are Dr. Wood?"

"The very same." He started to offer me his hand, but we both realized at the same time it was stained with blood. He drew it back quickly. "My apologies. I just finished a surgery and haven't had time to clean up properly yet."

"I don't want to take you away from your work, Doctor, so I will be brief. Do you remember treating my husband on Friday evening? I understand you attended to him before he died. He was Captain James Andrews. About six feet tall, with black hair and blue eyes. I understand he was beaten and shot."

"I do remember him. I assure you, ma'am, there was nothing I could have done to save his life."

"I am certain you did what you could. What I want to know is, what happened to him? I know he was attacked and brought here, but I do not know what happened."

The frazzled doctor looked briefly down the corridor, back to the ward, and then took the chair on my other side, wiping his hands on one of the cleaner areas of his apron.

"There were two of them brought in. They'd been attacked. Confederate sympathizers, maybe former soldiers, I expect. They saw them in uniform on a dark street, and took advantage of the opportunity."

I waited for him to continue. When it became clear I did not find the explanation satisfactory, he sighed and continued. "The Captain was shot twice. Once in the chest, and once in the head. Miraculously, he was still alive when they brought him here, but there was nothing to be done except make him as comfortable as possible and wait."

Nodding, I reached for my pendant, clutching the timepiece in my fist. "Was there anything unusual about the circumstances, do you remember?"

"Unusual? In what way?" he asked. He ran his fingers through his messy hair, making it stand up even more.

"I'm not certain, really, only I noticed some...inconsistencies. Some of my husband's valuables were missing, you see, but not others. I've spoken to Private Hamilton, and from his account it seems the men who attacked them were primarily interested in my husband. They did not bother with Mr. Hamilton, except to incapacitate him."

"Well, that's not entirely true. I believe the blow Private Hamilton took to the head was intended to be lethal, but it missed the mark. I think by rendering him unconscious, it probably saved his life by keeping him still and out of the way." He frowned, his expression darkening. "We tried to keep him here, but he insisted on leaving. Most of my staff has been sent away since the war ended, and I frankly don't have the time or patience to treat someone who doesn't want my help."

He sighed again, looking down at his feet. "He's

well, though? Well enough, anyway?"

"I spoke to him yesterday. He didn't show signs of an infection that I could see, but his room needs airing. He's resting. I've arranged for some medicine and other comforts to be sent to his lodging. I can give you the address. I would appreciate it if someone looked in on him."

He nodded, looking relieved. "Yes. I can do that."

"What else can you tell me? You agree Private Hamilton's injuries were less severe?"

"He is alive, yes. He will likely be discharged due to the damage on his knee."

"And?"

His mouth formed a firm line. "And that is all I will say on the matter, Mrs. Andrews. I understand you are searching for closure, but I don't think there is anything else I can tell you. No one at this hospital would stoop so low as to steal from a dead man." He stood stiffly, wincing a little. He looked in desperate need of a good meal, a hot bath, and approximately three days' worth of sleep. Not necessarily in that order.

"Please, Mrs. Andrews. Go home. Bury your husband. Grieve him as you see fit. But allow him to rest in peace. He feels no pain now, and it should be your own healing you are occupied with. It's too late to save him."

Once again, I felt tears springing to my eyes. With a throat too thick to speak, I stood as well, nodding, and offered him my gloved hand. He shook it briefly, neither of us minding the gore until it was too late.

"I did not mean to offend you, Doctor. I am simply trying to understand the last moments of my husband's life."

His expression softened and he nodded. "It's hard, I know. But all too often, there is nothing to understand, except that tragedy happens. All we can do is move on."

Someone called his name, and with a curt nod, he slumped back to his work.

"Doctor?"

He paused, turning back.

"By chance, do you know who found them?"

He shrugged. "I'm afraid I don't. Some men from his company brought him in, but from what I understand it was a civilian who found them. I don't know any more than that."

"Thank you."

I pulled the black veil back over my face as Colleen and I exited back into the autumn sunlight. "Find a cab, Colleen. I'd like to go back to the hotel for a rest. Please arrange to have a basket sent around to Dr. Wood, to thank him. It's time for us to go home."

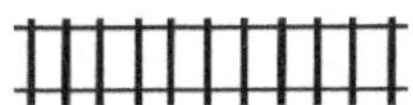

Usually, I slept better on the train than anywhere else. The rocking motion and the steady rhythm of the tracks lulled me to sleep within moments of laying down, but that night I found it distracting. I tossed and turned, staring alternately at the ceiling and at the thick green bed hangings.

Three years is a long time to sleep alone. I thought I would never grow accustomed to it, but I did. Even before the war, James did a lot of traveling, and I would remain in Buffalo, tending to our interests. I did not bother with our car for the few short journeys I needed to make after he took his commission. With coal and food and even fabric in short supply, it seemed wasteful, and certainly nothing I wanted to bother anyone with. Why go to the trouble of preparing an entire car for one person, expending the extra effort and fuel, when I could just as easily travel to New York City or Philadelphia in a normal first-class compartment? I even traveled second-class when the mood suited me, simply because I enjoyed watching my fellow passengers.

As I lay there, watching the telegraph wires flash by in the waning moonlight, attempting to count them in an effort to put myself to sleep, I wished I was even in a third-class car, just so I would not be alone.

I could ring for Colleen, of course. She was an excellent companion, and had been indispensable since the news of James's death, but I also knew she needed her rest. I had put more on her in the past few days than was typical.

Pulling on my dressing gown, I got up and went to the window. We were somewhere in the mountains, which meant we were probably in Pennsylvania. The train began to slow slightly as it climbed a particularly steep rise.

My reflection in the window was pale and ghostly, my eyes mere shadows on the glass. They ached from crying. The rest of me did not feel much better.

Exhaling slowly, I rested my head against the cool surface and watched my breath fog against the window.

The ground leveled out, and suddenly I was

plunged into absolute darkness as the train entered a tunnel.

I braced myself against the wall, heart hammering, and waited for the darkness to pass. The moonlight seemed almost blinding by comparison when it reemerged.

Below, the lights of an unknown town spread out, just a few twinkling candles in a city otherwise asleep. Then it was around a bend and the view was once again cut off as we were swallowed by the mountain.

This time, when I stared at the window, waiting for the light to return, another face stared back.

"James!"

This was not the face of the man in the casket, but of the man I remembered. When I looked over my shoulder, however, I was alone in the dark.

"James? Are you there?"

The light came back, but it did little to settle my pounding heart. The train began to descend, moving swiftly downhill. I gripped the edge of the window sill to keep my feet.

Watch...

"James? James, please! Watch what?"

Beware.

A pair of taps on the door startled me so badly I screamed.

"Ma'am? Mrs. Andrews! Are you well?" Colleen appeared at the door wrapped in a shawl, her hair still tucked into a night cap.

I pulled in a deep breath, trying to still my hammering heart. "I—yes. I'm sorry, Colleen. I thought—I heard something."

"Can I get you anything?"

"No. That's all right. You can go back to bed. I'm sorry I woke you."

"Begging your pardon, ma'am, but are you certain? You look very pale. Should I fetch--"

"No, Colleen. Please. I'll be fine."

Reluctantly she nodded, closing the door behind her.

Beware. I knew I heard James's voice. I had not imagined it, any more than I imagined his face in the window, or him sitting beside me on the bed.

My husband was trying to give me a warning.

chapter four

The night James came to sit by my bed was not my first visit from a recently liberated soul.

When I was nine, my mother gave birth to my brother. Her labor was long and difficult. As the midwife hurried in, my younger sister and I were whisked away to a neighbor's. Too excited to sleep, we finally settled down after midnight, with promises from Mrs. O'Neil to wake us if any word came. I strongly suspect the warm milk she gave us was laced with something to make us sleep.

At some point in the night, I woke to someone stroking my hair. Mother leaned over the bed, humming her favorite lullaby.

"Mama, what are you doing here?" I asked.

She smiled and kissed my forehead. "I just wanted to check on you. Be a good girl for Mrs. O'Neil, and look out for your brother and sister."

"When can we come home?" I asked. Why would Mrs. O'Neil look after us, if Mama was right there?

"In the morning, love. I can't wait for you to meet Daniel."

Eventually, I drifted to sleep, listening to her lullaby. The next morning, Papa couldn't understand how I knew my brother's name before anyone told me.

"Mama told me last night," I said. "She came to check on us."

Papa's face went very pale. Mrs. O'Neil gasped, gripping my shoulders hard. I relayed the message my mother gave me. Papa sank into a kitchen chair with tears running down his face. Mrs. O'Neil explained that my mother had not survived.

"It's very special that she came to say goodbye to you," she said. "It means your mama loved you very much, and you must do whatever you can to keep your promise to her."

There were similar visits over the years, though many of them were much less pleasant. When Danny met a bitter end in Five Points, his gambling and drinking catching up to him just as it had our father, I had a horrific vision of his face in the mirror as I was getting ready for bed. James resorted to giving me a drop of whiskey in some hot tea to soothe me.

Father made a downward turn after mother's death. Within two years he was so unfit to care for us, we were placed in a children's home. Mrs. O'Neil tried, but she couldn't take on three more mouths to feed in the long term. Bessie, Danny and I were separated. They were sent to a lower school, where we lost contact. It wasn't until after I was married that I found Danny again, but my sister remained lost to me.

I was old enough for the upper school, which was lucky. A group of benevolent ladies, conscious of the difficulty older children have with adoption, chose to sponsor three of the most promising girls, sending us to a proper seminary for young ladies.

I was in my third year at the seminary, in Miss Stein's elocution and deportment class. I had just stepped up to the podium for my recitation of Shakespeare when I felt it. In a moment, I knew my father was dead. When I looked over the heads of my classmates, I saw him standing in the doorway at the back of the room, clutching his brown felt hat and looking abashed—as though he regretted, finally, not being a better parent. It was both a heartbreak and a relief to know he would never remove me from the school, never try to take me home again. If not for the Kingston Seminary for Young Ladies, I never would have met James.

The visits were always somewhat shocking, usually unexpected, but in a way I had grown used to them over the years.

I never shared the secret with anyone except James, not since the day Danny was born. Mrs. O'Neil said it was a gift from God, to be revered. Papa said it was unholy, the Devil's work. When he was in a whiskey fueled rage, he would attempt to beat it out of me. Bessie always seemed torn between terror and intrigue, alternately fascinated and horrified. Danny never knew the truth, but always thought I was a little strange.

These thoughts and memories consumed me the rest of the long night and into the next morning. Our train arrived in Buffalo just before lunch. I disembarked, exhausted and stiff, having spent most of the night tossing and turning, contemplating the message and trying to decipher the meaning.

Where the weather was pleasantly warm in Washington, a harsh winter wind reminded us as soon as we disembarked that snow would not be far behind. I wrapped my shawl tighter and scanned the platform for a porter.

"You there, boy!" Mr. Richardson called, flagging one down. A few yards away he gave the boy directions on what to do with our luggage. I recognized the young man in the burgundy uniform with brass buttons. Colin was only fifteen, but reliable. He had always been very helpful whenever I traveled in the past.

Out of earshot, Mr. Richardson gave Colin his marching orders. I turned to Colleen. "Do you require your cloak, ma'am? It's quite chilly," she asked.

"No, Colleen, thank you. I'm fine with just the shawl." Honestly, the brisk wind was a relief. It reminded me I was home at last. It tore at the ribbon securing my bonnet and made my wide skirt sway like a church bell.

"When we get home, I'd like a few minutes in my room to rest. Please bring up any correspondence I've missed, along with the tea tray. Also, send a message to Father Hanby to let him know I've returned. I'll need to see him tonight if at all possible to make the final arrangements for the wake and funeral. Oh, and I'll also need to send a message to my mother-in-law; she will want to be there for the meeting." Mrs. Agnes Andrews lived only a few doors down, in a townhouse James secured for her once our fortunes turned around and we bought the house on Clinton Street.

"I'll see to it, ma'am."

We pushed our way through the wind and the crowded train station to the street, where a cab waited. Mr. Richardson gave me a hand up into the carriage, using his free hand to clamp his hat to his head. "I've arranged for your belongings to follow you. Shall I call on you tomorrow?"

"If you wish. Thank you for your help, but there is

no need for you to trouble yourself more on my account. Now that I'm home, I am perfectly capable of making the necessary arrangements."

"Of course."

A sudden thought made me grab his hand again quickly. "There is one thing you could do for me."

"Anything."

"I assume your business will at some point involve Mr. Coolidge?" Mr. Coolidge, a long time mutal friend, was also the company lawyer, and handled legal matters for both my husband and his business partner.

"Certainly."

"Would you arrange a day to go over the will? It would save me so much time if you could do that while I see to the funeral arrangements."

"Of course. I'll send a message once it has been seen to."

I thanked him, and the carriage started with a jolt. I leaned back against the hard leather seat and closed my eyes. Now that we were back in the city, all I wanted to do was go home and put the business of the past few days behind me.

Unfortunately, there was still so much to do. I sighed. I'd spent the entire journey longing for an occupation, something to keep my mind busy, but now faced with the necessary tasks, all I wanted was some peace and a little time to myself.

We stopped outside the brick three story and disembarked. I hadn't even straightened my skirts when Olivia came flying out the front door and threw herself into my arms.

"Mother! Oh, Mother. It was so awful! Thank

goodness you're home!"

"Olivia! Darling, what's wrong?" I asked, pushing her away just enough to see her face. Clearly overwrought, her blue eyes were wide and puffy and bore signs of earlier tears being shed. Not unusual considering the circumstances, but the policeman standing in the front door hinted it was not the loss of her father which had her so upset.

"What happened?"

Olivia pulled me into the foyer. The policeman stepped back long enough to allow me to remove my wrap and bonnet while Olivia relayed the story, her words spilling over one another in her hurry.

"It was this morning, very early. I was in bed asleep when I heard something downstairs, so I rang for Clara, but then I heard the shouting. Oh, it was terrible! I've never been so frightened in my life!"

I looked to the constable for clarification. "It seems in the wee hours, around three o'clock, an intruder broke a window in the study and attempted to enter. He didn't get very far, however. He was still in the study when the butler heard him and scared him off with the poker from the fireplace."

"Oh my!" I covered my mouth with one gloved hand, holding my daughter close to my side with the other, trying to imagine our ancient manservant defending the household. "Is Mr. Scott injured?"

"No, no. No injuries. The young lady didn't think anything had been taken, but you might have a better idea, if you'd care to have a look." He nodded in the direction of James's study, in one of the back rooms of the first floor.

I lead the way with Olivia and the officer

following at my heels. At first glance, it almost appeared nothing had been disturbed, save for the broken window, but as I approached the broad desk I saw several drawers were still open and some things on the work surface had been moved. The pastoral painting that usually hung near the window lay face down on the floor. Thankfully, the small safe it guarded still appeared intact.

Sitting heavily in the leather chair, I sorted through the drawers in turn, trying to remember what was in each one. The papers were out of order and in a general state of disarray, but I couldn't identify anything missing. Moving to the safe, I quickly dialed in the combination and the door sprang open. Inside were several stacks of bills and some ledgers, and the diamond and sapphire jewelry James had given me for our tenth anniversary.

"It's all here," I sighed, relieved, locking the safe once again. I sank down heavily into the desk chair. "Is there anything else you need?"

"Only a few questions, ma'am. The young lady says you were traveling?"

"Yes. I went to Washington to collect my husband's belongings and his remains."

The officer seemed a little caught off guard by the matter-of-fact statement. "My condolences, ma'am. I'll keep this brief, then. Have you seen any strange characters lately? Perhaps a workman hanging about when he shouldn't, or someone out of place?"

I shook my head. "I've been away for the past three days. I don't recall seeing anyone before that."

"Did anyone know of the safe, or of any valuables?"

"I don't think so. Mr. Richardson would know of the safe of course—he is—*was*—my husband's business partner. But he doesn't have the combination and he's been acting as my escort."

"Of course. I would still like to question the household, if I may?"

"Certainly. And while you are in the kitchen, please ask Mrs. Wordsworth to get you some coffee and something to eat. We certainly appreciate your help."

"Thank you for the kindness," he grinned, bowing briefly.

I rang the bell for the maid, and Clara escorted the constable to the kitchen where he could talk with the rest of the staff: Colleen, my lady's maid; Clara, the housemaid, who also looked after Olivia's needs; Mr. Scott, the butler, who had once also been my husband's valet and the only colored member of the staff; Mrs. Wordsworth, the cook; Charlie, Mrs. Wordsworth's son, who ran errands and fixed things about the house. He was only about fourteen. His sister Demelza was a year younger, and took the role of a scullery maid. Both children helped in the kitchen when they were not needed elsewhere.

Olivia sat beside me on the floor and I stroked her hair. Behind me, the broken window sent gusts of cold air, only a few degrees warmer than snow, against the back of my neck.

"Are you alright, pet?" I asked her again, gently.

"I'm fine, Mama. I'm just glad you're back."

"Me, too."

While the constable interviewed the female members of staff, Charlie and Mr. Scott worked together to cover the broken window in the study until a proper repair could be made. I attempted to give Mr. Scott the rest of the day off, but he steadfastly refused and insisted he would not leave his post when his mistress was in need. I half expected the old man to salute, as he stood there as straight as his stooped back would allow, November sunlight reflecting off his white hair.

Colleen offered to cancel my appointments, but I told her not to bother. "They are all things which need to be done right away, and nothing appears disturbed that a few moments of tidying won't fix. In the meantime, if you would prepare the parlor, I'll take Mrs. Andrews and Reverend Hanby there when they arrive. If anyone else arrives, tell them I will be home to callers tomorrow."

I spent the rest of the morning in the study, contemplating and cleaning up the mess. As I sifted through the papers, putting them back into their proper folders, I noticed it seemed the intruder had been more concerned with James's old journals and letters than with the ledgers or anything of monetary value.

I sank down into the leather chair again, pulling the worst of it towards me. The clothbound tome was filled with my late husband's sketches and drawings and his thin, messy handwriting, as well as several loose sheets of a related nature tucked inside. The corners were bent and torn now, wrinkled with the haste of the would-be thief.

Suddenly, my mind went back to the trunk in the baggage car, and the scratches along the latch.

If I didn't know any better, I would have thought

someone was attempting to steal his drawings. But who would do such a thing? James was brilliant in his way, but also somewhat fanciful. He enjoyed watching the way things moved and worked, and his best designs were the ones improving existing technology, like the train suspension responsible for our fortune.

But who would know they were there? Who would want them? Who would even know where to find them?

I pushed the book aside, then dropped it back into the drawer and locked it, tucking the key into the tiny pocket at my waist.

Retrieving the leather folio from my valise, I retreated to my room to examine the pages. For more than an hour I poured over them, laying out each page my bed and didn't look up until a soft knock at my bedroom door broke my concentration.

When I didn't answer right away, Clara's head appeared in the doorway. "Mrs. Andrews, lunch is served."

I looked up from the papers. My valise was still lying at the foot of the bed, my clothing and essentials spilling out. Sketches and notes formed a patchwork atop my own calico quilt.

"Hm? Oh, yes. Of course."

"Would you rather I bring up a tray, ma'am?"

"No, that won't be necessary. I'll be right down," I said, gathering up the pages.

She nodded and disappeared. I looked thoughtfully at the collection of drawings and notes. While I had picked up a few things simply from living and working with my husband for eighteen

years, I was hardly an engineer myself. Most of it
made about as much sense to me as the Chinese
characters I had seen once in a book. But the more I
looked at them, the more I wondered if there might be
something there someone else would want. If so,
would they want it badly enough to kill?

On my way to the dining room, I stopped to put
the portfolio, notebook, and assorted notes and
drawings in the safe.

Mrs. Andrews the elder was a diminutive woman
with iron grey hair under a lacy black cap. Bent
nearly in two, she walked with the aid of a cane.
During the war, she had taken advantage of the need
for bandages to cut six inches from the hem of every
dress and petticoat she owned—a not uncommon
practice. The higher hemline made it easier to walk
without tripping, particularly when going upstairs.

Hemlines were lowering again as things slowly
returned to normal. Of course, proper society ladies
still wore their hems at floor length, as I had been
reminded on more than one occasion. I always replied
that if my husband were in want of bandages, I would
gladly hand over my entire wardrobe to the cause and
go about town in nothing but what God and my
mother had given me, if it would help our boys to win
the war and come home safe. That resulted in several
shocked gasps from the wealthy wives of Buffalo,
though the president of our local Sanitary
Commission chapter had been quite amused and
applauded the patriotism, if not the practice itself.

Agnes hobbled through the front door, allowing

Clara to take her cloak before showing her into the parlor. Angela, the widow of her youngest son, followed in her wake. Thomas died in a prison camp a year into the war. With no children or family of her own, she was now the default caregiver for our mother-in-law, and an extra set of hands for Brigid, the fourth Andrews widow of Clinton Street.

Despite only coming up to my chin if she had been able to stand erect, and being as thin as a bird, James's mother was a tough old thing with a face like shoe leather, though it appeared even she was taking news of his death badly.

"Mother, Angela. Thank you for coming. Father Hanby should be here soon."

Agnes sniffled a little, but it was hard to imagine the dry, withered face holding back tears. Angela held out a hand to me from her place on the sofa, and I took it. "Sophia, dearie. How are you holding up?"

"As well as I can," I said, feeling the familiar prick behind my eyes.

Thankfully, Clara came in then with a cart bearing the Irish tea Agnes was so fond of.

"Where is Olivia?" she asked as I poured for her. Black, with no milk or sugar, and as strong as Mrs. Wordsworth could make it. I confided to James once that I thought his mother's tea could strip paint if applied properly, and he said it had once.

Handing her cup and saucer, I poured for my sister-in-law and myself—with generous helpings of both milk and sugar. "I think she's still in shock. She might come down later, but she was very upset when I left her room earlier."

The withered apple face seemed to fold in on

itself with disapproval. "The girl needs to get used to the facts of life. She's a grown woman. What does she think, she can avoid death her entire life?" The disapproval melted into profound sadness. "My poor, dear Jamie. Last of my boys. Oh, that I could have avoided his death a bit longer. A mother shouldn't have to bury her sons."

Setting aside my tea I took her hand, patting the frail shoulder. "I know. And she will come around in time. But she's only seventeen, and has never lost someone so close to her before. She hardly even remembers Mick and Thomas, and she never met Aiden." I offered her the handkerchief from my own sleeve and gave her a few moments to compose herself. I thought she would take offense that her granddaughter had no memories of her long deceased husband or her other sons, but she only nodded and dabbed at her eyes with the white linen.

The bell at the front door rang at the same time I heard the pocket door to the dining room slide open.

Voices in the hall, and then Clara was once again in the doorway. "Father Hanby to see you, ma'am."

"Thank you, Clara."

The Father and Olivia entered at the same time. Olivia bore the signs of having had her own small breakdown in the privacy of her room. She looked uncomfortable in her new black dress, just arrived that morning. We'd both needed new wardrobes to match the deep mourning period.

Father Hanby greeted us, his white collar standing out starkly in the room full of black. While I'd been away, the servants draped black bunting and covered the mirrors, taking down some of the decorative brick-a-brack and leaving our parlor feeling stark and hopeless. As the tall, thin Reverend and Olivia took their seats, black crepe billowing around them, I felt rather like I was at the center of a flock of crows.

"Granny Agnes!" Olivia and her grandmother embraced, the wizened crone planting a kiss on her granddaughter's cheek. They spoke in low tones while I offered the clergyman tea.

We dispensed with the formalities quickly enough, and the father offered up a prayer for James's soul and for our family. Agnes seemed to take comfort from it, though I myself was indifferent to religion on the whole. It was funny, really, how hard the ladies of the benevolent society tried to cure me of Catholicism, only to have me marry back into it.

When I was nineteen and newly married, I sometimes amused myself by imagining the looks of horror on the faces of those rich women when they found out I married a lowly Irish Catholic railway worker. Now, at thirty-six, I tried to imagine their faces if they found out the lowly railway worker had become one of the wealthiest men in the state of New York.

"Mrs. Andrews?"

My attention fluttered back to the priest. "I'm sorry. I lost myself to a memory. What were you saying, sir?"

"I was wondering if you had any particular requests in terms of music? For the service?"

He really does look like a bird of prey with that nose, I thought uncharitably, and hid an inappropriate smile behind my teacup. "Yes, of course. Colleen?" We'd compiled a list on the journey home. Hymns, flowers, and all the sundry details to make the funeral exactly what James would have wanted. A credit to his memory.

But as he looked over the list, taking suggestions from Agnes, Angela, and Olivia, I couldn't help but think it was all coming much, much, too soon.

With the arrangements attended to, there was nothing left but to get through the funeral itself. At ten o'clock the next morning, Olivia, Granny Agnes, and I took a coach to St. Joseph's. Angela and Brigid, followed in a second coach. Brigid's children, too young for such a service, waited in Olivia's old nursery with my household staff to look after them.

The new cathedral wasn't even a decade old. I felt a little ashamed to say it, but after the creaky wooden churches of my childhood it felt too new, too clean, to be holy. It made God seem further away, rather than the immediate presence Mama and Father Rourke had taught me about as a girl. But then again, God had seemed far away ever since Mama died and my visions of the dead began.

Olivia clung to my arm, her face averted from the casket as we walked down the long aisle, arm in arm. From behind my veil I stared at the gleaming black box and tried not to remember the scents of formaldehyde and decay, the waxy face of the corpse. I tried to concentrate instead on the lilies Granny Agnes insisted on, but there are few things worse than the smell of rot, except when someone tries to cover it with the fragrance of something else.

I closed my eyes, and when I opened them again James was there, standing behind the casket and smiling at me. Tears in his eyes, he clutched the brim of his hat. The buttons on his uniform shone in the weak daylight, though I could still see his injuries. For a moment, the smells of machine oil and his shaving soap overpowered the lilies.

I stumbled. I sob caught in my throat. Olivia had to hold me up, pressing her own tear stained face into my shoulder.

I couldn't do it. I couldn't walk toward the casket, knowing my husband was inside, that this was the end of everything we had built together. I couldn't say goodbye like this, not when his life had ended in murder instead of heroism.

A hand on my elbow. I looked up into Gunther Richardson's face. He nodded solemnly and gestured to the interminably long carpet leading to the front row where I was expected to sit and display my grief for all our friends and relatives.

"May I escort you, Mrs. Andrews?" he asked gently.

I nodded, clutching his arm with my free hand, the other still wrapped tightly around my daughter. My knees wobbled as he led us to the front row.

Agnes diverged from our party at the last moment, and went to kneel in front of the casket, crossing herself. Her sobs echoed against the high ceiling, mingled with a prayer. Her rosary beads banged against the wood of the coffin, loud as gunshots.

The noise struck me, each one like a blow to my own chest. The specter of James vanished, but it remained engraved in my mind. I saw him standing behind the polished wood box, and heard the shots, and felt them in my own breast as Father Hanby rose to greet everyone. As the congregation rose for the opening hymn, my corset seemed to constrict against the imaginary wounds. My vision went completely black.

chapter five

I woke up in the vestry, Olivia at my side.

"Mother!"

"What on earth happened?" I asked. My tongue felt as heavy as my limbs.

"You fainted," she said, pouring water into a basin and dabbing a wet handkerchief against my cheek.

"Ridiculous. I've never fainted in my life."

Olivia smiled tightly. "Well, I suppose there is a first time for everything."

The door to the little room opened and a round, middle aged man entered. "Ah, here is our patient," said Dr. Lynch. "How are you, my dear?"

"I've been better, but I'm fine now." I forced myself into a sitting position. The room wasn't spinning, but my head felt as if it only had the most tenuous of connections to my body.

"Let me have a look at you." The doctor pulled up a footstool and sat down. I had been deposited on a wood bench, not unlike the pews in the next room. My crinoline did indecent things while I was prostrate, as crinolines were want to do when one was anything but in the most upright of positions.

Our family doctor pushed open my eyelids, checking their response against a lamp, then took my pulse and listened to my breathing.

"I'm perfectly well, I assure you," I said, growing frustrated with his fussing.

"Well, everything seems to be in order. But you

should perhaps have a rest. I know these unfortunate circumstances can be very trying for the fairer sex—"

"I. Am. *Fine*."

Perhaps afraid he would pull back a bloody stump if he didn't, the doctor released my wrist and got to his feet. Behind him Olivia tried to hide a smile. I gave her a warning look.

"How much have I missed?" I asked, standing and attempting to straighten my dress. It was horribly wrinkled after my awkward nap on the bench.

"They are just moving to the cemetery now. But perhaps it would be better if you went home to rest..."

Inwardly, I was relieved. Bless Granny Agnes for insisting the show must go on. At least I wouldn't have to sit through Mr. Richardson's eulogy. "Nonsense. Come along, Olivia. We need to catch up to your grandmother for the burial."

The idea of "catching up" to Granny Agnes was laughable, since the woman generally moved slower than the average glacier.

We rejoined the family just as the procession entered the cemetery. Brigid, carrying her youngest on her hip, saw me over her should and held out a hand. I took it, pulling her into a half-embrace. "Are you better?" she whispered. I nodded, thanking her.

Up ahead, I recognized the backs of six men from the company, including Mr. Richardson, bearing the casket. The cold winter sunlight was a stark contrast from the interior of the church, though I could not shake the feeling of being watched as I pulled Olivia along after the long line of black-clad mourners.

Father Hanby gave a short reading when we reached the top of the hill. The hole was already dug, the stone in place. Baskets of flowers had been left, and someone handed me a lily I could throw down into the grave after the box was lowered.

I stared at it, not listening to the words of the priest. *James would have wanted roses*, I thought. He said roses were his favorite, because of me.

"A blue rose, that is what you are," he'd said the first night we spent in the Clinton street house. It was still mostly empty, and we sat on a pile of blankets, eating a cold picnic dinner in front of the fire. Olivia, barely a month old, was swaddled in her bassinette, the only furniture in the room.

"A blue rose, the rarest of all beauties," he said.

I snorted. "Hardly. I'm not some shrinking violet with milk white skin and golden blond hair and rosebud lips."

He only laughed. "Well, at least you have the cornflower blue eyes." I threw a biscuit at him. "But you are my beauty, with raven hair and the most steadfast woman I know. Who else would be as devoted to me, after the year we have had? Nearly starving, and now we have this whole house to ourselves, and a beautiful little girl who looks just like her mother."

Lilies are death. Lilies are a tragic end.

He should be buried with roses.

But I didn't have any. I hadn't thought to ask, or to stop for flowers on the way.

The priest finished his reading and nodded to me.

I threw the flower into the hole and walked away, knowing that if I ever smelled a lily again, I would be sick.

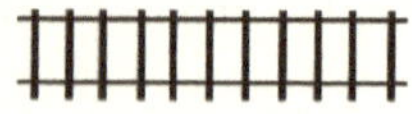

The house was filled to bursting with mourners. Agnes held court in one corner of the parlor, flanked by Angela and Brigid. Brigid's children, all under the age of ten, huddled around Olivia in another corner, unsure how to handle the strange energy of the crowd.

There were the men from the office, the high-ranking men who oversaw things. There were men from the board of directors, and from companies we had long standing relationships with. I even saw a gentleman from the Pennsylvania Rail Road and another from Boston.

Most of the guests were men with railroad connections of some kind, either through R&A, or through a competitor or a supplier. A few—the ones we were closest to—had brought their wives, all dressed and somber clothing and whispering over their wine glasses.

And they were all looking at my in-laws like they were something distasteful scraped from the bottom of their shoe.

Agnes was a harsh old crone until one got to know her, and she looked twice her own age. Brigid and Angela were working-class women with rough hands, whose only support came from James's generosity. Brigid still preferred to do most of their cooking. Angela spent most of her time caring for our mother-in-law, and the children went to a day school, instead of being tutored or going away to a boarding school. The greater problem was all three of them spoke with the distinct accent of an Irish American. To the guests, our family was of the same class as the help.

It took two extra elocution lessons every week for a year to beat the accent of my forefathers out of me, but at last Miss Stein managed to pass me off as a young lady of breeding instead of a fishmonger's daughter. There was no hope for James, though he tried to hide it when we were out in society. Agnes would rather cut off her own arm than change the way she spoke, and my sisters-in-law were largely ambivalent to the subject.

A hand on my arm drew my attention away.

"Oh, I'm sorry dear. I didn't mean to startle you."

I tried to smile on the round face beside me. Mrs. Lynch, the doctor's wife, was a sweet woman of fifty or so, and a terrible gossip, even if her heart was in the right place most of the time. Of all the women present, she was the only one who got invited to tea out of affection, not obligation. "Not at all. I'm afraid I was just woolgathering."

She followed my gaze, raising an eyebrow at the knot of family members several yards away. "Ah. Yes. I've just had a word with your mother-in-law. She's quite piqued. Says we're not giving the Captain his proper send off, since there's no whiskey or dancing."

I sighed, covering my face with one hand. *Oh, Agnes...* "It's an Irish custom. The wake is usually a party to celebrate the deceased's life, not an act of grief..."

I tried to explain, but Mrs. Lynch shook her head, apple cheeks rosy. "Oh, I understand. Personally, I don't think there's a better time to pull out a bottle of good whiskey than at a funeral. And there's been one or two I'd have happily danced at, but don't tell my husband that."

I raised an eyebrow in askance, and she hid a girlish giggle behind her hand. "You never met his mother, my dear. Or his older sister. Trust me, a dance at the funeral would be the closest either of them ever came to letting their hair down. But I'm not sure everyone is taking it that way." She nodded in the direction of Mrs. Watson and Mrs. Clark, who were staring at my in-laws in horror, and the children, who watched the whole thing with horrified fascination.

"Thank you. I'll see to it."

"No worries." With a wink, she wandered off to the dining room, where the long table had been pushed against the wall and laden with all manner of tiny, delicate foods for our guests.

"Do you need something, ma'am?" whispered Colleen, appearing at my elbow so suddenly I gave a little jump.

"So sorry, ma'am. I didn't mean to startle you."

"No, no. It's alright, Colleen. I seem to be rather tightly wound today. Would you take Olivia and the other children up to the nursery? Send them up a snack and something to drink. Oh, and if my in-laws ask for whiskey, tell them I donated it to the soldiers or something. Don't give them anything stronger than watered wine. I don't need them making a scene." Though on second thought, trying to come between the Irish and their whiskey might cause even more of a scene.

A proper lady never drank whisky in public. *Never*. But it did have a tendency to disappear at shocking speed if left within arm's reach of an

Irishwoman, as my mother used to say.

"Yes, Mrs. Andrews," she said, nodding.

The nursery was no longer used as such, though Olivia still kept her books and her old dolls there, and sometimes used it as an escape. James and I had hoped for another child, but nature was not forthcoming.

Well, too late for that now. At the moment, I needed to make sure Angela and Brigid didn't speak too loudly, and Mrs. Watson and Mrs. Clark didn't mistake them for the hired help, unintentionally or otherwise.

"...family. I knew they came from modest beginnings, but really..." Gloria Clark was saying as I approached. Both she and Prudence Watson clammed up tight when they saw me.

"Thank you ladies for coming," I said with as much sweetness and grace as I could manage. I made sure to keep the gravity in my tone as I added. "In this dark time, it is so important Olivia and I be surrounded by the loving kindness of family and friends. It means the world to me that you came today to show your support."

Momentarily taken aback, they stared at me wide eyed. "Of course, Mrs. Andrews."

"Captain Andrews was always such a lovely man. I hope now things won't be… too *difficult* for you, without him." The smile Gloria gave me was filled with venom. We had never gotten along; I thought she was insipid. She thought I was coarse, since I had the rather obnoxious habit of always having an opinion. It was a character flaw, I knew, but one not even Miss Stein and her fellow teachers at the

Kingston Seminary for Young Ladies had been able to break me of.

"I'm sure we will get along just fine. Tell, me, have you managed to find a new governess yet?"

Gloria's face went from chalk white to tomato red so quickly I half expected her head to shoot right off her shoulders like a champagne cork. It was common knowledge—though not commonly spoken of—that Mr. Clark had an eye for younger women, and their last governess had been dismissed quite abruptly. If the rumors were true, the poor girl was in a delicate condition. It was a state Gloria was unlikely to ever find herself in unless she herself moved to the wrong side of the blankets, since she was a good ten years older than he liked. He was a horrible man, but her vindictive, acerbic attitude and backstabbing nature were not inclined to make me charitable toward her.

The two of them stormed off in a huff, but I merely shook my head. *And good riddance.* With any luck, they would convince their husbands they simply must leave, *immediately.*

I moved into the dining room for a glass of wine, stopping at least two dozen times along the way to exchange pleasantries and receive condolences. Just walking across the room was becoming an ordeal.

"...future? After all, you and James were partners."

"Rupert, I assure you, everything is well in hand. Of course, Monday there will be the reading of the will, and everything will be settled."

"Have you a time for it then?" I asked, coming up behind Mr. Richardson. He turned abruptly at the sound of my voice, as did the two men he was speaking to—Mr. Clark, Gloria's husband, as well as Mr. Hughs and Mr. Dunlow.

"I'm sorry to intrude, gentlemen. I could not help but overhearing your conversation. Mr. Richardson has been so kind as to make the arrangements for the reading of the will."

"Not at all, Mrs. Andrews," said Mr. Dunlow with a bow. Always polite and usually in possession of a rapier wit, he was one of the few board members I didn't mind inviting to dinner. At least he kept the conversation interesting, rather than the other men, who were mostly old stuffed shirts with moustaches who cared for little except trains, politics, cards, and cigars.

They each offered their condolences, which I tried to accept graciously, though it was starting to get a bit tedious. Finally, I turned pointedly back to Mr. Richardson, and my original question.

"Ah, yes," he said, as though just remembering. "Monday. Mr. Coolidge has arranged an appointment for us at ten o'clock. It will be myself, Mr. Watson, and Mr. Dunlow here in attendance, plus yourself. And I suppose your mother-in-law, if she's so inclined." He nodded in the direction of Agnes, just visible through the dining room door. She seemed to be trying to convince Mr. Scott to bring her a brandy, if there was no whiskey in residence. Mr. Richardson couldn't quite keep the look of—was it distaste? Contempt?—off his face.

I decided to ignore it. I loved James's family like my own, but it was impossible trying to explain them to someone born with a silver spoon in his mouth. Gunther Richardson would never see them as anything but second class.

Just then, the front door opened letting in a rush of cold November wind that all but knocked Mr. Scott out of the way like a freight train.

When I saw who was framed in the opening, however, I nearly laughed. Leave it to Olivia Baxter to arrive in the most dramatic fashion possible. In fact, it may well have been the force of her personality and not just the wind to knock the butler out of the way.

"Sophia! Darling! Oh, my goodness. How are you?" she said, her resonant voice carrying through the room and seeming twice as loud as usual in the sudden silence following her entrance. She swept me up in a hug, crushing my face to her sable wrap, which was still chilled from outside.

"Oh, darling, I'm so sorry," she whispered into my hair, kissing my cheek.

"Thank you. Thank you for coming," I whispered back, squeezing her affectionately.

"As if I could stay away."

"Let me look at you. It's been far too long." I held her out at arm's length. Her dress, while technically following the rules of social etiquette by being black and dark grey, did not really follow their intent— since it was plaid, and shot through with thin stripes of deepest garnet, the same shade as the pea-sized baubles dangling from her earlobes.

Her mahogany hair was smoothed down and braided, covered by a beaded snood. With her bright green eyes, heart shaped face, and upturned nose, Olivia was the prettiest girl in our year at the seminary, and her marriage to a New York City banker had been the payoff. Even marriage to a stuffy banker, however, wasn't enough to cow her indomitable spirit.

"You haven't been sleeping well, have you, pet?" she asked gently, linking arms with me, like we were still girls of sixteen.

"Off and on." At night I slept hardly a wink until well after midnight, waking when the servants began their work, and then falling asleep at odd hours in the afternoon if left to my own devices.

"Well, we'll remedy that soon enough. Now, you must introduce me to everyone."

"So you can make scathing comments behind your fan?"

"Of course. What else is one to do at a dull social gathering? And you must admit it doesn't get any duller than a wake."

"Clearly you have never been to an Irish wake or hosted a dinner for thirty-five businessmen and their wives."

"My dear, clearly *you've* been doing it wrong all these years. You are in desperate need of my tutelage." She grinned wickedly, steering me over to the sideboard and releasing my arm long enough to pour herself a drink. Around us conversation resumed, but everyone in the room was shooting furtive looks in our direction.

"Well, I suppose we should introduce you around. Oh, and I can't wait for you to see little Olivia, my daughter."

"I can't wait to see her, either. It's been far too long. How old is she now?"

"Seventeen."

"Goodness! The last time I saw her she was only eight. She sounds absolutely charming from your letters."

For the next hour, we mingled and chatted, and I introduced my dearest friend and my daughter's namesake to the most prominent members of Buffalo society. "That's Lloyd Anderson, the banker."

"Oh, yes. We met last year when he was in the city. Dreadful bore."

"Indeed. I am half convinced one of these days at dinner his moustache is going to get up and walk away from sheer annoyance."

Mrs. Baxter was just taking a sip of her wine and covered her laugh with a bout of coughing. It was all I could do not to join her.

At last the guests began to trickle out, leaving just the family, Mr. Richardson, and Olivia Baxter. "It was good to meet you, Mrs. Baxter," he said with a perfunctory bow.

"Yes, an absolute pleasure, under the circumstances." My friend laid down charm so thick we could have laid tracks on it and used it to cross the Great Lakes. Mr. Richardson was so taken with her, he blushed like a schoolboy over her gloved hand. As usual, she enjoyed the effect immensely.

"Mrs. Andrews." He nodded to me.

"Until Monday morning, then."

"Don't trouble yourself. I can handle everything. You needn't bother." He managed to refrain himself from saying "a lawyer's office is no place for a lady," but I could still hear it in his voice.

"It is no trouble at all, I assure you. Mrs. Andrews and I will be at Mr. Coolidge's office at ten o'clock."

Did I imagine the displeasure on his face?

"Well. He's certainly...cold," Mrs. Baxter said, sipping her sherry once Mr. Richardson was out the door.

"Ach, don't mind that one. He don't like anyone. Except you, missy. He seemed to like you well enough," Angela said, coming to stand beside us. She had dark brown hair and eyes somewhere between brown and green. They flared green now, fueled by the power of agitation.

Much as I disliked him, I still felt it was my duty to defend him—if for no other reason than to be polite. "Now, Mr. Richardson has been very kind since James passed. He handled the trip to Washington and has been very kind in helping with the arrangements." He had also sent wonderful condolence gifts of flowers, wine, and cakes from a local bakery—crème de menthe, my favorite.

Mrs. Baxter pursed her lips. It was the same expression she give our teachers before disagreeing with them. "If you say so." She finished the last of her drink and set down the glass. "Well, I should probably take my leave."

"No, certainly not. Stay for dinner," I said.

"I don't want to intrude."

"My closest friend? Nearly a sister? Never. This is the first time I've seen you in years. I know our house is hardly the most cheerful place at the moment, but I would be honored if you would spend the duration of your stay here. I could hardly send my dearest friend to a hotel, when she has come so far to see me."

She smiled and pressed my hand. "Of course."

The wolfish grin came back. "It will be like the old days when we shared a room at school."

"Oh, heaven forbid." But we both laughed. Agnes gave us a rather severe look for it.

I linked my arm back through Mrs. Baxter's. "Shall we go to dinner, then?"

The next morning came far too soon. Mrs. Baxter and I stayed up long into the night talking, reminiscing and catching up on all we had missed in the past nine years, despite our many letters. For the earlier part of the evening my Olivia joined us, at once enraptured by her namesake. At the end of an hour, I could see already my daughter's spirit shining behind her eyes. Where there was that glint, shenanigans couldn't be far behind.

Sunday was much more of the same, with the three of us talking in the parlor. In the afternoon, they helped me write thank you cards too those who had come for the service and letters to those who sent their condolences from afar. Mrs. Baxter and I stayed up far too late again, drinking red wine on the floor of my bedroom in front of the fire, books and letters strewn around us—letters from mutual friends, old correspondence from each other.

She reached for my hand, giving it a squeeze. "I'm glad you sent me the telegram, instead of just a letter. I'm glad I could be here."

"Me too," I said, squeezing back.

"How are you? Really?"

I shrugged. I had good moments and bad. Keeping busy helped, but I still found myself overwhelmed by tears at odd moments. It had been three years since James and I shared a roof, and while regular correspondence helped to keep his memory fresh in my mind and heart, the time apart both dulled and sharpened my grief. "I spent so long expecting him not to come home. Then the war ended, and he was still alive, still writing weekly like always. He expected to receive his discharge papers at any time. Most of the boys were already home. We thought he would be back in time for Christmas." My eyes began to prickle again. Mrs. Baxter pulled me against her shoulder, and I didn't bother to wipe away the tears.

chapter six

Monday was grey and cold. As soon as I woke up, I could smell snow in the air, though it hadn't yet fallen. The burial had been timed just right; soon the ground would be frozen, and bodies would pile up in dead houses all over until it thawed enough to bury them.

Colleen helped me dress, reminding me I would have to wear a veil—so troublesome, but it was cold enough I was disinclined to complain—and then brought up tea and toast with apple butter for my breakfast.

I'd arranged for the carriage to stop at my mother-in-law's house, but walked down myself a little early. The brisk wind jolted me awake more effectively than tea or coffee ever could. I stamped my feet a little as I stood on the front step, waiting for someone to answer the door.

At last, it was one of the older children who came running in a jumble of pounding feet.

"Granny Agnes says she's not going out today," Thomas announced, bouncing on the balls of his feet. Behind him, his younger siblings crowded, jockeying for the first position at the door.

"Isn't she? Is she not feeling well?" I asked.

"Granny says cold makes her bones ache," piped up the older girl, Brianna.

I sighed, shivering a little in my wrap. I could just hear the clatter of the carriage coming down the street. "Very well. I'll come back tonight to let her know how things went."

I looked down when the littlest, Molly, tugged on my skirt. "Auntie Sophie, do you have any candy?" she asked, staring up at me with two fingers curled into her mouth. I crouched down so we were almost eye to eye and smiled. "Not with me. But when I come later I'll bring you some."

"Lemon?" Molly was positively addicted to the lemon drops from the dry good store two streets away.

I tapped her nose lightly. "We'll see."

"Is Olivia coming over?" Brigid asked. At seven, she idolized her teenage cousin.

"Yes, she'll come with me."

From the recesses of the house, a dry voice shouted. "Who is that out there? Why is the door open? We can't heat the entire street!"

I sighed, gathering the children in for a hug. "Tommy, why don't you run down and get some tea for your granny. Brianna, tell your mother and Auntie Angela that Olivia and I will come by later this afternoon. Oh, and we'll have Mrs. Baxter with us, since she's staying for a few days." I gave them each a kiss on the forehead, then retreated down the front walk to the carriage and the waiting brazier, climbing gratefully inside.

Having set aside extra time to accommodate my mother-in-law, I arrived at the third floor office of Shipley, Coolidge, and Hagen twenty minutes early.

"May I help you, madam?" asked the young man behind the desk when I arrived.

"Mrs. James Andrews to see Mr. Coolidge. I have an appointment."

He checked his calendar, but shook his head. "I'm sorry, Mrs. Andrews, but you're not on the list. Could you have mistaken the day, perhaps?"

I paused with the veil raised half over my face. "I don't think so. Mr. Richardson was quite specific. Ten o'clock on Monday morning. I am to meet him and some associates to address the issue of my late husband's will."

"Mr. Richardson, you say?" he checked the look again. "Mr. Richardson's appointment began ten minutes ago."

"Then I suggest you show me to Mr. Coolidge's office immediately."

"Ma'am, I really can't—"

"No, you really *can*. And you ought to, as it is my husband's will they are reading. Now either you can knock on that door and tell them I have arrived, or I will do it myself."

He stared at me though this outburst, color slowly draining from his face. For a full minute we stared one another down before he blinked, pushed out his chair, and scuttled off down the hall.

Not giving him a chance to leave me behind, I swept after him. He knocked quickly on the heavy, polished oak door before slipping inside. I pushed my way in after him.

"Thank you, sir, for showing me the way," I said quickly, before he could object. I yanked off my veil and dropped my wrap into the first empty chair I came to. "Gentlemen, I do hope you will forgive my tardiness." I gave a pointed look to Mr. Richardson.

"No doubt in your grief you confused the time," he said mildly.

"No doubt."

The young man from the front desk was still standing by the door with his mouth slightly open. I raised my eyebrow and he jumped, rushing forward to pull out my chair and collect my wrap. "W-would you care for a drink, Mrs. Andrews. Coffee, perhaps—?"

I waved my hand dismissively. "Nothing for me, thank you. I'm afraid I've held things up long enough. Mr. Coolidge, if you would be so kind?"

"Of course, Mrs. Andrews."

The lawyer produced a pair of pince-nez from his waistcoat pocket and held them to his face. The packet of papers was already unsealed and laid out before him at the head of the table. From my position at the opposite end, I had a good view of the three men from the company. Mr. Dunlow offered a small smile and a nod of greeting to me before turning his attention to the opening lines of the document, but Mr. Watson's face was dark and his irritation evident. Mr. Richardson did not look at me at all.

After the introduction, Mr. Coolidge read the short list of charities James and I favored and the generous sums they would receive. The men waited patiently while these were read out.

"For my family and dearest friends: to my partner in business and closest friend, Gunther Richardson. It is thanks to your steadfast belief in me that I want for nothing. There is little of material value I could leave to you that would be of any significance compared to what you already have, and thus I must leave something more sentimental: the inlaid cigar box in my study. I hope the contents remind you as much of companionship as it does me. May you share them with our compatriots, and have a drink for me."

Mr. Richardson bowed his head, for a moment overcome with emotion. Beside him, Mr. Dunlow nodded. I could hardly think of a more fitting gift, myself. James rarely smoked, but when he did, it was always those cigars, shared among friends.

"For my dear mother, Agnes Andrews, and my sisters, Angela Blackwell Andrews and Brigid Andrews McDonald, I leave the house at 42 Clinton Street and an additional sum of five thousand dollars per annum for their combined upkeep, for as long as they each should live or until they choose to remarry." It was a generous sum; perhaps not enough to live in the luxury women like Olivia Baxter or even myself was accustomed, but the Andrews women had simple needs and simple desires, and none of them overlapped much with the type of society that would require more.

"For my dearest daughter Olivia Andrews, I offer twenty thousand dollars, which shall be hers when she marries, or when she turns twenty-one." I closed my eyes, biting the inside of my cheek to keep the tears at bay. "Additionally, I leave my watch, which you have always so admired. May it remind you God works on his own timetable, and despite our best laid plans, we cannot deviate from it."

There were small sums laid aside for the household staff; Mrs. Wordsworth and Mr. Scott each had a small bequest for their years of loyalty, and there were small tokens of thanks to Clara and Colleen for caring for Olivia and I in his absence.

"Household staff, really," Mr. Watson muttered. "Truly, the thought of war made him maudlin." Mr.

Dunlow shushed him quietly, and Mr. Coolidge continued.

"Finally, for my dearest companion, and my partner in all things, my wife—" Mr. Coolidge paused, staring at the page. "Ah…"

I could guess the hold up. "Síomha Róisín. It's pronounced shee-va roh-sheen. It's Irish."

He blinked owlishly. "Of course." He cleared his throat. "Síomha Róisín, my dear Sophia Rose, I leave the only thing I have under the circumstances: the remainder of my possessions, assets, etc, not listed here, including but not limited to the house at 36 Clinton street and its contents, my stocks, bonds, etc; the balance of my holdings at Buffalo City Bank, and any other sundry items not listed here I have laid claim to."

"But what of the railroad?" demanded Mr. Watson.

"He signed it over to me two years ago."

"That's impossible. He couldn't sign over a business to a woman."

"By New York law, women are allowed to own and inherit property, including businesses. And in case you forgotten, I've been running the day to day operations in the office for years."

Mr. Wilson sighed, his lips smacking impatiently, like he was speaking to a small child. "But you were acting as his *custodian*. That's entirely different. It was tolerable as a temporary situation, but it is not acceptable for every day."

"And why not?" I arched an eyebrow at him.

"Women are far too hysterical for business. It needs to be handled by someone with a cooler head and some actual business acumen."

"Do I strike you as the hysterical sort?" I asked, deliberately lowering my voice.

Mr. Dunlow held up a hand. "Mrs. Andrews, I assume you can provide proof of this?"

"Of course. I have a copy on file at the house, and my husband had one as well. There was also a copy sent to the office, and there should be one on file with the lawyer who oversaw the transfer. Mr. Richardson, you are well aware of this. I know my husband wrote to you about it, when he sent a copy of the contract."

"I'm afraid no such letter ever reached me. As I said, to my knowledge you were acting as his custodian."

I stared at him, dumbfounded. James had showed me his letters, confirming the wisdom of signing over his half of the company until he returned from the war.

"This is absurd!"

We all turned to look at Mr. Watson. His face was the color of an overripe tomato. Beside him, Mr. Richardson was slowly turning scarlet, but he was glaring at the lawyer, not me.

"Pardon me?" Mr. Coolidge said.

"This was not what we discussed."

Mr. Coolidge's face turned ashen. He stared down at the will in his hands, then swallowed, his silver moustache twitching. "Mrs. Andrews, I trust that if you have these documents, you can produce them?"

"They aren't with me at the moment, but I can have one of the copies sent to your office this afternoon."

Mr. Watson's face was such an ugly shade of puce

at this point I doubted he could speak, even if he wanted to.

Mr. Coolidge nodded, clearing his throat. "There. I suggest we finish the reading, and set aside the finer points of the execution until later?"

Reluctantly, the men agreed and he finished reading the will. There was a moment of profound silence when he was done.

"Well, that was certainly interesting," I said, rising. "Mr. Coolidge, is there anything else you need from me?"

"Aside from the transfer papers? There will be documents for you to sign, of course, to make everything official...the deed to the house, for example..."

"Of course. I'll make an appointment with the young man out front, shall I? That way there won't be any confusion, if I make the appointment myself." I gave Mr. Richardson a smile so sweet even Olivia Baxter would have been sickened, and let myself out of the office.

"You should have told me!" Richardson roared.

The lawyer was quick to snap back. "You never asked. If I'd known—"

But what he didn't know was cut off as the door closed behind me.

I hurried down to the busy street as fast as I could without drawing undue attention. Mr. Hartly, the driver, was hunched against the cold. "Take me to Mr. Andrews's office. And hurry!"

A little off guard, he straightened up, drawing the whip across the horse's back, sending us into motion before I was even fully into my seat.

On the brief drive, I tried to think of a reason Mr. Richardson would have to lie about the appointment time or the transfer. Legally, even if I wasn't present for the reading, it would not change the facts. However...

What if his plan had, instead, been to convince me the will was different, in the hope I would not read it for myself? But still, signatures would be required for the land, the stocks...But if I failed to sign them, then what?

And if that were the case, why attempt to keep me from claiming my husband's property? Monetary gain seemed a foolish idea; Mr. Richardson was born to wealth long before going into business with James.

The coach pulled up in front of the plain red brick office. Everyone there knew me. I passed without question up to the third floor office on the western corner.

For three years, I came in four days a week to handle the essentials of business, and no one questioned my place—at least, not to my face. I read the reports and forwarded any necessary information to James. I corresponded with clients and suppliers (signing everything as S. R. Andrews), reviewed the accounts, and talked to the workers. I made sure orders were filled, documents signed, and things ran as smoothly as possible. In the upheaval following the start of the war, when so many men enlisted or drafted, many of those remaining learned to be grateful for my work.

Producing the key to James's office from my pocket, I unlocked the door and ducked inside quickly, locking it again behind me.

I tore through the desk drawers and then the cabinet behind, searching for the transfer papers. I knew they were on file. I'd put them there myself once it was all said and done. Mr. Richardson had told me to keep the copy in James's office, and I'd filed it neatly with the other contracts in the third drawer of the left-hand cabinet. The other cabinets were dedicated mostly to his drawings and such, which I didn't use with any kind of regularity.

The contract wasn't in the third drawer. I checked the bottom, then the other drawers, but it wasn't in any of them. I started checking the other cabinets...and realized just how many empty folders there were.

Patents. Drawings. Notes. Those folders, seldom accessed by me during my work, were much thinner than they should have been. What remained was out of order, and, I noticed, disturbed—bent corners, wrinkles. As if they had been put back carelessly, or in a hurry.

Or both.

A commotion in the hall. Slamming the drawer shut I returned to the desk, throwing my cloak down on the surface just as the key turned in the lock and Mr. Richardson barreled through.

He froze when he saw me. There was an instant of recognition between us.

"Mrs. Andrews. I did not expect to see you here."

You didn't expect me to beat you, you mean, I thought.

"I wanted to collect any personal effects James may have left, so they can be passed along to the relevant parties."

Mr. Richardson remained stiffly in the doorway. Behind him were Mr. Watson and Mr. Dunlow, both surprised by the apparent standoff between us.

"Certainly. I'll have one of the boys pack up his things and send them around to you tomorrow." The "boys" were the young lads, about twelve to fifteen, who ran errands in the office. I didn't think for a moment Mr. Richardson would trust the contents of the locked office to any boy, whether he was on the payroll or no.

A thought seemed to occur to him suddenly. "As we are dividing the assets, so to speak, I think it would also be prudent to remove any papers pertaining to the business to the office. A clean separation, hm?"

"To what end? I own my husband's half of the company now, as well as any of his patents not under company ownership. I will need his notes and records."

Mr. Watson made a very impolite sound. "This is utter nonsense. What business does a woman have in an office?"

"Plenty," I said, gathering up my wrap and coming around the desk to face the three of them squarely. "I own one half of this company. I was there when we rented the first office on Cumberland street. I unpacked the boxes and helped move in desks. I kept records and accounts for the first few months.

"I have been hostess for every banquet and ball. Every time the company has needed an investor, or attempted to woo a potential client, I have been the one to 'grease the wheels,' so to speak.

"Since my husband has been gone, I have stepped

into his place, and kept his end of things running for the past three years. I have balanced accounts and managed correspondence. I have trimmed unnecessary expenses and increased profits—how many other companies can say that during a time of war?

"You say I have no place in business because I am a woman. Because I run a household? I tell you, sir, running a company is not unlike running a household. There is staff to direct, money to manage, stubborn men to corral and infantile behavior to curb. You think I am inexperienced, but I have been at my work for eighteen years. And if you think I am emotional, well. I am not the one who resembles an overcooked beet at the moment."

Mr. Watson spluttered incoherently as I pushed past him, crushing my wrap to my chest in anger. I thought, for a moment, that I caught Mr. Dunlow smiling at me, but I didn't stop to look. I was on the first floor before I dared to breathe. I did not even pause to put on my cloak before plunging out into the street, where sleet had begun to fall. "Home, Hartly!" I called to the driver as I climbed inside the carriage.

I waited until we were two streets away before pulling the ledger from the folds of my cloak.

"That snake! That dirty rotten snake!" Olivia Baxter let out a string of unladylike language that would have gotten her caned in our school days. "Who does he think he is?"

"The other half of the company, unfortunately." I bit my lip, joining her as she paced the length of the parlor rug.

"He's trying to make you look bad, that's what he's doing. You said he's been perfectly supportive since your husband left?"

"Yes. He tried to get James to stay, of course, but he was supportive of his decision to leave. And he knows I'm perfectly competent. For the first year we were in business, we didn't have enough money to hire clerks in the office. James handled everything in the workshop, and Mr. Richardson traveled all over the country trying to gain interest from investors and customers. That left me in the office to handle the account and the paperwork. Though I will say, he wasn't happy about that. Before they started working together, he presented James with a contract. I found it on our kitchen table one night and read it. Mr. Richardson was not pleased that I informed my husband he'd be getting a onetime payment, signing over all claim to his invention, and would give Mr. Richardson the first crack at anything else he invented."

Mrs. Baxter's lips twitched up into a smile. "So he wanted to buy your husband out at the start, and you're the reason they wound up as business partners."

"Well, when you put it that way, I suppose so." I'd been fresh out of the seminary. I didn't have experience with contracts, but all of those elocution lessons had to be good for something—I spent a lot of time reading a lot of big words the other girls never saw. Once I realized the contract was written to be intentionally confusing, it wasn't hard to see through the fog to what it was really hiding.

"You said he wasn't happy about you working in the office. Not now, not then."

"Well, not any more. And I suppose to be fair, I *was* in a delicate condition when we first opened. James didn't like the idea of me working, either, but there was no one else to do it. At least, no one we could afford."

"So you worked for a year with no pay. Do you get paid now?"

I blinked at her. Where was she going with this? "Of course. James still received his royalty payments, and when we transferred the business, we also transferred his salary."

"Are you sure?"

"What do you mean?"

"You need to go to the bank, and make sure all of those payments were made in your name, not your husband's."

"Why?"

Mrs. Baxter grabbed my forearms. "Because if everything is still in your husband's name, then there is no record of you working for the company, not on paper. And it looks like your Mr. Richardson is about to make things very difficult for you."

We spent the rest of the afternoon pouring over my pilfered ledger, but could find nothing amiss with it.

"Well, it's no wonder. If you're the one keeping track of the accounts, then of course this book is accurate. But who's to say your Mr. Richardson doesn't have a second account book somewhere?"

I tapped my pencil against my chin, brow furrowed. "He's not my Mr. Richardson," I said offhandedly. I'd had to correct her several times already—just the phrasing was distasteful—but what she was suggesting—intentional duplicity on the part of my husband's oldest friend—made me ill at ease. I'd never much cared for Gunther Richardson, it was true. He certainly hadn't been my first choice of companion when it came time to travel to Washington. But I wasn't certain I believed he would wrong me or my husband in such a way.

The clock on the mantle chimed the hour. Mrs. Baxter looked over her shoulder, squinting at the face. With a yawn, she reached her arms over her head, stretching her neck from side to side. "Shouldn't we get ready for dinner?"

"Oh—blast it. We were supposed to go to my mother-in-law's for dinner." I'd forgotten to tell Mrs. Wordsworth after the excitement of the morning. The smell of something roasted was already wafting up from the basement kitchen.

I got stiffly from the couch and went to the foot of the stairs. "Olivia! Olivia, come down here please!"

She appeared a moment later, walking slowly from her room, nose buried in a book.

"Olivia! I need you to run down to your grandmother's. Tell your aunt Brigid we're running late. If they want to eat with us, they can come down here. Otherwise we'll have dinner tomorrow night."

Olivia finally tore her eyes from her book look behind me and out the windows by the front door. The snow I'd smelled that morning began to fall at some point after lunch, and a thick layer of it now covered the walk. She made a face and started back to her room.

"Olivia Agnes Martha Elizabeth Andrews!"

"I'm just getting my boots, Mama. I'll be down in a minute.

"Is something the matter?" Mrs. Baxter asked, appearing at my elbow.

"Oh, it's nothing. She's just angry with me, is all."

"Whatever for?" Mrs. Baxter scoffed.

I sighed. "The night before the funeral, she asked about her season. It was supposed to start with our Christmas ball, but of course now we're in mourning. It wouldn't be right for her to have a season just a month after his death."

"Oh. The poor thing."

I shrugged. "There's nothing for it. By the time the party comes around, it will only be a month since the funeral. It wouldn't be right. If we had more time..."

Mrs. Baxter put her hand on my arm. "You know, many girls have stopped waiting before they have their season. There's been too much death the last five years. If we stopped our entire lives to mourn, we would never move forward again."

I shook free, suddenly defensive. "I'm not asking her to put her entire life on hold. I'm just saying it's too soon for dancing and parties. She can come out next year. Eighteen is perfectly respectable.

"But her birthday is in January. She'll be eighteen in a few weeks, and then nineteen. Older than all the other girls. She'll be starting adulthood at a disadvantage."

"She's starting her adulthood without her father. She's already at a disadvantage," I snapped.

Mrs. Baxter drew back, hands held up in submission. "I understand. You just might consider her perspective."

Olivia reappeared then, cutting off the argument. She paused at the top of the stairs, watching us. "Am I interrupting something?"

"No. Please just go see your aunt."

She looked at each of us, then came down the stairs, boots clomping with every step.

"Olivia…"

"What? It's not like I have anyone to impress, Mother." She threw on her cloak and went out the door before I could reprimand her.

Mrs. Baxter clucked her tongue. "You've got your hands full with that one, Sophia."

"Don't remind me."

chapter seven

The next day, Mrs. Baxter and I dressed to go out. Me, once again in black, and my friend in a cheerful red dress trimmed with deep purple lace and white embroidery.

"You look lovely," I said, smoothing down some of the lace at her shoulders. "I miss wearing color."

She gave me a light hug, our argument the night before forgotten. "Did you get any sleep last night, dear? You look positively exhausted."

"Some." Not much. I'd gone to bed with everyone else around ten, but woke in the night after dreaming of James—or rather, the body in the coffin. The waxy, rotten face loomed over me, begging me for justice. For mercy. I tried to push him away, but my hand sank into his flesh. I woke drenched in a cold sweat, and immediately lit every lamp in my room. I couldn't chase away the shadows in my mind, however. I'd buried myself in a book until I couldn't keep my eyes open any longer, somewhere near dawn.

She gave me another hug. "Well, let's get some food and some coffee in you. What is the plan for today?"

"Well, I thought we could go to the office. I could give you a tour."

"A *tour*?" She raised an eyebrow.

"Among other things." I yawned. I was so tired, the floor seemed to sway beneath me. "I want a second pair of eyes."

"Of course." She linked her arm through mine and we went down to breakfast. Mostly through her coercion, I ate a griddle cake and had a cup of strong black tea with sugar—not as strong as Granny Agnes liked hers, but a nice Assam never went amiss when correctly brewed, in my book.

"What if we brought little Olivia along?" Mrs. Baxter asked, her question timed exactly to my daughter's entrance into the dining room. I shot her a look. I hadn't told Olivia anything about the will or the transfer, since it was always intended to go back to James when he returned. And I did not want her to think poorly of Mr. Richardson, not now when he was one of the few reminders of her father left.

"Brought me along for what?" She asked, pausing suddenly.

"We're going into the office. Your mother wants to give me a tour."

"It's all very boring. Just a bunch of men working," she said with a shrug.

"Oh, is that what you think?"

Olivia poured herself a cup of tea and reached for the covered dish of griddle cakes. "Mama does the accounts, but I like watching at the foundry better. I like watching the men make things, but it's very smoky and dirty. Papa said I wasn't allowed to go except with him."

"Well, would you like to come with us to the office?"

Olivia looked at me. She must have caught the look I was giving our guest, trying to curtail whatever it was she was up to.

"Yes. I think I will," she said, staring straight at

me as she plopped another cake down onto her plate.

"Are you certain? I know you find it dull. We'll mostly be looking at paperwork."

"I'm sure I can find some way to entertain myself," she said, smiling sweetly.

Too tired to argue and unable to come up with a good reason she should stay home—other than *because I said so*—a sure way to start another argument I didn't have the energy for—I sighed and sipped my tea. What on earth was Olivia Baxter up to?

While Mr. Richardson might suddenly have changed his mind about having me in the office, I did have other allies. Mr. Dunlow, for one. He and Mr. Coolidge had, in the past, always seemed more amused than annoyed by my forceful personality, though I think he mainly gave me free reign when he saw me working just to see what I would do with it— and if I would end up hanging by it.

The boys all liked me, after years of buying their loyalty with Molly's favorite lemon drops. The clerks all appreciated that unlike most of the men, I bothered to look them in the eye, say *please* and *thank you*,, and called for extra lights to be brought in on dark days. The board members, who spent most of their time in their clubs or at home, showed up only an hour or two a day, if that, and though the extra oil and coal for the stoves was a wasteful extravagance we could do without. I argued, however, that a warm clerk who can see his nose in front of his face is a more efficient clerk. Not to mention the fact that he writes better copy than one who is shivering with cold and can't see the end of his pen. That might have been a losing battle, had Mr. Dunlow and another board member not stepped up to validate my reasoning.

Just once, it would be nice if my reasoning could stand on its own, without needing a man's approval.

"Well, this is it," I said as we left our cloaks with the man by the door. "Down here is where the clerks work, since it has the best light." I gestured to the large open room, where twenty-five desks were arranged in rows. Men in black suits, hands covered in knitted mitts that left their fingers free to work, hunched over their work.

One of the boys spotted me and came trotting across the long room. "Hello, Trevor," I said, patting his head. He grinned up at me. He claimed to be twelve, but I was certain he was much younger. It was hardly uncommon for young children to take work running errands and the like in order to support their families. At least it kept him out of factories or mines where he'd be injured or even killed in short order.

"Anythin' I can do for ya, ma'am?" he asked, grinning at me, gaps where two of his lower front teeth should be.

"Not at the moment. Where's your coat? It's freezing out."

"It's naw bad," he said, lisping slightly around the gaps in his mouth. "My brodder needed it more."

"Well, we'll see that you're kitted out. Boys with pneumonia don't run many messages, do they?" I reached into my reticule. I knew I had a card somewhere…

"Ah. Here. Have you been practicing your

letters?"

He nodded, eyes bright. "I taught my brodder to spell his name."

I smiled. "Excellent. Go to this address, and ask for Mrs. Lynch. Tell her I sent you, and you need a coat. If your brothers and sisters need anything in the way of coats or shoes or any sort of clothing, tell her and she'll see you're taken care of."

He favored me with his gap-toothed grin again. "Thanks!"

Someone called him from across the room, and he started to run off, but I called him back, just long enough to get one of the hard lemon candies. He thanked me, then disappeared into the tidy rows of desks for his marching orders.

"Are you like that with all of your employees?" Mrs. Baxter asked with a raised eyebrow.

"Oh, Mama's like that with everyone," Olivia said, striding toward the stairs.

With a sigh, I followed the two of them. As we passed each office, I told them who worked in each. As we rounded the corner near my husband's office, we met one of the men in the hall.

"Oh, Mrs. Andrews. Good to see you. I'm so sorry for your loss," he said, bowing over my hand.

"I—thank you, Mr. Jories. Olivia, I'd like to present David Jories, our manager. Mr. Jories, this is my dear friend, Mrs. Olivia Baxter of New York City. I think you already know my daughter, Olivia."

He took Mrs. Baxter's hand and kissed it, but his eyes were on my daughter. "How charming. Two Olivias?"

"Mrs. Baxter is my godmother. I was named after

her," Olivia said when it was her turn to receive the same greeting. Mr. Jories lingered over her hand, eyes sparkling.

I cleared my throat. He was a young man, twenty-five or thirty, but my daughter was seventeen and not yet out in society. He pulled back quickly, nodding at us before making his excuses. For her part, Olivia didn't seem to notice the flirtation, though I did catch her wiping her hand on her skirt as he walked away.

I unlocked the office and let us in, grateful to close the door.

Already bored, Olivia went to the desk and threw herself into the chair behind it. Mrs. Baxter went to the big map framed on one wall. It was much abused, showing all the lines we currently had. During the war, pins and red string marked lines interrupted or unusable. Most of them were now repaired, except for a few in the deep south.

"What's all this string for?" She asked, gesturing. I came to stand beside her.

"The brown string is the proposed railway west. The government just awarded the contract for that, but we hope to put in our own competing line, here or here," I said, pointing to the green string running roughly parallel to it. Halfway through Kansas, it diverged, with one potential route curving slightly north and continuing to San Francisco, and another running south west.

"Through the south? By why would anyone want to go there?"

"That's where we're arguing right now. Mr. Richardson wants a more northerly route, to mimic the Union-Pacific line. He hopes to take business away from them. But I think if we go south, we'll be more in line with the military contracts. They're always sending soldiers to Texas. If we skirt the northern border of the fighting, we can have a line that is both convenient for the army, but safe enough to take civilian passengers. If we terminate here, they will be close enough to take ships across the Pacific, too."

"Los...Angels?" Mrs. Baxter struggled with the unfamiliar Spanish pronunciation. "I don't know. I've never heard of it. Sounds like a dead end to me. Nothing will ever come of it."

"I think it's pronounced Los Angeles. But I see your point. I think, however, if we built a hotel, and partnered with one of the sailing companies, it could be something. Everyone knows there's gold in California, and there are still people going from all over—I'm sorry. I'm rambling."

"It's alright, dear," she said, patting my arm.

I turned back to my daughter, who was staring at the empty filing cabinets. She'd pulled open one of the drawers, and stared into the empty depths.

"Mother...where are all of Papa's drawings?" she asked, staring over her shoulder at me, eyes huge with worry.

"They've been moved to another office," I said. It wasn't quite a lie; I was fairly certain they'd been moved to Mr. Richardson's office.

"But why? Shouldn't they be here? This is your office, isn't it?"

"I..." I wasn't certain how to answer that.

Mrs. Baxter pressed my hand. "Darling, I think it's time we said hello to that business partner of yours, don't you?"

Mr. Richardson was in his office. His secretary waved us through, narrowing his eyes at me as he did so. From the furtive looks I'd gotten from some of the men downstairs, it appeared no one expected me to be back at the office, let alone with my daughter and a strange woman in tow.

Perhaps it was only the exhaustion, but the weight of their stares, their judgment, pressed down on me. I did my best to shake it off. I would need my wits about me if I was going to face Gunther Richardson.

"Mr. Richardson!" Mrs. Baxter practically sang as she swept into his office. He looked up from his desk, startled.

"Can I help you?"

"We just wanted to say hello. Sophia has just been a dear, showing me around your wonderful facility. I told her I couldn't think of leaving without paying my respects to you." She was laying it on at least as thick as she had at the wake, but Mr. Richardson didn't seem to be as taken in. He did, however, rise from his seat to come greet her, bowing over her offered hand.

"It's a pleasure to see you again," he said, but the please didn't seem to reach his eyes. "However, I'm quite busy today. I'm afraid I'm about to leave for a meeting with one of our investors."

"And investor? How fascinating."

"Not really. It's quite dull." He was gently pushing her toward the door, but she seemed oblivious. Olivia, suddenly at my side, squeezed my hand. Her brows were narrowed, as though she'd realized there was something amiss.

"Oh, I don't think so. You see, my husband is a banker. I find anything to do with investments and stocks and the like utterly fascinating." She gave him a girlish grin. One corner of his mouth turned up in a smile, but his expression turned lascivious.

Suddenly light headed, I closed my eyes for a moment. When I opened them, James's reflection stared back at me from the window behind the desk. I blinked, and it was gone.

"Really, you need to leave now."

I turned back to Mrs. Baxter and Mr. Richardson. How much had I missed? I swore it had only be a second, but it seemed I'd missed part of the conversation.

"You have no right to be here. If the three of you don't leave right away, I will have a constable remove you."

"What is the meaning of this? I have every right to be here. Olivia and Mrs. Baxter are my guests," I said, stepping forward.

"Mr. Coolidge sent me a message this afternoon. He received that travesty of a contract you sent to him, and he has confirmed it is not valid. You will remove yourself immediately, before I arrange it for you."

"You can't do this! This is my father's company!" Olivia cried, stepping between me and him. Her cheeks were red with emotion. I tried to pull her back.

"Your father is dead. It is no longer his company."

Olivia's face turned white, then scarlet. She took a step closer—

Before I could stop her, one petite booted foot struck out, connecting with his shin. He let out a yelp as she turned and ran.

Mrs. Baxter and I exchanged a look and chased after her.

We finally caught up to her in the carriage. The brazier had gone cold, but it hardly mattered. We were all panting with the exertion of running through the office.

Olivia curled up in one corner of the carriage, sobbing into her cloak.

"Oh, sweetheart. I'm so sorry," I said, I tried to take her into my arms, but she pulled away.

"What did he mean? What was he talking about?" she demanded as the carriage lurched forward. I sighed, and explained about the contract. "It was done as a precaution, in case the worst happened. Mr. Richardson had a copy of the contract on file. He signed it. He had to, for it to be valid."

"Then why is he saying it was a lie?"

I was about to tell her I didn't know, but Mrs. Baxter gave an unladylike snort. "Because he's a greedy, two faced snake is why. Men like him are all too common where there's money or power to be found, unfortunately, but I think you handled him pretty well. Next time, though, aim higher."

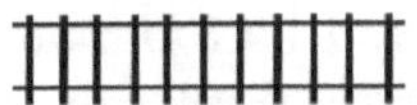

"You will tell me if you find anything suspicious?" Mrs. Baxter asked, hugging me tight. It was the second week of December, past time for her to return to her obligations in the city, and Olivia and I waited on the platform to see her off. The day was bright and cold, and a thin crust of dry snow covered each side of the tracks.

"Of course," I said, returning the warm embrace. "Write to me?"

"Always." She turned to Olivia, wrapping her arms around her. Olivia hugged her back. Our animosity had largely drained away under our combined efforts of thwarting Mr. Richardson. So far, they'd come to naught, but I was glad to have my daughter back.

"Be good to your mother. She takes too much on herself. And there is a guest room with your name on it the next time you want to come to the city."

Olivia smiled, "I'd like that."

The train pulled in with a cloud of steam. We stood together as the porters loaded her luggage, waiting until the last moment for her to board.

"It's been far too long. Come see me this summer. Both of you," she said, thrusting her hand out the open window to me. I clasped it as if she could take me along.

"We will," I promised, releasing her hand as the train began to move.

We waved until the train rounded a bend, and she was lost from sight.

"Can we go see her, Mama?" Olivia asked, coming to stand beside me.

"We will. I'm afraid I let too many friendships lapse after I got married. I think now is the time to rebuild them."

"What about your other friends? Mrs. Lynch? Mrs. Watson?"

"Mrs. Lynch is a dear friend, a wonderful woman.

But there is a difference between the friends a woman makes through her husband, and the friends she makes with her own heart."

Olivia thought about that for a moment, then linked her arm through mine. "I understand. The people we have to be around, versus the people we choose to be around."

"Exactly. But don't ever say such a thing to Mrs. Lynch. She's a dear friend. She's just..."

"Exhausting?"

I smiled a little, thinking of her persistent chatter. Wonderful to have at a party, but she could be overwhelming in close quarters. Much like Mrs. Baxter, now that I thought of it.

When we returned home, I had to lay down for a nap, exhaustion finally overtaking me. Still sleeping poorly, I would rise around eight, an hour later than I was accustomed, unless sleeplessness dictated I rise earlier. After breakfast and the newspaper, supervising the menu with Mrs. Wordsworth and the list of household chores to be completed with Clara and Colleen, the latter would help me dress while we reviewed my agenda for the day.

Normally, I would spend my mornings at the office, but now that I'd been banned I found myself with too much time on my hands. As it became more and more clear that Mr. Richardson would pursue some sort of lawsuit, and that Mr. Coolidge, as representative of both R&A and Mr. Richardson personally, would have to side with the larger client. I wrote to several law firms in New York City and around Buffalo, but found none willing to meet with me. Frustration and exhaustion threatened to overwhelm me as I struggled to maintain a cool head.

I did manage to convince them to compromise while Mr. Coolidge traveled to Baltimore to meet with the lawyer who oversaw the contract. While he was away, I was allowed to return to my duties, though it was under the close scrutiny of Mr. Richardson, and with very limited hours. That in itself redoubled my suspicions of him. I kept my head down and went about my business as usual, but I noticed there was a distinct coolness in the office which had nothing to do with the half-starved stoves heating the general work areas.

My feeble attempts with espionage were fruitless. More and more of the men refused to speak to me, acting under direct orders from those above. The board couldn't force me out—not yet, anyway—but they could make things unpleasant. More than once I found out about meetings after they happened, or was sent on wild goose chases with incorrect times and places.

In such difficult situations before, when faced with disagreeable people, my solution had always been to gather them together over a meal. I'd swayed men in favor of Mr. Richardson and James though the hospitality of my table, but custom dictated widows eschew all social gatherings for at least a year, preferably two and a half.

After nearly a month of this, I decided I'd had enough. The most recent meeting was to discuss the possibility of taking the company public. Once again, I'd been provided with the incorrect date. In a fit of pique I went to Mr. Richardson's office, intending to have it out with him. My temper was short and I was in no mood to willingly suffer the foolishness I'd been tolerating for weeks.

Much to my surprise, I found the outer office empty, his assistant presumably at lunch. Without bothering to knock, I barged right into the inner office, my lungs already full in preparation for the diatribe I planned to deliver.

The air rushed out of me at once when I looked around the empty room. I swore—twice—dredging up language I hadn't heard since my father was alive. For a split second, I considered walking out and returning later to give Mr. Richardson a well-deserved earful, then changed my mind. Closing the door, I listened, but no one was coming. With a few steps I crossed the room and examined the desk.

Unlike my late husband, Mr. Richardson was fastidious. There was nothing on the surface of his desk that would tell me anything, so I moved to the drawers. The bottom one was locked, but the two uppers were not. One yielded only writing supplies, but in the other I found a small box of letters. I took one, stowing it up my wide sleeve and closing the drawer just as footsteps sounded outside.

I hurried away from the desk, meeting Mr. Richardson at the door.

The surprised expression on his face turned quickly to anger. "Mrs. Andrews. What on earth are you doing here?"

"I came to speak to you, obviously," I snapped back, my tone going as sharp as his.

"And you thought you could just welcome yourself to my office?"

"I thought you were in residence."

The squabbling continued for some minutes, until I was quite as frustrated with him as he was with me.

"Never mind! Clearly it is useless attempting to speak to you, anyway," I snapped. I stormed off, fingers curling around the letter in my sleeve.

I didn't dare read it until I was at home again, in the privacy of my own room. I sat by the fire and unfolded the creased paper, which began with *Dear Brother* and ended with *Yours, Arthur,* but I found little of consequence in between. I knew Mr. Richardson had a younger brother by his stepmother, but understood them to be estranged. From the letter, I was able to glean that this brother was a doctor, and he had served as such during the war but was now back in New York, and had been for some time—the letter was dated June 15, 1865. Whatever his new venture was, it appeared to be going quite well for Dr. Arthur Richardson, but it provided me with no useful information.

I looked at the lines again. *Our patron, Mr. Talbert, has had to leave his post quite suddenly, but Dr. Glass has arranged new means for us, and our work shall continue uninterrupted.* So it was some sort of research, then, that he did. Hardly uncommon. The cadavers of soldiers had been in high demand, or so I'd read, as doctors tried to solve the riddle of death, to find new treatments for injuries and illness other than the butchery practiced in battlefield hospitals.

"Useless," I sighed, throwing the letter into the fire.

I went to my night stand and pulled out one of the bundles of ribbon-tied letters. I sifted through them

until I found August, 1862, and pulled out two
envelopes.

My dearest Síomha Róisín,
Wonderful news—not as wonderful as the end of
the war, but wonderful still. If you can get this letter
in time, I will have two days of leave next week, the
24th and 25th. If you can take a train to Baltimore, I'll
be able to meet you there. I've arranged a room at the
George Washington Hotel on Oak Street. Please
come. I have something urgent I would like to discuss
with you.
Love,
James

The letter had, understandably, piqued my
interest. I'd arranged the trip right away, but due to
the delays to mail during the war, hadn't gotten the
letter until the twenty-second. I'd set out
immediately, and after a long delay in Philadelphia,
finally managed to see him the morning of the
twenty-fifth. We'd only had a few hours before he
had to board a train south again. Rather than the
tender reunion we both longed for, we ate a cold
lunch in his room while he explained the transfer
contract and the reason behind it.

"It's just a precaution," he insisted. He'd seen his
first real battle, and wanted to make sure we were
provided for. "This way, no one can take it away from
you."

It took an hour for me to read the contract and
ensure everything was in order. By the time I signed
it, we hardly had time for a kiss goodbye before he

was off to the station.

Colleen, of course, had come with me. She knew the reason for the meeting; she'd been the one to post the letter and the copy of the contract to Mr. Richardson that afternoon while I rested in the hotel, waiting for my own train North.

I clutched at the letter. If I'd not seen the contract myself, waiting on my desk when I returned, I would suspect something had gone wrong with the delivery. But I knew it arrived. I *knew it*. I'd handled it, filed it in the third drawer, as was proper.

I looked down at the next letter in the stack, which was longer and smudged. Wherever it had been written, it hadn't been someplace intended for writing.

Dear Síomha,

I miss you so much I can hardly think. Those few hours were not enough, and I hope this war is over soon so I can return home to you.

I received a telegram from Gunther this morning, and everything is in order. I know you will do well. You were always much better in an office than I could ever be. I will always be a laborer at heart; I belong with the coal and the dirt.

Well, I certainly get enough of it here. We've been repairing telegraph lines all morning, and trying to get some balloons up to see the Rebels before they get too close. I've got an idea to make communicating with the balloonists easier. They've been dropping notes down to us, weighted with small stones, but if we don't have to chase them down, then they usually end up hitting someone on the head. I think if we can rig up some sort of telegraph wire, it might solve the problem.

He went on to give his love to Olivia and to talk about a hundred other pointless things. Pointless, but I hung on to every word, as though the letters themselves could bring him back. I sighed, stuffing the letters back into the drawer.

For all the turmoil in the office, our home stayed reasonably peaceful. At least two or three times a week Olivia and I bundled up in our furs and cloaks, trotting a few doors down on the slippery street to have dinner with my in-laws, or they would come to us, if Agnes was feeling up to it.

Due to the mourning period, none of us were obliged to return calls. I found the mere thought of it exhausting when Colleen brought in the silver tray with the cards. Where once I had loathed spending long, unoccupied hours at home, I now sought refuge in them, shutting the world away with the thick oak front door. I preferred to spend my time reading, my only contact with the world outside my company and my family through correspondence. Mrs. Baxter and I exchanged a letter or two a week, at least, and I sent one to Private Hamilton, to check on his recovery and to see if he'd remembered anything else about the attack. Olivia suggested I go back to my volunteer work at the hospital, but I couldn't face it. I couldn't think of the suffering of those poor souls now without remembering James, the body, and every nightmare since that telegram.

But life still went on. Due to the mourning period, we could not decorate as we had in the past for

Christmas, but we still put up a Prince Albert tree, just a small one. Olivia and I strung popcorn to decorate it.

"What is it?" I asked, sensing the words unsaid as she draped her string over the branches.

"The Spencers have a much larger tree. They have to set theirs on the floor. It's taller than I am." Ours was only about two feet tall, and rested on a small table draped with a cheery red shawl I'd found in my bureau. As it wouldn't get much wear for the next two years, I determined there was no harm in repurposing it for the holiday.

"The Spencers are not in mourning," I reminded her.

"I suppose we shall have to put black crepe on the tree, too."

"I think that may be going a bit far. But perhaps a black ribbon at the top, in honor of your father?"

She scowled. "I am so weary of black. It has only been a month, but I am sick of it! He was gone for so long, it hardly seems fair now..."

Setting down the bowl of popcorn, I rose to put a hand on her shoulder. "I know. We said our goodbyes a long time ago, in a way. We have learned to live without him. For us, day-to-day, little changes, except now the expectation of his return is gone."

"He was supposed to come home. I hardly remember his face."

"I know."

She threw her arms around me briefly, her tears leaking into my shoulder, then pulled away and ran upstairs without another word.

I sat back down in my chair and continued

stringing popcorn, staring into the fireplace without seeing the flames.

chapter eight

Unlike previous years, when the Christmas season had been filled with visits and visitors, holiday parties and teas, December plodded on quietly, and even the stiff lake wind could not force it along any faster. Outside, carolers and parties ran long into the night, but the cheerful holiday spirit did not cross our threshold. Even the thick coating of snow seemed duller than in years past.

To distract myself, I threw all my limited energy into planning the annual R&A Christmas party. At noon on Christmas Eve, all non-essential personnel would be to attend a casual gathering, in which Mr. Richardson and the members of the board presented the men with small tokens of their appreciation. There would be food and lively dancing until dusk, and at seven o'clock a more formal affair for those of a higher rank, as well as their guests and any interested business associates would commence, and likely wouldn't end until well after midnight.

Mr. Richardson was happy about that at least; with the party looming so close, it gave me something to think about other than business, and I slackened my death grip on the day-to-day business of the company in order to ensure both parties went off without a hitch. Though the company was in transition now, I would not let down the employees.

The first floor of the main office was mostly single, broad room. Normally, this was where the clerks worked but on Christmas Eve morning moved them all into lines against the wall and covering them with crisp white linen and evergreen boughs to serve as buffet tables. At noon, the whistle blew and the staff received a half holiday. From the rail yard to the foundry, men flooded into the office to partake of ham and potatoes, joined by their families. Some of them brought instruments, and an impromptu band formed in the corner, playing merry tunes.

The gift I'd arranged for them this year was a new pair of warm leather gloves for each man and boy on the payroll (much to my chagrin, women were still not employed in any capacity). I watched from the second floor balcony as the boxes were handed out.

"Where is Mr. Richardson?" I asked, spotting his secretary.

"He's not here, Mrs. Andrews."

"What do you mean, he's not here? He should be here. The men should hear a few words from him."

Mr. Crewe shifted uncomfortably. "He left at noon, ma'am. Said he had preparations for the gala tonight."

My lips pressed themselves into a thin, almost painful, line. "Very well, then."

He hurried off. I moved quickly through the gathered crowd to the staircase. When I reached the landing I turned to face the room. A hush fell over the workmen and their wives and families.

"Ladies and gentlemen. Thank you all for being here tonight." My eyes swept the gathered crowd, a motley crew of people in frayed tweed and stained wool. Many familiar faces were thinner than in years before, and many were missing limbs. I had insisted R&A provide as much work for the men coming back from war as possible, though Richardson insisted we weren't a charity. Thankfully, he'd been outvoted.

"It is a very different group I see before me tonight than I did five years ago. War took its toll on us all, in many ways. Some visible," I gestured to one of the clerks, who balanced himself on a pair of crutches, one empty trouser leg pinned up beneath him. "Some not as much." I touched my pendant, closing it in my fist.

"1865 has been a difficult year. A transitory year. We have won a war, but lost a president. Despite the challenges we've faced, our business has continued to grow and expand, though we've lost many of our own." Briefly, I listed a few of the most notable names—Jason Hammond, our old foreman. Nicolai Brown, a bright, friendly man from the steelworks who was always willing to help and had a joke at the ready.

"I know if my husband were here to address you today, he would tell you how proud he is, not only of how far we have come, but of how strong and united we are. Through all our trials, we have never failed to support each other." My eyes flicked to the clerks and the other men from the office, the ones who bowed under pressure from Mr. Richardson. They looked away quickly.

"For three years, in each of his letters, he never failed to ask after the wellbeing of the company. Not in terms of profit and loss, but to know the morale of his men. He asked me to give you each his love as if you were members of our family, because you are. Without you, we would not have made it this far."

There was a smattering of applause. In the front

row, one of the wives reached for her husband's arm, laying her head lightly on his shoulder. The coarse workmen bowed their heads, and we stood in silence for a moment, honoring the men we'd lost.

"Tonight, however, we celebrate. We celebrate lives well lived, worthy causes, and brighter futures. But most of all, we are here to honor you, and your hard work." I took a glass someone handed up to me and raised it. "So please, dance, be merry. You have all earned it. And happy Christmas to you all."

Around the room, glasses rose in unison, accompanied by a round of "huzzahs," and we all drank to the health of the men. I stepped down from my perch, and the band started playing again, picking up with a lively jig.

I spent another hour at the celebration before I, too, had to leave to prepare for the gala, but not before I'd made a point of speaking to each of the guests individually, even if it was only to say hello. They did not expect it; the heads of railroads did not say hello to the men who shoveled the coal. They didn't make a point of knowing people by name, or knowing what their job was.

That was why James and I always insisted on doing it.

With Colleen's help, I managed to greet everyone, thanking them for their work. Even if a man was new, or I'd forgotten his name, I tried to greet him as if we were old friends.

"Mrs. Andrews, it's after three," Colleen whispered as we left another cluster of well-wishers. We made our final good-byes and went for the carriage. Mr. Hartly was in a cheerful mood, having already partaken of the tankard of beer the employees were provided with.

At home, Colleen and Clara helped me change into something more formal. The black crepe with velvet trim and black buttons was a far cry from the plum colored silk and white fur I'd worn the year before.

"Is it too much?" I asked Colleen, examining the fabric in the mirror. Velvet wasn't supposed to be worn until deep mourning was over, not for several months.

"It's Christmas, ma'am. Anything less would be too little."

The gala was a grand affair hosted by Mr. Richardson at his sprawling mansion on the north end of town. The foyer alone was larger than our parlor, with marble floors and great columns supporting the next story, a curving staircase with a carved banister, and more artwork than a New York City gallery.

I was early—intentionally so.

"Mrs. Andrews. We were not expecting you until much later, ma'am," said Green, the butler. Through his English accent, he pronounced the last *marm*.

"I just wanted to check on a few things before we get underway," I replied as he helped me out of my cloak.

"If you'd care to wait in the parlor, I can have someone bring you refreshment while you wait for Mr. Richardson."

"That won't be necessary. Colleen, do you have the new seating chart?" She produced it from her bag. "We'll have to move Mrs. Spencer and Miss Alexander. I just found out the Thompsons won't be attending, which means there will be nothing between the ladies and Mr. Stern, and when he's in his cups he is no fair partner for any lady at the dinner table. Green, have the musicians arrived yet?"

"Yes, ma'am. They're setting up in the ballroom now."

"Wonderful. Colleen, tell them there will be a pause in the music at eight o'clock so Mr. Richardson and I may address the guests. Mr. Richardson will speak first, then me, and then we'll get back to dancing. Then check to make sure dinner is coming along, and make sure the help is polished up like a new penny."

"Yes, Mrs. Andrews."

She scampered off to perform her tasks. Green watched me with a stern expression, clearly miffed that I'd declined his offer of tea and cakes in the parlor.

"I'm sure, madam, everything is well in hand, if you would just—"

"Green, how long have you known me?" I asked, unfolding the new seating chart as I strode toward the dining room.

"I'm not certain, ma'am."

"I'm estimating about ten years, ever since you came to work for Mr. Richardson. Which means for at least ten years now, you've been present for these galas, and have watched me plan them—no, no dear. Those should go in the entry. They're too tall for the dining room," I told a passing maid, carrying a large vase of flowers. "Just there. Put it on the table by the door. And we want evergreens in the ballroom, but not around the tables. The fragrance is too strong when one is trying to eat," I explained as another tried to arrange pine boughs on the table.

I turned back to the butler. "Where was I? Oh, yes. For ten years, you have watched me oversee these galas, making certain every detail is correct. As Mr. Richardson is unmarried, I am the designated hostess for these affairs, and that has never been truer or more necessary than it is tonight. Now, you can either attend to your own duties, which I am sure are numerous on this occasion, or you can follow me around like a lost duckling. It doesn't matter which you choose, but I assure you things will be much more efficient if we divide our efforts."

He nodded. "Yes, Mrs. Andrews. My mistake. It is only that Mr. Richardson told me you would not be overseeing things this year, in light of…" he glanced pointedly at my black dress.

"Nonsense. I'm mourning, not dead. I promise, I will be the picture of dignity once the guests arrive, but until then, there is quite a lot to get done and I haven't the time nor the patience to sit around doing nothing."

Green hesitated, then bowed quickly and hurried away. I hid my annoyance behind the seating chart, and set about finding some poor gentleman I could seat across from Mr. Stern, to spare the finer feelings of our female guests.

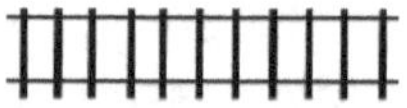

Mr. Richardson, though he was a single man who lived alone, save for his household staff, had a grand house built for entertaining. Colored glass windows, marble staircases, inlaid wood floors, flocked papers in all the rooms. He had more guest rooms than a hotel, and a cistern on the roof to provide running water to the entire house. There were gas lamps and every modern convenience that could be wanted. He employed a small army to keep it ready at a moment's notice, should anyone happen to visit. While my own home could boast of gas lights and an actual water closet, it was less than half the size and not nearly as grand. Ours was a comfortable family home, not one built to impress.

The guests began arriving at six. The long dining table could seat twenty, and on this instance, it did.

The most important guests—the board members, their wives and our most important business contacts—would join us for dinner after the dancing.

But before that, there was dancing. I noted with some chagrin that while addressing the workmen was less important to Mr. Richardson than ensuring he was dressed properly for the gala, he was very eager to stand up and propose a toast to a prosperous year when men in crisp jackets and silk bow ties were the ones listening.

"Though this year has been difficult for us in many respects, we are moving forward now, full steam ahead, so to speak." He laughed a little at his own joke, and the others joined him. "My late partner would be so pleased to see you all here." He droned on a little longer, about how well the business was doing, and how important all our investors and partners and friends were, before finally lifting his own glass and proposing a toast to James. I joined in, sipping lightly at my champagne and opening my fan. With so many people in the room, I felt rather over-warm. I started to move to the front, but Mr. Richardson signaled the band they began to play again.

"We agreed that we would both address the guests," I said when I caught up to him a moment later.

"Well, I think what I said just about covers it, don't you?" he asked, hands dangling from his pockets. A waiter passed behind him and he turned to collect two glasses. "Don't be so dour, Sophia. It's a party! A celebration. Here." He handed me one of the glasses and slipped his arm around my waist, leading me back to the guests. "Why don't you take a turn around the room, hm? You've always liked the more personal touch, anyhow."

The pat he gave me was more than a little familiar. I hid my annoyance behind the fan and settled myself onto a chair next to a potted fern taller than I was, throwing back the champagne and wishing it was something stronger.

"Can I get you anything, ma'am?" asked one of the footmen, passing with a tray of empty glasses. He looked at me with concern.

I started to answer, but then there were two of him. I swallowed sharply, taking in a deep breath. "Water, please. A glass of water."

I was near the door. I waited for the worst of the dizzy spell to pass, then crept out onto the terrace and sank down onto a stone bench, panting, and laid my head back against the side of the house. The cold air bit into my cheeks pleasantly.

It was here the footman found me with a tumbler of water, and Mr. Richardson in tow.

"Are you quite well?" he asked, concern coloring his face. Or maybe it was just the cold.

I held up a hand, downing the water quickly and taking a deep breath. My unsteadiness vanished. "Yes. Quite well. I'm afraid I just got a little warm."

"Well, I wanted to find you. I've had something prepared."

"Oh?" What a surprise. He'd been more than happy to leave all the party arrangements to me, refusing to express an opinion on anything other than the quality of the port, champagne, and whiskey we would serve.

He offered me his arm, and led me back into the ballroom. At the end of a polka, he signaled the band, who lowered their instruments.

"Ladies and gentlemen, Christmas is a time for acknowledging our friends and family, for showing our appreciation for them. Many of you know of our humble beginnings. My partner, James Andrews, was a simple man, but one with infallible taste, be it the color we should paint our cars or the quality of the steel and glass we would employ. Though I have worked tirelessly in his absence to maintain these same high standards, there is one department in which I fear I shall always fail miserably.

"You see, James had an eye for quality, and there was no area where he recognized quality more than in women."

Our audience seemed to think it was a joke. Nervous titters rippled through the ballroom. I, still on his arm, started. *Where, exactly, are you going with this?* I wondered. Surely, he would not be so crude as to allude to an affair—which did not exist, I knew—in front of not only all of Buffalo's polite society, but also in front of a dead man's wife.

"This is most noticeable in his choice of wife," Richardson said, gesturing to me and offering a smile. I tried to be gracious, but I still wasn't sure where his train of thought was leading.

"Our first office would not even have filled this room. We had ten employees we could hardly afford, and had to do much of the work ourselves. Mrs. Andrews was a new bride at the time, and I'm sure was much more eager to raise a family than to spend long hours in our drafty office acting as clerk and secretary until one could be found, but she did, working tirelessly both in and out of the office to ensure R&A had as good a start in the world as any newborn.

"Today, her work has continued, even through her grief, to ensure her husband's progeny can continue without him."

Polite applause, and Mr. Richardson gestured to one of the footmen, who brought forth a large white box tied with a red ribbon. "In thanks for your dedication," he said with a smile. "From a foundering infant we thought would not make it through the night, to a company that is strong and proud."

Unsure how to take that last, I instead pulled on the ribbon. The bow fell away and I lifted the lid on the softest, finest sable I'd ever laid eyes on.

"Oh…!" I reached in, lifting it out of the box to raise to my cheek, closing my eyes in the sheer bliss of it against my skin.

"It's beautiful," I said, laying it back down. "Thank you."

Mr. Richardson took another glass of champagne. "To Mrs. Andrews."

"To Mrs. Andrews," the guests repeated.

I smiled like a fool through the rest of the evening.

"Mama, do we have to wear black? Even for Christmas dinner?"

"Yes, Olivia," I said, glancing at her reflection in my looking glass.

"It's just so dreary." She threw herself down on my bed. "It's hard enough to celebrate this year. Do we have to look like we're attending a funeral all over again?"

I laid down my comb. It was difficult to summon the joy of the season. We had gotten used to the empty place at the table, but this year there wouldn't even be a letter to read after dinner, or a box of comforts to pack. We wound black ribbon with the garland on the banister, and tied a black bow to the top of the Prince Albert tree.

"Olivia, come here."

Vacating my stool, I gestured for her to sit. From a drawer, I produced a bright silk ribbon of red and green plaid that I fixed in her hair.

"It's only among family, so I don't see the harm in being a little festive. Your father wouldn't want Christmas ruined for his sake. He would want you to smile and be merry."

Olivia didn't even crack a smile as I tied a bow above her braided crown, and then slid a bright pair of silver earrings with red beads into her lobes. For a finishing touch I added a drop of my rosewater to her neck.

"May I wear my red gloves, too?" she asked, examining the effect in the mirror.

"Yes. Just for Christmas. And why don't you get the book from downstairs? You can do the reading from Dickens this year."

It was a solemn group that gathered around Agnes Andrews' dining table. Agnes, often irritable from the pain in her joints, was even more difficult to get along with than usual, snapping at the young ones, on whom all sense of decorum was lost.

"Olivia, perhaps you could take charge of the boys," I whispered, dropping my cloak over a hook in the entryway. From above came a shrill screech and the "Pow! Pow! Pow!" of young boys in rambunctious play, followed by an annoyed "Be quiet!" from Agnes.

Olivia scampered up the stairs to the boys' room while I went to the drawing room to check on my mother-in-law.

I took a deep breath before pushing open the pocket door to the parlor.

"Good day, Mother. Happy Christmas."

"Speak for yourself. Where are those lazy girls? Foolish things," she growled. Within arm's reach was a brown bottle of morphine.

Hm. So she was in one of *those* moods. The only way to cope with it, really, was to ignore it.

"Can I get you anything? Tea? An extra pillow?"

"You can tell those girls to hurry up with dinner. Shouldn't even be celebrating anyway. Not with my boys gone..." Her pale eyes welled with tears, but an instant later she was glaring again.

"I'll go check on dinner, then," I said, taking advantage of the excuse to leave. Agnes glared into the fire, my presence already dismissed.

I found Angela and Brigid in the kitchen, hard at work on dinner. The kitchen was filled with the smell of turkey, pie, and bread.

"Oh, it smells heavenly in here," I said slipping through the door.

"Oh, Sophia. Good. Can you carry up the first tray? We're almost through here," Angela said. Her face was flushed from the heat of the kitchen.

"Of course. Maybe we could get the boys to carry a few things up?"

"That sounds like an excellent idea. Molly? Would you run up and fetch your brothers and Brianna?" she turned to her little niece, who was clinging to Brigid's skirts by the stove. The girl nodded silently and ran off like a startled mouse. Only four, she was shy of most people outside of her immediate family, even taking a while to warm up to Olivia and I every time we visited.

Brigid was stirring a large pot of something aromatic, her curly hair escaping from her snood and forming a ruddy halo around her face.

"Do you need anything, Brigid?"

"No. Almost done." She smiled through the steam.

Ten minutes of minor chaos saw us all seated around the table. Once all the dishes had been brought up, I escorted Agnes to the table. She grumbled the entire trip from the parlor to the dining room.

"Can't see what the sense is in having servants

and then sending them home when there's a big meal
to fix. I'd have given my right arm for a cook back
when I was making Christmas dinner."

"Mother, we told you. Mrs. Monroe and Mary
both deserve to spend Christmas with their families.
Besides, for just us, we don't need much. We can
cook and wash up, just as we did for years," Brigid
said.

After the formality of the night before, it was a
relief to gather around the scarred dining table with
Brigid's brood and listen to the talk and laughter as
plates were passed around. Through the front
window, carolers sang "Merry Christmas" in the
snow.

A few sips of wassail brought a general good
humor to Agnes—unsurprising considering the
amount of rum it contained—and she stopped
snapping at the boys, who were eager to open the
Christmas crackers, and instead asked Olivia about
her school work.

"When I was a girl, a little thing like death
wouldn't stop a girl from coming out," she said. "No,
her mother would be even more eager to marry her
off. You know what this is, it's the damned English.
That chit they have on the throne and her obsession
with that dead husband of hers."

I would hardly call the Queen of England a "chit"
but Agnes was very attached to her Irish roots, which
meant everything, in her opinion, was the fault of "the
damned English," from her rheumatism to the
economy. She even blamed the secession and the war
on the English, saying the Rebs never would have
tried such a daring move if they hadn't thought the

English would support them. Well, at least they had been mistaken in that. Officially, anyway.

Across the table from me, Angela rolled her eyes and smiled. She'd heard these diatribes before, many times. "Olivia mentioned you received a lovely new gift last night," she said, ignoring her complaints.

"Oh, yes. I'll have to show it to you after dinner. I wore it over." I described my new fur to her. "Olivia's already attempted to steal it from me," I teased.

Olivia latched onto the new thread of conversation. "It's so soft," she agreed. "Granny Agnes, you should try it on. It's like wearing a cloud!"

"That was a very generous gift of Mr. Richardson," Brigid said, raising an eyebrow.

"Well, it wasn't really from him, it was from the company." After the tense few weeks we'd had, I couldn't help but smile at his words. It was so rare that my work received praise or even thanks. A lady, of course, works for the satisfaction of a job well done, but it was still nice to be acknowledged. I thought it a very fine apology, even if the words weren't said.

"He's been so considerate. First, escorting you down to Washington, and then that lovely fur. And he's even been checking in on us from time to time," Brigid said.

"He brought us toys last time!" Kevin said brightly.

"Did he now?" I asked, genuinely surprised. Mr. Richardson had never shown an interest in children for as long as I'd known him.

The boy nodded enthusiastically. "He brought us new cars for our train set!" he said. Before anyone could stop him, Michael bounded up and went to retrieve it. In no time at all, the carved wooden train cars were being passed around the table with the bowls of mashed potatoes and greens to be admired by all, even those who had already seen it.

Once things had settled down a bit, I expressed my surprise that the uptight businessman was playing Father Christmas.

"Well, he came to pay is condolences, and brought the gifts for the children. He didn't stay long—mostly he just wanted to see how we were holding up. We talked about James for a while, and then he left."

"Is that so?" My eyebrow arched, almost of its own will.

"Yes. He was very kind. I think he just wanted someone else to reminisce about James with."

Mr. Richardson was certainly taking an unusual interest in our family, more than ever before. I wondered what sparked his sudden burst of friendliness, and felt a now-familiar tingle crawl down the back of my neck.

chapter nine

January left me with a sense of despondency. The city bowed its head against a wall of snow that came in from the north, burying us to our knees in white powder. Anything not covered in snow became coated in ice, and the sun did not show its face for days on end. Occasionally it would peer out through a curtain of cloud, then decide it was far too dreary and cold to be out of doors and retreat once again, leaving us poor souls on the ground to suffer.

Olivia loathed her walk to school each morning, and would arrive home in the evening chilled and red with cold. I made sure Mrs. Wordsworth always had a pot of chocolate waiting for her, and then she would be whisked up to her room to warm up before coming down to dinner.

Mr. Coolidge, returned from Baltimore and his extended Christmas holiday in Boston, withdrew the compromise, and I was once again fully barred from the office.

Melancholy settled over me like the heavy blanket of snow outside. Things that had seemed urgent in November and December suddenly felt less so. The tray of calling cards remained stubbornly empty after the New Year; It seemed Mrs. Watson was doing her part to assist her husband and Mr. Richardson in seeing me exiled from R&A by ensuring none of the other company wives would receive me.

It hardly mattered. I was too tired to go out, anyway. I hated the cold. I walked down to Granny

Agnes's house most days for tea, always bundled in my new fur, but otherwise I sat in my room or in the parlor, with a book open but unread, or the packet of James's old letters spread out in front of me. After the flurry of activity preceding the holiday I felt adrift, without purpose or direction, and I could pass hours in idleness without even noticing. Angela and Brigid both expressed concern, but there was little I could tell them. I didn't sleep more than two or three hours a night, and meals became a dreaded chore. I insisted on a normal schedule—at during the hours Olivia was home—but could barely bring myself to eat more than my tea and toast in the morning, for fear anything heavier would make a repeat performance.

As though trying to make amends now that I was out of the office, Mr. Richardson stopped by on occasion, once with a gift of chocolate and then again with wine, but things were too strained between us and he never stayed long. If I hadn't known any better, I would have said he was trying to woo me in his awkward way, but it didn't take much to put us at loggerheads once again.

"Mrs. Andrews?" Colleen knocked gently on my bedroom door. It was already partially open, so she poked her head in. Her face was a pale orb in the darkness that had settled unwittingly around me.

I looked up but didn't say anything. "Mr. Richardson is here to see you. I…I wasn't sure if you were at home," she said.

Rousing myself slightly, I set aside my handkerchief and the letter I'd been rereading "Thank you. Yes. I'm at home. I just..." My words trailed off into the unknown as I moved from the fainting couch to the stool by my looking glass. My hair was braided but not up, loose strands curling about my face.

"Shall I—"

"No, I'm alright. Tell him I'll be right down. Have Clara bring in tea. No, ask him if he'd prefer coffee. I think Mr. Richardson prefers coffee..."

"Are you sure you're well, ma'am?"

"Yes. Please, don't leave him waiting. I'll be down shortly." I was already re-plaiting my hair, twisting it up into a knot at the base of my neck. Jabbing it several times with pins, I tucked the entire thing under a black snood. My cheeks were pale, setting off the shadows under my eyes.

Well, nothing to be done about that, I sighed.

I arrived in the parlor just as Clara was leaving. Mr. Richardson stood to bow in greeting and I gave him a polite curtsy.

"Mr. Richardson. It is good of you to come. To what do I owe the pleasure?" The words were mere politeness; the lie tasted of bile on my lips.

"I apologize for coming so late. I know you have been unwell, and wanted to see if you were feeling better. When I spoke to Dr. Lynch yesterday, he expressed some concern."

I gestured him back to his seat and moved to pour the coffee, my back ramrod straight. I would have to have a word with Dr. Lynch. "That is very kind, but I assure you I am quite well. I simply find the task of venturing out in this weather to be a bit daunting."

"Certainly. I quite agree." He winced at the memory, I noticed his face was still flushed with cold, though he must have been indoors a good ten minutes at that point.

Adding a small spoonful of sugar to his cup, I offered it to him, then proceeded to pour one for myself. I gave myself a generous helping of cream and three sugars, but still set my cup aside after hardly a sip. The bitter flavor of coffee has never been to my liking.

"I admit I do have another reason for my visit," he said, setting aside his drink to look at me squarely. "I think you are aware your presence is...disruptive in the office."

I felt color, so long banished from my complexion, begin to rise, beginning at my neck. "It is only disruptive to those who choose to be disturbed. I fail to see how it interferes with anyone's work, when I am in my office attending to my own tasks and lifting a burden from others."

"That is just the point, you see—it is not your office. It is the office of your late husband, a man sorely missed and in desperate need of replacement." Odd. In three years, he'd never spoken of replacing James at all.

"I see. And you have found a suitable replacement?"

"Indeed. Horace Westcomb will begin his work on Monday."

"Why am I only hearing of this now? As co-owner, I should be informed of any major appointments and be able to vote on them, just as any other member of the board."

He sighed. "Mrs. Andrews, your ownership is still under contention. I know Mr. Coolidge has written to you regarding that so-called contract. The company has no record of it."

"You handed me a copy of it yourself, with a letter from my husband." My hand began to shake. I put down my cup quickly so he wouldn't see. "We've been through this. James sent you a copy of the contract. You told me you would see to the transfer of his salary to my name yourself, but now I find that you did no such thing. In fact, after all we've gone through the past few weeks, I begin to wonder if you had any intention of following through at all from the beginning."

He put down his cup. "We have already discussed the questionable legality of that contract *ad nauseum*. Mr. Westcomb has already been approved by the board. I only came to see you today as a courtesy, and to inform you that your personal belongings need to be removed from the office post haste. If you don't collect them yourself, I'll have one of the boys pack them up and deliver them.

"I also came to give you this." He reached into his jacket and produced a folded piece of paper, handing it over to me.

"What's this?" I unfolded it, my eyes skimming the words without recognition. I read it again, more slowly, to make sure I understood. "You wish to buy me out?" I asked in shock.

"The *company* wishes to buy back your interest. I know you are an independent, intelligent woman, but the role you are attempting to take on is one I fear is ill-suited to your temperament. You must agree the sum is impressive. You and Olivia could live like royalty for the rest of your days."

"This is quite a lot of money. If I understand this correctly, you are asking me to walk away and cut ties completely with R&A."

"Not completely. After the inconvenience of this legal trouble, we're prepared to allow you to retain the use of James's private car—"

"But you want me to walk away. You want me to have nothing more to do with the company, to have no more say in it. I would not speak of R&A, nor seek any further contact with its offices or those who work there. Am I to assume you include yourself in that?"

"Certainly not. Our friendship goes far beyond mere business. You are the widow of my dearest friend in all the world; I would feel I had failed him if I turned my back on you now."

"But you do not feel you are failing him by attempting to take away the one thing he left me other than our daughter that meant the most in the world to him? That it is not a betrayal to take the company public, after he desired it to remain in our hands? Is it not a betrayal to cut me out of the meetings, to lie to me, when I am the one he chose to act in his stead?" Losing my composure briefly, I thrust the paper back at him. All attempts at solicitude dropped from his face. "No. I refuse. James and I built the company. I will not walk away from it just because he is gone."

Mr. Richardson snatched at the contract, stuffing it back into his pocket. "James and *I* built the company, madam. R&A will go public by summer; the board has already voted on the matter."

"Is that what your secret meetings have been about? The ones you have been trying to keep me away from?" It took all my strength not to hurl my cup at his head. There had been discussions about the decision all last summer, but I'd moved to table the discussion until James resumed his post, since his return seemed imminent. The vote passed, but after his death, murmurings began again.

"I have hardly excluded you, Mrs. Andrews. You have no further obligation to the company. While I appreciate you volunteering your time during your husband's absence, I promise you, this is the best offer you will receive. It is more than generous. If you decline it now, you will not get a second chance."

"Good. I don't want one." Snatching the bell from the tea cart, I rang for Mr. Scott.

"Please show Mr. Richardson out," I said, without taking my eyes off my erstwhile guest.

Slamming his hat back onto his head, he stormed out without a backward glance.

As soon as I heard the front door shut, I called for one of the servants. I didn't care who answered, but Clara took that dubious pleasure. Only fifteen, she cowered slightly in the face of my anger.

"Summon Mr. Hartly. Tell him to bring the carriage 'round."

I shivered all the way to Shipley, Coolidge and Hagen, even with the hot brick, thick rug, and fur trimmed cloak I wore. For once I was grateful for the veil, as it meant there was an extra layer between my face and the cold, flimsy as it might be. I burrowed deep into my black fur, feeling like a half-frozen turtle as the carriage rocked in the stiff wind, the horse plodding slowly over icy streets.

The cold was enough to calm my temper slightly. Not knowing how long I might be, I sent Mr. Hartly home to warm up. Fifteen minutes was long enough to cause frostbite in weather like this, and I had a suspicion I would be much longer.

Mr. Coolidge was in his office when I arrived, and though he was surprised to see me, he was gracious enough to meet with me. "I have twenty minutes before my next appointment," he said, gesturing to a chair. "I am at your disposal until then."

I briefly outlined my conversation with Mr. Richardson. While I tried to stick to the facts, a reference or two to Gunther Richardson's character and parentage may have slipped out in my anger. Mr. Coolidge hid his amusement behind his hand, stroking his clipped white beard as he thought. "Based on the wording of the will, you have inherited his stock—it falls into the category of 'assets not listed here.' But you can't legally inherit his position within the company, or his income, though the company can choose to award you a pension based on his service. I believe Gunther considers the payments you've been receiving through the war as that pension. As to your half of the company, they can't force you to sell, not legally. But they can make things uncomfortable for you, to the point you *wish* to sell."

"Uncomfortable in what ways?"

"Oh, anything. I've seen this before with other large businesses, or in any case when someone has something of considerable value someone else wants. There are the usual, distasteful methods—rumor mongering is popular, slander. Skeletons tend to come out of the closet, be they real or imagined.

Considering your position, I suspect this would be the most likely tactic, should they choose to force the issue. There are few things which can cause more harm to a woman than the loss of her reputation."

"Of course. A new widow, chaperoned by her maid in public places, and shut up in a private office is clearly up to no good."

Mr. Coolidge had been sipping from a glass of brandy and made a slight choking noise.

"That wasn't entirely what I meant, but I think you get the general concept," he said at last.

I looked down into my cup of tea, thinking of the empty tray in the hall. I was still in deep mourning, and therefore exempt from social gatherings, but it was still considered polite to send an invitation. I knew of at least three dinners and a ball I'd been excluded from already, based on the social column in the newspaper.

"What about the contract? I gave the information on the lawyer in Baltimore."

"And his office has moved, with no forwarding address, if it existed at all."

I closed my eyes. It was all too much. "What would you have me do?" I asked quietly. All of a sudden, I felt completely exhausted. It would be so easy to simply send Charlie around with a message for Mr. Richardson, to tell him I had reconsidered. I could take the money and be done with all of it.

"I can't really advise you in this situation," he said, eyes softening. "You know I represent the company and Mr. Richardson as well. It is a very generous offer. I helped draw it up myself."

Somehow, I'd forgotten. I set down my cup and

moved to leave. "Of course. I understand."

"However, if I found myself faced with a similar decision, I would ask myself what my motivations were for hanging on so tightly." Then, quietly, "You can't bring him back."

I nodded. "Thank you for the tea," I said, my throat tight.

I took a cab home. My thoughts were still reeling after the conversations I'd had. I fairly floated up to my room, my mind so far detached from my body. Demelza built up the fire while I paced on the rug. I felt her eyeing me, but she looked away quickly and scurried off when I glanced in her direction.

I needed advice; a friend. A sounding board. In the past, I would have gone to James or Angela, but James was gone and Angela was hardly a businesswoman. She'd tell me to sell and be done with it. It was too much trouble to hang on, and there was too much money to be made by selling.

But I wasn't ready to let go, not just yet.

I went to the window and looked out. On the street below, a man in a long black coat strolled down the street, heedless of the wind. He stopped at a street lamp just outside the house, produced a newspaper from under his arm, and proceeded to unfold and read it. He didn't seem to notice the cold or the sleet, his broad brimmed hat pulled low over his face.

I backed away from the window, closing the curtain quickly.

Sitting down at my writing desk, I folded down the lid and pulled out paper and ink, and began to compose a letter to Olivia Baxter. She had written two or three times since Christmas, but my responses had been short and to the point. December was too busy, and January too dreary for me to express my deepest thoughts.

My letter stretched on to some six pages before I managed to conclude it. Folding it up, I copied down the Baxter's address and went downstairs. Dinner would be soon; I'd already heard Olivia come home some time ago.

I was on the landing when the bell rang. Who on earth could be calling so late? I wondered. It was nearly seven o'clock, far too late for regular calls.

Mr. Scott answered the door, conversing briefly with the person outside before letting in a hunched figure covered in snow and ice. At first, I thought it was the man from the lamppost. A panicked scream began to build in my throat, until the butler peeled off the coat and hat, and I caught sight of his face

"Mr. Hamilton! What are you doing here?" I asked, before I remembered myself. His cheeks were red above his beard, and what I could see of his lips were nearly blue with cold.

"M-my ap-p-pologies. I d-did n-not realize it was s-so f-far f-from the r-rail l-line."

"Do you mean to say you walked all the way here?" I asked, noting the cane he leaned heavily on and the stiffness of his right leg.

He nodded, teeth chattering too badly to form another response.

"Come in! Clara! Where's Clara? Mr. Scott, send Clara to the kitchen for some of that hot cider from Mrs. Wordsworth. And add some brandy to it." I showed Mr. Hamilton into the parlor myself. As he hobbled through the door, his cane slipped on the floor, damp with the snow melting off his person. I caught his elbow and helped him to the chair nearest the fireplace, which had burned down to glowing coals. I threw on another log and found a thick blanket and wrapped it tightly around the poor man. He tried to object, but I shushed him and pushed him back down in the chair. "You are practically frozen solid, and with your injury, too."

"It's not so bad, r-really—"

"Nonsense. Here." I'd already crossed the room to the sideboard and filled a glass with two fingers of whiskey, pushing it into his hands.

At last, Clara appeared. She had a stoneware pitcher and two cups. Demelza followed in her wake and made quick work of restarting the fire. Slowly, the poor man began to thaw. Once he had finished the whiskey, I took the glass and poured him a cup of the hot cider.

"Now, tell me what was so important you risked life and limb to see me this evening," I said, once he was capable of finishing a sentence.

"I'm sorry. You really must excuse me. I feel an absolute fool now having come here, but by the time I'd realized my error, I felt I had no choice to go on— I thought you might at least have pity on me and give me shelter from the cold before I returned to my lodging."

"Well, you were correct in one estimation, at least," I said with a small smile. I wasn't sure if the color to his cheeks came from cold, spirits, or embarrassment.

"I've only just arrived in Buffalo. My train came in last night, and I am still learning my way around.

This afternoon, I went down to the R&A office. I think I told you that your husband mentioned giving me a job once the war was over."

"Yes, I remember." James had written to me of his comrade, who had an eye for detail and an inquisitive mind. I had at least two letters from him in which he stated Joshua Hamilton would make a fine addition to R&A, helping to design the next generation of locomotive.

"He wrote me a letter of introduction before he died. He said he didn't want to forget." He patted his breast, and I heard the crinkle of paper under his jacket.

"Yes, that sounds like him." James could be terribly absent minded when it came to small matters like correspondence, or remembering to come down to dinner. Once he became involved in a project, it took nothing short of an act of God to pull him away.

Mr. Hamilton set down his empty cup and tucked his hands back under the blanket to warm them. "He said if for some reason he wasn't there, I should ask for his partner, Gunther Richardson, present the letter, and ask to be placed in Engineering and Development. He said he was always looking for good men with new ideas."

I pressed my lips into a thin line. "Let me guess. You arrived at the office to find it in a mild state of chaos. Mr. Richardson refused to see you at first, but finally consented when you produced the letter, but was in a foul mood for the entire interview, and ultimately refused you a place, likely for some flimsy excuse?"

A small smile distorted his closely trimmed beard.

"Ah. I see you are on familiar terms with Mr. Richardson."

"Indeed." I sipped the last of my cider and heaved a sigh. "I'm afraid his temper is my fault—at least on this occasion. We had a bit of a disagreement earlier and it made us both a bit unpleasant."

"If that is the case, madam, I hope you will not think me too bold if I humbly beg you to intercede on my behalf? I could very much use the work at the moment, and it is difficult for wounded soldiers like me to find any now the war is over and there are so many of us."

"Certainly. I will go first thing in the morning."

There was a soft tap on the door and Olivia appeared.

She looked a little surprised to see Mr. Hamilton, a strange man, in the parlor so late, but took it in stride. "I'm sorry to interrupt. I hope I am not disturbing anything."

"Ah, of course not. Mr. Hamilton, this is my daughter, Olivia. Olivia, this is Mr. Joshua Hamilton; he was your father's secretary in the Army."

My daughter bobbed a curtsy, and I turned back to our guest. "I believe Olivia has come to summon me to dinner. You must join us, Mr. Hamilton. We are dining *en famille* tonight, if you don't mind."

"I don't want to intrude. I fear I've already taken advantage of your hospitality more than I should."

"I insist. We have had few visitors these past few weeks, and I would like to thank you."

"Thank me?" he asked in bewilderment.

"Yes. For being a good and loyal friend to my husband, and looking out for him when I could not.

And for tolerating the incessant questions of a rather nosy widow."

He made a polite objection, but I waved it away. "No, I insist."

He peeled back the blanket, and I noted his trousers were damp up to the knee from the snow. Handing him his cane, I watched as he got stiffly and unsteadily to his feet, the damaged leg unwilling to move properly.

"I am quite glad to have you as our guest, Mr. Hamilton. Our table has felt so empty with only Olivia and I to share it," I said, resisting the urge to take his arm and offer assistance, instead walking slowly beside him until we reached the dining room. I took the seat Mr. Scott pulled out for me at the head of the table. Olivia sat on my left, and our guest took the seat to my right, resting his cane against the edge of the table.

"I am glad to see your recovery is going smoothly. Mama said you injured your leg very badly," commented Olivia.

"Olivia, not at dinner!"

But Mr. Hamilton only smiled. "Yes, but I deprived those military sawbones of a chance to ply their trade. Butchers, all of them."

Seeing Olivia was about to ask another question that would likely not be appropriate in front of a guest, even were we not at table, I cut her off with a warning look and turned back to Mr. Hamilton. "That is such a unique cane. Very lovely." It was, in fact. Made of polished wood, the grip at the top was carved to resemble the climbing branches of a rose bush, complete with delicately carved blooms. The hand rested in this nest of vines, providing a broad, flat place to support the palm.

For unknown reasons, I found my eyes growing a little damp. I tried to dab at them discreetly, but it was no use.

"Are you well, Mrs. Andrews?" Mr. Hamilton's voice had an edge of panic at my sudden burst of emotion.

"I'm sorry. I—I don't know what's come over me. I sometimes find myself quite overcome for no apparent reason." I could not tear my eyes away from the carving.

Olivia looked from me, to the cane, and back again. "Oh. I see. It's the roses."

"Roses?"

"'Rose' is Mama's middle name. Papa used to always call her that, or her Irish name."

"Her Irish name?" This time it was Mr. Hamilton's eyes who bounced back and forth.

I nodded and attempted to regain my composure enough to explain. "My parents were from Ireland, but I was born here. After my mother died, I was taken up by a benevolent society, with the intention of making a lady out of me. They thought introducing me as Síomha Róisín O'Cleary, a Papist, would be 'too Irish' and limit my prospects. So, I was made to attend services at the nearby Episcopal church, and my name was anglicized to Sophia Rose Cleary."

He smiled warmly. "Well, it seems they've achieved their goal. You are certainly the finest lady I've ever had the pleasure to meet." Suddenly realizing his words, he backpedaled suddenly. "That is, you hold yourself—I mean—I'm sorry, that was too forward."

Olivia laughed. I couldn't help but join in, and then all three of us were laughing. "It's quite all right, Mr. Hamilton. But as I was saying before, your cane is…it's a work of art."

A broad smile split the bearded face as he lifted it slightly to show the workmanship at a better angle. "Thank you. I had so little to do during my recovery, and I've always found carving to be a very soothing occupation."

Olivia leaned over slightly for a better examination. "It's lovely. And so unique!"

"I found the shape of it was easier on my hand," he said, then laughed. "I'm afraid I made quite a few while I was convalescing. And I think I have caught up on all of the reading I couldn't do during the war."

"Are you fond of reading, Mr. Hamilton?" Olivia asked, her soup forgotten as they talked for some minutes about literature.

"And what of you, Mrs. Andrews? Are you as voracious a reader as your daughter?"

"Oh, Mama is more so. She used to read to me every night when I was little, but I don't think you want any recommendations from her." Olivia's grin was as wicked as any to ever cross the lips of her namesake.

"Olivia!"

She stage-whispered conspiratorially across the table: "Her favorite books all come from the bookshop at the train station."

Mr. Hamilton's laugh was full and loud. "Penny dreadfuls, eh? Are you fond of those, Mrs. Andrews?"

My face was the same color as the wine. "I find them diverting. Of course, I read other things as well."

We had exchanged one or two letters since our initial meeting, but I'd forgotten the sense of familiarity I had with him; he was very easy to talk to.

"Were you ever able to track down that boy?" he asked, after Clara brought in the after-dinner tea.

"What boy?" Olivia asked.

"The boy who…who helped your father, after his injuries. The one who called for help. I wanted to thank him, you see." And to question him about what he might have seen.

Olivia scowled into her cup. "He didn't do much."

"Olivia! He did all he could. You father…he had the best care. And it's likely because of him that Mr. Hamilton is still alive."

She wiped her eyes. I wasn't sure if her tears were from anger or grief. Probably both. I could feel the familiar itch in my own eyes.

"I've been trying to help your mother find him," Mr. Hamilton said gently. "I've asked some of the men from my company if they remember anything, but no one seems to know who he was. I'm afraid it's a dead end."

"I'm going to keep trying." I wanted to say more, but didn't want to voice my suspicions in front of Olivia. Bad enough she'd lost her father. I didn't want her to know he'd been murdered, as well.

The room filled with a tense, sad silence. I cleared my throat, refreshing my cup of tea. "Tell me, Mr. Hamilton. All those books you caught up on. Was there a favorite?"

The dark moment passed and we spent the rest of the evening in lively conversation. I realized I had not smiled or laughed so well since Mrs. Baxter returned to New York City.

The clock in the hall chimed the hour, and I was surprised to see it was already after ten o'clock.

I was not the only one. Olivia yawned widely, her attempt to cover it with her hand unsuccessful. I felt one tugging at my own jaw.

"Well, I think I have taken up more than enough of your time for one evening," Mr. Hamilton said, reaching for his cane.

"No trouble at all. If you would care to call tomorrow, about ten o'clock, we can proceed to the office together and I will have a word with Mr. Richardson."

"That sounds like a very fine idea."

"If you'd like to stay the night, we do have a guest room. I don't like the idea of you walking home in the dark in this cold."

"No, please, don't trouble yourself—"

"I insist. I've already had to defrost you once tonight, and I highly doubt there will be someone waiting at your lodging to repeat the process, considering you've only been in our city for a day."

"No. I couldn't." It was the only polite thing he could say; gentleman callers did not say with ladies as their house guests, even if the weather outside was dreadful.

"In that case, at least wait and I can have the carriage brought around for you."

He was ready to object, but Olivia stopped him. "I wouldn't argue if I were you. Mama takes her duties as matron very seriously. And she hates the cold."

"You seem to live in an odd place, for one who hates it so much," Mr. Hamilton said, raising one eyebrow.

I shrugged. "I was born here. What can I say? But I certainly will not stand for anyone to freeze to death under my watch if it can be prevented."

Mr. Scott, who had been standing unobtrusively in a corner should he be needed, had already seen to it Mr. Hartly prepared the carriage and a brazier.

By the time he bundled himself back into his heavy coat, muffler, gloves, and hat, our horse and driver were already waiting, the lantern at the front of the coach sending a warm glow over the snow.

"Until tomorrow, then." Mr. Hamilton bowed as low as he could. As he passed out the front door, I signaled to Mr. Scott to follow at a distance, to ensure he didn't slip on the walk, but despite his limp he made it without incident. I peered over their heads in the dark, but there was no sign of the man at the lamppost. I breathed a sigh of relief.

"Mr. Hamilton is a very nice man," Olivia said, standing beside me at the door, watching the carriage rattle off into the darkness.

"Yes, he is."

"I can see why Papa liked him so much."

"Mmhm. Come on. Time for bed. It's late."

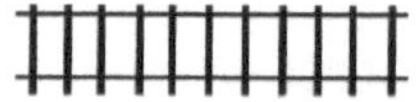

"I think it might be best if you wait here for the moment. Allow me to speak with him first," I said the next morning as we entered the R&A office.

Mr. Hamilton nodded, sinking down into a chair.

"Do you think you can convince him? I did not mean to force you in any way, or to put you in an awkward position..."

"Think nothing of it. I must speak to him, anyway, and I do have a plan."

"May I ask what it is?"

I held up the wooden box I was carrying. "I have a peace offering. I also have something he wants."

Mr. Richardson's office was on the same floor as James's, but in the eastern corner. Similarly fashioned, it was also lined with bookcases and filing cabinets, furnished with a heavy desk, leather chairs, and a drinks cart against one wall. Unlike James's office, however, this one did not sport the slightly cluttered, absentminded look of a man who is more accustomed to creation than business. Instead, it was neat as a pin and arranged to impress with an expensive oil painting on the wall and any trinket he could find to show off his power and wealth, right down to the thick smell of the cigar smoke lingering in the room.

His secretary announced me, and after a wait I was allowed into his office. He did not bother to rise when he saw me, barely looking up from his papers.

"And what do you want? I know you too well to think you've changed your mind after a good night's rest."

My general lack of sleep notwithstanding, I held out the box to him. "I realized last night after you left that you never collected your bequest."

When he made no move, I set it down on the desk. Carved of polished maple, the lid was inlaid with six different kinds of wood, mother of pearl, and copper, to create mountain scene with a lake and forest. In the background, a train crossed a bridge over the lake, opalescent smoke curling out behind it.

Mr. Richardson set his pen down and reached for the box, pressing the hidden catch to open the lid. Inside was a neat row of my late husband's favorite cigars.

He closed the lid quickly and pulled back his hand as though burned. He turned to me, eyes still blazing. "Unless you have changed your mind, we have nothing to discuss."

Though he hadn't offered, I helped myself to one of the brass-studded leather chairs, spreading my skirts about me. "We have plenty to discuss," I replied. "Yesterday you caught me unawares. I was not expecting such a... generous offer. I have not changed my mind," I said quickly when he opened his mouth, "But I would like to ask...a few days. To think it over. I think perhaps I can come up with a counter offer, one that would be satisfactory to both of us."

He frowned; it was a look I was familiar with from the various parties and dinners I had hosted for investors and businessmen. It was the frown that said he strongly disagreed with the statement, but in the interest of diplomacy, he would keep his opinions to himself. For the time being.

I continued. "There is one thing you can do which would go a long way to...fostering good will between us."

"And what is that?" He sounded more than a little doubtful.

"You have known me for eighteen years. You know money and social standing are of little interest to me."

His lips twitched. "Everyone says that, until they don't have it to depend on."

"You forget I have done without it in the past, and I can do without it again, if necessary. However, kindness, fidelity, and honor—those are things I put stock in. Even more than in railroad companies."

I waited. He raised an eyebrow.

"Downstairs there is a gentleman who came you yesterday seeking employment. He bore a letter of introduction from my husband, which you ignored. I would like you to offer him a position. I know for a fact James mentioned him to you in his letters. He's a brilliant man and would be an asset to the company."

"Absolutely not."

"On what grounds? Can he get a better testimonial than from my husband? Did you yourself not say only yesterday that R&A needed fresh ideas? Mr. Hamilton is a clever man, forged in the fires of war, and tutored by one of the greatest scientific minds in this business."

"He also has no experience with what we do. He has drawings, nothing practical. He has wooden toys he thinks represent the next generation of transportation, but they are little more than fanciful ideas. Untested. And as I told you yesterday, we have already found a new head for that department. If Mr. Westcomb approves of him, then that is all well and good but I will not get involved in his decisions. It is his duty to find the most qualified candidates."

And you certainly won't try to influence him in any *way*, I thought. No, it was just as I had feared. My speaking out on Mr. Hamilton's behalf only solidified

Mr. Richardson's position against him. I would have been better off to come in maligning his character than to say anything good about him.

There was nothing left then, but to push. "Very well. If you are set in your decision, then I suppose I am set in mine as well."

He narrowed his eyes. "Mrs. Andrews, I think you have misunderstood the situation. The board has been tolerant of your antics thus far out of respect for your late husband, and in recognition of the unfortunate situation you find yourself in. But our patience is wearing thin. Now, we have made you a very generous offer, but should you choose to decline it, I'm afraid there may be legal ramifications. You'd hardly want to find yourself in the position of the former first lady, would you?"

I pursed my lips. Mrs. Lincoln, so recently widowed, had been cast out of the White House and now depended on the charity of family. Rumor had it she was an emotional wreck, deep in debt, and completely hysterical.

"R&A may choose to challenge you in court if we can't settle this amicably. You know the law so rarely sides with women. Could you really afford the scandal and the expense? Your one source of income frozen, the loss of your place in society? Surely even you realize your place is precarious, what with your husband so newly dead, after so long away. The amount of time you spend in the company of men, even myself. Attempting to have something that amounts to an occupation. And that is even before we touch on your...modest upbringing." He sneered. "Of course, such things do not bother *me* in the slightest, but you may find you are no longer welcome in every drawing room in the city now."

We stared each other down coldly, neither of us willing to flinch, neither daring to blink.

"Can the *company* afford the scandal, I wonder?" I asked softly when I saw his lips begin to twitch into a triumphant sneer. "Profits have been down, lately. Fewer people traveling. No more Army contracts. We lost our place as the most extensive rail network in the North East, and there are rumors the New York-Pennsylvania line has built an engine twice as efficient as the model we have been using. How will it look then, if you go to court with the new widow of your former partner, squabbling over the ownership of an already weakened company? Will you be able to tolerate the public scorn it would stir up? Would customers still purchase tickets from R&A, or would they go elsewhere? Would the other rail companies support your dealings, or would they go to Pullman for their passenger cars, instead?"

The smirk became a scowl. "Well, it seems we are at an impasse."

"One week. In one week, I will return with my counter offer."

"You said a few days."

I shrugged, standing and brushing down the soft wool of my skirt. "You threatened me. Now it's a week. Good day to you, Mr. Richardson."

I swept out of his office with regal bearing the Queen of England herself would envy.

Mr. Hamilton struggled to his feet when he saw me. He was reading from a slender pocket volume of Dickens, gold rimmed spectacles on his nose.

"Mrs. Andrews. How did—"

"My coat please," I demanded of the boy behind the coat check. "And Mr. Hamilton's, too. Sir, if you would care to come with me, I have a proposition to make you."

chapter ten

If the servants were surprised to see me home so soon, and with the visitor from the night before in tow, they did their duty and did not show it.

Mr. Scott helped us with our wraps. "We will need the study for at least half an hour. Have Demelza build up the fire, and bring in tea. Or do you prefer coffee, Mr. Hamilton?"

Still looking slightly confused by the abrupt change in plans, he shook his head. "I have no preference. Either way, it will undoubtedly be an improvement over what we were served in the Army."

"Very good. Tea it is, then."

I led the way back to the study at such a brisk pace Mr. Hamilton had difficulty keeping up.

The room was cold after so many weeks of being shut up. The window had been repaired, the mess from the break-in cleaned up, but seeing the room properly for the first time in weeks brought back with a jolt how foolish I had been. How careless.

Demelza hurried in after us, building up the fire with some difficulty.

I offered Mr. Hamilton one of the armchairs on the hearth rug, and he sat gratefully, his bad leg stiff from the cold. I took the other and waited for the girl to finish her work before speaking.

The room was papered in burgundy, lined with shelves and glass cupboards. There were books of literature and books of science, as well as history and art. Small models of ideas James had and sketches of some that bore promise. Aside from the desk, there was also a drafting table. A row of jars on top held a selection of pencils and charcoal. The table remained untouched since his departure. I had been encouraged to learn the rudiments of art while at school, but never showed any real talent for it. I had always leaned more towards music when it came to the arts a lady should know. That, and penmanship. I would never wield a paintbrush with any skill, but my penmanship was second to none.

"Mr. Hamilton, I hope you will not find it impertinent of me, but I would be very grateful if you would tell me something of yourself."

Thoroughly confused, Mr. Hamilton stared at me.

"I assure you I have a very good reason for asking, if you will only bear with me for a little while. Please, where do you come from? What was your occupation before the war?"

Clara entered just then with the tea cart. I poured while he began his tale. "My family is from Ohio. We owned a mill there. Lumber."

I nodded for him to keep going. He swallowed, then took a fortifying sip of tea before continuing. "I suppose that was what sparked my interest in mechanics and invention, watching the wheels of the mill turn, and seeing how everything worked together." Another sip, and he began to relax into the tale. "My brother was set to inherit the company, so I was sent to school. I studied in Philadelphia."

"What did you study?"

He gave a lopsided smile. "I was a very indecisive youth. At my father's suggestion I started in law, but found it tiresome and dull, so I changed to business with the same result. Father was at his wit's end when he finally consented to let me study engineering. I had just graduated when the war started. I didn't really fancy the thought of going back home, so I joined up. I knew the army was short of men with my training. Father was livid, but I was assigned to Captain Andrews' unit, and the rest is history, I suppose."

I did a quick calculation. "So you are not yet thirty, then?" I was surprised, but then, the beard and the hardship of war added years to him, particularly around the eyes.

"Only just."

"And what of your family?"

"Mother died when I was a boy. My brother joined up a year after I did. Father was killed in an accident at the mill a few months later. Edward was taken to Andersonville sometime in '64; I don't know when, exactly. I think they were marching through Kentucky when he was captured." He pressed his lips together grimly, and I knew his brother did not survive the Southern prison camp. Few managed to live through the deplorable conditions. The broadsheets had been filled with the horror stories for weeks after the camp was liberated.

"I'm very sorry for your loss."

"When I was finally discharged and well enough to travel, I thought about going back home, to the ruins of the mill, and I couldn't do it. The good thing about Xenia is there is always a demand for lumber. The trade off is that we have to rebuild every year. A storm leveled the mill in April, just after Mr. Lincoln was shot. I couldn't rebuild something I never really loved, not when the people who truly loved it were gone."

There was a faraway look in his eyes. He was no longer seeing me, or the fire or the study. His mind and heart were back in Ohio, in the ruins of his former life.

"I took what we had in the bank—it wasn't much. Father lost a lot during the war. And then I came here. I still had the letter from your husband, and I thought it would mean something. I wanted to start over. I've no family to speak of, and all I have to my name is what was left of my father's estate, the clothes on my back, and that letter."

I nodded, refilling his cup. His eyes had taken on the same sad, haunted look I remembered from our first interview. It made him look fifteen years older.

I couldn't fathom the thought of losing my entire family, a dear friend, and my home in the span of four years, on top of the trials of war. "I can certainly understand your desire to start again. In a way, I find myself attempting to do the same thing."

He looked up at me, as though for the first time noticing the room around us, that we were in New York and not a faraway town of memory. "Yes. Of course."

"Which brings me to my proposal: I was unable to argue on your behalf to Mr. Richardson. I doubt he will change his mind. There are…legal complications in the way. As long as you are associated with me, your hope of working at R&A in any capacity is, I'm afraid, non-existent."

He nodded, looking down into his drink.

"However, I do have another position to offer

you."

Surprise colored his face.

"It is not so illustrious as working for the railroad. In fact, it will require a great deal of discretion. But it would give you access to the company, and it would, perhaps, give you a chance to prove yourself to those in charge, should the opportunity arise—and I will do my best to arrange for such an occurrence."

"What is this position?"

"I am in need of a secretary of sorts. A man who, well, to put it simply, is a *man*. Legally, I may have more freedom now than I did before the war, but there are still places in society which are closed to me, and I need access. There are still people who would treat me differently because of my sex, or refuse to speak to me at all in matters of business. I need someone who is trustworthy, intelligent, and creative who can act on my behalf."

"And you want me?" He was utterly incredulous. "I'm flattered you think so highly of me after such a short acquaintance, but are you certain? We scarcely know each other."

"How long did you work with my husband?"

"Nearly three years."

"Yes. And from his letters, I know he trusted you implicitly. He relied on your judgment and said there was never a more courageous, bright man under his command, either with the railroad or in the army."

His cheeks colored, and I plowed onward. "He trusted you, and so do I. Some might argue my offer is rash, but I assure you I have a very good sense of people, and I trust you.

"There is more to this, but you may feel free to

decline. At our first meeting, you made a statement, one I have been unable to forget, though I have tried to ignore it. These past few weeks, I'm afraid I have allowed myself to be lulled into complacency, or overrun with melancholy, however you prefer to view it. But I now find my passions and my anger renewed.

"I want you to help me find the man who murdered my husband."

His cup clattered against the saucer, and he choked on his tea. I waited for him to recover. He stared at me with eyes made bluer by the rush of blood to his face, which now resembled a furry radish. I forced myself not to smile.

"You want...You want me to track down a murderer?"

"I understand if you decline the position. You have spent the last four years risking life and limb for your country, and have suffered nearly unbearable loss, not to mention your own injuries. But I know my husband's death and your injuries were not the result of a random attack of Rebels who set upon you by chance. I have become aware of too many things since then to think they are not all connected."

"And what things are those, if I may ask?"

"Between the time I first saw you and the time we left Washington, my husband's belongings were tampered with. Someone attempted to steal something from his trunk, but either lacked the proper tools to completely the job, or was interrupted.

"I think this person, frustrated at their inability to search my husband's personal effects, then attempted to break into this very house." I gestured to the new window, which did not quite match the others behind the desk. "He was not so subtle in his attempt. He broke into my home the night before I arrived. I cannot help but think the two things are connected, especially since some of my husband's belongings were taken from his person after the attack—but not those of the most monetary value."

Mr. Hamilton did not so much as twitch at the revelations, his eyes locked on to me.

"Once my initial shock and anger passed, I allowed my grief to take me. I allowed the urgency of the situation to pass me by when I failed to gather additional information at the time, but I know you share my opinion on this. The attack was not random, and it was not perpetrated by Rebels.

"The police in Buffalo are scattered, weak, and easily bought. I know they will not coordinate properly with the Army or the police in Washington, and the Army has no reason to involve itself in the break in of an old widow, even if her late husband was a decorated captain."

He set down his cup, resting his hands in his lap and staring into the fire, digesting the information I had just fed him. "You are certain of this?"

"I am. I want to bring his killer to justice. I want to settle this, and I know there is no other man in this city who will be as motivated to find the truth as you."

"Mrs. Andrews, I am flattered by your confidence in me, but I'm a cripple. I'm new to this city and have no connections to anyone, save yourself. You would do better to hire a Pinkerton."

I made a rather unladylike noise. "The Pinkertons are ruffians. I want someone who is subtler."

"If it's as you say, then we are dealing with someone who so far has had no qualms about physical assault, breaking into a woman's home, or even murder. You may wish to have a ruffian on your side before this is over."

"But none of them knew my husband. None of them have my trust. And none of them witnessed his murder.

"I do not ask for your help because of your record as a soldier or any physical prowess. I come to you from shared loss, and because in you I see a bright, active mind and a soul of honor."

He closed his eyes, exhaling loudly. "Your confidence in me is...overwhelming."

I did not respond. My tea had long since grown cold, but it hardly seemed to matter.

"Do you accept my offer? I will, of course, offer you pay commensurate to the work to be done."

He looked at me with eyes like coals, the blue heat at the center of a flame. "I do."

Mr. Hamilton stayed for luncheon. We moved to the dining room, bringing some of James's papers with us. We ate with them spread around us at the table and Mr. Hamilton pulled out the familiar notebook to make a list of everything we knew.

"And you think the person responsible for the attack was searching for his designs?"

"Yes. I know he always carried a small notebook with him when he was working to scribble ideas in." I should have noticed it was missing when I went through his belongings, but it was only now, going over the evidence again that I realized it.

"He didn't have it with him that night. He filled it up that very afternoon as we were working, so he left it in his quarters when we went out. It was in the items I packed up."

"This one?" I picked up the slim volume and he nodded. "Yes, I remember seeing it. When I realized someone had attempted to force their way into his trunk, I moved it and some of his other drawings to my own luggage."

"And then at the break in, it was once again his drawings that were disturbed?"

"Yes. He didn't keep many here. Most of his drawings were for the railroad and were kept in his office. The ones in his study were mostly things he did for his own pleasure, or ideas that didn't pan out."

"And the safe?"

I hesitated. "Money. Jewelry. I don't know the exact value of the jewels, but there's a few hundred dollars in the safe. And the most important papers. Deeds, titles, and the like. He never locked up his drawings, but I put his notebook there after the break in. James always seemed to think of his sketches as worthless doodles until Mr. Richardson gave his stamp of approval. To be fair, most of those slap-dash drawings would mean little to anyone but him. It would take a very experienced person to make heads or tails of his initial drawings and notes."

Mr. Hamilton grinned. "Well, then, it is lucky you have me. I've spent three years learning his style, and I promise war did not afford us the time to create finished drawings or plans. I would like to see what was left behind. It may give us an idea of what they were looking for in the first place."

"As far as I can determine, it's all still there. At least, what was here. I looked through his files at work afterward, and they had all been cleaned out. I don't know how I missed it." Well, I did. I didn't need to use his drawings. My work never involved his designs, and I never even opened the filing drawers save the two pertinent to my own work. I was essentially a clerk and social secretary for the company. I took out my anger on my pork chop, savagely cutting it into smaller pieces.

"Do you have any idea when they might have been removed?"

"None. It could have been at any point after he left. I kept regular hours, so everyone knew exactly when and where to find me."

We ate in silence for a few minutes. Finally, he stopped scribbling in his notebook and gave his meal some proper attention. "There are other, more mundane matters I require assistance with as well. I need a new lawyer." I explained about the complication with Mr. Coolidge. "So you see, I really can't employ his services any longer."

"And you want me to engage a replacement?"

"Yes. As soon as possible. I can provide you with a list of some of the more reputable lawyers in the city; the ones our clients, partners, and friends have dealings with. I've exhausted the list of reputable firms here in Buffalo. I may write to my friend, Olivia Baxter, in New York City to see if she has any recommendations. But I think this will go more smoothly if you are the one to make the actual inquiries."

He nodded. "Of course."

"There are other things, but I think they can wait for the moment. That is the most pressing issue."

"Do you...I'm sorry, this is a very indelicate question. Do you suspect someone from the company? Mr. Richardson, or Mr. Coolidge, or someone else altogether, of involvement?"

For a moment, I didn't answer. "I don't know who else to suspect. Clearly, Mr. Richardson wants the patents I still hold, and what is left of my husband's designs, presumably so he can patent those as well. He's not a particularly nice man, but he was a good friend to James and I've always considered him a part of the family. Mr. Coolidge is a man of business; he has more to gain by siding with the company than with me. If he can arrange for us to settle our differences amicably, then it means he won't lose a client—at least, the way he sees it. He's always been fair and kind in his dealings with me, and never seemed concerned with my sex; he was one of the few men who would speak openly to me about business.

"I don't want to think ill of Mr. Richardson. I have known the man for years, and without his investment, we would still be living a slum near the railyard. But since my husband died, he has cajoled and threatened me, and proved himself to be much less honorable than I initially thought."

"If your beginnings were so humble, how did Captain Andrews end up in business with Mr. Richardson?"

"James was working at a factory that belonged to Mr. Richardson's father. He made train wheels. He had an idea one day for a method to make the ride smoother for passengers. A smoother ride means less strain on the engine, and an engine that doesn't have to work as hard is more efficient and can travel faster.

"He created a mock up, and then a full-size model. He managed to persuade a few men down at the yard to allow him to install the model onto an unused boxcar, and then with the help of the foreman convinced Mr. Richardson's father to pay a visit. He demonstrated it, but the elder Mr. Richardson was not impressed. He said it would be too expensive to produce, and it would require altering the entire fleet. But Gunther Richardson took his entire inheritance, and used it to purchase a small, outmoded factory right from under his father's nose with the help of Mr. Coolidge. James made some slight alterations to the design, so it could be fitted to any railcar, regardless of manufacturer. James and Mr. Richardson were able to round up a small number of investors—Mr. Coolidge, for one, and a few others—and they put together enough capital to employ a skeleton crew for three months. We were so short of cash I ran the office and handled all of the clerical duties myself while James oversaw production and Mr. Richardson attempted to drum up business.

"It was difficult, at first. His father worked against us, saying neither James nor Gunther knew what they were doing, and the entire venture was doomed to fail. There were a few small buyers, enough orders to fit half a dozen cars at a time, but not enough to keep us afloat. After six months, we were days from shutting down when an order to supply one hundred and ninety-seven cars for the Boston & Maine

Railroad came in.

"Once we had that, everything else fell into place. We went from making just a few parts, to entire rail cars based on my husband's designs. Seats that absorbed the motion of travel. Long-distance cars with separate sleeping compartments. Cars where meals could be served, or passengers could play cards. He even designed a car where meals could be prepared for passengers while they traveled, without stopping, but it's hardly practical. He said the technology isn't there yet.

"When a small line between here and Rochester was about to go under, we bought them out, and began our own rail company. Not just making the cars, but sending them all over the country. Before the war started, we had plans to expand as far as Kansas City." Before the war, there had been so many plans. We were going to partner with a Canadian railway to provide service into Ontario and Quebec. There were to be additional lines in Ohio, Indiana, and Illinois, and then further south into Kentucky, Tennessee, and Georgia. There were plans to lay over five thousand miles of new track between 1860 and 1870, but now it was 1866, and only a fraction of those lines had been laid.

I laid down my knife and fork. My appetite had deserted me. "Would it sound strange to you, if I said I felt certain we were the only two who could do this?"

"No," he said softly. "It doesn't sound strange at all. I confess, I feel it is almost as if...the hand of fate has intervened to bring us together again in this manner." He opened his mouth to expand on the idea, but then closed it again, brow furrowing.

I looked down the long table towards the window facing the street, which was all but deserted. In the bright reflection of the snow, I thought I could see James in the glass. *Beware*, he had said. *Watch.* But what did that mean? What was I to watch for?

"The more I think on it, the more I think you should hire a Pinkerton. I know you find them distasteful, but if we're dealing with a murderer then it will do better to have someone a little more disreputable on our side."

I sighed. "If that is how you feel, I will look into it."

His eyebrows rose again.

"Don't look so surprised. I'm employing you for your knowledge and expert advice, am I not?"

His lips twitched under his moustache. "Well, yes, but you do not strike me as the type of woman to actually use it."

I smiled. "Well, I suppose it is never too late for those fresh starts we spoke of earlier."

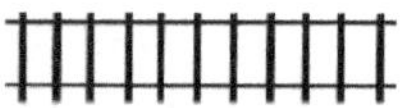

After lunch, I saw Mr. Hamilton off and once again engaged Mr. Hartly to take him home through the cold, icy streets.

While I waited for the driver to return, I summoned Colleen to help me rearrange my hair.

"Are you going out, madam?"

"I am, in fact. Have Charlie put on his suit, and find him a warmer coat. I'm going visiting."

Technically, a widow was under no obligation to return social calls, and, in fact, it was generally frowned upon. But now that my blood was moving again, I suddenly couldn't stand the idea of more seclusion. There was only so much I could learn of the world from the newspaper.

Once Mr. Hartly returned, we were off. Normally, my first stop would be to Mrs. Watson. As the wife of the chairman of the board, she was the most important woman in R&A circles after myself.

The day before, I'd sent Charlie around to the homes of women like Mrs. Watson, the wealthy, influential ladies of Buffalo who might be able to sway the opinions of their husbands. The new calling cards, bordered in black, had white roses and poppies on the front with my name in elaborate script. On the back where the days when I was "at home" to visitors.

The sleigh pulled up in front of the Watson's elaborate brick home, which resembled a small castle more than anything else. Charlie leaped down from the back of the sleigh, where he was acting as footman, and bounded up the walk to ring the bell, clutching another card in his glove.

When he returned, I started to climb out of the sleigh, but he stopped me, holding my own card back out. "Sorry, ma'am," he mumbled, as though it was his fault Mrs. Watson had chosen to snub me. If her visiting hours had simply changed, then Charlie would have been provided with one of her cards in return, with the correct days.

"Very well. On to the next, then," I said, directing Mr. Hartly to the next residence.

The day was cold and clear, but not as cold as the preceding week. February was on the horizon, and even nature seemed eager to be rid of January.

At the Brandt's, too, my card was returned. As the sleigh glided past the parlor window, I caught a flutter of movement at the window. When I looked over my shoulder, three faces quickly vanished behind the curtain.

Pursing my lips, I tried a third residence, that of Mrs. Lynch. Dr. Lynch had been the one to tend to me at the funeral. Unlike the others, they had no connection to the railroad. His wife volunteered with me at the hospital during the war, occasionally acting as a nurse and sometimes simply as a nursemaid, reading to patients, fetching glasses of water, and generally keeping the sick and injured company. She was a kind, caring woman—and the world's worst gossip. Even if she disapproved of whatever the rumor mill was spouting out about me, she would certainly invite me in, just to get the story straight from the horse's mouth, and to have conversational fodder for the next person to call on her.

She did not disappoint. I was shown into the parlor, which was filled with brick-a-brack, all of it in blue and white. The blue and white wallpaper was covered with cheery prints and watercolors of domestic life. The shelves built into the wall on either side of the fireplace were filled with ceramic cats, decorative figurines, elaborate china sets, and more framed artwork. Every couch, chair, ottoman, and horizontal surface had been draped with crocheted lace. In the summer, it was a pineapple pattern, or something floral. In the winter, it was snowflakes.

Mrs. Lynch rose from her seat to greet me, setting aside her crocheting. Between her deep blue day dress and the white lace cap covering her greying brown curls, she was a perfect match for the furniture.

"Oh, Sophia! So good to see you. We've missed you at the hospital. You haven't been by in an age!" she said, coming to take my hands and placing a kiss on each of my cheeks. She was a round woman, nearly a head shorter than myself and I had to stoop to accommodate her.

I smiled, and felt tears prick my eyes. It had been so long since anyone had greeted me as a friend, I'd forgotten the sensation. "I'm very sorry. I... I've not been well."

"Nothing serious, I hope?"

"No, nothing that would require Dr. Lynch's attention. Just a bit of the melancholy, I think."

"And no wonder, my dear," she said, with sympathy, not pity. "I'm surprised you are out and about at all."

I sank into the offered seat and she began pouring tea. "I needed to get out. Fresh air. Change of pace, and all that. If I stayed in my room, I don't think I'd ever come out again."

"There, there. Have you thought about taking a cure somewhere? I was just reading in one of Dr. Lynch's journals that they are all the rage in Europe. Rest, relaxation, good food, and exercise. A nice change of pace from the everyday, and exactly what the doctor ordered."

"Is it helpful, do you think? It seems...wasteful, somehow. Shirking one's duty."

"Oh, yes. They have very good results with it. They're treating all sorts of complaints." She set down her cup long enough to tick the items off on her fingers. "Consumption is the most popular, and female complaints. Very common for women of a hysterical nature. Switzerland is a very popular destination, especially for lung complaints. All of that cold mountain air."

I raised an eyebrow and looked pointedly towards the window. "I don't think a lack of cold air is my problem."

Mrs. Lynch laughed gaily, bright spots of pink appearing on her apple-round cheeks. She resembled one of the porcelain milk maids on her shelves. "A rest cure might do you good, though. That's what they're calling it." She picked up the little silver bell and rang for the maid before I could object. "Mary, go into Dr. Lynch's office and bring me the Journal of European Medicine. It should be on the shelf with the others. I'd like Mrs. Andrews to borrow it."

I tried to stop her. "Oh, I'd hate to be an inconvenience."

"Certainly not. Besides, Dr. Lynch never has time to read all those journals, anyway. They mostly collect dust after I'm done with them. And you might find something useful. You've not traveled further than New York City since the war started, and you've never been abroad, have you?"

"I went to Quebec City once with James, back when we were trying to build a line through to Canada."

She waved a hand dismissively. "No, that's not what I mean. Europe! Italy! London! Paris! Switzerland! Germany! You know, Dr. Lynch took me on a grand tour just after we married? We traveled by steamship to Spain and England, and then down to

France. It was much different, then. Railways weren't as common, and the European lines aren't nearly as comfortable as ours."

She spent the next several minutes telling me all about Europe and the places she had visited. The warm sea breezes of Italy and southern France sounded particularly enticing as the wind outside rattled the shutters and whistled down the chimney.

Her "rest cure" began to sound very appealing indeed, but I could not allow myself to be distracted from my goal in coming.

"I really don't think I could consider doing such a thing right now. I have too many responsibilities here, and I am not sure I could do with being out of society for so long," I said, attempting to steer the conversation in my chosen direction.

"Oh, but you wouldn't have to go for months or even go far. Dr. Lynch was just telling me the other day of a new facility, right here in New York. They've been open for a few years, apparently, and are achieving very good results. I'll see if I can find the information for you. If only I could remember that doctor's name—Robinson, I think. No, that's not it. At any rate, they've been doing wonders, from what I've heard, and it's only a few hours away by train."

Clearly subtlety would not win the day. "Perhaps in a few months. I seem to have slighted some persons, and would not dream of leaving the city until the damage had been repaired."

Mrs. Lynch looked into her teacup, clearly avoiding my gaze. "Slighted? In what way?"

"Well, that's the trouble. I'm not certain. Of course, Mrs. Watson has always been very...*particular* in her tastes, but I should think Mrs. Brandt would at least speak to me, should a difficulty arise between us."

"Oh, now dear. You know it is very unbecoming to beg for social acknowledgement."

"I am hardly begging. But there is little I can do. While in mourning I cannot act as a hostess or even attend functions I have been invited to." Had there been any invitations, that is.

It wasn't that I was so concerned with my own social status. Financially I was secure, even if I did loose James's income, and I had good friends I knew would not desert me, like Olivia Baxter and Charlotte Lynch. But within the next year, Olivia would be out in society, and I could not risk her chances. Women might have more opportunities than before the war, simply from sheer necessity, but a young lady of quality was still expected to marry well, and she could not do that if her widowed mother was in disgrace, no matter how much money she brought to the table. And the man who risked disgrace for the sake of money alone was not a man I would consent to marry my daughter.

"It is only this business with the company, I think. None of us want to disturb you in your time of mourning. But there has been talk of a lawsuit. Very unflattering talk indeed."

I waved a hand dismissively. "It's a minor misunderstanding, nothing more. Mr. Richardson and I hope to reach an agreement on our own by the end of the week." This was technically true, however unlikely it was. I made a mental note to have Mr. Hamilton look into the lawyer in Baltimore who had suddenly gone missing. Was he really missing, or was it only a ruse to further discredit me?

I rubbed the bridge of my nose. Perhaps I was getting paranoid, seeing malice at every turn. Maybe Mrs. Lynch was right and I did need a rest cure.

Misreading my expression, she patted my hand warmly. "I think you will find these things blow over in time. Old fashioned people like the Watsons and the Brandts tend to take offense at the slightest provocation, but they are also more than willing to ride on the coattails of another's success. Give them time, and they will come around."

"That's your advice then, to wait it out?"

"Well...Of course, dear, I know nothing at all could be improper where you are concerned. Especially with you still in mourning. But, well, a gentleman caller..."

At first, I thought she meant Mr. Richardson, who for so long had been the only gentleman to call on me. Until I remembered Mr. Hamilton's late arrival, and his even later departure. My, news traveled quickly. How had she even heard?

"Oh, that?" I laughed. "You mean to tell me they are concerned about a visit from my husband's secretary? The poor man arrived in the city late, and had the misfortune to misjudge his distances in an unfamiliar city. He arrived on my doorstep half frozen. I could hardly turn him away without allowing him to join us for the dinner we were about to sit down to. He's a very dear man, very dedicated to Captain Andrews. As a mark of gratitude for his service, James offered him a position at the factory. I merely sought to fulfill that promise."

"And that's all?" Charlotte chuckled. "Well. He sounds like a charming man. Tell me about him. Is he married?"

As simple as that, I knew the story of Mr. Hamilton would be to all of the pertinent parties as quickly as the story of his arrival. It was a shame Mr. Hamilton did not have wealth or position on his side; as a single, well-educated gentleman he would have made quite the catch. Unfortunately, with men, one could choose only two of three key traits at best: wealth, personality, and appearance. I'd married for love, choosing the latter two. Thankfully, the wealth followed later. I supposed the same could happen to Joshua Hamilton. He was still young, after all, for all that his eyes spoke of decades.

The bell rang, and a few moments later the maid came in with a card on a tray.

"Well, I should be moving on, myself," I said, taking my cue to leave. It was terribly rude to overlap one's call into another visitor's time. I'd already well exceeded the quarter of an hour afternoon calls typically took, but such things were not uncommon occurrences at Charlotte Lynch's tea table.

Much to my surprise, it was Mrs. Watson waiting in the foyer, half out of her cloak as I emerged from the parlor.

She froze, staring down her long nose at me. "Mrs. Andrews. What a surprise to see you here."

Deciding the best revenge was a life well lived, I smiled brightly, sweeping my wrap around my shoulders. "Delightful to see you Mrs. Watson, but I really should be going. Do enjoy your visit."

No doubt there would be gossip about my so-

called cheer—inappropriate in a widow, no doubt—
but the reason behind it would have Mrs Watson in
knots for weeks. She had to know everything about
everyone, if for no other reason than to hold it over
them later.

Mr. Hartly and Charlie were already waiting by
the time I got outside. Charlie was still nibbling on a
muffin with his gloved hands, pilfered from the
Lynch's kitchen, where they'd been sent to warm up
during the visit. I found the pair of them perched in
the driver's seat, sharing a drink from Mr. Hartly's
flask. "Enough of that. Home, if you please, Mr.
Hartly."

"Yes, Mrs. Andrews."

We lurched off into the gathering gloom. It was
nearly five o'clock when I returned home. Olivia had
just returned from school, and changed from her blue
and white uniform dress—which now sported bands
of black mourning trim—into something drier and
warmer after the walk home through the snowy
streets. She was curled up in the parlor with a book,
wrapped up in a blanket with slippered feet tucked up
under her.

"Hello, Mama," she said, smiling brightly. She
pulled back the blanket so I could sit next to her. "Oh,
your feet are freezing!"

I bent down to kiss the top of her head, burrowing
my stockinged toes under her legs. She squirmed,
trying to shoo me away. I caught her in a hug and we
both laughed. "How was your day?"

"Oh, dull as ever. Verity Steward is 'out' this
season, and everyone has been talking about the ball
her parents had for her last Friday. It was the absolute

talk of the season, from what I've heard. And Rachel Moreson's entire wardrobe was ordered straight from Paris. I am so sick of hearing about everyone else's seasons and everyone else's balls," she said, folding her arms over her chest in a determined pout. All of our colorful dresses had been put away for the time being, even the new ones never worn and ordered specifically for her aborted season. Her only consolation was a quilted yellow dressing gown embroidered with red flowers—the only thing left in her wardrobe that wasn't black, since it would never be seen in public. She pulled the yellow cotton more tightly around her shoulders.

"I'm sorry we had to delay your season. I wish I could make it up to you somehow."

"Verity's first dance was with her father," she said quietly. There were tears swimming at the corners of her eyes. "She set aside the first place in her dance card, just for him."

I didn't know what to say. There was no comfort for either of us, it seemed. What platitude could make up for the loss of a father, of a partner? Olivia had always been the light of her father's eye and he doted on her completely. It was a good thing she was generally a sensible child anyway, or he would have spoiled her completely and we would have been left with someone unbearably selfish and cruel, like Mr. Coolidge's granddaughter. She was a few years older than Olivia, and had made a horse's ass of herself at a dinner party when she criticized the floral arrangements and the hostess' dress, then complained about the seating arrangement. Her father had been forced to raise her dowry, but it still took her the

better part of three seasons to receive any offers.
Society has a long memory where rudeness is
involved.

All I could do as my daughter wept was wrap my
arms around her, and join her in her grief, hoping the
old saying about pain shared was, in fact, true.

The following morning after breakfast, I decided
it was finally time to address the issue of the study.
I'd been tiptoeing around it for weeks. My
conversation with Mr. Hamilton was the first time I'd
spent more than a few moments in the room since the
break in.

It wasn't something that could be put off any
longer. It was a miracle whomever had chosen to
break in hadn't attempted a repeat performance.

With so much interest in the patents, it only
seemed prudent to catalog them all.

This is something I should have done ages ago, I
thought, searching through the desk until I found
some blank paper. James was very precise in his
work, but only as long as a project was active in his
mind. Once he set it aside, either through completion
or disinterest, it entered a veritable wasteland of
discarded ideas.

I searched every drawer and cabinet until I
collected all drawings and their notes, stacking them
up on the desk. When it became clear the desk was
not large enough, I moved to the hearth rug, pulling
the two heavy chairs and the little table out of the way
so I could work in front of the warmth of the fire.

I was soon surrounded by an enormous fan shape of paper, three rows deep, with more balanced on the seat cushions and the table. There was an occasional pang as I read a note or two scrawled in his hand, or saw a drawing I'd watched him work on. I retrieved paper and a box of pins from the desk, pinning notes to each stack, listing the status of each invention if I knew it—ideas that had never left the drawing board; patents that belonged to the company or to myself; and the location of any known prototypes.

I got up once to add another log to the fire. The pot of tea I'd brought in with me grew cold, but there was still more work to do. Once I was sure every page had been accounted for as much as possible, I began stacking the different types together. I was left with piles: unpatented projects, patents that belonged to R&A and would have to be returned to the office, and patents belonging to the family. There was also a small pile of miscellaneous papers I knew belonged to some design or project or another, but could not identify—partial pages of notes, a scaled up drawing of a specific part, unidentifiable without the whole. I thought I might ask Mr. Hamilton for his expertise, as he was knowledgeable of not only mechanics, but of my husband's particular brand of shorthand.

I was just scooping up the stacks when Mr. Scott knocked gently on the door frame. "Luncheon is served, madam."

"Thank you."

He entered the room, offering me a hand as I struggled to my feet with the armload of papers. A feeling of lightheadedness swept over me, and I realized just how long I'd been sifting papers.

"Do you require assistance, ma'am?"

"No, thank you, Mr. Scott. I think I have this well in hand."

I left the piles on the desk. When I turned around, I caught the butler scanning the room. He was looking particularly at the new window. The glass had been replaced, but the wood sash did not match the ones on either side. That was a task that would wait until spring.

"Are you well, Mr. Scott?"

"Perfectly, missus. I was just remembering the devil who broke that window. Who knows what he might have done if he made it up to Miss Olivia's room."

"Indeed. I'm certainly glad you were here, watching out for her." I took his arm affectionately and allowed him to escort me to hall. I closed the door of the study behind us.

"I shall never forget his horrible face," the old man mused, seemingly lost in thought. "Clearly up to no good. Looked like he'd been on the wrong side of everything."

"What do you mean?"

The butler gestured to his cheek with his thumb. "Awful, jagged scar, right here. Like he'd been caught by a fisherman's hook."

My thoughts flashed once again to a sketch of a man, simply done with a draftsman's touch, but clear enough in the pertinent details.

I hurried back through the study door, snatching up the pad of paper and reaching so hastily for the pen and ink that I blotted the page.

Come immediately. Bring your notebook.

Realizing the note might be thought rude, I hastily added a "please" before signing my initials and stuffing it into an envelope. "Tell Charlie to take this to the boarding house on Elk Street. He is to deliver it to Mr. Hamilton personally."

Mr. Scott's eyes widened briefly in surprise, but he bowed. "Right away, missus."

If I was right, then it meant we were in more danger than I had originally thought.

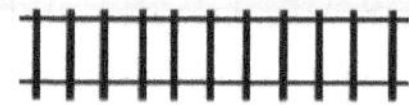

I barely touched my lunch. Pushing aside my soup, I paced up and down in the dining room, looking out the window every time I reached it. Once, I thought I saw a figure watching me from the end of the street, but then the man moved on. I shook off the idea like a wet cloak.

Paranoia, one part of my mind insisted.

Caution, whispered the other.

Watch. Beware, warned a third.

Finally, a knock on the door. I didn't wait for Mr. Scott to answer. I was already halfway there myself.

"Come in, come in. Quickly. Did you bring it?"

"Mrs. Andrews, what's happened?" Mr. Hamilton asked, hurriedly peeling off his coat and hat.

"Do you have the notebook? The one with the drawing in it?"

"What drawing?"

"The one of the man! The one who attacked you!"

He held up a hand as though trying to calm a screaming child. "Yes, it's right here." He produced it from the inside of his coat. I snatched it out of his hand, not even caring if it was rude, thumbing quickly through the pages until I found the one that looked back at me.

"Mr. Scott! Mr. Scott, is this the man you saw? The one that was in the study?"

The old butler was already in the entryway, too late to open the door but never too late to attend to my needs. He held the book at arm's length until the page came into focus, squinting at it. His eyes became round and his mouth fell open. "Yes, missus. That's a rather remarkable likeness, there."

I took the book back, rounding on Mr. Hamilton and jabbing the drawing with a forefinger. "This is the man. This is the one who broke into my house while I was in Washington. I think he was trying to search my husband's papers, looking for patents, maybe, or—or drawings that might have some value. Notes, maybe, on his research and experiments. He—"

Mr. Hamilton took hold on my elbows, looking me forcibly in the eye. "Deep breath. Now, slow down and tell me everything."

chapter eleven

It was Mr. Hamilton who had the presence of mind to ring for Clara and ask her to bring tea. He was the one who took my elbow and led me into the parlor, seating me on the couch as the entire story spilled out.

I was powerless to stop the words. "He's been in my house," I finished. I clutched my cup and saucer without drinking. "He was in my house with my daughter. I am not foolish enough to think Mr. Scott's presence was enough to actually frighten him off. He could have done...anything." My throat constricted at the thought of what I might have come home to instead of a broken window.

"The fact that Mr. Scott did frighten him off says his mission valued stealth above the actual end target. His fear of being seen was greater than the cost of leaving without what he came for."

"The drawings. The patents! Oh, I left them out—"

Even though there had been no trouble since that night, I had a sudden fear he could return at any moment when my back was turned.

Abandoning both tea and guest, I went back to the study, where the papers were still laid out on the desk, just as neat and orderly as I had left them. I took the family-owned patents and put them immediately in the safe. The ones for the company, I tied up with string. I was already reaching for a sheet of stationery and a pen when I became aware of Mr. Hamilton standing in the doorway.

I sighed, closing my eyes briefly. "I'm sorry. I don't know where my thoughts are. This can wait. My apologies. I'm..."

"You are agitated. Worried. Perfectly understandable under the circumstances." He hobbled into the room, his cane thunking heavily on the carpet. He was using the climbing rose cane again. He appeared to have added some kind of stain to the flowers and leaves, tinting them red and green.

I glanced down at the pages. "When you have the time, I have a few of these I would like you to look over. I can't make heads or tails of them, and some of them seem to be random, unconnected to anything I have been able to identify."

"Of course."

I placed a hand on the stack of papers to go to the office. "I should write a note to go along with these. They should be sent back to Mr. Richardson as soon as possible. Oh, and that blasted promise I made...I must develop an offer to counter the one he gave me two days ago." There was so much to do, and suddenly it felt like there was too little time to do it in. Time seemed to alternately speed up to twice the rate it should be working, and then suddenly coming to a near complete halt. My fingers wound around my watch. I wished I could make things work the way they should, to go back to normal, but we abandoned normal with the declaration of war, and then again when James left. And again when he did not come home. For an irrational moment I wondered how many more times "normal" would have to change before it would be satisfied with the new permutation.

It will never be satisfied, I reminded myself. *It is the lot of us on earth to live through the changes as best we can. We can't hang on, we can only let go with grace and find some new place to hang our hats.*

I took several deep breaths. Mr. Hamilton was still standing on the other side of the desk, watching me patiently.

"You are taking all of this very calmly, considering we now have someone else who can identify the man who injured you," I said at last.

He gave me a bland smile, more mask than expression. "I am reserving my vigor for when I meet him face to face."

"Do you plan to kill him?"

One honey-brown eyebrow rose into.

"I'm sorry. That was overly blunt. But I have been honest with you in my motives and my plans, and I hope you will give me the same consideration."

He looked thoughtfully over my head at the window, so recently replaced. "I don't know yet. I find there is a sort of poetic irony in a permanent but non-fatal wound."

"An eye for an eye?"

"Something of that sort. There are days when I would not hesitate to put a bullet in his breast, the way he did to Captain Andrews, and others when I think a simple bullet is too kind, and there are better horrors that could be visited on him for the lives he has ruined." A dark look crossed his face, reminding me that despite his mild demeanor, Mr. Hamilton was a soldier who had lived through the most gristly war our nation had ever seen. That the *world* had ever seen.

I nodded. "I often feel the same way."

A smile twitched his lips. "Pardon me, I have a difficult time picturing you visiting any kind of punishment on him."

"Do not underestimate me simply because I am a woman."

He conceded the point with a nod. "Of course not, Mrs. Andrews. If I have learned anything in our brief acquaintance, it is not to underestimate your tenacity or force of will."

Pushing back the chair, I put the remainder of the papers in a drawer and locked it, fixing the key to my chatelaine.

"Despite the circumstances, it is fortuitous you called me," Mr. Hamilton said, changing the subject slightly as we returned to the hall. I already felt calmer after our brief conversation. There was something in his honesty and the plainness of his speech that I found endlessly reassuring.

"In what way?"

"I have made some inquiries. It turns out I have more connections in Buffalo than I first thought. I've narrowed the list of potential lawyers to three."

"Three? Already?"

He reached once again for the notebook, sliding out a folded piece of paper with several names and addresses.

"The first one there, though not on the list you initially gave me, is the one I liked the best. It is a lesser known firm, not as established as the others, but it is owned by the brother of a man Captain Andrews and I served with, and I can vouch for his character. I've already spoken to him, and he's willing to meet you in person tomorrow afternoon, if you are agreeable."

"Yes...Tomorrow will do," I said, not looking up from the sheet. Spying Colleen in the hall, I called her into the room and handed her the page. "Put this on my writing desk. And make a note I will be meeting with a Mr. Purcell tomorrow afternoon."

"Yes ma'am." She curtsied and hurried off.

"I have another bit of news, as well, one I hope you will find to be as good."

"And what is that?" We returned to the parlor, resuming our seats. Clara brought in a fresh pot of tea almost immediately.

"I also looked into the possibility of engaging a Pinkerton's agent." When I started to object, he held up a hand. "I know you dislike them. But please believe me when I say they were invaluable to our cause during the war, and they maintain a stringent standard of ethics in their work, if not in their personal lives. They are...driven individuals."

I pursed my lips, but allowed him to continue. "I have asked one of their agents to call on you tomorrow during your receiving hours, but with your permission I would like to move that meeting up. I...I do not like the idea of you and Olivia being in the house unprotected."

I thought briefly of the man by the lamppost. Rising, I went to the window, as much to stall for time as to check the street. I did not see him, but still felt eyes watching me through the window. Perhaps a professional—a professional ruffian, as Mr. Hamilton put it—was not such a bad idea.

"Very well. I will tell Mr. Scott I am not at home

to guests once this detective arrives."

Mr. Hamilton let out a sigh of relief and leaned back in his chair. I resumed my seat, hiding my amusement at his expression behind a fresh cup of tea.

"Good. Where is the boy you sent for me? I'll send him straight away with a message."

Once Charlie had been dispatched with the messages for the Pinkerton and the lawyer, there was little to do but wait. Perhaps sensing I was still uneasy, Mr. Hamilton proposed to wait with me until the detective arrived. I did not say it, but I was relieved. His calm nature helped ease the tangled mess of my nerves.

To pass the time, I retrieved the drawings I had spent the morning organizing. While he examined the pages I was not able to identify, attempting to place them in one of the three stacks, I wrote a note to Mr. Richardson, turning over the papers to do with what he would—so far as the drawings and patents in the company name were concerned.

Once that was complete I began a list, drafting out my rebuttal to his offensive offer. If Mr. Hamilton's lawyer friend was as good as he said, then I would have him draw up a proper version of the contract the following day.

Finally, the bell rang.

Whatever I expected, it was not the woman Mr. Scott showed into the parlor. Small and neat, she wore a mauve and gray plaid skirt and matching vest and jacket. Her light brown hair was braided over the top of her forehead, and a snood of the same pristine white as her blouse covered the bun at her nape. The crinoline under her skirt was of a modest width; she was well dressed for middle class, but clearly not a society woman.

Mr. Hamilton stood to greet her, and I followed his example belatedly. "Mrs. Perry. Thank you for coming to promptly. I apologize for the short notice."

"No trouble at all. I understand there have been developments in the case you enquired about."

"Indeed. Mrs. Andrews, may I present Mrs. Lydia Perry, of the Pinkerton Detective Agency. Mrs. Perry, this is Mrs. Sophia Andrews."

"How do you do?"

After more bowing and curtsying, and the formalities of pouring and seating, Mrs. Perry reached into her reticule and produced a small notebook and pencil stub. "Let's get right to the point, shall we? Mrs. Andrews, Mr. Hamilton has told me something of your situation, but I would like to hear the particulars from you."

I opened my mouth, then closed it again. Finally, I said: "I'm sorry, but there seems to be some mistake..." I looked over at Mr. Hamilton. "I thought you wanted to hire a Pinkerton for my protection, not...I'm very sorry, Mrs. Perry, I don't mean to insult your abilities. I'm sure you are a wholly capable detective."

"But you were expecting someone...taller, perhaps?" her lips quirked into a smile that was half mirth, half agitation. I got the feeling she had been second guessed more than once in her career. My cheeks warmed. It was a feeling I was all too familiar with myself.

"Among other things, yes."

Setting the notebook on her lap, she folded her hands over it. "Then let me begin by saying I am well versed in all of the ways in which a lady might defend herself, from throwing off an assailant unarmed to shooting a man at twenty paces."

"Goodness!"

The smile broadened almost imperceivably. "I also happen to be excellent at blending in wherever I am needed, be it a dinner for the upper crust, or hunting for crusts in a slum. My work has taken me all over.

"Secondly, I am but one half of a team. Mr. Perry is at this moment examining the exterior of your home for security risks and also noting anything or anyone who might be out of place."

"I should like to meet Mr. Perry, in that case." Imagine! A strange man examining my home without even introducing himself first!

"When do you receive deliveries for the kitchen?"

"Pardon me?"

"Dry goods, or from the butcher. When do you receive your deliveries?"

I was so caught off guard I forgot to ask why she wanted to know. "Mondays, I think, for the most part. The butcher's boy also comes on Wednesday and Friday. Mrs. Wordsworth prefers to choose her own vegetables, and she gets those on Tuesday, Thursday, and Saturday."

"Very good. And who provides your dry goods?"

"Weston's, I think, on Hampton street."

"Excellent. Tomorrow is Wednesday. If you are in the kitchen at six-thirty tomorrow morning, then you will meet Mr. Perry."

Though I looked at her in askance, she did not elaborate as to why I had to be up at such an ungodly hour, nor why her husband would be delivering my groceries.

For the time being, I decided to let the issue pass and reserve judgment until I met the enigmatic Mr. Perry.

In the meantime, Mrs. Perry and I negotiated the terms, and I gave her the basics of the case.

"So we need to track down the man with the scar, who will in turn lead us to the missing articles, and find out why he wanted Mr. Andrews dead in the first place. This man with the scar...it seems fairly obvious he was hired by someone at the company, or perhaps by a rival, to eliminate your husband. Did your husband have any disagreements with the other men of the company? Any tension over profits or control of the patents?"

"Anything that went into production for the company was controlled by the company. There were a few designs James thought had potential, but were simply not practical to produce. There were also one or two designs he patented on his own, which were later adapted for use on the railway, such as the steam powered coffee pot."

"I'm sorry, the what?"

"We have one in the kitchen, the first he ever made. It's a copper drum heated by a brazier. It's something like an overlarge tea kettle. If it is maintained throughout the day—that is, someone continually adds water and coffee beans—it can produce hot coffee from first thing in the morning until well after dinner, without it ever getting cold or tasting poorly. Colleen is a dab hand at maintaining it, though I'm not overly fond of coffee myself. James always had a cup at hand, though."

"Very...interesting."

"It was a grand idea, though one that never really caught on. The men at the office are quite fond of theirs. James had one installed in the dining hall at the office, and two in the factory so the men could have something hot to drink on cold days, but it never went further. I'm afraid must be rather diligent to keep it from burning."

"How ingenious. But, back to the topic at hand. What of his rivals?"

I tried to think, but could come up with no one we'd had quarrels with. "We have competitors, to be sure, but I can't think of any company or individual who would go so far as murder. We did beat out several other companies for the contract with the Federal Army, and there was the line to Canada...I think there were three other companies competing for that...but the contract eventually fell through due to the war, and our Army contracts are over now. Of course now the attention is on the Pacific line, but we haven't even put in an official bid yet, and James had only a minor part in the discussion. It was primarily myself and Mr. Richardson, and the board."

"I will need a list of all of them, and of all of the patents, particularly those that may be contested."

I nodded, making a mental note of it.

"And what sort of income is derived from these patents?"

I named the sum from the previous year, blushing slightly. I tried not to look at Mr. Hamilton, or remember his threadbare suit.

"That is a considerable amount of money on the line."

I nodded. Sometimes the idea of it still terrified me. I remembered the day I left finishing school, and was awarded five dollars for the literature prize. Back then it seemed a fortune, but now I had several thousand times that amount in the bank, and more tied up in investments and property.

We spent the rest of the afternoon examining every detail of the situation. I recounted the trip to Washington and what I learned while I was there. Mr. Hamilton told the story of the attack in brutal detail at least a dozen times, to the point I had to leave the room for several minutes. Mrs. Perry took furious notes. After half an hour, we moved to the study so I could show her some of the designs.

I started with the packet I had put together for Mr. Richardson. "These are all set to go back to R&A. They're all designs owned by the railroad. Some of them are just sketches, concepts that later went on to something else."

"Where are his notes and drawings from his time in Washington?" Mr. Hamilton asked, examining the neat stacks, his hand hovering over each in turn as though he expected divine intervention to direct him.

"It's this one here," I said, pointing to the stack on my right. I went to the safe, dialed in the combination, and removed the abused book. For a moment, I imagined it still smelled like gunpowder.

He took it, settling himself into one of the chairs by the empty fireplace, and began leafing through the contents, slowly. Mrs. Perry took her stack to the chair opposite, creating a list of everything.

I took the seat behind the desk, staring absently at the remaining pile—the unknowns. Thanks to Mr. Hamilton's help, it was the smallest of the three.

"Mrs. Andrews…tell me, your factories. Do they only make railroad cars?" Mr. Hamilton inquired after some time.

I looked up, blinking dazedly. It took a moment for my mind to catch the thread of conversation he had thrown in my direction. "Well, mostly. But all of the accoutrements, as well. Fittings and rails and seats. Anything that would go into the different types of car."

"So in theory, the factories could make anything out of metal or any other material?"

"Well, yes, I suppose. The same machines we used to make the Andrews suspension were later adjusted when we started making entire rail cars. And all of the different pipes and things of that nature are made in the same building."

"Have you found something?" Mrs. Perry asked.

At first he didn't answer. "Mr. Richardson…how did he feel about the war?"

"Feel?" I gave an unladylike snort. "I'm not certain the man feels much of anything. He tried to convince James not to go. He said there were plenty of willing men to fight, and he needn't go. I felt much the same, but it was more because I didn't want him killed than because I think our immigrant population needs culling."

I rose from my seat to see what it was he was looking at. At first, I could not tell. The page was all gears and levers; a close up view of something unidentified.

Hamilton placed the drawing on the table between him and Mrs. Perry, where all three of us could see it. His face took on a tinge of pale green I hadn't seen since his days convalescing in Washington. "I presume you are both familiar with the Gatling gun?"

It was hard not to be. The newspapers had been filled with praise for the newest weapon of war: a gun that could fire three hundred fifty rounds per minute with just the turn of a crank. There was even talk that a new, four hundred round per minute model might be available soon. Invented in 1864, they helped turn the tide of battle in our favor.

"This is their inner workings. You see this here?" he pointed to a portion of the drawing. "This is where the gun takes in the ammunition, which is filtered down through a hopper that sits to the side. Later in the war, we started using a magazine, which would be mounted here. It helped to reduce jamming.

"Jamming is always a problem. When the guns work correctly, they work like a dream—or should I say, a nightmare. I've never seen so many men fall at one time before. They fell like dominos." He shook his head. "But they always jammed eventually, and some men were injured trying to clear them. But see here, where this lever is, and this spring? That's not on any Gatling I've ever seen. This is all James. By changing that part of the mechanism, I think he hoped to correct the problem. You see, this would allow for a top-loading magazine—much faster. The sights have been moved, just here." He tapped the page where two little x's had been drawn. "So by adopting this method, you have a faster gun, and one that's safer and more efficient to use. At a guess I would say it would be fifteen to twenty percent more effective."

"I don't understand," I said slowly. "The war is over. Why would someone murder my husband to steal plans for a gun when the war is over?"

"Because he didn't share this with me. I don't think he wanted to make something intended for killing, especially not when peace had been declared. The war might be over, but we are still fighting. The troops are just moving further west, to deal with the Indians. And did you say that while he was away, you were expanding the line westward?"

"Well, yes, of course. We've only gotten as far as the Mississippi. There will be more tracks laid, eventually, but there are some problems with land acquisition in the plains."

Mrs. Perry raised an eyebrow. "In other words, the natives are restless and not at all willing?"

"Well…no."

"Tensions are already high. If he already has the tracks to the area, and the relationship with the Army, and if he can provide them with a better weapon…"

"Then why not take advantage of it?" I finished softly. I picked up the drawing, examining it closely. *Oh, James. What have you done?*

I swam up from the nightmare like fighting my way to the surface of a lake. My limbs were weighed down as if with sodden garments, but it wasn't water filling my lungs.

I was buried. Smothered. I knew not with what, nor did not matter. All I cared about was the pressing weight on my chest and the way my arms and legs were restrained.

I was going to die. Death stood over me, leaning over my body, reaching for me with a clammy hand—

Shooting bolt upright in bed, I gasped for breath. The bands around my chest loosened. I was alone in my room, curtains drawn, fire dead in the grate.

My book lay spread eagle on the floor, the heavy thud of its fall saving me from the terror of my dream.

Even though icy air permeated my room, the thought of staying under the covers was unthinkable after such a nightmare. The weight of my blankets felt like six feet of earth, crushing me and threatening to swallow me whole. With slippered feet I dashed across the room to the grate and set about stirring some life into it. I'd nearly succeeded when there was a light but insistent tap at the door. The clock on the mantle said it was ten minutes after six.

"Come in, Demelza. I'm awake. I've already got the fire started, though."

But it wasn't young Demelza Wordsworth at the door. Colleen hurried in, not bothering to close the door. Her cheeks were red and her cap askew. Melting snow clung to the hem of her skirt and she was still wearing her outdoor wrap.

"Colleen, whatever is the matter?"

"I'm sorry to call so early, ma'am, but I found it! I saw it this morning on me way to work," she said, her accent growing thicker in her excitement. She came and knelt beside me on the hearth rug. "Well, I saw it last night, actually, but the man was closing up, and—"

"Saw what?"

"The ring! The red jewel Mr. Andrews used to wear. Remember, you told me to look for it in Washington? I found it yesterday, as I was walking to me mam's. I saw it! It was in a shop window off Swan street."

"You found it? You found Mr. Andrews' ring?" I could hardly believe it. She nodded excitedly, grinning from ear to ear.

"Oh, Colleen, this is excellent news!" Forgetting myself, I clasped her in a tight embrace. "Hurry, help me dress. Tell me everything. I shall go at once to collect it."

She helped me to my feet, clucking her tongue when she felt how cold my hands were. "You'll catch your death, ma'am. We must get you dressed right away." She rang the bell for Demelza, so the girl could build up the fire properly, and then wrapped me in the blanket from the settee while she went about laying out a warm, black wool dress, stockings, corset, crinoline, chemise, one quilted petticoat and two plain, gloves, and a bonnet and veil.

"It was in this shop, on Apple Tree lane, near Swan? I saw it last night as I was walking home, just as the man was shutting up for the day. I begged him to let me in to look closer, but he said no, not unless I was planning on buying it. I asked him how much it was, and he said it was ten dollars. And I said that was more than I had, but I knew the ring belonged to my employer, and he just laughed and said it didn't no more and unless I could pay for it I wasn't gettin' no closer, an' then 'ee slammed the door in me face."

While she'd been working, I took the seat at the

dressing table and began combing out the plait I slept in, re-braiding it and pinning it up into a simple knot. She continued as she helped me out of my nightgown and into my under things: "I came back again first thing this morning. Pounded on the door until 'ee came down. I told him you would be back for it right away, and he had to hold it. He just laughed again, so I gave him two dollars—all I 'ad—and told him he had to wait. He said we've only got until he opens the store at eight. Waste of two dollars, that was."

"Don't worry about the money," I gasped as she laced me tightly into my corset. Skillfully tying off the laces, she reached for my crinoline. I raised my arms so she could drop the cage of fabric covered wire over my head.

Demelza finally arrived, carrying a fresh armload of wood for the fire. "As soon as you are done, tell Mr. Hartly to ready the carriage." It was sheer luck we hadn't had a good, heavy snow recently. Usually Buffalo in February resembles nothing so much as a block of barely-inhabitable ice.

After the crinoline came the petticoats, as much for warmth and fullness of the skirt as to hide the ridges created by the crinoline.

Another plain black dress. I waited impatiently as she buttoned the myriad of tiny black buttons running up my spine.

The clock on the mantle said it was just after six thirty. How long would it take to get to Apple Tree Lane?

Colleen helped me into my coat. I ran to the street carrying my bonnet and muff, gloves forgotten somewhere in the house.

Colleen told Mr. Hartly where to go, and to make as much haste as possible. The streets were slick with frost and a thin layer of ice, but the horses' hooves broke through it easily and we crunched loudly the entire way.

We alighted in a shabby neighborhood, filled with teetering wooden buildings blocking out the sunrise and creating a dark, cave-like atmosphere.

It took all of my self-control and every single lesson on carriage I had not to leap to the street before we even stopped moving. Precisely, deliberately, I stepped down into the frozen mud and made my way to the front of the shop, veil covering my face and numb hands inside my muff.

The shop was even dingier than the street outside and full to the brim with the cast offs of the local inhabitant's valuables. Used clothing, that might fetch a few dollars in a time of need. Instruments and jewelry, pawned against gambling debts and hard times. Furniture, leftover from a dead relative, or too heavy or fragile to take to new lodging. How many times had we pawned this selfsame ring for food, nearly losing it before getting the money to buy it back?

I allowed Colleen to enter first as I picked my way over frozen garbage and horse droppings, and things that were probably much worse.

After ten minutes pounding on the door and several obscenities thrown down from a second story window, someone finally answered. "And what have we here? Came back for it, did you?" jeered the thickset man. He was still wearing a night cap and shirt, but had tucked it into his trousers. His boots and waistcoat were both unfastened, flapping like limp, broken wings when he moved. His scraggly hair and an unkempt beard trailed down over his stained shirt. "Come back at a decent hour!"

When he tried to close the door, Colleen stuck her foot in the way, drawing up all the pluck a country-born Irish lass has to offer—which is a considerable amount. "We're here now."

The gentleman—I use the phrase loosely—tried to push her out of the way, so I stepped in, producing one of my cards. "Sir. Before making a scene, perhaps you ought to let us is. I believe you are in possession of stolen property. Either let us in now, or we will return with a watchman and you will have much more to worry about than an early wake up call."

"You got my money this time?" he demanded of Colleen. She stared him down without replying until he opened the door to let us in.

A single lamp, mounted on the wall behind the L-shaped counter, was the only illumination. Somewhere in the back, something small scuttled into hiding, and I shuddered.

Once in the shadows of the shop, he moved back behind the counter, eyes darting anywhere but in my direction. I smiled slightly behind my black veil, allowing it to do its work.

"It's just there, Mrs. Andrews." Colleen gestured to the case by the window.

Nestled in a worn velvet tray was the ring.

"I need to see that ring, please," I commanded. He fumbled the case open, and fished out the tiny ring with one filthy, meaty hand, dropping it into my waiting palm.

"It's a very nice piece. Antique, like. Very fine detail. Just came in the other day—"

"It *is* antique. It belonged to my husband's grandfather." There, the Andrews crest. I even recognized a small scratch running along one side of the stone; it had been there as long as James had had it, as long as I'd known him. "Who brought it to you?"

He blinked at me several times, as if he had suddenly forgotten how to speak English, or I had suddenly begun speaking Gaelic.

"Who sold it to you?" I repeated, putting some steel into my voice.

"Now, ma'am, I can't go telling all of my customers—"

"You will tell me, sir, because this ring was taken from my husband's finger as he lay in the street bleeding to death. The man who sold it to you was most likely his murderer!"

The man's jaw snapped shut audibly. We stood locked in a silent battle of wills over the counter, until the shock and fear in his beady eyes turned to something like anger.

"Now, see here. You can't just come in here with crazy stories like that thinking I'll just give you anything you want. I got a business to run. You want a piece, you pay for it just like anyone else."

"I don't care about the price. I just want to know who sold it to you." Ridiculous man! I intended to compensate him for his trouble, anyway. If only I wasn't so tired. It was so difficult to rein in my emotions these days.

"I don't remember," he replied flatly. "And the price just went up. It'll be fifteen dollars now."

Oh, if I weren't a lady, I'd throttle him myself, I thought. "You've already taken two dollars from my servant, and the ring is only worth five, anyway." That was a lie. I had no idea what it was really worth. "I'll give you eight, and my word I won't tell the police you're selling stolen property."

"You don't have no proof—"

I held up the ring. "Eight dollars, final offer. Or I could go straight to the watchmen. I'm sure they would find all sorts of interesting things here." I glanced pointedly at the rest of the jewelry, a few pieces far too fine for a shop of such low caliber.

The man's face turned a livid shade of beetroot. Inside my muff, I clenched my fist and tried to keep my expression as neutral as possible under my veil.

"Fine," he snapped at last.

"Done." I nodded to Colleen, who produced the money from her reticule, the one she always carried when she was with me. Inside would be her personal effects, tucked into her own bag, as well as the notebook, pencil, shopping money, and other miscellanea a lady of quality would need but should not carry on her own person. It wasn't proper for a lady to handle money, nor to jingle.

I closed my fist over the ring, tucking it into my muff before he could object. Soon we were bundled back into the carriage. I slipped the ring onto my finger for safekeeping. He's worn it on his smallest finger; it fit the middle of the right hand perfectly.

Colleen had two spots of color and a pleased grin on her face as she watched the city pass. "Thank you," I said, finally, staring at the stone.

"I knew that was it, ma'am. I knew it. I knew I'd find it eventually. I just didn't think it would be here." There was a righteous sort of vindication in her features. With the morning sun creating a halo out of her red curls and the white lining of her bonnet, she looked like an avenging angel. *Colleen Boyle, avenging ladies' maid.*

The women from church would be horrified to hear me describe my maid in such a way. They'd be horrified in general, to hear half of what I thought and did. I got a strange sense of satisfaction from it, and couldn't help but giggle just a little.

"Ma'am?"

"Nevermind, Colleen. I'm just a little giddy from not sleeping, is all."

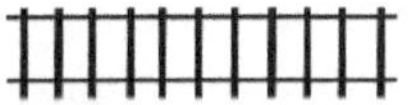

The first thing I did when I returned home was send Charlie with a note for Mrs. Perry, asking her to call that afternoon. I had missed my appointment with her husband in all the excitement that morning.

Yawning, I paced in the parlor for a while, turning the facts over and over in my head. I was exhausted, but too wound up to lay down. I could hardly sit still. Colleen offered to get me something to help me sleep, but I told her no.

I'd had to take laudanum for a brief period several years earlier, and had not tolerated it well. It opened my mind up in exactly the wrong way. My dreams turned to nightmares, and the visions I saw normally were even more intense, more terrifying. As night terrors were already the thing keeping me from my bed, I could only shudder at the thought of mixing them with an opiate. The drowsiness had been like a veil I couldn't throw back. I could only imagine being caught in a nightmare I couldn't wake from.

No, I would rather pace until I collapsed from exhaustion than take something to make me sleep unnaturally.

Instead, I whiled away the morning in reviewing my notes and lists of tasks for the staff. I'd been ignoring them for weeks. Thankfully, Mr. Scott was a dab hand at keeping things running, Colleen and Clara were both steady, hard workers, and Mrs. Wordsworth would no sooner neglect her duties than burn a pie.

"Make sure the front steps are cleared and put down a bit of sand. I noticed it was slick this morning. And the fireplaces are getting a bit untidy. Have Demelza sweep them up and wipe down the hearths. She can be so messy when she's clearing up the ash."

"Yes, Mrs. Andrews," Mr. Scott said with a bow.

I tried to think what other tasks had been neglected. "My room could use a bit of airing. Fresh linens. Tell Clara to leave the window open for an hour or so while she's cleaning. I do hate winter and how we must all be shut up like this." I was feeling particularly constrained at the moment. What I wouldn't give to be able to take a nice, brisk walk down the street, or in a park. But winter in Buffalo goes a bit beyond "brisk." I would be risking any exposed skin if I went out for more than a few moments.

When lunchtime came, I was too agitated to eat. I thought about taking a nap instead, but still felt the shadow of my nightmare every time I closed my eyes. No, I would discuss the situation with Mrs. Perry. I would feel better afterward, and perhaps take a short rest before dinner.

I paced the parlor, twisting my husband's ring on my finger, still unwilling to take it off. Wearing it made me feel as if his ghost were watching from across the room. Every time I reached the end of the rug and turned, I expected to see him standing opposite me, arms folded, eyebrow raised.

"Why don't you sit down, dear?" he would say. "Really, Síomha, there's no need for this. It will work itself out in time."

My stomach twisted in on itself.

"What do you know? You're dead. You probably thought *that* would work itself out in time, too," I muttered, scratching my neck. There was a red, irritated patch of skin just below my jaw.

The bell rang. I jumped. In the hall, I heard Mr. Scott open the door and greet the guest, but he did not present Mrs. Perry.

"Mr. Hamilton! What are you doing here?" It was rude, I knew, but I was caught off guard. My mind was jumping from one thing to the next. My heart hammered against my ribs so hard I could feel it throbbing against my corset, as though it intended to burst out.

"I came because...are you well?" he asked, concern creasing his brow.

I shook my head. My words began tumbling over each other in a frenzied disarray as I continued to pace the carpet. "I found it this morning. Or, Colleen did. The ring. The one that went missing after the attack. It was in a pawn shop, here in Buffalo. That man was in Buffalo. It had to be him. There's no other way that ring could have made it here. Which just means it was definitely the same man who broke into the house. I'm sure of it. *That man has been in my house*. He was under the same roof—as my *daughter*—" My breath came in short wheezing gasps. I could hear the rush of my heartbeat in my ears. It roared like the engine of a locomotive, racing at four times the normal speed.

Black spots began to appear in my vision. No matter how hard I tried to inhale, I couldn't. My knees wobbled. For a moment my frame of vision was filled with Mr. Hamilton's worried face. He said something, but I couldn't hear it over the sound of the train.

My lungs expanded with such force I was thrown into nearly a sitting position. I coughed, convinced there was dirt in my mouth. My arms and legs were limp and numb.

Then I managed to cover my mouth as I gasped. My feet twitched involuntarily. I wasn't bound.

I lay on the floor of my own parlor. Mrs. Perry and Colleen knelt beside me. In a corner, I saw Mr. Hamilton's back. Even from this angle, I could see the red flush running upwards from the collar of his shirt.

It was then I realized my dress was torn open, the laces of my corset cut. Mrs. Perry clutched a wicked, pearl handled knife in one hand.

"Madam, are you well? Can you breathe?"

Colleen asked, her voice high and thin with fright.

I tried to pull my dress closed, but couldn't over the open corset. The cool air felt good on my hot skin. My heart was still beating too fast. I felt as if I'd just run a great distance.

My mouth worked, and words formed awkwardly on my cottony tongue. "I—I'm all right now."

"We've sent for the doctor," Mrs. Perry said calmly, taking charge of the situation with her dispassionate firmness.

From his corner, I could see Mr. Hamilton attempting to turn, to ensure I was, indeed, well, but also fighting to remain within the bounds of propriety. "Are you certain you are well, Mrs. Andrews. You gave me—*us*—quite a fright."

"I don't know what happened. I was just talking, and then..."

"You've overexerted yourself," Mrs. Perry said, helping me to sit. Colleen retrieved a blanket from the sofa, wrapping it about my shoulders in an attempt to protect my dignity. "I've seen it happen once or twice before to women who get overset with emotion. Your...restrictive garments made it worse. I tried to remedy the problem as expediently as possible. I apologize for the lack of modesty and for the damage, but I assure you it was necessary."

I nodded. Words still felt too taxing for my mouth, my lungs, and my brain. After the nightmare, and then the brief flash of it I'd had when regaining consciousness, I began to wonder if I would ever be able to lace myself into a corset again without thinking of that smothered feeling, of not being able to breathe.

"We should get you off to bed. You need a rest. Dr. Lynch will be here soon," Colleen said. Together, she and Mrs. Perry helped me to my feet. My corset flopped uncomfortably, held in place by the waistband of my skirt, but only just. Now that I was covered, Mr. Hamilton turned around, regarding me with a concerned gaze. "Is there anything I can do?"

"Go home and let her rest," Mrs. Perry said, attempting to shoo him towards the door with her free hand. I was clinging to the other.

I stopped him. "No, please stay. Give me a moment to change."

He waited at the bottom of the stairs while the two women helped me to my room. They peeled off the layers of clothing, and Colleen dropped a nightgown over my head. My limbs trembled like pudding.

"There. We'll get you settled," Colleen said, pulling up the blankets.

"No. No, I need to talk to Mr. Hamilton."

Mrs. Perry raised an eyebrow. "I think that can wait."

I glared at her. "I *don't*."

The maid and the detective exchanged a look, Colleen's eyes wide, unwilling to contradict her mistress out loud.

At last, Mrs. Perry sighed. "Very well. But only for a few minutes. Just until the doctor gets here."

Wrapped in a robe and covered by the quilt, Colleen declared me "decent enough," with a disapproving look, and went to get Mr. Hamilton. Mrs. Perry started to leave, but I called her back. "Please wait. You should hear this, too."

"Now we are all here, I think we can get started?"

Mrs. Perry said a few moments later. She pulled out her little notebook and pencil stub.

I pulled the ring off my finger and passed it to Mr. Hamilton. His brows furrowed as he examined it, and then shot upwards in surprise. "This—"

"My husband's ring. The one that went missing when he was killed. Yes. We recovered it this morning." I related the tale for their benefit as Mrs. Perry scribbled notes. When I was done, I leaned back against the pillows, inhaling deeply. It felt like a great weight had been lifted, but now I had even more questions.

"Miss Boyle, I'll want to speak with you when we finish here," the detective said to Colleen. "I need to know everything you saw and heard."

"Yes, ma'am."

"This is good news. We have a lead to work with. If we can find the man with the scar, we can work on building a connection between him and his employer." She refrained from saying Mr. Richardson's name. I was still loathe to think of him as an enemy. I glanced at the stack of novels on the night stand. In all the really good stories, the person who appears to be at fault never is. It's always someone operating from the shadows. That meant it couldn't possibly be Mr. Richardson.

Unless the Confederate sympathizers were the ones meant to redirect us.

I let out a breath. It was so confusing, and my head ached abominably. Mrs. Perry asked to take the ring with her, just for the evening. "I'll be back tomorrow. We have more to discuss. But for now you should get some rest." She looked pointedly at Mr.

Hamilton. He nodded, starting to move towards the door, but I reached automatically to pull him back, catching his sleeve.

He looked down at my hand. I let go quickly. "Just a moment. I'd like a word, if you don't mind. It won't take long."

Colleen escorted Mrs. Perry out, leaving the door open. Mr. Hamilton pulled up a chair, sitting a respectable distance from the bed and leaning his cane against the nightstand. This one was shaped like an upside-down L. The body of a cat reposed at the top, forming a grip roughly the same shape as the interior of his fist, and the tail traveled down the length of the shaft. I wondered how he found the time to make so many intricate carvings. It seemed I seldom saw him with the same stick twice.

He waited expectantly for me to begin. Words failed me. With my heart and mind in such turmoil, it took several moments to gather myself.

"I'm afraid I got things backward. I—you came today to tell me something? I wanted to know the purpose of your visit."

Mr. Hamilton shook his head slightly. "It's of no consequence now. We can address it another time, when you're feeling better." He glanced away for a moment, his eye landing on the bedside table. He reached for the pamphlet there, the one from Mrs. Lynch. "Are you considering a sanatorium?" he asked, surprised.

"It was recommended by a friend." My cheeks were burning brighter than a coal fireplace. I needed to return that to Mrs. Lynch as soon as possible.

"It might not be a bad idea."

"What?"

He held up the paper. "I realize our acquaintance has been brief, but even I have noticed...a change. In your demeanor."

I stiffened. "In what way?"

"I'm sorry. I meant no offense." He made as if to leave, reaching for his cane.

I placed my hand on the wooden cat, holding it in place. "In what way?"

He sighed, drawing back both hands and folding them in his lap. He looked at them as if they held the answer to my awkward question.

"The woman who barged into my room in Washington was bold. Sad, but bold. She was strong and sturdy; she knew her way and her mind.

"The woman we just picked up off the floor was frightened. It is very clear you have not been sleeping, or eating. Your mind is unsettled, your words muddled." He hesitated, then placed his hand over mine on the cane. "I know you are scared. Anyone would be in your situation. But I have seen this before in my fellow soldiers. If you don't rest, your mind will fracture. Better to take some time now to recover from the strain, than to try to pick up the pieces later."

I pulled back my hand, lacing my fingers together. "Thank you for your opinion."

Another sigh. "I know you don't want to go. No one as strong willed as you would be willing to walk away in the middle of this. But please, for the sake of your health—for the sake of your daughter—consider it?"

I stared pointedly at the window. After a moment's pause, I heard the unsteady three-legged gait of his departure. The pamphlet stared up at me from the quilt. I glared at it fiercely and shoved it into a drawer.

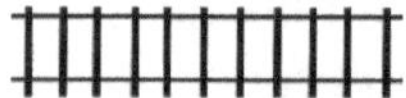

Dr. Lynch declared I would be fit as a fiddle after a night's rest, but I should refrain from exertion. I was hardly willing to comply, but he left a sleeping draught and insisted Colleen give it to me, supervising its administration. As Colleen was showing him out, I watched through heavy lids as they stood on the landing outside my door, whispering. I thought I heard the words *nervous hysteria* pass between them, but I was so tired it hardly seemed to matter.

I woke up some time in late afternoon with Olivia curled up at my side, watching me.

"What are you doing in here?" I asked with a sleepy yawn.

"Just checking on you," she replied in a near whisper. Her hand rested on a book. There were usually books on my bed these days, since I spent so little time sleeping.

"You don't have to do that. I'm fine."

"Colleen told me Dr. Lynch came to visit."

"That was nothing."

"She said you fainted."

"Psh. I don't faint. You know I'm not wilting violet."

"It's 'wilting flower' and 'shrinking violet.' Not wilting violet."

I waved a hand dismissively. "Does it matter?"

She frowned. "For someone who doesn't faint, you're sure doing a lot of it lately. First Father's funeral, and now this?"

I took her hand, clasping it over the pillow. She had her father's black hair and blue eyes, but my face shape. "It's nothing to worry about. I just haven't been sleeping well. Dr. Lynch gave me something that will help." Of course, I had no intention of actually taking it, but there was no reason to worry the poor girl. The last thing I needed was for my daughter to become a tangled ball of nerves like her mother.

"Promise?"

"Promise." I gave her hand a squeeze. She inched closer to me until she could put her head on my shoulder. She threw one arm around my waist, and I pulled her into an embrace.

What would I do if something happened to her? The man who killed James was still in the city, according to the pawnbroker. What if he came back to the house, made a second attempt to find what it was he had been looking for? What if, instead of waking Mr. Scott, he happened to meet Olivia on the stairs? What then?

"Mama, why are you so afraid?" she asked.

"I'm not afraid. I just haven't been feeling myself lately." Much as I worried, I couldn't tell her. I couldn't tell a mere child her father's murderer was so close at hand.

We lay there in silence for several moments, and, very quietly, she asked, "Are you going to go away?"

"Heavens, no! Whatever gave you that idea?"

"I heard the servants talking when I came home.

They said Dr. Lynch said you should go away for a while, to recover."

Hm. As soon as Olivia left for school in the morning, I would have to have a very firm talk with Colleen and the other servants. Just because we tended to treat them as family did not mean they could speak freely about my personal affairs in front of a child.

"Well, that's a load of nonsense. I'm staying right here, right where I need to be. Besides, where would I go that would make me feel better?"

"You could go to the country house. It's not far."

Our country house was much grander, much more stately and impressive than the one in the city. James purchased it on a whim—his one, ridiculous, grandiose purchase once we realized just how well-off we truly were. It was built in the style of an English manor house, or so I had been told. Fancy carved staircases. Stained glass windows. Marble floors. So many rooms a small army of servants was necessary to maintain the place. In summer, it was nice for parties and guests, and there was a small park surrounding it with some very well-tended gardens. But it was not a house one occupied without company. It was simply too much for just the family, and as pretty as it was to look at, it never felt like home to James and me. Our tastes were much simpler.

But Olivia continued: "We could have Colleen pack everything up and you could be there by tomorrow afternoon. You do love the gardens. And it would be so peaceful, out in the country. And Mr. and Mrs. Benton would take such good care of you." The

Bentons, the housekeeper and butler who came with the place, where a kind elderly couple who kept everything in order when we weren't in residence.

I wrinkled my nose a little. "I'm sure they would, but that house is very drafty in the winter. And so far from everything." Even in good weather, it was at least two hours by coach. Mr. Richardson tried to convince James to put in a light rail line to the house, as a few of their peers and competitors had done to their private estates, but James thought it was wasteful to install a single line for personal use. I agreed. "Besides, there's not much of a garden to enjoy with three feet of snow on the ground. And what about you? I couldn't just leave you here."

Olivia answered without missing a beat. "I could stay with Granny Agnes and Aunt Brigid and Aunt Angela, and come out to see you on Sundays."

"Clearly you have thought of this a great deal."

"I could go out with Mr. Hamilton. I'm certain he would go to visit you frequently."

"No, I don't think so. I will stay right here, with you, where I belong," I said finally, giving my daughter a squeeze.

chapter twelve

I woke suddenly and completely, well before dawn. The grate was cold and so were my feet. For a moment, I felt a stiffness around my ankles, as though they had been bound. My chest was tight and my mouth gritty; I half expected to see dirt on my hand when I passed it over my lips.

Feeling any attempt to sleep would be pointless, I procured robe, slippers, and candle, and took a book to the kitchen. The tall clock in the hall indicated it was not quite five o'clock.

The kitchen, which was half submerged underground, with high, narrow windows peeping up just above eye level, was even colder than my bedroom. The barest whisper of warmth remained in the stove. I stirred the coals, put on the kettle, and lit a few of the gas lamps, just enough to read by. Then I sat down at the table and waited.

I was at the end of chapter nine when Mrs. Wordsworth came in. She greeted me awkwardly, Demelza hiding behind her skirt. Behind them, Charlie blinked sleepily, a wide yawn cracking his jaw.

"Don't mind me, Mrs. Wordsworth. I'm just waiting on the kettle. I'll be out of your way soon enough."

"You sure you don't want one of the girls to take you up a tray? I can have breakfast ready in two shakes. You'll be more comfortable in the parlor, maybe, or your room..."

I gave her a gentle smile. I knew my presence made her uncomfortable; I was in her realm, now. It might be my house, but everything below stairs was her domain. She was Hades in this underworld, and I was clearly not Persephone.

"Don't trouble yourself. I think I'll just have a cup of tea and go back to bed. You can wait on breakfast, at least for me. Let the others eat first."

The kettle was steaming by then. I got up and removed it from the stove before Mrs. Wordsworth even moved from the doorway.

"Where is my tea?" I asked, scanning the shelf. The familiar green tin was missing.

"Used up the last of it last night. There should be more in the delivery this morning. But there's a tin there," the cook said, reaching for a frying pan.

I followed the direction of her gaze and spotted a red tin on the same shelf. "Where did this come from? I don't think I've ever had it."

"No, ma'am. It's from one of the baskets we received after Mr. Andrews passed."

Prying off the lid I took a deep sniff of the earthy leaves. "Not bad." I took my time taking down a cup and saucer and finding a strainer, spoon, milk, and sugar. Eventually, I was aware of the cook beginning her own work, though I could feel her sending glances in my direction.

It was hardly the first time she found me in the kitchen making tea at odd hours. I'd always had a bit of insomnia, though it got worse after James went to war. Still, she did not like having me in *her* kitchen.

I was just putting back the sugar bowl when someone knocked at the servant's door. Charlie answered it.

As soon as the door opened, a gust of frigid wind blew inside. The stranger was ushered indoors, where he set down a large crate of paper wrapped parcels, tinned goods, and vegetables.

Rather than the usual delivery boy from the grocer—I knew him by sight from my early morning tea break, though of course we never spoke—there was a large Negro man, so tall he had to duck to get through the door. A brown tweed overcoat covered him from neck to knee, adding an extra layer of padding to his already broad chest and shoulders.

When he saw me, he took off his flat cap and nodded. Even with his dark skin, I could see he was red from cold.

I pulled my dressing gown tighter. "Well. You certainly aren't the boy who usually comes," I said, offhandedly. This man was easily twice his height.

The Negro mumbled to the floor. "No, missus. I'm new. Silas Perry, at your service."

"Well, I thank you for venturing out in this cold. I can't say I envy your task."

He nodded again, this time his eyes flicking up to meet mine. "I appreciate it, ma'am."

He was still playing the dutiful errand boy; the lower-class worker. It was rather brilliant, really. Allow the pretty Mrs. Perry to wheedle her way into everything upstairs, where a woman could hear all the latest gossip and ply the men for information, while Mr. Perry, in the guise of servant or laborer, could infiltrate any place less savory.

They were an odd pair. But, taking in the symmetry of his face, and the intensity of the dark brown gaze, I found I could not blame Mrs. Perry in the slightest for her taste. His large dark eyes filled me with peace and calm. This man was loyal and fierce, but also watchful and kind.

I gave him a nod of approval, then collected my book and my cup, and went back upstairs to bed. A few drops of the sleeping draught in my tea, and I was out like a light once again.

When I finally woke the second time, it was well after sun up. I lay stiffly on the mattress for several seconds as my brain attempted to sift out my disjointed dreams from reality. I couldn't remember them, only vague impressions of danger; an ominous presence and perhaps being chased. I thought I remembered familiar faces, but couldn't place them.

My limbs were heavy and numb. I couldn't tell if it came from the sleeping draught or the insomnia; more than once in the past I awoke to lifeless limbs and a bounding heart, feeling as if some hell beast crouched on my chest, or something stood over me, waiting only for my eyes to open before visiting waking horror.

On mornings like that, I was never certain if it was a good thing or a bad thing I was not a regular guest of the confessional at St. Joseph's. I hated to think how many Hail Mary's I might be assigned to drive it away, or what ritual the priest might find necessary to drive out the demonic influence that clearly haunted me.

My fingers and toes twitched, almost involuntarily. I sat up, reading the time on the mantle clock as half past eight. My heartbeat was still quick and light, my eyes darting to every shadow in the room. I pulled my seldom used crucifix from the bedside drawer and said an "Our Father," just in case.

The ritual complete, I felt a bit more myself. I rang for Colleen. While I waited, I stacked up the books scattered over my bed, and set them on the night stand on my late husband's side of the bed, where they would be out of the way. I created two stacks: one of the books I was finished with, and one of the books I was still perusing.

"Good morning, Mrs. Andrews," Colleen said, appearing at the door with a tray balanced in her arms. She waited for me to settle back against the pillows, and then laid it across my lap. There were eggs, a pot of tea, some bacon, the day's paper and the slender notebook where I made all my lists and plans.

I spread out the paper and nibbled on some toast. The debate about Reconstruction continued, and there was more trouble in Texas—when wasn't there trouble in Texas? At the bottom of the last page was a short article blaming a fortune teller in New York City for duping a wealthy young lady into trusting her sweetheart. The young man was married with two children, but of course the girl was a silly fool for believing the fortune teller, and the fortune teller was a wretched confidence trickster for telling her what she wanted to hear. The man, of course, suffered no blame nor rebuke for betraying his wife and family, while the poor dear girl was ostracized for cavorting with a married man.

"It's never the man's fault when a romance goes sour. It's always the woman who was foolish enough to believe him." I glowered at the newspaper before tossing it aside in disgust.

"Did you say something, ma'am?" Colleen asked, looking up from where she poured water into the wash basin.

"No, nothing." Removing the tray from my lap, I moved to join her by the fire. She helped me disrobe, and I wiped myself down with the warm water. I felt absolutely wretched for lying in bed for so long, like my skin had been imprinted with the weave of the sheets. I could hardly stand the smell of myself.

"Oh, dear. What's this?" Colleen asked, leaning close.

"What is it?"

She fetched the hand mirror from my dressing table, holding it up to show a series of red marks on my neck.

"Looks like biters, ma'am."

I sighed. I was all too familiar with the types of things that liked to live in unwashed bedding. "And we just changed the sheets, too. When we're done here, change them again. And replace the pillows. Do we have any pennyroyal or arsenic? We'll have to wipe down all the bed frames. Oh, and we'll need to put the legs in dishes of oil. If you and Clara can't manage on your own, let me know. I can offer another set of hands."

Colleen sighed, mumbling assent, but she glared at the bed. A bedbug infestation meant a great deal of extra housework.

Once bathed, Colleen summoned Demelza to empty out the water and start stripping the bed. I sat down on the stool of my dressing table, wrapped in a robe, and allowed the maid to wash my long hair.

Colleen moved the end table from the chair by the fire behind me, arranging the empty basin and other tools she would need.

She began by letting down the plait. With a towel wrapped about my shoulders, she applied a mixture of egg yolk, rosemary, and water with a brush. She piled my hair on top of my head, wrapping it in the towel. Once more able to look down at my hands, I flipped through my diary and my lists of daily tasks while waiting for the egg mixture to set.

There was so much that needed done. It had been four days since my promise to Mr. Richardson, and I had yet to engage a new solicitor, let alone draw up a counter offer. I needed to meet with Mrs. Perry and Mr. Hamilton. And now that my reputation had been somewhat cleansed, I had social obligations to fill. There were letters to write, and I needed speak to Dr. Lynch about some kind of rest cure.

And then there were the household chores. The parlor rug needed swept, and I had noticed dust on the mantle. My room was a mess. I would have to see that Clara tidied up. It looked like someone had taken a bookstore, torn off the roof, and shaken its contents down onto my bed. And as much as I hated to admit it, something would have to be done about my husband's belongings. Men's clothing did me little good, and I was hardly so sentimental I would keep his entire wardrobe.

Without thinking, I glanced over my shoulder at the tall clothing press. I opened it occasionally, pulling out a shirt or a jacket to try to catch his scent. After three years, however, the scent was mostly gone.

"Time to rinse now, Mrs. Andrews," Colleen said cheerfully, bustling back into the room with a steaming pot of strong, black tea and a pitcher of clean water.

I leaned back in my chair so she could loosen the towel, dropping it back down around my shoulders. Unwinding my hair into the wash basin, she poured tea mixed with a splash of vinegar over the strands to rinse out the egg, gently massaging it into my scalp. The tea had the added bonus of helping disguise some of the strands of gray coming into my hair. I didn't consider myself especially vain, but I'd been somewhat annoyed to discover the first one just after James left. They'd only gotten more numerous since.

One last rinse, this one of plain water, and the washing was complete. She patted my hair dry with a spare towel, combed it once again, and then began working it into my usual style: a straight center part, with two braids looping over my ears and back into a braided knot at the nape of my neck.

Colleen helped me into my clothing, and then the entire coiffure was covered with a snood and cap.

My face having already been washed and scrubbed, I applied a cream to keep the skin supple, then a dab of powder to hide the red marks and a bit of rosy tint for my lips. Fashion is a fickle thing; it dictated a woman must always look her best, but prevented a lady of quality from applying cosmetics. Only a tart would do such a thing. Still, every woman I knew had her secrets—like my lip tint, just a few shades off from my natural coloring. Powder, to even the skin tone and make it fairer. A bit of lemon juice to wash light hair, to turn it golden—or tea, to darken hair tending to gray.

I was just finishing when there was a soft knock at the door. "Enter."

Clara pushed it open. "Mrs. Andrews, Mr. Hamilton to see you."

"Thank you, Clara."

As always, Mr. Hamilton was waiting in the parlor. His head was thrown back against the chair, eyes closed, bad leg extended when I entered. He straightened quickly, but not before I saw a slight wince as he drew in his right foot, and the bare condition of the sole. He started to rise, as custom dictated he must when a lady entered the room, but I gestured for him to stay where he was.

"Please, don't get up on my account. We are friends here. There is no need to stand on formalities. Or to stand at all, really," I added, taking the seat opposite him. The smile I offered was a little rueful as I added, "You certainly saw me in poor enough form yesterday. I can certainly excuse an unnecessary gesture today if you are in pain."

Though I had meant it to be comforting, his expression was a mixture of shame and frustration. I immediately regretted my choice of words, but the moment and the expression vanished quickly. Mr. Hamilton plowed on before I could apologize.

"I've not had any word from Mrs. Perry on what we discussed yesterday, but they are looking into the situation. She has assured me Mr. Perry will be in the area, keeping an eye on the house at all times."

"I met Mr. Perry this morning," I said with a nod. "But surely one man cannot watch the house at all times, as you say."

"I believe they are also employing a network of errand boys. If Mr. Perry cannot be here, one of them will be watching discretely, and will get a message to him as soon as possible. She said you will likely not see him. He'll be working mostly in the evenings and after dark, when the danger is strongest."

"Of course. That is very logical." Mr. Perry would indeed be difficult to spot after dark, save for that bright white grin. I didn't like the idea of trusting my safety to a gaggle of errand boys, but could not think of a better solution at the moment. To hire a full guard like some medieval queen, seemed a bit excessive even under the circumstances.

"Are you well enough today to go out?" he asked.

"I think so. What do you have in mind?"

"Do you remember the lawyer friend I told you about? The one I knew though the Army?"

"Yes."

"I thought you might want to meet with him. It was what I came to ask you yesterday, before you became unwell. I know you would prefer to meet with anyone who would be handling your affairs personally."

"Quite so. I think I can manage."

"Excellent. The appointment is arranged for one o'clock, so we should have you back in plenty of time for your afternoon calling hours."

I glanced at the clock in the hall, which was ticking slowly towards ten-thirty. Beside the clock, I spotted Mr. Hamilton's hat, hanging from the rack by the door. The band was coming loose and even from a distance I could see it was certainly the worse for wear.

When my gaze returned to the man himself, I remembered once again my earlier impressions of him, when he first arrived in Buffalo: the jacket, well cut, but thread bare and obviously intended for a more vigorous man, and not one who spent several years on Army rations. The style of his waistcoat and tie were both out of fashion by roughly eight years; they certainly came from his pre-war wardrobe. The hems of his trousers were worn, and the sole of his right shoe was beginning to pull away from the upper. They wouldn't last the winter.

"Mr. Hamilton, do you have any plans between now and one o'clock?"

He seemed a little surprised by the question. "Well, no, not really. I confess, I had hoped we might dine together for luncheon, if you were feeling up to it."

I nodded quickly. "And so we shall. In the meantime, however, I would be most appreciative if you could join me upstairs."

Mild surprise turned to shock. "I'm sorry, I'm not certain I heard you properly."

I allowed my smile to turn slightly wicked. "Oh, no. You heard me correctly. And I shall need you to remove your clothes."

I shall cherish the look of absolute shock and horror Mr. Hamilton gave me at that moment to the end of my days. Without waiting for him to answer I went out into the hall to summon Colleen and Mr. Scott, leaving him no choice to follow. For a moment, I considered loitering to assist him on the stairs, or perhaps asking one of the servants to give him aid, but finally decided against it. I had no desire to humiliate or insult him, though I did whisper a quick word to Mr. Scott as I passed him, and asked him to keep an eye out in case he had too much difficulty.

While he navigated the stairs to the second floor, I joined Colleen in the bedroom, where her arms were loaded down with pillows. Demelza was tucking fresh sheets around the mattress.

I threw open the doors of my late husband's wardrobe. "Colleen, fetch the name of Mr. Andrews' tailor and barber, please," I said, sifting through the stacks of shirts and collars and jackets. "And pull out the dressing screen. Set it up over there, by the fire. Oh, and your mending basket. We may be able to tweak a few things right away without too much effort."

The maid looked nearly as bewildered as my guest, but nodded quickly and scurried off to follow orders. She was smart enough—or at least, loyal enough. Or perhaps only shocked—not to comment. But then, no one ever accused me of doing things by halves.

I spread three or four shirts over the bed, then pulled out collars and silk cravats. I was trying to decide between waistcoats when Mr. Hamilton appeared hesitantly in the doorway.

"Mrs. Andrews?"

"Come in, come in. Did Mr. Scott come up with you? Good, good. Mr. Scott, please show our guest behind the screen and help him to undress. Here, start with these." I handed the manservant a pair of plain wool trousers, suitable for everyday wear, a shirt and collar, and a plain jacket. "Colleen, if you would be so kind, once he is ready, to make any necessary changes, if they can be done?"

"I'm sorry, I seem to have missed something here," Mr. Hamilton said, bewilderment on his face. His eyes went wide as he watched me giving orders.

I took a moment, but only a moment. I knew if I stopped to contemplate, to consider—to be sentimental—then I would spend the rest of the afternoon weeping into my husband's shirts. "We each have a problem, Mr. Hamilton. I have a wardrobe full of my husband's things, which he shall never wear again. Clearly, I cannot wear them and there are no men in my family who could make use of them. Even were I to give them to Mr. Scott here, which I did briefly consider, he is not of a size with my late husband." Mr. Scott, stooping though he was, was a reed thin man a good six inches shorter than James.

"You have just come to a new city, and are...in reduced circumstances." He started to object, but I held up a hand. "You are also now in my employ, and as my representative, I cannot have you wandering the streets looking like a vagabond. While I understand your current situation is temporary, I also understand you are perhaps the closest friend my husband has had these past three years, who has done a great service to him, and you continue to provide a great service to me. If you must, consider this your uniform, as when you were in the military. Or a one-time perk of your position. If you decline, then all of this will go to charity, and what would a recipient of charity do with a silk waistcoat? It would be sold immediately to a reseller for God only knows what, only to be sold again. I would much rather you have his things. If you so desire them."

Mr. Hamilton considered me for a moment, his cane braced squarely in front of him, both hands resting on the curling rose vines. At last he nodded. "Very well. Just this once, I suppose." He said it with a slightly indulgent air, and I hoped I had not offended him once again.

"You are about of a size with my husband," I said, turning quickly back to the wardrobe. "I also have shoes and socks and underthings here, should you require them. And his shaving kit...let me see..."

Mr. Hamilton disappeared behind the screen while I dove into the contents of the clothing press, pulling things out by the armload and sorting it all into piles on the bed. I decided the blue, dark green, and red waistcoats would be the most flattering, while the yellow and light green would have to go to charity after all, as they were clearly unsuitable for his complexion.

"How is it?" I asked as I attempted to match ties to the waistcoats from the pile of bowties stacked up in a drawer.

"You've a very good eye, ma'am. A bit loose in the shoulders, but otherwise it should be a good fit," Mr. Hamilton said. A moment later, Colleen disappeared behind the screen with her pin cushion and a measuring tape, assisting Mr. Scott as he pointed out minor adjustments. The sleeves were a bit long, but easily fixed. Mr. Hamilton, though about the same height as my husband, had longer legs, and could the hem of his trousers be let down slightly?

I approached the screen, standing just on the other

side. "Colleen?"

The maid's face appeared. I handed her a pair of polished back shoes, and she ducked back behind the screen. I went back to sorting, the soft murmur of their voices as they discussed whether or not the trousers should be taken in, and would anyone notice if the shoulders of his shirt were half an inch too broad, creating a pleasant background noise. After a while, Colleen came out to retrieve another waistcoat, jacket, and tie.

At last, I had three piles. At the foot of the bed were two suits for every day wear, and one for more formal occasions. Five shirts for daily use, and two that were nicer. A handful of detachable collars. One blue plaid waistcoat, one dark green with leaves and vines embroidered on it, one of a red tweed, and one each in solid black and solid brown. A bundle of silk ties, each coordinated to match a particular combination of suit and waistcoat.

At the head of the bed, I placed a few things to pass on to charity—the unsuitable waistcoats, a stained collar, and the ties which matched neither the selected waistcoats nor their intended's coloring.

The middle pile was more problematic. I neatly folded the flannel underthings, and placed them on the far end of the bed. I thought those might end up in the charity pile.

Then there were the shoes. Should the pair I provided fit, Mr. Hamilton would go home with three pairs of shoes and two pairs of boots in various stages of dress and wear, but all better suited than his current pair.

Last, there were the socks.

I'd made all of James's socks myself. He said mine were the most comfortable. I'd dutifully sent him two pairs every month since he'd left. Most went to his men, many of whom had to do without decent coats, hats, gloves, socks, and even shoes, on top of the lack of food and decent shelter. The Engineers Corps was better off than most regiments, but they still had their challenges.

The socks he left behind were worn, with darned patches at the heel and toe. In the first weeks he was gone, back when we thought he would be home in a matter of months, I repaired all of them. As the war dragged on, I replaced the worst of them completely.

It was a silly thing. Who gets sentimental about worn out, used socks? But I hesitated at the thought of giving them away, even to Mr. Hamilton.

"Ma'am?"

I looked up at the sound of Colleen's voice, hastily wiping my face.

Mr. Hamilton emerged from behind the screen, flanked on either side by Mr. Scott and Colleen.

The transformation was stunning. The jacket fit like a glove, and Colleen and Mr. Scott had pinned so artfully the tucks were hardly noticeable. It was as if the pieces were made for him.

They put him in a crisp white shirt and the blue plaid waistcoat, which made his eyes even bluer. He glanced at himself in my dressing table mirror, and raised an eyebrow.

"My. I look almost the gentleman, don't I?" he mused. With the hand not leaning on his cane, he reached to adjust his tie, the bow of which was slightly crooked.

"Here, let me." Without thinking I reached up to tug gently on the silk, smoothing it flat over the cotton shirt front and smoothing down some of the wrinkles that had set in from such long disuse. He held perfectly still under my hand.

"There." I brushed some lint from his shoulder. He looked down on me solemnly, expression unreadable. For a fraction of a second, our eyes met, and I backed away quickly. "Colleen, did you retrieve those names?" I asked, clearing my throat of a sudden catch.

"Here, ma'am," she said, sliding a slip of paper from her pocket.

"Excellent, thank you."

I held the page out to Mr. Hamilton. "Please take this as merely a recommendation, as you are still new to our city. I've had Colleen write down the addresses of Captain Andrews's tailor and barber, if you need them. Colleen can adjust the day clothes well enough, but I do have some more formal wear, and we should have Mr. Collier see to that. I'll have those sent around this afternoon with your measurements." It reminded me that I had another package to send, as well, for Olivia Baxter.

Mr. Hamilton coughed slightly, the spots of color once again appearing over the top of his beard.

Both Colleen and Mr. Scott were too well trained to say anything if they caught the moment before it was gone, but I thought I saw a smile under the butler's thick white mustache, and Colleen was staring very intently at the pincushion in her cupped hands.

I brushed my hands off on my skirt, as if I could

brush off the awkwardness suddenly filling the room.
I cleared my throat. "Colleen, would you please check
on lunch?"

She nearly bolted from the room. I let out an
inward sigh. The entire household would be gossiping
by the time the plates were on the table. I really
would have to have a chat with them. The last thing I
wanted was for word to get around that I was entering
into a flirtation with an employee before I was even
out of my mourning weeds.

Mr. Scott helped Mr. Hamilton to change back
into his own clothes, and I asked him to make the
arrangements with the tailor before I led my guest
down to the dining room for a quiet meal—too quiet.
From the silence of the house, at least one of the
servants—probably Demelza, I thought, likely with
her brother or Clara—was listening at the door to the
kitchen to confirm the story Colleen had no doubt
related. As if I didn't have enough to worry about
already.

Mr. Purcell's office was on the first floor of a
crowded building at the edge of downtown. It was
placed a little too far northwest to be fashionable,
attempting to straddle the fine line between a prime
location and a lower rent, and failing slightly at the
former.

I raised an eyebrow at the neglected brick
building behind my veil, but Mr. Hamilton didn't
notice, merely offering a hand down from the carriage
and leading me across the icy pavement to the front

door.

Remember, you hired him for his judgment, I told myself firmly as I got a whiff of the entrance, which smelled of old cabbage. At the moment, his judgement was looking rather questionable.

The office facing the street was a bookmaker. The second office was empty, but filled with garbage and things the former tenant apparently didn't need. Several rough looking workmen were in the process of sweeping the contents out into a rear courtyard that appeared to double as a garbage repository.

Mr. Hamilton took me up to the second floor, leaning heavily on his cane and the railing. I opened my mouth to offer assistance, but closed it again, following quietly in his wake instead. At last we reached the landing on the second floor. There were two doors with frosted glass windows and painted lettering. 2A belonged to a shoemaker, and 2B was the law offices of Purcell & Co.

As he held open the door of 2B, he gave me the same small smile and nod as always—the smile mostly hidden by his beard, but visible in his eyes. His confidence helped me lay aside some of my worries.

It was clear from the first step into the waiting area that "Purcell & Co" was an aspirational name. The room was nearly bare, with a wood stove in one corner pumping out as much heat as is possibly could while still leaving a chill in the air. Four straight backed wooden chair lined one wall, and opposite was a desk and filing cabinets. It was all very tidy and clean, but in need of upkeep. The wallpaper was peeling and there was evidently a leak in the southwest corner.

Behind the desk was a small, bespectacled man, who put me in mind of a rat I once saw a street performer with. He trained it to do all manner of tricks, from climbing on people's shoulders and retrieving a lady's hat pin, to jumping through hoops and passing obstacles to ring a bell. At the end of the performance, the sleek black creature, who bore little resemblance at all to the pests we left poison for in the pantry, ran up the man's shoulder to kiss his cheek.

The little man in front of me had beady eyes and a pointed face, but the sort of friendly expression one might associate with a cherished pet, rather than disease-ridden rodent. The thin black mustache balanced on his upper lip twitched like rat's whiskers, and I suppressed a smile.

"How can I help you today?" he asked, in a voice much lower than my imagination supplied.

"Mrs. Andrews and Joshua Hamilton to see Mr. Purcell," my companion said. He held out a hand to help me remove my wrap while the secretary consulted his appointment book.

"Of course. Mr. Purcell is currently out for his lunch, but he should be back in a few moments. You're a little early," He said, checking his fob watch.

The movement made me think once again of my husband's missing watch. I wondered if Mrs. Perry's investigation would lead her to retrieve it. I fingered my own, hoping its match would soon be returned to me.

We sat down next to the little coal stove, warming appendages gone stiff with cold on the ride over. I was just getting the feeling back into my toes when the office door opened.

The man who entered was tall and ungainly, dressed in a suit of subtle gray plaid trimmed in black. He had a shock of red hair and a day's growth of beard, but if, like the office, he was in need of upkeep, he was at least clean and tidy—at least, until the pie he was holding in his mouth leaked brown juice down the front of his waistcoat. He tried to stop it, but the greasy paper bag in one hand only made it worse. He saw us waiting just as the crust of the pie fell apart. Meat and gravy spilled all over the folders in his other hand. He tried to move the folders out of the way, but the contents slid out, scattering all over the floor. The greasy bag, objecting to such rough treatment, split, and two more pies splattered on top of them.

Mr. Purcell's long arms dropped limply to his sides. He was still clutching the empty cardboard folders. Swallowing the mouthful of pie, he heaved a sigh of resignation.

His secretary was already out of this chair, armed with a rag and a bin for the garbage. The lawyer attempted to clean himself up with a handkerchief before addressing us. "So sorry about that. How clumsy of me. Joshua?"

Mr. Hamilton stood, grinning and shaking his head. "It's a good thing your brother did the fighting in the family. With luck like yours, you'd shoot yourself in the foot, William."

"Why do you think I stayed in college as long as possible?" Mr. Purcell laughed at his own clumsiness, and turning to me. I stood slowly.

"Mrs. Andrews, this is William Purcell. His elder brother was in the same regiment as the Captain and me."

"It's a pleasure, ma'am," he said, bowing over my hand.

I nodded in his direction, once again questioning my choice to come. "And you are a recent graduate of…?"

"Harvard, ma'am. Graduated in '63 and spent a year with a firm in Boston before coming back up here. My family's from a little town just south of the city."

He smiled again and gestured for us to follow him back into his office. We brushed past his poor assistant, still trying to wipe up the mess and salvage the soiled papers, and into a tiny, windowless office that was probably intended as a large storage cupboard.

"So sorry to keep you waiting. I hope you weren't kept long," he said, squeezing past us to get behind his desk.

The office was narrow, with hardly enough room for my wide, crinoline supported skirts, let alone my skirts and two men. A pair of straight backed chairs sat opposite the desk, and the little remaining space was taken up by shelves and cabinets, full of books and papers. It was a far cry from the opulent rooms of Shipley, Coolidge and Hagen. There was no cart of spirits, no one offering to bring tea or coffee. No carpets softened the scarred wood floors, and there was only one small window, which hardly let in enough light to supplement the gas lamps.

My first thought on taking my seat was it was a

good thing Mr. Purcell had the same build as a lamppost, because a man like Mr. Coolidge would never make it through the door.

"No, it wasn't long," Mr. Hamilton said, sinking into the seat next to me. He rested his cane between his knees. I was a little surprised to note the smile he greeted the lawyer with was not the mild, businesslike one I had grown accustomed to, but something more genuine; less polite and more cheerful.

"Well, I suppose we should get down to business, then. Mrs. Andrews, my friend here has told me a little of your situation. You are seeking representation should your current arrangement with your late husband's company deteriorate. Is that correct?"

I nodded, drawing back my veil. It was too dim to keep my face covered.

Mr. Purcell, who was about to reach for something in a drawer, froze with his mouth half open.

I raised an eyebrow. "Is something the matter, Mr. Purcell?"

"I-no. I simply wasn't—When Joshua told me he represented a widow, I was not expecting—"

The second eyebrow joined the first. "We have had nearly five years of war in this country, Mr. Purcell. There are thousands of widows much younger than myself."

"Yes. Yes. Of course." The drawer slammed shut and he plunked a folder down onto the stained blotter. "I apologize, I meant no offense."

I glanced at my companion. *I do hope you know what you are doing,* I thought. *I hope he is better spoken in court, and more graceful with his litigation than he is with his paperwork.*

The lawyer cleared his throat, opening the folder to spread out the contents. With precise movements that seemed almost choreographed, he pulled a pair of spectacles from the breast pocket of his jacket and settled them on his long nose, adding to his bird-like appearance. If his assistant was a circus rat, then Mr. Purcell was some variety of stork or other long-legged creature. Perhaps some variety of crane.

"Are those the papers I asked for?" Mr. Hamilton asked, leaning forward slightly.

"Yes. I just finished with them last night."

Hamilton turned to me. "I knew you would want...an assurance. A test of sorts. I asked Mr. Purcell if he would draw up a contract between the two of us, to solidify our arrangement. Just as an exercise, you understand. He is very gifted at mediation and striking agreeable balances between parties."

My eyebrow was getting something of a workout. I reached for the pages Mr. Purcell offered, and read them in silence.

For the next thirty minutes the three of us discussed the various points in the contract. While Mr. Purcell's large hands were clumsy, his mind and words were clearly not. He also had the courtesy to speak directly to me, and to ask for my preferences and opinions on various points, rather than telling me the way things *should be*, as men in his position usually did.

"Yes, I think we should be able to forge a good working relationship," I said at the end of an hour, handing the pen and papers back to Mr. Purcell. He blew on the damp ink, initialing the bottom of the pages himself as witness.

I promised to have the relevant papers from Mr. Coolidge sent over as soon as possible, and he saw Mr. Hamilton and I out. The front room had been cleaned up during our meeting, and another gentleman was waiting in the chair by the stove, melting snow from his boots.

It was coming down thick and fast when we emerged onto the street. The skies were heavy and gray, and though it was midafternoon, the streets were filled with a twilight darkness.

"Well, that went well," I said, adjusting my muff and pulling the heavy rug over my lap as we climbed into the sleigh. "Though I do wonder what you told your friend to have him expect some decrepit matron."

Hamilton's mustache twitched with a hidden smile. "I assure you, I made no illusions as to your age. I merely told him I was in the employ of a widow of a particular nature, who preferred to manage her own affairs."

"Hm." My lips pressed together in something that was not quite a smile, but he still laughed a little in amusement.

"I promise I would never be so indelicate as that," he assured me. "I would never mention a lady's age, even in passing. In truth, I do not even know your age. And I would not presume to ask." He added the last very quickly, perceiving he had made a verbal misstep. "That is—it is not my business. And I do not care to know. What I mean is—"

I finally laughed, to end his misery. His face was

going red above the beard again, and I did not think it was from cold. I took pity on him. "You have been the soul of discretion in our acquaintance," I told him. "Please forgive my jest at your expense."

Leaning forward, I told Mr. Rigby to take me to the company office. "I may be some time, so do take Mr. Hamilton home."

"Are you sure you will not require any assistance?" he asked.

"No. I need to speak with Mr. Richardson. I'd like to set a few things straight, and I'm afraid I can't do that with you there. Mr. Richardson is the type of man who always refuses to deal with a woman when a man is in the room, and in his case, I would rather handle him myself. This is one matter I will insist upon."

"Very well."

There was a hesitation at the end of his sentence, as if there was more he wanted to say but was holding back.

"Yes?"

"I only wondered...have you thought more about the proposal...to spend some time away?"

At first, I didn't respond. "I am taking it under consideration. That is all I can say for now. My mind is not made up." Today was a good day. I did not know how I would fare tomorrow, or the day after.

Hamilton nodded. "Very well, then. Only...know whatever course you decide to take, I—we, all of us—your family and friends, if I may be so bold to number myself among the latter—we only want what is best for you. And speaking as someone who has suffered...*trauma*...it may be in your best interest to take some time away and recover yourself. Some heal better when among familiar surroundings. Others benefit from a fresh perspective."

Inside my muff, my hands clenched into tight fists. I stared firmly ahead, my eyes boring holes into Mr. Rigby's back.

For a moment, it looked like Mr. Hamilton would reach out to place a hand on my shoulder or arm, but he pulled back.

"Merely an observation," he said at last. "From my own experience. But your feelings may be different. You must do what you think is best."

"That is all any of us can do."

Whether from necessity or simple spite, Mr. Richardson kept me waiting for nearly three quarters of an hour. His secretary, Johnson, bent nearly backwards to ensure I would be as comfortable as possible in the hard-backed wooden chair, but no matter how flustered he was, he could not hurry his employer.

"Is there anything else I can get for you, Mrs. Andrews?" he asked for what was probably the fiftieth time in thirty minutes.

I took a sip of the horrible coffee he had provided and attempted not to let my disgust show on my face. Someone had clearly been neglecting the boiler. "No, Mr. Johnson. I'm perfectly fine."

"Mr. Richardson should be with you any moment."

I nodded. He'd said this line almost as many times in the past forty-five minutes; there was no need to reply at this point. We both knew he was only trying to placate me, and to reassure his frayed nerves. Johnson had been with the company long enough to remember my husband, and for me to have learned of his wife and children. We'd already exhausted the polite forms of conversation, and now it was a matter of Mr. Richardson's whims.

At last, the door to Mr. Richardson's office opened and he stepped out.

"Mrs. Andrews. I did not mean to keep you waiting for so long."

"Of course not," I said mildly. *I'm certain you meant for me to give up and leave after ten minutes.* Much as I would have loved to say it aloud, I tucked my uncharitable thoughts away, just as a lady was supposed to, and took the seat offered across his desk. "I presume you received the documents I sent?"

"I did indeed. I am merely wondering where the rest of them are."

"'The rest of them?' Those are all of the patent documents related to the railroad that were among my husband's things."

"I assure you, Mrs. Andrews, they are not. I know with certainty he was working on other designs prior to his death."

"While he was in Washington? I would think the Army would have more claim to them than you." I was glad I was wearing gloves. My knuckles would be white with the way I was clenching my hands together. At least the black leather disguised my anger somewhat.

Mr. Richardson rose and went to one of the filing cabinets behind his desk. "You may not be aware of this, but part of the agreement with James was that all of his designs were property of R&A. He received his payments through our company, as a set fee for his work." He pulled out a sheaf of papers and waved them about. "Look for yourself, if you do not believe me."

The pages were thick with legal writing of the sort the average person can understand no more readily than they can read the language of a foreigner. Nonetheless, I thumbed through them slowly, giving the impression I was, at least, reading them in detail.

The contract itself was completely unfamiliar to me. There had been no copy kept in the study at home, and no mention of it had ever been made. Despite his own natural uncertainty of his designs, I knew James would never sign over his life's work—not the patents, and certainly not the unregistered designs.

"If there is something in particular you are looking for, I could certainly go through his things again," I responded slowly, waiting for him to mention the Gatling gun.

"What I want, *specifically*, is for you to honor your obligations to this company, and do what is best for R&A and its employees by turning over what rightfully belongs to us. Really, this has gone on long enough. I'd hoped to avoid such ugliness, but if I must get the law involve, I will."

"Why was this not brought to my attention at the first, when you made your...generous offer?" I asked sharply, but my glare was reserved for the final page of the contract, not Mr. Richardson. I stared at my husband's signature on the page. It was his name.

There was the same curl in the J, the same slant and curve in the capital A, the flourish at the end of *Andrews*. But my limbs felt numb and cold as I stared at it. For three years, my only communication with my husband had been through letters, usually written every week, but sometimes only once a month if things were bad. Sometimes, at the beginning of the war, or when he was traveling, he would save up a stock of letters, and send me three or four all bundled together. My husband's handwriting was more familiar to me than his face. It might have been his name. It might have been his flourishes. But it was not his signature.

"I did not want to distress you," Mr. Richardson said. His moustache quivered with the effort of hiding the triumph in his expression. He leaned back in his chair to savor it.

The pages shook in my hands. It took all of my strength of will not to ball them up and hurl them at his face.

"This is the first I have seen these papers. James did not have a copy of them in his files at home. I presume, then, his copy would be in his office here?"

"Perhaps. That office has been cleaned out so Mr. Westcomb could make use of it."

"Where are his papers, then? I would like a copy of this document, so I may look into it further."

Mr. Richardson sighed. "Really, Mrs. Andrews. Must we go through all of this? Simply hand the designs over to me. They do not belong to you."

"If James already signed a contract stating all of his designs were property of the railroad, why would he leave me his patents and designs in his will?"

But Gunther Richardson only shrugged. "Perhaps it slipped his mind. You know he could be absent minded at times."

"Not about something like this." This time, I didn't try to keep the hard edge out of my voice. "If you cannot provide me with a copy of this contract, then I will take this one."

He shrugged. "The original is on file with Mr. Coolidge."

"Good. I shall have my lawyer look this over. You understand, it doesn't do to be hasty in situations like this," I said, bringing back the charm and stuffing my anger away, like unwanted kittens into a bag to be drowned. A southern belle couldn't be sweeter. "If he tells me what you've said is true, then I'll send those documents right over, along with my counter offer at the end of the week."

His eyes narrowed. "Your lawyer?"

"Indeed. I'm just a simple woman, you understand. I don't understand things like business or law or anything like that, and I'm still so upset at the loss of my husband. I simply can't fathom making any big decisions like this without solid advice." I was laying it on a bit thick, but then, he knew me well enough after all these years to know I was more capable of handling my affairs than most. But we both knew the steps in this dance, and we were both determined to see it through, rather than show our hands too soon.

"You speak as if you no longer employ Mr. Coolidge."

"Oh, yes, I nearly forgot. I'm not. I was informed there was a... conflict of interest, I think is the term.

So I have found new representation. I'll see he is in contact with you presently.”

Mr. Richardson was on his feet and by my side instantly. He pressed his hand to the office door, keeping me inside. “And was this change at the advice of your...companion?”

“As you can see, I have no companion except yourself today. But if you are referring to Mr. Hamilton, yes, he did assist me in this matter.”

I could not read the expression on his face, except to say it filled me with unease. “As you say, Mrs. Andrews, it wouldn't do to be hasty in a situation like this. I'd hate to see you taking bad advice.”

“I assure you, Mr. Hamilton's advice has been extremely sound.”

“Has it? Did you not say he was a confidant of your husband? His sudden, tragic death...I would hate to think perhaps your Mr. Hamilton might have had a hand in it, and is now, somehow, attempting to manipulate you to his advantage. There have been many stories of men inflicting injury on themselves to get out of the fighting. Considering what is at stake, I can’t see how this would be much different.”

Finally growing fed up with the dance, I favored him with my sternest glare. “Let me pass, please, Mr. Richardson. If you have no purpose other than to slander a dear friend of my late husband, then I believe our conversation is over. Joshua Hamilton has proved himself to be remarkably good character on multiple occasions, both in his service to James and to me. He was, himself, injured in the attack, and attempted to save my husband!”

When he did not move, I pushed past him and

jerked the door open, sweeping out into the hall. I collected my cloak, bonnet and muff with forced calm.

The look Mr. Richardson had given me as I left made me want to run from the building, and not stop until I was far, far away.

The more I thought about Mr. Richardson's words, the more uneasy it made me. As much as I hated to admit it, he had a point. I had no one's word about the attack that had killed James other than that of his aide de camp. There were no living witnesses I knew of, aside from the attackers themselves, who could hardly be considered trustworthy sources on the matter. Though I'd given Mrs. Perry all the information I had about the boy who had found them, it wasn't much to go on and it was doubtful it would come to anything.

I could think of no motivation Mr. Hamilton might have had for instigating the attack, but then much had changed in the past three years. James's letters were usually cheerful. He spoke of conditions, but not situations. Aftermaths, but not battles. He did his best to keep me from worrying.

But he always referred to his secretary in glowing terms. They become fast friends, forming the tight bond not just of brothers-in-arms, but also of men with a shared passion and interests.

In desperation, I decided the answer must lie with the trunk of James's belongings, so carefully packed by Mr. Hamilton.

As I knelt in front of the trunk, I remembered

Hamilton insisting on packing the trunk himself, despite his injury. He left the hospital against the physician's recommendation to do so. He aggravated the injury, and was feverish when I saw him in Washington.

Now, cast in a new light, I wondered if his actions spoke not of dedication, but desperation. Was he searching for something? What could he hope to gain?

I had not touched the trunk since the incident in the train car. I hadn't even allowed Colleen and Clara to unpack it, stating I would do it myself, when I was ready. More than two months later I still did not feel ready, even though it was sitting before me on the hearth rug in my bedroom. I already gave away his clothing; it was time. I could not put it off any longer.

I told the servants not to disturb me until dinner. Olivia would not be home from school for several hours yet.

The longer I sat there, reaching for the lock and then changing my mind, the more my doubts seemed to accumulate. I examined every conversation I'd had in the past eight weeks, agonized over every letter, every glance.

What if I'm wrong? I thought.

But then, and equally terrifying, *What if I'm right?*

There was no choice. Sucking in a deep breath, I twisted the key into the lock and flung open the lid.

For a brief, horrible moment, I thought the trunk looked like an open grave—full of maggots, reeking of death. The barest whiff of the smell from the coffin seemed to glide past my nose, and I found myself gagging.

I scrambled away, snatching up the glass of water from the bedside table and gulping it down.

When I turned back, it was just a trunk. Just a traveling case, just like a thousand others that passed through rail yards every day. It was full of papers, nearly worn out socks, and soiled clothing. It smelled of wool, sweat, paper, and more faintly, the lavender sachets I packed the day James left.

I approached it with caution, as one might a sleeping dog prone to biting. It was ridiculous, and I knew it, but I still tasted bile in my mouth and my heart drummed "When Johnny Comes Marching Home" against my corset.

With deliberate detachment, I removed the clothing and personal effects and set them aside, out of sight.

I was left with the detritus of a creative mind: half-finished sketches, a stack of notebooks filled with scribbles and images anyone who was not the creator would be hard pressed to decipher. The folio containing the projects James had been working on at the time of his death was filed away, of course, but there were a million other ideas stashed away in the trunk, waiting for the right time to develop and mature.

Olivia found me like that, kneeling on the hearth rug, with one of the notebooks open in my lap.

"Mama? What are you doing?" she asked, coming to sit beside me.

"Just going through some of your father's things," I said quietly. I traced a finger over the letters on the inside flyleaf: *Property of Captain James Andrews,*

Army of the Potomac.

Gently, Olivia pried the book from my fingers, closed it and set it aside.

"Are you well, Mama?" she asked.

I glanced up at her.

"Mary Barton's mama wasn't the same after her brother was killed at Gettysburg. And Miss Stanton, she's my French teacher, she says her sister down in Virginia watched the battle at Winchester from her bedroom window. She was so close, she had to dig bullets out of the walls when it was all over, and now she can't sleep in any room with a window because she has nightmares about getting shot at and wakes up screaming. And Eliza Martin told me her brother's fiancé's mother wears all back and doesn't smile, and she just wanders around their old house wailing and crying for her son, who died in Andersonville. And Millie Carter—"

"What's wrong, sweetheart? Why are you telling me all these stories?"

Olivia swallowed hard, looking down at the book in her hands. "Well it's just...all of the girls at school...they all know someone who's...*not right* after the war. There's the men, of course. The brothers and fathers who came back in pieces. And the ones who wake up with nightmares, and the ones that drink and swear and don't laugh the way they used to. But there's also the women. The ones who get so wrapped up in grief they don't come out of it again."

"And you're afraid that's what's happening to me?"

She still didn't look at me, but I saw the tears glistening on her lashes that she wouldn't let fall.

"You're not yourself, Mama. For a while I thought you were better, but you've been acting so strange. And Mr. Hamilton—"

I looked at her sharply. "What about Mr. Hamilton?"

She sniffled. "You smile when you're with him. And I don't like it! You talk to him like you used to talk to Papa, and now Clara says you've given him all of Papa's old things—"

"Don't you pay any attention to Clara," I ordered sharply. *I swear, if that girl kept it up, I'd have to find a new maid.* "Yes, I gave him *some* of your father clothes. Things we can't possibly use. But I'm hardly giving away everything he owned. Mr. Hamilton was in difficulty, and I did was I could to assist him. As for the rest...are you saying you don't want me to smile? That I've no right to pleasurable company, because I'm a widow?"

Olivia bit her lip, shaking her head.

I softened my tone a little. "It is true. I like Mr. Hamilton a great deal. He has done much for us, and for your father, which I have done my best to repay. He is a kind, clever man, and I enjoy his conversation. In that, he reminds me a great deal of your papa."

"The other girls...they say it isn't right, the way you spend so much time with him," she whispered.

Jesus, Mary, and Joseph. Does Buffalo have nothing better to do than critique my social life? I took a deep breath and tried to calm my ire. "Do you dislike having him here? Do you think it is inappropriate?"

"I—I don't dislike him at all..."

When she didn't continue, I tried to find the best way to phrase my thoughts. "If that is the case, then you must learn to weigh public opinion against your own heart. I don't care what the gossips say. They have no idea what goes on under this roof, and if the best entertainment they can conceive is imagining improprieties, then their minds are far too idle for me to waste any time trying to convince them otherwise. The ones who know us—*truly* know us—will know better."

She nodded again.

"You are right about one thing, however. I am not myself. I find myself questioning decisions that in the past I would have made without hesitation. I doubt everything I say and think and do, and I doubt those around me. And I cannot do that. Not now."

Our eyes met briefly, and I tried to smile for her. "Dearest, would you forgive me if I *did* decide to go away? Just for a little while? Just to catch my breath?"

Once it had been decided, things fell into place very quickly. I asked Doctor and Mrs. Lynch for a recommendation for a nearby sanatorium, and they recommend Talbert House, just fifty miles from Buffalo, nestled in a picturesque little valley. Far enough for me to gain some perspective, but close enough for Olivia to visit, if she chose. I doubted she would, however. After a quick exchange of telegrams with Mrs. Baxter, it was decided Olivia would go to the city to stay with her. I put Colleen in charge of packing—unbeknownst to Olivia, not a single dress in her trunk would be black.

"Are you certain, Mrs. Andrews?" she asked when I gave the order.

"I am," I replied, remembering my conversation with Mrs. Baxter. "The color of a dress does not change what is in one's heart. I know Olivia grieves for her father, but it is not fair of me to put her life on hold for the sake of my own mourning. And really, if she is going to be in New York City for several weeks, during the season, she might as well take advantage of it." I could just picture Mrs. Baxter breaking the news to her. My only regret was not being able to see her face when it happened.

"So you have chosen to leave then," Mr. Hamilton said a few days later when he came to call. I met him in the parlor, where he stood with his hat in hand. He was wearing one of the suits I'd given him, newly tailored to a perfect fit. The blue of the waistcoat and neckcloth suited his eyes perfectly.

"Only for a little while. Two or three weeks, I think. Just to get a…a fresh perspective. I think those were your words."

He bobbed his head, as though regretting them. "That can be helpful. I only hope you return fully recovered."

We stood in awkward silence for a moment. Mr. Hamilton twisted the brim of his hat. It was the first sign of nervousness I'd ever seen from him. He opened his mouth to speak, but then closed it abruptly when Colleen brought in the tea cart. She smiled and bobbed a curtsy to him before she left; the entire household was fond of Mr. Hamilton.

"Won't you take a seat?" I asked quickly.

"Should I?" he asked, looking slightly baffled. I tilted my head in askance.

"That is...have I angered you in some way? Offended you?" he asked, sinking down onto the couch. I perched on the chair across from him to pour. "No."

"It is only...The last few days, you have received my messages? I sent a few...and Mrs. Perry said she was in contact with you. She told you she found a name to go with the face of our mystery man?"

"She did." Jake Black. He was an itinerant worker of dubious reputation, who had caused trouble from Georgia to the Canadian border. He was wanted in at least three counties for everything from theft to assault. When she came to deliver the news, I gave her the contract from Mr. Richardson, and asked her to look into it.

He was still looking at me through those thick lashes, looking something like a dog that has been smacked and comes asking forgiveness.

I turned away, setting down the teapot. "I am not angry with you, Mr. Hamilton. I am simply...I have been otherwise occupied."

"I am surprised you plan to pursue your trip when we now have a name to go with the face."

"Honestly, I find this whole ordeal so strenuous...I am happy to let Mrs. Perry and her husband handle the matter."

"Now that I find surprising, indeed. You have never been a woman to allow others to do your work for you."

"Tracking down murderers is not my job. I am a lady. Ladies do not go traipsing about after criminals," I snapped.

He pulled back into the thick upholstery of the couch. "I'm sorry. I... I phrased that poorly. I meant no offense." He set down his tea, untasted, and stood. "I seem to have come at a bad time. My apologies. But I promise I will keep an eye on things while you are away. I'll check in on Olivia. Will she be staying here or with your family?"

"No, that won't be necessary. She'll be staying with a friend."

"I... I see. Well, then I'll just be going." The meaning was clear on his face as he turned towards the door. *You don't trust me.* There was pain and confusion mixed there, as well.

I wanted to call after him, to apologize, but I didn't know what to say. *Please don't come near my daughter until I'm certain you didn't kill my husband?* Was there anything I *could* say that wouldn't make the whole, terrible situation worse?

"Talbert House," I blurted quickly.

"I beg your pardon?"

"Talbert House. It's the name of...it's where I'll be staying. Colleen is coming with me. It's about an hour and a half from here by train, just outside a little village called Great Valley. Should you need to contact me, that's where I will be."

He nodded, silently tipping his hat. The door clicked shut behind him.

Almost as soon as the parlor door closed, I knew I had made an error. Joshua Hamilton was kind and attentive, proving over and over his loyalty to both James and myself. He had been a friend when I had none, a comfort and a joy when both were precious and few.

But whether it was pride, doubt, or fear, I could not bring myself to call him back. The very next day I boarded a southbound train amid the swirling flakes of a light flurry.

The swaying car seemed to shake my thoughts loose. I felt them tumbling around in my brain until they rolled into their correct places, like the wooden maze Mr. Hamilton carved for Brigid's children, with the little ball that tumbled through the channels until it found the end.

Traveling by rail soothed me, like a mother rocking her child. I closed my eyes and listened to the tracks and the wind rushing by.

Colleen and I shared a first-class compartment. She knit a pair of gloves while I stared out the window, thinking. I wished suddenly I had brought my traveling desk; I needed to apologize to Mr. Hamilton for our last meeting. There would, of course, be ink and stationary at our destination. Dr. Lynch assured me Talbert House was as grand as any hotel, but with the benefit of doctors on staff to treat anything which might ail a body.

Late afternoon sunlight flashed in and out of view as the trees grew denser. Their limbs were bare, but there were many of them, and they were tall. Every time a shadow passed over my window, I thought I saw the reflection of James's face in the glass, and once more remembered his warning: *beware the brothers.*

At first, it startled me. But, as we traveled further south, I began to think of it as comforting. I knew he was watching over me. I left Buffalo in order to get

guidance, perspective. There was no one more suited
to guide me, I thought, than the spirit of my beloved
husband. After all, no one could have a better
perspective than one of heaven's angels.

After two hours by train, we hired a wagon at
Great Valley to take us the last five miles of lurching,
frozen road.

We finally arrived, shivering, just after dark. The
driver lashed the horses, encouraging them up the last
treacherous incline, and there it was. A fifteen-foot
wrought iron gate set into a brick wall nearly as high.
By the fading light, I could make out the looming
form of a huge, sprawling complex of brick and
stone. Three stories high and almost as long as a city
block, "imposing" felt like an understatement.

Beside me, Colleen's mouth formed a wide "o" as
she took it in. "This is where we're staying?"

I nodded. "Yes." As we drew nearer, I could just
make out the engraving next to the gate: *Talbert
House, est. 1858.* "Dr. Lynch says it's one of the most
modern facilities in the country. They have all kinds
of treatments, and the latest scientific research. They
have the most well-respected alienists in the union."

"What's an alienist, ma'am?"

"It's a doctor who looks at ailments of the mind,
instead of the body."

"Is that what's wrong with you? An ailment of the
mind?"

I gave her a sharp look for saying such things in
front of a stranger, but the driver was already leaping
down from his seat to open the gate and didn't give
any sign of hearting.

"That's what we'll find out."

The grounds seemed to vanish into shadow the closer we got. The only light came from two lamps on each side of the front door. As we drew up, I saw they were candles, likely lit for our expected arrival. Talbert house would be much too far from town to receive a gas line.

A woman of about forty in a grey dress and crisp white pinafore waited in the foyer. She drew her heavy shawl around her shoulders and came out to greet us.

"Sophia Andrews?" she asked, without smiling.

"Yes. And you are?"

"Mary Beaton. I'm the matron of our ladies' ward. Come on down, now. You must be frozen stiff."

The driver helped us down from the wagon. Mrs. Beaton scanned Colleen up and down. "And who are you?"

"This is my ladies' maid, Colleen Boyle. I wrote and said she would be accompanying me."

The matron frowned. "Our guests have their every need attended to. Outside staff if unnecessary, and can hinder the process."

I shivered, rubbing my hands together inside my muff. The driver was already turning his wagon around, driving back to the gate. "Perhaps we could discuss this inside, where it is warm?"

Still reluctant, she showed us into the building and tugged on a bell pull by the door. Within moments, two young men with shoulders like Fort Sumter appeared to carry our things inside.

Though all of the lamps were lit, the building felt unaccountably dark, as though the walls themselves devoured candlelight.

"You should have received a telegram stating what to bring. A ladies' maid most certainly was no on the list."

I pulled myself up to my full, if not considerable height. "I understand. But Colleen is my companion. Either she stays with me, or we both leave first thing in the morning."

Colleen looked ready to object, and so did Mrs. Beaton. I shot the former a look, silencing her. Her jaw snapped shut with an audible click.

The matron's mouth formed a thin, white line. "I'll discuss it with the doctor. You'll need his approval."

I raised an eyebrow defiantly. "Then discuss it."

She huffed, turning on her heel.

"You've come just in time for dinner. We eat at seven o'clock, precise, every night. You'll be with the ladies in A ward. I'll show you the way up to your room. The other wards are locked; you'll want to stay clear of them. Those are the patients that require more care.

"Men are on the south wing, women in the north. Meals are shared, but otherwise there's no mixing except for our Friday evening socials."

She led us up a grand staircase to rival any of the great houses I had visited. In fact, the curling marble banister, the broad steps with the red carpet, the cherubs carved into the niche at the landing—it reminded me quite a bit of Mr. Richardson's home.

Up into the highest reaches of the institution we climbed. At the top of the stairs, my guide produced a key from her chatelaine and unlocked number 312. Already, a card with *Andrews, Sophia* in curling script waited in the frame by the door.

"What's down there?" I asked, spying a solid looking door at the end of the hall, only a few doors down.

"That's the door to B ward. It stays locked at all times."

"What's B ward?"

The look the matron gave me showed plainly I'd reached the end of her patience. "Don't worry about them. You'll not be mixing with them. We keeps all the wards separate, based on the needs of our guests."

While she found the correct key, I gave the hall a swift appraisal. A ward was characterized by light green walls and honey-colored wood floors covered in a floral rug. In between each door was a small table with a vase of silk flowers, or a small painting of some inoffensive still life.

"This'll be your room, then, Mrs. Andrews, if you would care to freshen up a bit." She looked at Colleen. "I'll see what we can do about accommodating your…companion." She said it as though I'd packed a box of roaches in my luggage.

Colleen stood very close to me. "Just a blanket and a pillow is all I need. I can stay in here. That way I'll be prepared should my mistress need anything."

The thin white line came back. "They've already started serving downstairs, but if you want to freshen up a bit, I'll see they keep a plate for you. Doors are locked a ten o'clock, you must be in bed by then. No candles are permitted in the bedrooms, and your luggage will have to be searched for sharp objects."

"I beg your pardon!"

"This facility specializes in the treatment of

disturbed minds, Mrs. Andrews. We house many veterans here who are prone to various kinds of fits. It is a measure for your safety and that of those around you. It is *not* optional." With another sharp turn, she strode away. Like the hallway downstairs, the corridor where she left us also seemed to absorb the light, until it swallowed her up, too. I shivered and went inside.

"Well! This is...nice..." Colleen said, taking my cloak and muff. From the hesitation, "nice" was not her first choice of description for Talbert House. More likely the fourth or fifth.

"I'm sure it's very cozy by daylight," I sighed. I resisted the urge to look around the room; it felt like someone was watching me, but I would not give in to the feeling of paranoia. I was *safe* here. This was a place where women like me came to recover from physical and emotional strain. The idea someone was *watching* me was ludicrous.

The men hadn't been up with my things yet, so I did the best I could with the tiny looking glass over the dressing table. It was mounted so high I could only see myself from the chin up, and only if I stood on my toes.

The room was illuminated by a gas sconce hanging from the ceiling. Contrary to my original assessment, they must have had some kind of gas line. It only made sense, if candles were not allowed in the room.

My lodging was very plain: a bed against one wall with a nightstand. On the opposite wall, the dressing table and a wash stand. There was a small shelf, presumably for personal effects, and a stout looking chest of drawers. The only ornamentation in the entire room was a painting of a little girl with golden ringlets and rosy cheeks at prayer.

"It looks like a convent in here," I mused. Dr. Lynch made it sound like I would be staying at a very fine hotel, but with a specialized staff; the reality fell somewhat short of the expectation.

"Me mam says a simple room makes for a clean soul," Colleen said, but she was frowning as she joined me in my examination of the painting. "But I think that was just because we were so poor. Is it just me, or is her head on wrong?" she asked, tilting her own slightly to the side.

I did my level best not to laugh, but I couldn't keep my lips from twitching. "Not wrong, exactly, but I do not think the artist has more than a passing familiarity with human anatomy. I'm afraid that child may have a goose hidden in her family tree."

Colleen's laugh was bright and loud, and succeeded in dissipating some of the gloom. The room itself even seemed a bit brighter. I knew I wouldn't be able to sleep with that deformed child looking down on me from the other side of the room, however, so I removed the painting and slid it between the dressing table and the wall, where it would be out of the way.

I took a few moments to freshen up at the washstand, then left Colleen to see to the unpacking. She would have her dinner in the kitchen with the other staff.

Once I was back to the first floor, I had a few wrong turns before I found the dining room, since it was in the north wing. On the south side there was a library and a common room, and then a heavy door blocked the end of the hallway.

"Can I help you, ma'am?" asked a young woman in the same grey dress and pinafore as Mrs. Beaton.

I jumped. I could have sworn the hall was deserted; I hadn't even heard her footsteps.

"I was looking for the dining room, I thought I heard something." I turned back to the door, but the sound stopped. For a moment it had sounded like a scream.

"Dining room's this way," she said, pointing back in the opposite direction, with the obvious expectation I would follow.

I hesitated. She couldn't have been more than twenty, but here were shadows under her eyes the gas lamps accentuated. She didn't smile, and barely seemed to breathe or blink.

"What's through here?" I asked instead, gesturing to the door.

"Private rooms," she said unhelpfully. "You should be getting to dinner, ma'am. They're almost done."

"I—yes. Thank you. Of course."

A cold chill ran down my spine as I passed the grand staircase and the entry once again. The building seemed to pulse around me, as though it was a living entity and devoured me whole, along with all of the light. I shuddered and hurried in the direction the woman had indicated.

chapter thirteen

The dining room, at least, lived up to Dr. Lynch's description: mauve wallpaper, cut glass sconces, and a lovely china pattern contrasted sharply with the spartan guest rooms. The table had been arranged so the ladies sat on one side, while the men sat on the other. The ladies were dressed in evening wear, and the gentlemen in good suits, but the conversation was subdued.

I, of course, was not dressed for dinner. I was still in my wrinkled black traveling suit, the hem with snow. The ladies at the table all gave me an appraising look. The men, though they looked up at my entrance, did not seem to mark it as unusual.

"Ah, Mrs. Andrews," said the tall, bearded man at the head of the table. "So glad you could join us. Here, we have a place set aside for you. Grace, see that Mrs. Andrews gets a plate." A maid standing against the wall hurried off to fetch another place setting, while another pulled up a chair from the corner of the room and placed it next to the man who had spoken.

"I'm so sorry for my late arrival. The roads were rather terrible," I said awkwardly, taking the indicated seat.

"No trouble, no trouble. We weren't sure what time to expect you, is all. It can be rather difficult to get out here in the winter. We're so remote, you know."

"Indeed."

Grace reappeared with a plate, flatware, glasses, and a napkin. The man continued. "I am Dr. Leiter. I have charge of this establishment, so we will be seeing much more of each other over the next few days." He laughed a little, and I nodded. "It's a pleasure to meet you."

The conversation slowly began to pick up again. With Dr. Leiter on my left and an older woman who was also dressed in widow's garb on my right, I began to relax slightly. The woman was in her sixties, at my guess. Mrs. Mary Lou Hurst wasted no time in introducing herself, and everyone around us.

"I've always been in poor health," she said. "Always. Even as a girl. But after my Byron died, it just got so much worse. My daughter finally sent me here, and Dr. Leiter has taken such good care of me. I've been here since '58, just after Dr. Talbert opened the doors. Dr. Leiter says I may as well be the lady of Talbert House." She smiled and batted her eyes at Dr. Leiter like a coquettish young girl, but he had turned to speak to the gentleman on his left and didn't see.

I nodded and cut a sliver off my roast beef. A part of me wanted to know what was wrong with her that she had been in the sanatorium for so long, but the greater part of me recognized asking would be unbelievably rude. At any rate, I had a feeling it had more to do with Dr. Leiter's thick, dark hair and elaborately tied neckcloth than any actual *medical* care.

When it came time for the dinners to adjourn to their after-dinner pursuits (did that include cigars and brandy in an establishment such as this, or perhaps cards and dancing?), I still had a few bites of food left on my plate, but I was so tired I couldn't finish them.

Mrs. Hurst had already formed an attachment to me. She linked her arm through mine as we left the dining room. "After supper we have two hours to spend in the common rooms. The gentlemen have theirs, of course, and we have ours. It's just down this way. But you seem ready to drop, my dear. You must be exhausted after your travels."

"I am a little tired," I admitted.

"What room are you in, dear? I'm in number twelve, so if ever you need anything, just give a shout. Some of the girls who work here, you know, they're so *dour*. I don't like calling on them if I can help it. So if you've any questions at all, just ask."

I tried to smile, but it was swallowed up by a yawn. "I certainly will. But for now, I think I shall just retire for the night."

We parted at the stairs, and I managed to drag myself up to my room. I didn't even bother to ring for Colleen; she would be at dinner, and after such a long day she deserved to eat in peace. I found my belongings had been hung and folded. The tintype of our family James had carried while at war was open on the little shelf above the dresser, and my books were lined up next to it. As far as I could tell, nothing was missing after the mandatory search, and Colleen had put everything in good order.

I stared at the photograph, thinking regretfully at the face of my daughter. The nagging feeling I had failed her somehow tugged at me, but I yawned again as I peeled off my dress, undoing the buttons and my corset with some difficulty and dropped into bed.

Despite my exhaustion, I hardly slept. The strangeness of the building drove Morpheus away completely once the lights were out. I lay awake, tossing and turning on the lumpy, unfamiliar bed, until the nurse came down the hall and locked the door.

I got up to sit by the window. I had no candle to read by, and no way to turn the gas back on from inside the room. When I closed my eyes I thought I could see the disturbed child from the paining staring at me, even though her frame was hidden.

I went back to bed and stared pointedly at the ceiling until I fell into a fitful dream.

James. He stood not fifteen feet from me, just out of arm's reach. He held out a wordless hand, but when I tried to go to him a chasm opened between us. I could not walk around it. If I tried, he would surely vanish. The only choice was to jump over the breach, into his arm.

I reached, straining as best as I could for his hand, but at the last moment he pulled away. From the skeletal trees surrounding us, a murder of crows suddenly alighted, aiming their sharp beaks at my face. The lumpy landscape congealed into a graveyard, full of misshapen headstones. The rift became an open grave.

Try as I might to shoo them away, the birds kept coming. I pulled back to cover my face and head, but it was no good. They continued to peck, beating me with their broad wings until I lost my balance and tumbled into the gaping black hole.

I woke with a start, face streaming with sweat,

heart hammering. Someone tapped lightly on the door.

"Ma'am? It's me. I've come to help you dress," Colleen said. I must have slept through the nurse unlocking the doors.

I bundled myself into my wrapper, croaking for her to enter as I half fell out of bed, unwilling to lay still and horizontal any longer.

"Mrs. Andrews! You look a fright! Are you well?" She asked, hurriedly setting down the pitcher with the fresh water for the wash basin.

"I—I'm fine. It was only a nightmare," I said. Though the light from my window was clear and bright, reflecting off the snow with blinding ferocity, it did not seem to reach inside my room. Were the shadows in the corner deeper than a moment ago?

Colleen *tsked*, then proceeded to bustle about the room, selecting clothing and laying out soap and a clean towel. "Well, we'd best hurry. One of the maids said breakfast is served right at eight, every morning, and it's already after seven. She also said you'll want to be there since it's your first day, as they always make announcements and such."

Quick as anything, Colleen helped me to wash and dress. I'd realized the night before that the price Talbert House payed for its grand appearance was all of the rooms were frightfully cold and drafty. There were two thick blankets on my bed, but my toes still felt chilled, even though I'd slept in my stockings.

Once I'd been buttoned into a plain black wool dress and donned a horrible widow's cap, I was ready to face the day. I hated the cap with a passion, but it would be improper for me to appear with my head uncovered, and I was grateful for the extra warmth. At least I didn't have to wear a veil.

Mrs. Hurst saved me a place at the breakfast table. We were further down the line this time, at about the middle of the table. When I looked around a little, she waved her hand and patted my seat. "Don't bother about it, dear. It's first come, first served here. We only bother with seating placement at dinner," she informed me with a broad grin. Like myself, she was dressed head to foot in black, but her dress was trimmed in white lace with tiny white specks scattered over the material, like stars. Her cap was black with more white lace, but had been trimmed with red ribbon and a pair of wax cherries, which matched the red border on her thick black crocheted shawl. It also matched the cheerful flush in her cheeks. The night before I'd attributed it to wine, but I began to think it was her general disposition, leaning towards the latter. I could not help but return her smile.

"Good morning, Mrs. Hurst. Are you well today?"

"Oh, yes. I am feeling much better today than I have in a long time. It seems having a good companion is a soothing balm on my soul. Which means you must call me Mary Lou. No more of these formalities." Her smile was less of friendship, and more of friendly mischief. I thought, for a moment, I was seeing Olivia Baxter at the age of sixty or seventy, and had to suppress a laugh. I did not have many friends I called by their Christian names; it would be nice to add another to the list.

By morning light, I took another look at my

fellow patients. There were very few men—one for every three or four women, I estimated but the men almost all had some sort of visible injury. One man had burn scars on his face, and other was missing his right arm. He ate awkwardly with the left, and kept bumping his right side against the table as though trying to us the missing limb. The patients ranged in age, but it was very clear everyone at the table came from means.

"Are there so few patients for such a large building?" I asked, counting only about twenty persons, though there were still empty chairs.

Mrs. Hurst laughed, which turned into a chesty cough. She produced a handkerchief and was occupied for a few moments. When she could speak, she asked, "Have you traveled much, Mrs. Andrews?"

One of the serving girls deposited a large scoop of porridge into the bowl before me. It sucked wetly against the bowl, and I tried to hide my revulsion. Porridge and toast have always reminded me of my childhood, growing up in the Irish tenements, or of the early days of my marriage. For this reason, I would generally prefer to subsist on tea alone until lunchtime. "Some. More than most, I expect. My husband was in the railroad."

Her face lit up brightly. "Oh, how wonderful! I have always loved rail travel. But that is a conversation for a different time. Think of your stay here as being in a hotel. We, of course, are the first-class guests, which is why we have the nicest dining room and the best sleeping arrangements." She coughed again and took a sip of her coffee, making a face. "Though I don't think anyone gets the best coffee! Really, dear, I advise you to avoid it, if you can," she said in a stage whisper. I took a sniff from my own cup, and set in down quickly. The smell alone could have peeled the paper from the walls.

"There are others, of course, but we don't mix with them. The difficult cases. They keep to themselves. Of course, they get the best care possible, but some just aren't fit to mingle, you understand."

"Of course."

Mrs. Hurst lifted her spoon, but instead of eating she continued with her favorite occupation, explaining the ins and outs of Talbert House: who was a friend, who to avoid. Dr. Glass was pleasant enough around the dinner table, but completely insufferable when providing treatment. "Very arrogant, that one. Very proud indeed of his title." Miss Temple was a sweet girl, but prone to hysterics, which was why her parents sent her away. "Female complaints," Mrs. Hurst whispered behind her napkin. "Wholly given over to emotion. And there was a rumor when she first came that there was an incident with the milkman."

"So there are all kinds here, then."

"Oh, indeed there are. Generally, they divide us up into groups. Dr. Sawchuck and Dr. Glass handle the hysterical patients and the ones with nervous disorders. Miss Temple and Mrs. Gray are two of their patients."

"What's wrong with Mrs. Gray?" I asked before I could stop myself. I was following Mrs. Hurst's gaze to the end of the table, where a woman of about thirty stared listlessly at her porridge.

"I don't know the fully story—not yet, anyway,"

she added with a slight chuckle, tapping the side of her nose, "But from what I understand she had a child not long ago and hasn't been herself since. She talks to herself, sometimes, about what a horrible creature she is. It's very sad," she said, her humor suddenly turning to quiet empathy. "I don't know if it is true or not, but from what I understand Dr. Glass is in favor of a hysterectomy, but her husband is opposed to it. Apparently, the child was a girl, and their eldest died two years ago, and he is adamant she give him a son. I suppose four daughters are a poor substitute."

"Poor woman."

Mrs. Hurst turned back to her breakfast, shaking off the melancholy air. "Well. At any rate, on the other side, you have Dr. Richards and Dr. Wellman— very well named indeed! They take care of all of the other complaints, like me. There's several of us that have weak lungs, or general complaints. And of course, Dr. Leiter oversees everything."

"Mrs. Andrews?"

I turned around. One of the female attendants appeared at my elbow. I hadn't decided yet if they were more maid or nurse; they seemed to handle most everything, from the little I had seen. "Yes?"

"When you are finished with your breakfast, Dr. Glass would like to speak with you."

"Oh, thank you," I replied. She curtsied and fell back to her place against the wall.

"That's just standard," Mrs. Hurst said, noting the slightly confused look on my face. "The doctors always meet with new patients to examine them and discuss their care and symptoms."

I glanced down again at my bowl. The contents

had congealed into a solid mass. "I think I'll go take care of that now, then." There was certainly no way I would eat *that*.

Dr. Glass had a cozy office on the first floor, just a few doors down from the dining room. It wasn't large, but it was impressive, with heavy bookcases filled with innumerable books and expensive ornaments.

"Wait here a moment, ma'am. He will be right with you," said my guide. She closed the door behind her, leaving me alone in what appeared to be a miniature library.

The wallpaper was deep blue, which made the room feel smaller—more intimate. Outside the broad windows behind the desk, I could see the sun had taken shelter behind a cloud; the grounds were no longer blinding with the reflection on the snow. Ignoring the chair, I took a closer look.

The garden was large, and surrounded by a stone wall about six feet tall. The trees were all bare, the flowers covered by snow, but walking paths had been cleared between the evergreen hedges, and there was evidence these were frequently walked. Considering the emphasis on "clean air and exercise" to cure every ill, daily walks were probably essential to recovery. I shivered at the very thought of it as the wind kicked up, blowing clouds of white powder that temporarily blocked my view of the landscape.

When it cleared again, I saw two men weaving through the shrubbery with what appeared to be a rolled up rug swinging between them. One of them slipped on a patch of ice, but was able to catch himself on a tree. Passing a large greenhouse, they left the garden via a gate set into the far wall, and disappeared into the forest on the other side. Above the high wall, I could see the roofs of several other outbuildings. Talbert House was clearly even larger than I'd first thought.

The office door opened and closed, pulling me from my reverie.

"Mrs. Andrews, I presume?"

I turned around. A stout, cheerful man with pink cheeks and a white beard—the only hair on his head—smiled in the doorway, hands tucked into his white coat.

I returned the smile and offered a small curtsey. "Dr. Glass. A pleasure. I hope you don't mind me enjoying your view. I did not see much of Talbert House last night due to my late arrival."

"Oh, no trouble. I'm afraid there isn't much to see this time of year, but it really is quite lovely in the summer."

"Where does that gate lead? I only ask because I just saw some men go through it with…something."

"There are some walking paths in the woods some of our guests use in the summer, and some outbuildings that way. I imaging they were just making some repairs. We had high winds a few days ago that did some damage, and they need to clear away some of the snow in order to make the repairs." I meant to ask about the rug, but he gestured to the studded leather chair on the other side of the desk. We traded places and took our respective seats.

"Now, what is it we can do for you? From your

letter and the information I received from Dr. Lynch, it seems you have something of a nervous complaint since your husband died."

"Yes. I..." I described the heavy melancholy weighing on me; the lack of appetite and difficulty sleeping and rising in the morning.

"I feel as though I can't accomplish anything. I go through bouts in which all I seem to do is sleep, to cry, and others in which I have a great flurry of activity, but everything I accomplish is purely mechanical. What I do feel is nervousness. I... I find myself mistrusting those around me, even those I have no reason to doubt. I question every decision I make."

Dr. Glass nodded, making notes on the pad in front of him. "Of course. Perfectly understandable for you to feel uncertain now that your husband is no longer the decision maker in the household."

I fought down an offended reflex. "I have been the decision maker in the household since he went to war. He trusted me completely, and I managed things very well in his absence. It has only been recently..."

But Dr. Glass had already waved off my concerns. "Of course, of course." He continued writing, and then asked me about other symptoms.

I shrugged a little. "I get headaches sometimes, or stomachaches. From not sleeping or eating, I expect. They usually go away with a little rest."

"And what is that?" he asked, pointing.

I reached up to the area indicated. "This?" The red patch along my jaw had been coming and going for weeks.

"I'm not sure, honestly," I replied. "It usually

fades in a day or two, but has been more persistent this week."

"And how long have you been getting it?"

I tried to think. It seemed to have started around the time the weather turned bitter. "Since Christmas, I think?"

"Any other complaints?"

I was suddenly reminded of my fainting episodes. "I have on occasion had some little trouble breathing. I am not prone to histrionics, you understand. I have always been very calm and pragmatic. But on two separate occasions I swooned. I thought perhaps my corset was at fault, so I have instructed my maid not to lace it as tightly."

We chatted for a few more minutes, then he closed the file and pushed it aside. "Well, this all seems fairly straightforward, Mrs. Andrews. We'll have you right as rain in no time. It's nothing a little rest can't cure."

By then, it was fairly clear our interview was over. When I pressed to find out what exactly my treatment would entail, he merely said, "Don't you worry. You just concentrate on relaxing, and leave the rest to us."

Though Dr. Glass made it sound easy, it was not so simple for me to relax and place everything in the care of someone else. After exhausting my list of correspondents on the second day and finding the contents of the library severely lacking in the fiction department (likely because the reading of novels was sufficient cause for a husband to have his wife committed), I found myself increasingly bored and desirous of an occupation, to the point Ijoined Mrs. Hurst at her quilting circle.

"We made all kinds of things during the war," she said as we sat at our work. I pieced several small blue and white squares together into a nine-block that would be joined to the larger quilt. "We sent boxes and boxes of things to the soldiers. Quilts and socks and shirts and gloves and anything you can think of. We practically had our own chapter of the Sanitary Commission."

Mrs. Hurst was capable of keeping up a ceaseless stream of chatter on everything from her sons, who had both died at Shiloh, to the indiscreet activities of the staff and other patients. This latter was always communicated in something of a stage whisper, and was greeted by the other ladies of the circle with a nervous titter. This was how I learned one of the nurses for our floor, Anne Price, had an arrangement with one of the gentlemen on the other side of the building, a Mr. Morton, who lost both legs in the war and suffered from nostalgia after spending two and a half years in a Southern prison camp. Mrs. Hurst said crowded rooms made him nervous, so he seldom joined us for meals, and he frequently woke from violent nightmares.

"Rumor has it he nearly strangled one of the orderlies his first morning here. They almost moved him to C ward, but he's recovered well enough. He's mild as a lamb, as long as he's not startled. But oh! Last July there were fireworks to celebrate Independence Day, and it set him off something awful. You could hear him all over the building. He was shouting about how the Rebels were going to get him, and they'd never take him alive, and he wasn't going back, not ever." Mrs. Hurst *tsked* sadly. "Poor, poor thing. When I see what those dirty Rebs did to him, it almost makes me glad my boys didn't come back." She paused here to dab at her eyes with her handkerchief, and then had to excuse herself from the circle for a few minutes.

She was also a wealth of information about the doctors. It seemed Dr. Leiter took a special interest in the young ladies who were sent by parents concerned about their virtue. I pursed my lips at that, and for the first time wondered if I had perhaps made a mistake in coming to Talbert House. It was not terribly uncommon for young girls who showed certain...interests to be sent away so they could be corrected, but the way Mrs. Hurst spoke, I was not at all sure I approved of the treatment.

My second night at Talbert House, Dr. Glass prescribed something to help me sleep. I objected, but he insisted. "This will help get you back onto a normal schedule. Many of our patients have difficulty sleeping, and find this to be very helpful." At his insistence, I took it dutifully every evening, under the watchful eye of Colleen and one of the nurses. When I complained of the vivid nightmares it gave me, he assured me it was a temporary side effect and would go away soon enough.

I wasn't sure I believed him. Worse, the food seemed to disagree with me. On my second morning, a nurse reminded me gently that I must eat. On my third morning, the reminder was less gentle. Mary Lou touched my arm gently and leaned over to whisper, "You must eat dear, just a little. If you refuse food for long enough, they will send you to B ward, and it's only downhill from there."

So, I choked down a few bites every morning. The coffee and tea fluctuated between something that was little more than colored water, and something that could be used to remove wallpaper. Our lunches were usually light, consisting of boiled meats and vegetables with very little seasoning (so as not to aggravate the nerves, according to my mentor) but even this seemed to bother my digestion.

At the end of two weeks, however, I felt worse than when I had arrived. My stomach was in a constant state of agony, and I nearly gave up food altogether. In the morning, I joined the quilting circle in the ladies' common area, but then retired to my room to read or write letters. I received no mail after my arrival, but continued to write endless letters, anyway. There was little else to do. I sent cheerful missives to family, but was more candid when writing to Mrs. Baxter. My letters to her seemed to be the one place I could express the fear and anxiety that had riddled me for so long. While I unwell at home, I avoided doing all I could, including keeping up with my correspondence. Being unwell at the sanatorium, however, seemed to have the opposite effect. I felt as though I *must* work, I must continue on as I would normally—even though there was really nothing for me to do. I wrote four short notes to my daughter, three missives of epic length to Olivia Baxter, and one carefully crafted letter to Mr. Hamilton.

I had intended to send it immediately after my arrival, but could not seem to find the words. I started it half a dozen times, but always found myself hesitating after the initial greeting.

So much time in bed, however, gave me plenty of time to think and reflect. I found I missed his conversation and wanted his humor and level-headed advice, which I had so foolishly disregarded.

I missed his smile and his blue, blue eyes, and the way he seemed to take absolutely everything in stride.

When it was finally complete, I gave the letter to Colleen. "See this is posted right away," I said as she cleared away my traveling desk so I could rest.

"What? What is it?" I asked when she bit her lip.

Colleen glanced over her shoulder at the door, which was partially open. "I don't think they've been posting your letters, ma'am," she whispered.

"What are you talking about?" I asked. "Why wouldn't they?"

She looked again, as though she expected us to be interrupted any moment, and lowered her voice again. "Yesterday, I put your letter to Miss Olivia in the bowl, just as usual. But when I came by a little later, I saw one of the attendants from the men's ward, he was all wrapped up to take them to town, but I saw him sorting through the letters, but he pulled some of them out and put them in the fire." All of our letters were collected in a large ceramic bowl on a small table in the dining room, and the mail was handed out every day at lunch. "When he was gone, I went to look, and I think Miss Olivia's letter was in the fire, along with several others."

"Did you say anything to him?"

Colleen shook her head. "No, ma'am. I was afraid of what he might say. Or do. I didn't like the look of him, not one bit."

"He wasn't one of the regular men?"

She hesitated. "I've seen him around. I think he runs errands. I've seen him come and go a few times. He was with one of the nurses in a storage room the other day." By her frown, I thought perhaps the nurse hadn't been so keen for the company.

"Help me dress," I said, throwing back the covers.

"Ma'am, you should be in bed—"

I was weak from lack of food and my stomach ached something fierce, but I planted my feet on the floor and managed to stand up. "Colleen, help me dress."

By the time I was buttoned and laced into yet another black wool dress, I was pale and sweating, but I only waved off Colleen's entreaties. "I must go downstairs. I want you to find that man. Watch him, but don't let him see you. If he does anything suspicious, I want you to find me immediately."

"Oh, no! Please don't make me, Mrs. Andrews. He's such a fierce man, and with that awful scar!"

I froze at the word and turned to look at her. With one finger I traced a line down my cheek, the same place the man in Mr. Hamilton's drawing had his own deformity. Wide eyed, Colleen nodded.

I clutched her arms for balance and tried to think. I knew there was no way I could make the three-mile trek back to town, even on horseback. Trying to take a wagon or cart would take too long and attract too much attention.

I went to my trunk and dug around inside until I found my reticule. "Take this. Get to town, and send for the police. If you pass a farm along the way, pay someone to give you a ride. Do whatever you have to do to get to the telegraph office and send for help. Do you think you can get out without anyone noticing?"

"But what about you, ma'am? I can't just leave you here alone!"

I looked at her steadily. "You can, and you will. I have a plan. But I need you to get to town, to get help."

She glanced out the window, where heavy gray clouds filled with rolled across the already lowered sun like an invading Confederate army.

"Hurry. Dress warm." I went to the wall where my own things hung on a peg, and handed her the leather gloves lined with cashmere, my rabbit fur muff, and my cloak, which was far thicker and warmer than hers. "Take an extra pair of stockings, too. But don't dawdle. If anyone sees you leave, I'll try to create a distraction." A sudden idea occurred to me. "I know. I'll tell them I'm going for a walk. Keep the hood up, and with luck anyone who glances you outside will think you are me. I'll tell them whatever stomach complaint I have has kept you to your bed, so no one will miss you."

Colleen plopped down on the bed to untie her boots and pull on the extra pair of wool stockings I gave her. The purse was already tucked deep into the pockets of her brown calico work dress, where hopefully it would remain out of sight.

Though I felt ill, I walked as straight as I could to the common room. Dinner would be soon, and everyone would be migrating into the large hall where we mingled on Friday evenings.

Mr. Morton was already there, his wheeled chair

positioned in the corner near the piano. His fiddle was out and he tested the bow against the strings.

He looked up when he saw me and smiled. It was a good day for him, then. He only attended one meal in six due to his dislike of crowded spaces, but Mrs. Hurst said they were trying a new course of treatment with him. Playing his violin calmed him; it could often be heard echoing through the corridors of the men's ward, if one got close enough—a fact some complained of, but he was a very good player.

"Are you well this evening, Mrs. Andrews?" he asked, brows knitting when he saw my pale face.

"Well enough, thank you," I said. "Is dinner over already?" It was not even dark yet.

"No. I just like to come down a bit early when I plan on playing. The acoustics in this room are the best in the entire building. Warm up a little, you know, before everyone comes. The food here isn't really good enough for me to miss, though it is better than battlefield rations." He frowned slightly, but raised the instrument to his chin and began the opening strains of the apt, "Hard Times Come Again No More."

I lingered in the doorway until I saw the bright cherries on Mrs. Hurst's cap.

"Sophia, my dear! It is so good to see you out of bed. But, pardon me, it looks like that is where you belong still," she said, dropping her voice down to a more concerned, discrete tone as she got nearer.

I pulled her into the common room, closing the door behind her. It was the closest thing to a private conversation we could have. I hoped the music would keep Mr. Morton or anyone else from overhearing us.

"I need you to tell me quickly. There's a man with a scar here. One just like this." I traced my finger down my cheek again. "Have you seen him?"

"Him? Oh, that's just Mr. Black. He's our groundskeeper. He came a few months ago. Why do you ask?"

"Do you know where I might find him?"

"Well, he's probably in the basement with the other staff, or working outside. Why?"

I hesitated, but decided my time and options were short. "I think I am in danger. I need to see him. He matches the description of a man—a man who has hurt my family."

Mary Lou drew back slightly, and I suddenly realized the absurdity of telling her, considering our surroundings. I grabbed her hand and held it fast. "Listen to me, Mary Lou. You have become my friend these past weeks. You know why I came here. It was not for delusions or hallucinations. If I am paranoid, then allow me to see him and put my fears at rest."

She looked uncertainly to the window, where the light was beginning to fail behind the weight of the clouds. Fat flakes began to fall.

"I think he's in the ladies' common room. Mrs. Proust was upset this afternoon and threw a book out the window. He'll be boarding it up."

"Thank you."

I turned to hurry off—well, as quickly as I could manage—but Mary Lou took my arm and tucked it through hers. "I'll go with you. I want to see for myself."

We never made it to the common room, however.

No sooner were we back in the hall than a voice stopped us.

"Mrs. Andrews. Up and about? You really ought to be in bed," Dr. Glass said. He was accompanied by another doctor, Dr. Richards.

"I don't think I could stand another moment in bed," I replied honestly. "I think an occupation would do me more good—"

"I didn't realize you were a doctor, Mrs. Andrews," frowned Dr. Richards.

Color rose to my pale cheeks, and I inadvertently gripped Mary Lou's arm harder.

"I was just taking her back to her room," she said. "We've had a short turn around the dancing hall so she could stretch her legs, and now we're going back upstairs." Bless that woman.

"I think we'll take it over from here," Dr. Glass interjected. "We've talked it over, and think you might be best served in a different ward, Mrs. Andrews."

I looked from one to another in confusion. "What do you mean?"

"Your symptoms are clearly more severe than we first thought, and there has been a decline in your physical health since your arrival. And I've been hearing rumors of your paranoid delusions. It's time we gave you more…*specialized* care."

I stared up at Dr. Richards. Like Dr. Glass, he had brown eyes, but his were hard and cold, with none of the humor or warmth of Dr. Glass. They were frighteningly familiar.

I clung to Mary Lou, but the men pulled me away. I was too weak to put up much of a fight. I caught one

last look of her frightened face before a door
slammed shut between us.

I couldn't tell which ward we were in now, but it
wasn't one I wanted to be in. The rooms all had heavy
locks. There were no carpets or paintings or end
tables full of flowers. Instead, they threw me into a
cold, bare room with bars on the single, small
window. The bed was plain, with a steel frame bolted
to the floor.

My trepidation gave way to panic. I tried to run
for the door, but Dr. Richards threw me back, hard
enough to bruise. The other doctors nodded and left,
and were replaced with two of the male orderlies.
Cornered against the wall, I fought back as they lifted
me bodily onto the bed. My heel connected a jaw, my
elbow with a stomach. There was a confused flailing
of limbs for a moment before they pinned me down
on the hard mattress. I screamed for help, but a meaty
hand clamped over my nose and mouth, so hard I
struggled to breathe.

Richards closed the door.

"What do we do with her, sir?"

"For now, we just keep her here. Make sure she's
secure. Find the maid. Bring her to my office and I'll
take care of her."

They my wrists and ankles to the sturdy metal
frame. My wide crinoline bunched uncomfortably
under my legs.

Once we were alone, Dr. Richards sat down on
the edge of my bed. "Your friends and family are
very worried about you, Mrs. Andrews. This sudden
paranoia, the way you have distrusted even your
husband's closest friends since his death, and then

taken up with a strange man. It's all very concerning. My brother expressed his concerns to our mutual friend, Dr. Lynch. As I have much more experience in the field of nervous disorders and their treatment, he was more than happy to recommend my facility for your care."

I wanted to spit in his face. I recognized the eyes now. "Your brother—it's Richard*son,* isn't it?"

He smiled, reaching into his pocket for a small bottle and shook it in front of me, the liquid sloshing against the glass. "Half-brother, technically. My mother was only a lowly mistress, but father would have done anything to take care of us. Well, anything except claim me. Gunther helped with that. We were fast friends from the start. He's the one who helped me find this position. You know, I did brilliant work during the war. It could have changed everything if the fighting had only gone on a little longer. But at least here I can completely my research in peace, among like-minded individuals.

"Now, you're very weak. You've been ill. It's time for you to get some rest."

He pulled off the cork. I suddenly realized all of our food was communal, served from the same platters. The same pitcher filled every glass at the dinner table.

But my nightly sleeping potion, that came exclusively from the bottle the nurse for my floor carried in her pocket. I had initially assumed the bottle was shared among other patients, but what if it wasn't?

He held out the bottle of bitter liquid. I turned my head away.

"Don't make me get unpleasant. We'd like to ensure your stay here is as comfortable as *short* as possible, Mrs. Andrews."

His hand latched on to my jaw, vise-like, squeezing until my lips were forced open and he could pour some of the ether inside. I tried to spit it out, but once again he held his hand over my nose and mouth until I was choking, coughing on his poison.

Some of it dribbled out the side of my mouth, but an unfortunate amount managed to get down my throat.

"Now, why don't you have a nap? When you wake up, we can discuss your future treatment, and the terms for your release."

The door slammed shut behind him, a bolt sliding into place. The last thing I heard before I lost the battle against the spirits of ether was the ferocious wind howling outside my tiny window, battering the glass with hard, dry snow.

Someone slapped me.

"Where is she? Where is she, dammit!" an angry voice demanded.

I cracked my eyes open. Even though I was laying down, it felt like I as rolling on the deck of a ship. The wind still whistled outside. My room was dark except for the single lamp Dr. Richards held over my face.

"Where is the girl, Mrs. Andrews?" he asked again. "Where has your maid gone?"

My tongue was thick and heavy in my mouth. It didn't want to respond any more than the rest of me did.

He slapped me again.

"Gone," I managed at last, my dry throat creaking. I desperately needed a glass of water. Ether left a bitter aftertaste.

He pulled back, jaw working as his teeth ground against themselves in frustration. He set down the lamp and went to the window. All I could see was the black sky above, and a little drift of snow against the sill. Slowly, his jaw relaxed. He nodded once.

"I hope you're happy, now you've given that girl a death sentence," he said.

"What do you mean?"

"It is nine o'clock. You've been asleep for five hours. In that time, we've had nearly eight inches of snow, and it is still coming down. It looks like it could keep going all night. How long do you think it will take her to walk to town in snow that deep? What of the cold? It's three, nearly four miles to town, and there are very few houses on the road."

My blood turned as cold as the snow outside when I realized what he was saying, but he continued: "Come spring, I'm sure we will find her huddled up somewhere along the side of the road. An unidentified woman, frozen to death on a fool-hardy quest."

"You're wrong."

"Really. So she didn't sneak out to try to get to town, then?"

I kept my mouth shut and turned away.

"Now, there are a few small matters we need to take care of." He reached into his jacket, and produced a folded packet of papers, which he slapped down on the night stand.

"My brother had these sent over when he heard you would be staying with us. All we require is your signature, and then we can put all of this behind us."

If there was one thing I learned from my father that was reinforced as a woman surrounded by men, it was to always hold a few cards in reserve. If they didn't get what they wanted from me—or even if they did—who was to say they wouldn't go after Olivia next?

I ran my tongue along the inside of my mouth, tasting the sour flavor of ether. No. Even if I played along, he would still kill me. That much was obvious. I just needed more time. If I could last until morning, then Colleen might have enough time to get help. I refused to believe she was trapped in the storm or dead. Not yet.

I decided my safest bet was to play dumb. "I don't know what you want from me."

"It's quite simple. Sign over your half of the company, and all of the patents. You have no use for them, anyway."

"They are my only income without my husband."

"Perhaps you should have thought of that before rejecting my brother's generous offer." Dr. Richards leaned in close. "I'm going to leave these here. The storm will likely blow itself out by morning. At which point, I will return to collect these papers and hand them off to Mr. Black, who will then with all possible speed ride to town to post them back to Buffalo."

"No one will believe I actually signed them. Especially not Mr. Coolidge."

"But it will be your signature. And did you not

come here to contemplate the troubles and worries that have been plaguing you? Did you not come to set your mind at ease? It only makes sense you would bring the documents with you, so you could meditate more fully on their contents."

"And if I don't sign?"

"I have heard you have a pretty daughter. It would be a shame if something happened to her."

"She's nothing to do with this."

"No. But if, for example, she were to...have an accident. And it seems with your husband gone, your home has become a target for thieves and brigands. What if one were to make their way into the house while she slept?"

"Don't you dare touch my daughter!"

He leaned back, a small smile gracing his lips. "The power to keep her safe lies with you. You have until morning."

One of his men undid my restraints, and I was left alone with the contract, ink, pen, and a single lamp to wait for dawn.

It was, perhaps, the longest night I have ever spent. Though I was no longer tied to the bed, I was no more free than before. Both bed and table were bolted to the floor. Even with aid of the chair, I could not reach the high window of my cell, and there was no knob, lock, or hinge on my side of the door. I tried crying out for help, but I was not the only person in my ward who spent the night screaming. After a time, one of the large male attendants came down the hall carrying a club, threatening anyone who didn't quiet down.

I wondered how many other "patients" were held against their will, and how many were truly ill. How many of them had fortunes the doctors coveted?

At last, I sank down onto my knees and wept with defeat. What could I do? There was no escape. I had no doubt they planned to kill me, regardless of whether or not I signed the contract. There would be no reason to keep me alive, and it was so easy for a patient to die in a place like this, where fevers could spread so easily. I had spent enough time volunteering at the soldier's hospital to know.

With the roads blocked, it could be days—weeks, even—before help arrived, even if Dr. Richards was wrong and Colleen managed to find shelter, or even to get all the way to town. I had no hope of delaying them that long.

I read the contract until I had it nearly memorized. This was not the version Mr. Richardson brought to me. I would lose everything if I signed it; my daughter, my mother and sisters in law and I would be destitute in a matter of years, despite our generally thrifty way of life. Property, holdings, patents, everything, would become his.

At some point I became aware of the wind howling less fiercely. The sky was no lighter, but exhaustion overtook me. I collapsed onto my bed and started into the light of the kerosene lamp.

I sat up.

The room was small. The walls and floor were made of brick and stone.

I stood and slowly began to peel off my under things, piling them up on the bed. My crinoline. Both petticoats.

Carefully, I removed the globe from the oil lamp and set it aside, then scattered the pages of the contract over the bed. At the last moment, I pulled back the first page, folding it, and tucking it into my bodice.

Then I stepped back, picked up the lamp, and dashed it on the floor.

Oil splattered all over the floor. In an instant, the iridescent pool caught and flames leapt up at the bed clothes and my dangling undergarments. The entire room began to fill with foul smoke.

I stood by the door, waiting, until I began to cough. My head ached. I pounded on the door and began to scream again. "Help! Help me! Fire!" I fanned the smoke at the crack under the door until at last I heard someone unlocking it.

Two orderlies burst in. The flames jumped higher, as though performing just for this new audience. I backed toward the door.

"Fire! Get a blanket!" One of them shouted. The other pushed past me and out into the hall to get something to battle it. I was just beyond the threshold. A few more steps and I might run—

The second man started to grab me. I wheeled back, and straight into someone else's arms.

"I've got her! Hurry up! Get some water or something! I'll move her to another room," said a female voice. I tried to turn, but strong hands on my arms pulled me down the hallway.

"You're Mrs. Andrews?" the nurse asked. She was one I'd seen before, a petite brunette with a heart shaped face.

"Yes. I am. Please. You need to get me out of here. They're going to kill me. I can prove it!"

"I know. Come on. I'm going to take you someplace safe."

"I don't understand…"

"I'm Julia Price. I—I'm a friend. Well, a friend of a friend."

"Mr. Morton…"

"He asked me to look in on you. He's very worried. So is Mrs. Hurst." She unlocked the door at the end of the hall and pushed me through, locking it again behind. "Hurry. We haven't much time before they realize I've let you out. Come on." She tore open another door and pushed me inside.

We were in some kind of storage or scullery. There were shelves with extra linen, a laundry chute, and cleaning supplies. One wall was dominated by a locked apothecary cabinet, full of all the medicines the nurses might need to administer to their patients.

"Thank you. But I still don't understand…"

"I've worked here long enough to know something isn't right about this place. I know when a patient is delusional. Hugo—Mr. Morton might have his moments, but he's completely lucid so long as he remains calm. And Mrs. Hurst has consumption, not hallucinations. You might be anxious, but I do not think for one moment that you are paranoid. You said you can prove it?"

I nodded, pulling the single page of the contract from my dress. I held it out to her.

She scanned the contents quickly, then handed it back before turning to one of the cupboards. "Here. Put these on. They should be about the right size.

Hurry and change. No one will look twice at you if you're in uniform. Just make sure to keep your head down." Any moment, another nurse or employee could come in, and I would be undone.

Faster even than Colleen, she helped me out of my dress and into the plain gray worsted the women who worked at Talbert House wore day in and day out.

Gray was not my best color, especially when combined with the plain white cap and the already ashen tone my complexion had taken on. I grimaced when I checked my reflection in the tiny mirror on the wall.

Once I'd been buttoned and pinned into place, she took me out into the servant's corridor, which ran along the back side of the building. It was darker and duller than the main hallway, but if it kept me away from the orderlies, I was glad. From deeper in the bowels of the building, I heard shouting. Either the fire had grown out of hand, or someone had realized I was missing.

Nurse Price heard them, too. "We need a place to hide you for a while. Some place where no one will come looking for you, or at least where they won't look too close—"

Two more nurses and a valet for one of the male patents—recognizable by his plain suit, and not the livery of the sanatorium—came up the narrow staircase on our left. Price changed her tone so quickly I nearly gave myself away with my startled expression.

"And once the beds are made, then you'll be working on the floors and cleaning up the common areas. Start with the dining area in the North wing, B ward. They'll be done with breakfast by then, and then you'll need to sweep up in the entryway. Always make sure dirty dishes are collected promptly. We take them down here to the kitchen."

"Hey, Julie! What are you doing, showing around a new maid? Isn't there someone else to do that?" laughed one of the nurses.

I looked demurely at the floor while Price, exasperated and irate, explained how she'd found me in the wrong wing and was attempting to set me right. "I already told her next time, I'll tell Matron. Besides, you know the girls in housekeeping. Slatterns, all of them. They're always leaving messes that get in the way of our work."

"Truer words!" laughed the nurse.

"Merciful Mary'll chew her up and spit her back out again. You want to scare her off?" asked the other. "We want to keep her in line, not send her running for the hills!"

"If it happens again, she'll get what she deserves," Price shot back. She turned to me. "Come on, you. This way." I had no choice but to follow her down the dark, narrow corridor to the bustling kitchen down below.

Below stairs was a rabbit warren of dim corridors and staircases barely wide enough for one person. The steps were uneven, and I had to watch every footfall to avoid tripping.

We took a left, then two rights, and then Nurse Price glanced over her shoulder and pulled me swiftly to another staircase, this one leading up.

As we climbed, my limbs started to shake. I was

winded by the time we reached the top, but I couldn't stop. There were servants everywhere, coming and going. Nurses, maids, attendants. Some belonging to Talbert house, some to the wealthier patients of A ward. One or two of them glanced at me quizzically. At least one, the maid belonging to Mrs. Stout of number sixteen, surely recognized me. She was a negro woman with sharp eyes. I turned away and studied the floor, following close behind Nurse Price as she came out of the servant's entrance on the first floor.

We were near the ladies' common room, but Price kept walking until she reached the patient rooms.

This ward did not have a guard at the door. We were able to walk straight down the plush carpet runner, down the gas-lit hall which was bright and cheerful compared to my spartan accommodation of the night before.

At first I thought she was taking me back to my old room, but she went right past it to number twelve and pushed open the door.

"Wait here," she said. "If anyone comes by, you're a maid, and you're here to change the sheets. There's another storage room at the far end of the hall, if it comes to that. But I'll be back in just a moment."

"Thank you, Nurse Price. I owe you my life." The woman had a poker face to rival my father's, and was much wiser in her bluffs.

"Don't thank me yet. They've realized you're not in your room by now, and the fire's probably out. They'll be looking everywhere for you." At least the building was so large no one in this wing even had an inkling of the fire.

"But hopefully they'll think I've tried to escape, and won't be looking inside the building."

"Exactly."

We exchanged smiles that were equal parts triumph and grim hope. "One day I may ask where you developed this devious mind of yours, but now is not the time."

Her smile broadened. "No, not just now."

When she was gone, I collapsed onto the mattress, my knees unable to hold me up anymore. I took a few deep breaths. There was a full pitcher of fresh water on the washstand. I borrowed a glass and drained it twice. My throat was parched.

Out the window, I could see snow two feet deep. The roads would be impassible for some time. How long could I hide inside Talbert House before I was found? They would realize soon enough I hadn't run off when they realized there were no trails leading from the building. My disguise would only hold up for so long, and there were only so many places to hide.

Footsteps in the corridor. Hastily, I set down the cup on the nightstand and moved to the bed, pretending to straighten the quilt.

"Sophia!"

"Mary Lou!"

Nurse Price closed the door behind them. Mary Lou enfolded me in a hug. "My goodness. Is it true? The nurse told me some of what had happened, but I simply don't believe it."

"It's all true. Richards is the younger brother of my husband's business partner. The two of them have some kind of scheme cooked up. All the doctors are in on it." I did my best to explain my suspicions. "They're using the patients for their money, and I think they're experimenting on the poorer ones. I'm not sure if they're fleecing patients to make them stay longer, or if they just kill them for money, but all of the doctors are in on it. I know it sounds crazy, Mary Lou, but you have to believe me." I pulled out the page of the contract and pressed it into her hand, but even with written evidence she didn't want to believe Dr. Leiter was capable of such a thing.

"I'm sure if you go to him, he will help you," she insisted.

I took back the paper, stuffing it back into my bodice. "At least one other doctor is working with him, and I don't know how many other staff members. If I go to him, then I'll give myself away. I need a place to hide."

She scoffed, and I felt heat rising in my cheeks. I was tired and hungry and I didn't feel well, and not at all in the mood to be explaining myself to someone who was so willfully ignorant of the situation.

"Matron."

We both turned to look at Nurse Price. "Matron works very closely with Dr. Richards. And she has a very fine watch, something she surely could not afford on what we make here." She blushed suddenly. "There are rumors she has a very...close relationship with Dr. Richards."

"Oh, yes, I've heard that, too," Mary Lou chuckled.

"Yes...her watch." I remembered seeing it now, the night we arrived, but the foyer had been too dim to see it clearly. "She carries a man's watch, doesn't she?"

Price nodded. "She said her brother died in the war, and his wife sent up his watch to remember him by for Christmas."

"You think Richards gave it to her, instead?"

Another nod. "It's fairly simple, but around the time she got that watch, Dr. Richards got a new one."

Outside the room came the sound of heavy footsteps and slamming doors. The orderlies were definitely searching for me now, and they were coming closer. Soon, they were going to reach Mary Lou's room, and there was nowhere for me to hide, except perhaps under the bed. I didn't think would fool them for more than a minute or two.

"We don't have time to debate this. They're looking for me. I need a place to hide until I can get out of here. Mary Lou, can I trust you not to give me away?"

She hesitated, looking toward the door, and then back at me, then to Nurse Price.

"You really think Mr. Morton is right? That there is something going on?"

"I'm sure of it. I just don't know what yet."

So perhaps Mr. Morton had not been as engrossed in his music as I had thought. He must have asked Nurse Price to check on me. Bless his soldier's paranoia. The man was known for jumping at shadows, half convinced the "them damn dirty Rebs" were sneaking around every corner, but for once his instincts had been right.

They were nearer, now. My heart fluttered nervously.

"How do you feel about laundry?" Nurse Price asked suddenly.

We were almost to the back staircase when they caught us.

"You two! What are you doing?" demanded one of the attendants.

"Morning rounds. Number Twelve isn't feeling well." Nurse Price said quickly.

Mary Lou, who had followed us to the door, coughed convincingly. Nurse Price looked at her very sternly and ordered her to bed. When it looked like she was going to object, she nodded to me. "Help her back to her bed, Mary."

I nodded and took Mary Lou by the elbow.

"Wait."

I turned.

"Never mind that. There is a patient on the loose. Mrs. Andrews. You know who she is?"

"Afraid not. I'm just covering for Sally this morning. She's sick. I work in the men's ward."

He made an annoyed sound. "We need to find her. She's delusional, wandering around the place. Set her room on fire this morning. She's the lady who came in two weeks ago—dark hair, always wears black."

"We'll keep an eye out."

"Everyone has been ordered to take part in the search. You two finish this floor."

The nurse glared at him. "That's your job. I have patients to take care of. If your bunch had been doing their jobs, she wouldn't have got out in the first place."

"Listen here you—" His tone and language was so abrasive I actually flinched, but Price just stared at him steadily. "—These are orders from up top, so unless you want to explain to Merciful Mary why the two of you were ignoring direct orders, you'll do as you're told."

"Fine, then. But you had better get out of our way. You'll scare all of the female patients."

He gave a short, sharp laugh. "Fine with me!"

As soon as he was gone, we went for the staircase at the opposite end of the corridor. By then, I was keeping up on adrenaline alone; Exhausted beyond measure, it was all I could do to put one foot in front of the other and not fall on my face as we descended once again into the bowels of the building.

She wove through a dizzying maze of dark, narrow passages, always threading through clumps of other servants and staff. Everyone was in such a hurry, searching for the delusional arsonist hidden right under their noses.

It was easy to tell when we were close to the laundry. Steam billowed out into the hall. My escort slowed down, looking around for anyone who might overhear.

"I'm going to leave you here for now. Just follow my lead. Staff eats in shifts—the laundry maids are in the 11 o'clock rotation. If you eat with them, though, you'll give yourself away. If you can get back up to Mrs. Hurst's room, I can bring you food there when I take around the lunches to the bedridden patients."

I nodded, but before I could even open my mouth she grabbed me firmly by the bicep and dragged me into the clouds of steam.

"...And if I ever catch you shirking, you can bet I'll be taking you straight to the Matron!" she said, loudly enough the women closest to us stopped what they were doing.

"What do we have here?" asked a stout, red faced woman who appeared to be in charge. She had her arms folded over her ample chest, and looked something like a slightly wrinkled apple.

"I caught this one lollygagging in Ward B. I thought she might want to come down here and see what a bit of real work is like." Nurse Price's glare was so fearsome, for a moment I thought I really was in trouble.

I stammered out an apology, but the stout woman just snorted. "We've no time for that down here, do we girls?" she asked the room at large. There was a chorus of "Aye's" and they all hurriedly went back to their tasks.

She looked me up and down. "Bit skinny, but we'll make sure she earns her keep. Over there. Help with the bed linens." She jerked her head in the direction of a vast pool, easily twice the size of my bed back home, where three women with long poles were stirring white cotton and linen in hot water and lye soap. Unlike the rest of the building, most of the faces down here were dark skinned and grim; they left the hard, manual labor to the colored help.

I was provided with a pole and set to stirring. After a while, each sheet would be pulled out and moved to another basin for rinsing.

The rest of the morning passed in this way. My back and shoulders ached. There was no talking, save for a simple "Pass the soap" or "Thank you" as items were handed off, but the women did sing as they worked, mostly folk tunes I didn't know the words of.

I was positively faint when the stout apple woman banged a mop handle against the copper gong hanging on the wall. Nearly synchronized, women began emptying tubs into the pools, and plugs on the pools were pulled so the dirty water could drain out. To where, I didn't know, and didn't care. The floor started to roll beneath me. At the door, I spied a jug of water and paused to take a drink. It was just enough of a delay that the other women left before me.

I realized I had no idea how to get back to the patient wings. I thought the laundry maids had turned right to go to their meal, and I didn't think we'd passed the kitchen on our way down, so I turned left, grateful for the cool, damp air of the basement, and the fact that Talbert House was perpetually cold.

My face was flushed and my uniform damp and bedraggled. My front was completely soaked through.

At last, I found a sign pointing to the staircase, Ladies Ward A-D and followed it. A ward was the upper class section, I knew. It was where Mary Lou and I had been staying. I could only assume my cell had been somewhere in Ward D. I wondered briefly if the D stood for *dungeon* or *demented.*

I emerged from the servant's stairs at the far end of the hall, but there were already two people in the passage. Without hesitation, I turned right and ducked into the storage room for that ward.

It was the mirror image of the one Nurse Price snuck me into. When voices came near, I pulled down an armload of towels and pretended to be folding and stacking them. My hands shook and I could barely stand. I needed food and rest—it had been days since I'd had a proper meal, and it was now a full twenty-four hours since I'd had anything at all.

The voices passed without anyone entering the storage room, and I sagged against the wall briefly. *Only a little further,* I told myself. *Just a little more.*

I poked my head out into the empty hall and tiptoed to Mary Lou's room.

It was blessedly empty. I poured myself another glass of water and forced myself to drink it slowly. Then I collapsed on her bed and covered myself with the blankets. I didn't even have time to remove my shoes or worry about getting caught before I drifted off.

chapter fourteen

The first thing I heard when I woke up was a soft creaking noise.

The second thing I noticed was the abominable ache in my shoulders and back. I wondered how I had even managed to fall into such a deep sleep while still wearing my corset.

I cracked open one groggy eye and peered out of a gap in the covers.

Mary Lou was in her rocker, head nodding over the needlework abandoned in her lap. She'd changed into a night dress and white lace sleeping cap.

Out the window, the last rays of sun faded, streaks of red smeared across the snow. Mary Lou had a view of the front of Talbert House. The walk had been cleared and a path leading to the gate, but there was a man in the gate house and two more cutting a path through the snow.

Dr. Richards said nearly two feet of snow had fallen in the night, but it appeared the sun must have been unseasonably warm; if I wasn't mistaken, it was already beginning to melt. I felt a surge of hope. Maybe all was not lost after all, and his ominous prediction about her would not come true.

A tray of food caught my attention on the night stand. There was a bowl of soup, a thick slice of bread, a slice of ham, some cheese, and a pot of tea. All of it was stone cold, but it didn't stop me. Though my stomach still clenched painfully around the food, I ate the bread, ham and cheese. The soup was not very appetizing cold, but I sipped it, anyway. Mary Lou didn't wake up until I moved on to the tea.

"Oh, goodness, you startled me!" she said. One of her knitting needles dropped to the floor.

"I'm sorry. I didn't want to wake you. But thank you for letting me use your bed. I was completely exhausted."

"Oh, think nothing of it. I told them I had a headache and was not to be disturbed for the rest of the evening. One of the nurses did come to check on me, but I put her off." She smiled wickedly, then pretended to have just been awakened from a deep sleep. "My headache? Oh, I'm sure it would go away much sooner if I could get some peace and quiet, instead of everyone banging on the doors at all hours!" Immediately the grumpy expression vanished and she giggled. "She bought it right away. Not very bright, our Nurse Collins, though she's sweet as can be. Though I did have a time of it keeping her out of the room. I was terrified she'd see you sleeping there, and then I'd have some explaining to do! You, of course, were dead to the world through the whole thing. Poor dear. You must have been absolutely worn out."

"I was. Thank you." I really didn't have words to express how grateful I was for Mary Lou and Nurse Price. I drained my cup and refilled it. "Are they still looking for me?"

"I don't know. I've been in here with you." She squinted at the clock on the dresser beside her. "It's a little after six now. They'll be calling us all down to dinner soon. They shouldn't bother us, however. I told Nurse Collins not to bother me again under any circumstances."

As if on cue, there was a commotion in the hallway, and then a loud knock on the door; a masculine knock.

Mary Lou and I exchanged panicked glances. There was no place for me to hide. The room was a simple square, the bed too high off the floor to be a good hiding place, and there were no large pieces of furniture for me to hide behind or inside.

The knock came again, much louder.

"Who is it?" Mary Lou called, rising from her chair.

I had a sudden inspiration. I gestured for her to go to the door, then began dragging the bedclothes towards me, draping them haphazardly off the mattress, as though Mary Lou had suddenly flung them off in irritation at being awakened.

"Open the door," said the deep voice on the other side of the door. I thought I recognized it as one of them men who would watch us in the common room in the evenings, something of a guard, but I didn't know against what. None of the patients in Ward A had been violent or dangerous in any way most of the time, though there had been a few who had violent nightmares. I knew some of the men—sons of wealthy men, mostly, who had come back...*different* after war. Men who no longer fit into societies tight constraints. Their families sent them away to avoid any awkwardness, sweeping them delicately under the rug just as husbands, brothers, and fathers sent of young ladies who happened to fall for unsuitable men, or women who fell into deep melancholy, or argued with their husbands too much. They were heroes, all of them, but paid a heavy toll for it. Now no one knew what to do with them as they adjusted to life without arms or legs, or simply with too many memories.

"Why should I? I'm sleeping!" Mary Lou demanded, jutting out her chin. By then, she was at the door, holding tight to the knob to keep him from entering before we were ready.

"Orders!" he hardly gave her warning before pushing open the door. I dropped to the floor just in time, barely hidden from view by the dangling quilt. Mary Lou's slight form was no match for him. She stumbled back, but didn't miss a beat. I could hear her eyes narrow and her lips pursed when she snapped "What do you think you are doing, entering a lady's room uninvited! And by force! I'll have you reported—"

"Shaddup! Do what you want. But orders are, everyone downstairs to the Central Hall. *Now,* " he barked.

For once, Mary Lou was completely speechless. Talbert House employees were charged with being unfailingly polite to the patients in ward A.

Though my stay had been short, I was beginning to pick up on a few things. For starters, the patients in wards A and D paid the highest price for care. Ward A had the best food, the most comfortable rooms, and got the most service from the cleaning staff. They were also largely insulated from the rest of the facility, and meant to think they were simply staying in a hotel.

Ward D, however, was where people who were meant to disappear went.

The more I'd thought about it as I stirred sheets and sweated over vats of boiling water that morning, the more sense it had made. Richards had the perfect set up.

A wealthy family had an inconvenient relative they wanted disposed of, so they were sent to the sanatorium. Perhaps they started off in Ward A, but then they began to fall into a decline and had to be moved to another ward for "additional care."

Since the patient suddenly went from ham and bread and tea to porridge and water, the cost of their care suddenly went down. Meanwhile, Dr. Richards could charge more for their care since they required more of it.

And then came the tricky part. The horrifying idea that my mind had been more than willing to supply in my exhausted state. For an extra fee, that relative might have an accident. A fall down the stairs, maybe, or perhaps they might come down with a case of typhoid, thus freeing up any estates that might otherwise be disputed or divided.

I could think of other things, too. There were several long-term patients, like Mary Lou. What if, in thanks for their exemplary care, they decided to leave a bequest to the organization that had taken such good care of them? If they were pliable, maybe it would be more profitable to simply keep them on long term, even if they didn't need doctors and nurses looking after them. But if they were made to *think* they did…

Of course, this would require coordination. It would mean all of the upper level staff would have to be complicit and the lower level staff wouldn't be able to ask questions without being dismissed. But how was that any different from a maid working in the house of a predatory man, or someone working in a factory, or risking their necks in a mine? Employers always did what they wanted to their employees, and the workers had no recourse.

What about Nurse Price then? She said she had doubts. Had she figured out what was going on?

"If you gotta know, there's a dangerous patient in Ward D that's escaped. We need to search every room to make sure she's not hiding somewhere."

"Well as you can see, there's no place for her to hide here. Now if you please, I'd like to get back to bed!"

"No can do. Everyone has to go to the big hall until the search is done."

Though Mary Lou objected fiercely, the orderly pulled her from the room. I waited until the door slammed shut behind them before I came out of my hiding place and listened.

I could hear more people being chased from their rooms and ushered down to the Central Hall, and then silence.

I waited until the hallways became quite again before cracking the door open to peer outside. The entire area was deserted, the ward silent. It felt like I was the only person in the entire building.

I crept to the end of the hall, to the door that opened into the central part of the building where the common rooms and dining room were. There was no guard for moment, but all of the staff and patients were flooding into the large central hall—the biggest room in the building.

"This is outrageous!" shouted one of the other

women from ward A. I recognized Mrs. Spencer from the dinner table. She was one of the few who insisted on dressing for dinner, and was already turned out with feathers in her hair and pearls around her neck.

"This is only temporary," the matron was saying her firm, flat voice. "As soon as the search is complete, you will be allowed to return to your rooms."

Mr. Hubbard, one of the men who had been my dinner partner the week before, was glowering at her, his empty sleeve pinned up and flapping wildly, as though the missing arm was trying to gesticulate what his left arm was too restrained to. "This is an invasion! You cannot treat us this way!" he bellowed. Mr. Hubbard was the sort who was belligerent in his disability, taking out his perceived impotence on all around him. It got worse when he had a reasonable outlet for his fury. For a moment, I thought he would strike at the Matron, but two of the stewards heard him shouting and came up behind him, grasping him firmly despite his shouts and hauling him bodily into the hall.

This sent a wave of outrage through the ladies clustered at the door—to treat a gentleman in such a way!—but the staff merely pushed them on into the hall despite their increasing protests.

Then, they barred the door.

"That wasn't wise," the Matron snapped to the two broad men who had restrained Mr. Hubbard.

"Doesn't matter. If we don't find her quick, then the boss says we're all done for. Besides, who are they gonna complain to? It's not like anyone out there will believe them, even if they did manage to get a letter out. They're all daft anyway." He tapped his temple pointedly. "And we tried it your way, and got nothin'. The boss wants results."

The matron made a noise of disgust. "If we don't handle this correctly, then it will all be over whether we find her or not. Some of them have to write home, or else people will get suspicious."

"Isn't that what you're here for, Mercy?" he said with a toothy, demonic grin. "Ain't this the time of year people tend to get sick? And its close quarters here. It's just ripe for some kind of outbreak. Typhoid, maybe."

Mary grumbled. "We did typhoid last time. It would have to be something else."

His grin broadened. "Well, I'm sure you'll come up with something."

I let the door close softly. I could barely breathe; I hadn't wanted to believe my fevered nightmares were true, but it appeared I had been right in my guess. "Merciful Mary" was disposing of patients at the order of one or more of the doctors. At the very least the stewards were part of the plan; when I looked at them again, a collection of large, rough men in the clean pressed uniforms of the Talbert, I suddenly realized they were employing what amounted to their own army; a cadre of men spoiling for violence and gain, all of whom undoubtedly were without purpose now the war was over. Where else would they find outlet for their violent whims without a Rebel army to subdue?

I needed to get out, and soon. Even if Colleen managed to get to town, I knew now there was no way for help to arrive in time if they no longer cared what happened to the other patients.

We did typhoid last time. How easy would it be to wipe out a few dozen troublesome souls, and lock away the rest?

A stab of fear struck my chest; not for myself, but for the few friends I had made. Mary Lou, Miss Temple, Mr. Morton. Mr. Morton, missing his legs and wheeled about in a chair by a nurse or steward, who would have no hope of escape without help. Mary Lou, who was strong in mind and spirit, but frail in body. And timid Miss Temple, who barely spoke above a whisper, and would surely not fight back if confronted.

It was no longer just my life Dr. Richards intended to take, but dozens—maybe hundreds—of others.

I ran down the corridor to the storage room connected to the servant's stairs, scouring it for anything that might be useful. If only I could create some kind of a distraction, to draw away the guards at the front gate and allow me to escape.

There was nothing I could think of that would help me now.

Think, I told myself. There had to be a way I could get myself, and as many others as possible, out of this.

One thing was for certain: I would need to arm myself if I was to put up any kind of fight.

With staff and residents alike trapped in the main hall, the rest of the building was deserted except for those searchers, who seemed to be taking a more methodical route this time, as they cleared rooms and locked doors behind them.

The servant's area below stairs felt eerie and haunted without the overwhelming activity I had witnessed earlier in the day. For a moment, around every corner, I expected to turn and see James, but I was alone.

I followed the signs until I got to the kitchen, where I procured two knives. The large butcher knife I put into my apron pocket, and the paring knife I slid into my boot, just in case.

My stomach clenched painfully, and I didn't know if it was from illness—poison? —or fear.

I could hide and hope for rescue, but both the chances of rescue and avoiding capture until it came were almost nonexistent.

If I ran, my chances were even more abysmal, even if I managed to get past the front gate. While the walks inside the compounded had mostly been cleared, the road outside was covered with at least a foot and a half of untouched snow, and it was dark out now. The clock on the kitchen mantle read 6:43. It was infinitely more likely I would freeze to death on the road than make it to help.

Lastly, I could stay and attempt to release the prisoners, and perhaps attempt to take back the building. But only a small portion of the prisoners were functional under normal circumstances, and organizing them would be nearly impossible, even if I could get them to believe me.

No, too many of them would get hurt.

A sudden thought struck me. I felt like a ninny for not realizing it before.

I was in the *kitchen*. There would have to be a servant's entrance, a place to take deliveries. If I was very lucky, that might also mean there was a cloakroom nearby, where I might find something warm before making my escape.

A kitchen door would almost certainly lead directly outside, circumventing the front gate. Wouldn't it?

Footsteps. The search had moved to the basement.

On tip toe, I dashed towards a dark opening at the back of the kitchen I thought might lead to a pantry or perhaps a scullery. Most of the gas lamps had been turned off, with only a few here or there that cast more in the way of shadows than light. I took them to my advantage.

The next room was filled with solid black, with only a thin slice of sky visible from a high window. I felt my way past one door (which smelled like it might be a pantry of some kind), to another room that was silent and dark. I slipped inside and waited.

I could no longer here the footsteps. I felt around and found the sconce of a gas lamp, and next to it a box of matches. I lit one, and heaved a sigh of relief so big it left me nearly giddy. It was a tiny, cramped, cloak room.

There was a quilted bonnet on the peg nearest me. I snatched it up as the match burned down to my fingertips. I shook it out, sucking on the burns for a moment. I tied the bonnet on in the dark.

A second match was spent taking a more detailed stock of my surrounding. There were five matches left in the box. The warmest thing hanging from the pegs appeared to be a thick men's coat, which was also hung with a muffler. When the second match burned out, I put on the coat, which was far too large, and wrapped the scarf several times around my neck and face.

In the pockets of the coat I felt a pair of rabbit lined mittens and some knit gloves that had seen better days. I put on both, though like the coat they were far too big. The coat hung down past my knees, and the sleeves were easily six inches longer than my fingertips.

Stuffing the matches into one of the pockets, I went to the door again and listened. Voices echoed on the stone walls, but they didn't seem any closer than before.

I found the kitchen door primarily by the draft leaking around the edges. I pulled off the mittens to feel for the handle and tried to open it as quietly as I could, but nature had other ideas.

A gust of wind nearly knocked me off my feet. I stumbled back as cold air and sleet slammed into my face.

Someone shouted. I didn't have time to doubt, to catch my breath, or to think twice. I plunged out into the snow.

The door opened into an icy stairwell, but both the stairs and the walk above had been cleared at some point in the day. Wind blew some of the white powder back over the bricks, but it was manageable. I slipped on the steps but didn't fall, and took off at a run when I reached the top.

The partial melting of the snow made sense now. Rain pelted down in the dark, some of it melting the snow only to freeze again immediately, some of it turning to ice on the way down. The path was slick with the new ice, and even the sand and ash that had been spread over it wasn't enough to stop me from slipping in the near total darkness.

Much to my chagrin, I was still inside the compound. I bolted for the side gate only to find it locked.

The kitchen door slammed open and booted feet pounded against the pavement. I muttered a few choice phrases I hadn't used since my days in the Irish tenement and took the path leading to the right.

There was another low gate into the garden where we took our daily walks. The latch was partially frozen shut. The men were getting closer. I pounded on it with a fist, but my hands were too padded, too clumsy.

I took a step back and kicked as hard as I could. The ice shattered, and a moment later I was through the gate.

They were too close now. I tore at my scarf as I ran diagonally through the path, hitching up my skirt with one hand.

The snow was deeper than my boots. I leaped across the lawn, crunching through the thin layer of ice over the snow. My breath came in short, shallow gasps. I wished I had abandoned my corset when I took off the crinoline. Well, it would be something to keep in mind the next time I had to run for my life.

I made the back gate, the one I had seen the men with the shovels go when I first arrived. My pursuers were clearing the last threshold. Unencumbered by ridiculous feminine fashions, they gained quickly.

Beyond the garden wall, I had no idea what I would find. There was a single path leading around the wall. I skidded left and kept running, slipping as much as stepping and trying to keep to the shallower drifts, where my leather-soled boots had slightly more purchase.

Around the corner there were a series of outbuildings. One I thought might be a staff dormitory, based on the path worn between it and the main building.

I could see movement, but didn't dare scream for help. I was still inside the large outer wall; there had to be another gate somewhere that would get me out of the compound. But where?

My throat and lungs burned from cold and my knees began to quake with exertion. *There!* Behind the dormitory. That had to be it.

If I could only make it to the gate. I didn't dare think of what might happen after that. Somehow, the gate meant hope. Never mind the three miles to civilization I would have to traverse with only a stolen coat and no provisions, in the dead of winter. If I could only make it that far...

Eyes on my goal, I put on one final burst of speed. Past the dormitory and a dormant, snow covered garden. Past a stable and a chicken coop and a hog pen. Abandoning the right angles of the walkway I darted diagonally towards the gate, high stepping like a Spanish parade horse until I practically crashed into the wrought iron bars.

As quickly as hope surged in my breast, it faltered and died. A great iron lock was fixed the bars, partially covered in ice and snow.

"No!" Tears of frustration and terror made tracks down my cheeks. I tried to squeeze through the bars, or to reach for one of the cross pieces, hoping to climb over, but the verticals were too close together and the horizontals too far apart. My mittened fingers barely grazed the bottom of one before firm hands grabbed me, lifting me bodily from the ground.

Though I screamed and flailed, it was no use. I was caught, two at my head while another locked both of my feet under one of his arms. Even if I had use of my hands, I realized the butcher knife was trapped beneath the long, thick layer of my coat.

The three men began to carry me back to Talbert House. "Shaddup!" one of them snapped, striking me on the head. The bonnet took most of the blow, but I was still left seeing stars.

"I will not! Let me go!" I shouted, twisting and kicking as best I could. Almost by accident, I pulled one arm into the body of the enormous coat.

The sudden change made the man on my left stop suddenly to adjust his grip, but I had an advantage now. I managed to plant one heel firmly into the ribcage of the man at my feet. He dropped me, but before I could escape the third had me around the middle.

"Stick her in here. I'm not dragging her all the way like that." said one of them, exasperated, nodding at one of the little buildings behind me.

Though I couldn't see it, I could hear the smile in the voice of the one holding me. It was reflected in the faces of the other two.

"Might as well. Save ourselves a trip."

Once again I was lifted up, and one of them took my feet, squeezing my ankles painfully. "Keep fightin'. I like I feisty woman," he leered. "We'll see how fast you run on two broken legs." His grip tightened. I let myself go limp. He held one foot on each side of his hips, the threat clear in his eyes.

A door was forced open behind us, ice cracking after a firm jerk from the third man. They dumped me onto a dirt floor.

"You, watch the door while I go get the boss. No one in or out until I come back."

As the door started to close, I lunged for it, one last, desperate effort to escape. A heavy fist threw me back, and then I was sealed into total darkness.

Time seemed interminable in that dark space. My breath rattled like Marley's chains.

I felt around my prison. There were no windows, that was clear. I took off my mittens and felt around the walls, where boxes had been stacked one on top of the other, forming a horseshoe shape around the door. I could find no other exits, not even a mouse hole.

I sat against one of the stacks of crates, drawing my knees up to my chest for warmth. My skirts were wet to the knee, my stockings soaked and frigid. After several moments of rocking back and forth fruitlessly, I crawled to the door and listened the wind whistling through the tiny cracks around the door.

At least my prison provided shelter from the wind and sleet.

I could have been there for hours for all I knew, but at last there were voices outside and then the door swung open.

The light from a single lantern seemed blinding after the complete and utter blackness of my cell. Dr.

Richards was wrapped in a snug fur coat. The lantern
threw the planes of his face into sharp relief,
accentuating his resemblance to his brother and
enhancing the pure evil of his soul.

"Well. You've lead us on a merry chase today,
haven't you?" he asked, the corner of his lip turning
up in something that might have been a smile, or
possibly a snarl.

He came to crouch next to me setting his lantern
on the floor and leaning in close. I was tempted to
bite off his nose, just to spite him.

"If you think this is going to convince me to sign
those papers, you're wrong. Even if you kill me, I
won't sign them."

He sighed. "Well, then it's a good thing I don't
need you. Of course, it would be better if we could
get your signature in your own hand, but that's not
really necessary. My brother has done his part and
convinced that wretched lawyer it is in his best
interest to honor any contracts we give him."

I stared at him, as frosty as the ground around us,
but he only smiled. "My brother tells me you recently
changed lawyers, just before you came here. So
really, no one will be surprised if, after weeks of
contemplation and rest, after carefully considering
your husband's death, you decide to compose a new
will, rectifying the offenses you have made to your
close friends in the last few months, and leaving a
healthy bequest, in gratitude, to Talbert House for
your recovery. Such a shame measles has been such a
problem this winter."

"There isn't a single person with measles in that
building."

He raised one eyebrow. "Are you certain? You yourself came in with skin rash, complaining of difficulty breathing. It's really too bad you spread it to your friends."

"So you would kill all of those innocent people just to hide the fact you killed me?"

Dr. Richards smiled. "Where better to hide a tree than in the forest?"

"You are sick. Depraved!"

That got a laugh out of him. "No, I'm a problem solver. You see, my half-brother, Gunther, and I, we each had a problem. We found by working together, we could find a solution. And then it occurred to me, what if others had the *same* problem? And thus, a very lucrative venture was formed. A risky one, it's true, but we are very careful about who we treat. Only the *best* members of society. For some, it is more profitable to send them away fully cured. But others, sadly, succumb to the weakness of their spirits."

"It almost feels as if things have come full circle now, with you. Gunther and I hadn't spoken in years, but then he came to me with a proposition. A few well-placed words in the right ears, and his problem was on its way to me for solving. For a share of the profits, of course. He already gave me a handsome advance."

I opened my mouth again, but he was already getting to his feet. "It's been lovely chatting with you, Mrs. Andrews, but I think we are done here. I'll make sure you receive a proper burial. We have a lovely cemetery just back through those woods. Very peaceful in summertime."

"It's February. The ground is frozen."

He raised an eyebrow and then his lamp. For the first time, looked at my surroundings.

The crates were coffins. Plain pine boxes, of the type there had lately been so much demand for.

"Cold storage. Until the ground thaws." He gestured to my guards, setting the lantern down on top of the nearest stack. There had to be at least a dozen of them.

I backed up. The stack behind me wobbled unsteadily, and I jumped away. There was no room to hide, no way to escape. They backed me into a corner.

"You know, chloroform is a funny thing. So useful. Excellent for breathing treatments, for example, and of course invaluable in surgery. But it can be so fussy. The same amount that will put one man peacefully to sleep will ensure another never wakes up again." He produced a glass bottle from his coat pocket, and poured the sweet-smelling liquid onto a handkerchief. "Hold her still."

One of the burly stewards reached out. I let the butcher's knife slide down out of my sleeve, into my gloved hand and slashed at his belly.

He jumped back with a startled yelp. "The bitch has a knife!"

"Well then take it away from her," Richards ordered, exasperated. He spoke like he was talking to a very slow child.

Then they were both on me. I struggled and fought, stabbed and bit. One of them shouted and stumbled back, but when it was over I was left with my arms pinioned to my sides by the bigger of the two. I threw back my head, hoping to crack a nose or a jaw or at least a tooth, but even with my toes barely touching the ground he was too tall.

The other one was bleeding. He held a hand to his side, and with the other struck me across the face.

"Now, now. You know I dislike violence," Richards said, holding out the handkerchief. "Keep her still."

He pressed the cloth to my face. I held my breath until my vision began to spot. I was never getting out of this alive. I would never see my dear Olivia again. What would they do to her when I was gone? What would happen to her, and Agnes and Angela and Brigid and the children?

I had no advantages left. I couldn't reach the paring knife. I couldn't hold my breath much longer, but I had to fight. There had to be something they wouldn't expect.

Something they wouldn't expect.

I allowed myself to go limp. Let my eyes close. But the fabric stayed in place. I had no choice left but to breath. I couldn't hold it any longer.

The last thing I heard before darkness came was the sneering voice of the doctor. "Make sure it's nailed tight. And bind her hands and feet, just in case. You know how superstitious these Irish are when it comes to dead bodies walking abroad."

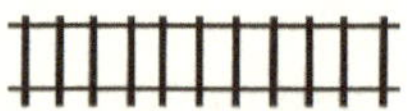

The nightmare consumed me.

I breathed it, I felt it in every pore. The darkness of the grave as it pulled me down deeper. Above me, James held out a hand, but I couldn't reach him. Someone else had me by the throat and was pulling me down deeper into the pit.

I screamed for him, and woke up in utter blackness and cold so absolute it stole the air from my very lungs.

At first I thought I was still in the grip of the nightmare. I couldn't move. My hands and feet were numb. I screamed and tried to break free, but there were no hands holding me, though my shoulders were wedged tight.

I began to shake uncontrollably. Fear or cold, it made no difference. I was trapped—nightmare or reality, or both? *Nail it tight. You know how superstitious these Irish are when it comes to dead bodies walking abroad.*

A coffin. They bound me hand and foot, and put me in a coffin.

They had either assumed I was dead or nearly so from the combination of chloroform and whatever else they had given me, or they were planning on letting the cold finish me off.

From my current vantage point, I couldn't say I faulted the logic, though logic was the furthest thing on my mind. For months, the nightmare of being buried alive haunted me like my husband's ghost, and now I was here. I was going to die in a plain pine box.

"S-Someone! Help me! Please! Help!" I screamed. For once, I felt no shame at the hot tears that began to roll down my cold cheeks. If ever there was a time to give way to hysterics, I thought this might be it. I screamed and banged my bound hands against the lid until I was sure they bled. There wasn't even room to bring them to my chest, where I might have more leverage.

The feeling of immobility, being completely powerless, only added to my panic.

Kicking, screaming, pounding. My entire body convulsed with the effort.

The next thing I knew, I was falling. It was a short drop, like falling out of bed. I landed hard on my side, banging my nose into the lid of the box—it was much easier to think of it as a box than a coffin. Nails wrenched apart. I kicked out with all of my might. Once. Twice. The boards split and I tumbled out onto the dirt floor of the dead house.

Over the blood roaring in my ears I made out someone at the door. The rattle of a lock. I fumbled in my boot for the paring knife with fingers nearly dead with cold and pain.

A thin strip of light appeared under the door. I hacked at the cords around my ankles until my legs— now tingling as blood began to return—flopped apart.

With no time to even attempt to free my hands, I clutched the knife handle as tight as I could in both hands and held it up to the door.

The lantern was blinding. I closed my eyes and turned away, brandishing the knife with arms I could barely raise.

"Good god," someone breathed.

A clatter. A thump. A series of unsteady footsteps, and then I was being wrapped in something warm.

"Mrs. Andrews!"

"Colleen?"

"We're in here! We've found her!"

Someone took the knife and cut my restraints. I opened my eyes. Colleen chaffed my hands in hers.

Fresh tears came. "Dear girl, I've killed you," I cried.

"No you didn't, ma'am. It was a near thing. I got as far as a farm, about two miles from here, before the snow came. Mr. Hannigan took me into town first thing this morning, and wouldn't you know, no sooner had I made it to the telegraph office then I hear there's been another telegraph from Buffalo from the police, wanting someone to go to the sanatorium. And so I talked to the officer there in town, and by the time we finished talking then the tracks were clear and the trains came again, and the first ones off the train was Mr. Hamilton and Mrs. Perry!" She gestured over my shoulder, and I looked up into Mr. Hamilton's face, not caring that being held in a gentleman's arms was so far beyond the rules of propriety as to be inconceivable.

"Can you stand?" he asked gently. "We must get you inside where it is warm. You are positively blue with cold."

I nodded, despite my own uncertainty. Colleen helped me to my feet. My legs tingled painfully, but I thought that was good—the return of blood meant they weren't frozen. My hands might be another story.

The two of them helped me back to the main building where I sat in a quiet room with a blazing fire—one of the offices, I thought, though I wasn't sure whose.

Mr. Hamilton pulled a chair up to the hearth and I sat as close to the flames as I dared. Colleen took charge, bringing hot tea and a basin of warm water to soak my hands and feet. Thick blankets and dry clothes were all brought from my room upstairs. She

waited on me hand and foot until one of the officers
who came in their party asked to speak with her, and I
was left alone in the quiet with Mr. Hamilton.

I was shaking too badly to drink the tea; it merely
spilled over the edge of the cup.

"What a-are you s-smiling f-for?" I stuttered
through chattering teeth.

"I'm merely remembering the time when you
pulled me in out of the snow and bundled me up
much as you are now," he said. "I don't remember the
last time anyone has taken such care with my
wellbeing as you did that afternoon." His eye landed
on the drinks cart next to the fireplace. "Perhaps a
drop of brandy—"

"No. Never. I will not eat or drink anything
prepared here. I may never eat or drink anything I've
not made myself ever again!"

There was a question in his face, but he didn't
voice it when I looked away into the fire.

With difficulty, he rose from his arm chair and
came to sit on the footstool beside me. With his cane
leaning against the side table, he reached over to take
my hand. The feeling had returned, but they were still
unbearably cold.

He rubbed my fingers gently in his calloused
palm. "Whenever you're ready. The police will want
to talk to you. As will Mrs. Perry, I think, but that can
wait until morning."

"I can't stay here any longer. Please, don't make
me stay the night here," I begged, my tears starting
anew.

"Shh." He reached up to brush them away.

I clung tightly to his other hand. "Please.

Please..."

"Don't worry. I think they intend to remove as many as they can tonight, but we need to get you warm, first. You'd never make the journey as you are now."

"I'll walk back to town if I have to. I can't get any colder than I am now."

"No worries about that. I've offered to go back to town to send for more assistance. It's going to take a small army to get this under control."

Mrs. Perry swept into the room, her traveling suit remarkably neat for the circumstances. "I don't think they'll mind if I commander the sledge. I've promised to keep you under my watchful eye until someone from the proper authorities has a chance to speak with you. We'll leave in an hour, once you've warmed up a bit." She took a swig of the tea, then held it out to me. "Drink up. You're going to need all the warmth you can get."

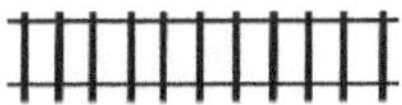

I woke up in a lodging house several steps down from my usual traveling accommodations, wondering if the entire thing had been a dream.

My hands and feet were still cold, but no longer frozen. The doctor Mr. Hamilton had summoned said it was a very near thing; any longer and I likely would have lost a few toes and fingers, but I had been bundled into a veritable fortress of heated bricks before we set off. Mrs. Perry drove the two horses hard. When Mr. Hamilton questioned her, she merely grinned over her shoulder. "Didn't I tell you? My husband was a teamster in the war. He's the one who taught me how to drive!"

I must have dozed off along the way, only waking when the doctor came. He performed a brief examination, and then ordered me off to a bed that had been warmed by the landlady. Colleen and Mrs. Perry slept beside me, as much to add their own warm as to keep an eye on me.

The bed was empty now, however, but someone had reheated the bricks from our travels and wrapped them in flannel, placing them at the end of the bed. Colleen was nowhere to be seen, but Mrs. Perry sat in a chair a few feet away, framed by morning sunlight. She was cleaning a revolver and had another on the table next to her.

"Good, you're awake. Sleep well?"

"'Well' isn't the word I would use for it," I croaked.

She handed me a glass of water. When I didn't take it immediately, she set it aside. "I can't be your taster forever, but I do promise no one has tampered with the food and drink in this house." She took a sip and then handed it back to me with a raised eyebrow. I took it, taking a tiny sip. I was so thirsty, though, it wasn't long before I had consumed the entire thing.

Colleen came in with a tray—toast, bacon, and a pot of tea. The bacon smelled so divine, I almost didn't care who had cooked it.

"It's after nine, now, ma'am. The doctor and the police are waiting downstairs to speak with you. When you're ready, I'll send them up. Doctor says you are to stay in bed for at least two days," she added sternly when she saw my try to get up.

I ate slowly, uncertainty making my stomach roll. Finally, I set the tray aside. Colleen frowned at what was left on the plate, but didn't say anything. I wrapped myself in the shawl Mrs. Perry handed me. "Doctor first, Colleen, then the police."

The doctor pronounced me "well enough" with a sigh, but cautioned against exertion and told me to stay in bed. "Two days. In two days, then we can talk about sending you home. But for now, you need rest and quiet."

The police were a different matter. Mine was a difficult tale to tell. I had to go back three months, to the death of my husband, for it to make any sense at all. Just the telling of the tale took all of an hour, and for two more hours after they asked questions. They asked a lot of questions about the poison. I described the bottle to them as clearly as I could, though I didn't think it was any different from any other medicine bottle.

"And you said you had the rash when you arrived at Talbert house?"

"Yes." I gestured to my neck and jaw. The marks had faded now.

"I noticed something like that on the maid," said one of the officers. There were two. Mrs. Perry called for Colleen, who came in and at my bidding tilted her head so they could see the red welts on her cheek.

"It's nuthin' though, sirs," she said, nerves pushing her accent back to the surface. "It's just the fur on Mrs. Andrews cloak. She lent it to me when I ran, you see. Sometimes cats make me sneeze, and that fur had me sneezing all the way to town. You'd a thought I had a cat draped 'round me neck."

The men exchanged a look and asked for the cloak. When it was brought, they bundled it up and said they would have it tested.

"You think the fur is poisoned?" I gaped.

"It is possible. Mercury and arsenic are both used to preserve furs. Where did you get it?"

I closed my eyes. "It was a Christmas present. From Mr. Richardson." The man behind the whole thing. Had the cloak been an early attempt to get me out of the way subtly?

Finally, noting my exhaustion, Mrs. Perry shooed them from the room and told them she could fill in any other missing pieces.

I fell back into my pillows, sleeping through lunch. I didn't wake until midafternoon.

For the first time, I was alone in the room. The light was beginning to fade as the window fell into shadow. The door was open only a few inches. A pitcher and glass had been left on the table within easy reach, and someone had taken away the now-cold bricks. I pushed myself up into a sitting position, but held perfectly still when I saw something move in the hall.

The familiar *thump-shuffle* of Mr. Hamilton's uneasy gait calmed my leaping heart, however. I could tell by the cadence—a heavier *thump*, a longer *shuffle*— the cold and activity of the past few days wore on him.

He tapped lightly on the door. I reached for my borrowed shawl and draped it around my shoulders. I was in nothing but a shift, hardly decent for callers, but in all the flurry of the morning's events, there had been one face I had sorely missed.

It peered around the door when I bid him to enter, worried lines relaxing instantly to those of the familiar, gentle smile when he met my eye.

"I'm glad to see you are feeling better, Mrs. Andrews. You had m—all of us, very worried."

"Are you guarding my door, then?" I asked, but then my eyes narrowed. There was a bruise on the side of his head I had not noticed the night before. "Do not tell me you have already had to fend off some violent cur?"

He touched a finger lightly to the mark, as though reminding himself it was there. "Oh, this? It's nothing, really."

"Come sit with me a while. I still have many questions for you, and that is only one of them."

He pushed the door open a little wider, nudging a brick doorstop into place for the sake of propriety. Sometimes, I felt enslaved to it. I wished nothing more than to shut the door and speak candidly, but that was not an option.

He limped over to Mrs. Perry's abandoned chair, dragging it a little closer to the bed and sinking into it. "Well. What can I do for you?"

"Tell me how it is you came to my rescue, just in the nick of time. Colleen said you arrived in town not long after she did."

"Well, for that, I need to explain this," he said, pointing to the bruise.

"It was...two days ago? Has it only been two days?" he wondered aloud, then shook his head in disbelief. "Yes, I think it was only two days.

"I was making sure everything was running smoothly, per your instructions. I met with Mr. Purcell regarding the transfer of your papers from Mr. Coolidge's office. We've been working on building a case against Mr. Coolidge and Mr. Richardson. Mrs. Perry was able to uncover some very interesting information regarding some of Mr. Coolidge's clients."

"I don't understand. Mr. Coolidge represents the top of Buffalo society." To be fair, Buffalo society wasn't much compared to New York or Boston or Philadelphia; Gunther Richardson and my husband—now myself—occupied the top spaces on a comparatively short list.

"It seems in the past few years there have been some disputes over wills. A few of his former clients have claimed the documents he has on record do not match the ones they are in possession of."

"Let me guess—suspiciously large donations to Talbert House?"

"Among other things. The mentions of Talbert House only got back a few years—it is a new facility. But before that, there were hospitals and charitable organizations in New York City, Albany, Rochester, and Hartford. Mrs. Perry is still waiting to hear back from her contacts in that city, but it would appear at least one of the wills is a forgery. It turns out one of his clerks is quite the dab hand with a pen and brush."

"And it's taken until now to catch him?"

"As I said, we are still uncovering more information, but it appears he was very selective in the wills he chose to alter, and very specific in the changes."

"It's a wonder then, he didn't change James's will."

"Did Captain Andrews change his will before he left?"

"He did."

"I think—and this is pure conjecture— Mr. Richardson, frustrated by his failed attempts, failed to give Mr. Coolidge the proper warning to make the changes. Unaware the captain had made changes prior to his departure, he assumed the status quo would not change."

"He tried to keep me away from the reading," I remembered. "He changed the time. It was only by coincidence I managed to be there at all."

"Then perhaps he planned to discuss the necessary changes with his partners."

I stared at him, open mouthed. "With the entire board of R&A?"

"If, by chance, Coolidge managed to warn them— too late to make the changes, but perhaps with enough time to gather the necessary people—they could have planned what their next move would be, how they wanted to approach things. Of course, they couldn't do that with you in the room."

My head was spinning with this revelation. Were there really so few people I could trust?

"We are getting off topic. You promised to tell me the story of that injury."

"And so I shall. I'm getting there.

"I left Mr. Perry to keep an eye on the household, just in case. I convinced Mrs. Angela Andrews that a man-of-all-work would be a good investment for them. They have a lovely house, but the children are rather hard on it." He chuckled slightly and I smiled. I was very familiar with the gouges in the parlor floor, the nick in the banister, all of the damage rambunctious boys can make in an unsuspecting house.

"Has there been any word from Olivia?" I asked desperately.

"You have some letters waiting for you, and she did write to her aunts. She did write to me once. She's worried about you. We all were. We had no letters—"

"He destroyed them—oh, goodness—did Colleen tell you about him? The man with the scar? He was running errands—"

He placed a calming hand on mine. "Yes, I heard. But I have more to tell as well, and he features very prominently in this tale.

"As I said, I left Mr. Perry to keep an eye on the rest of the family, just in case. I went with Mrs. Perry in the morning to interview Mr. Richardson. This was not long after the discovery of Mr. Coolidge's duplicity.

"We saw him around eleven o'clock. Mrs. Perry was sharp as a tack in her questions. Remind me to never be on her bad side. It was clear we were making Richardson uncomfortable, to the point he threw us out of his office.

"At some point in the conversation, however, it came out I had been with your husband at the time of his attack. This was just before he finally lost his temper.

"He must have realized I was a liability then, for when I returned to my boarding house for dinner, the man with the scar was waiting for me. I nearly met the same fate as your husband, though I did sacrifice that lovely top hat you gave me to the cause. It took a bullet when I leaped out of the way.

"Of course, I recognized him immediately, and was more than willing to repay him for his own treatment of me in Washington. I don't think he was expecting a cripple to put up quite such a good fight, but I have had three months to imagine how I might be revenged upon him.

"In the middle of the fisticuffs, Mrs. Perry arrived and put her pistol to his head as coolly as if asking for the time. He did attempt to fight back, and in the end he escaped, but not before I left a bruise of my own, though unfortunately I snapped my favorite cane in half in the process."

"He came back here, then. Colleen saw him destroying the mail just last night. Two nights ago, I mean."

"He came here intending to go to ground. It's a secluded area where he might find work; we think he has been going back and forth between Talbert House and R&A, acting as messenger and muscle for whichever brother needs him.

"We narrowly missed him at the depot. Mrs. Perry wired ahead, but there was a line down. With all that had been uncovered, I feared that you were in great danger, but we had to wait for the next train south. We were more than halfway to Great Valley when the snow made the tracks impassible. We were delayed for several hours until they could be cleared. While we were stuck at the station, Mrs. Perry managed to send a cable to the local police, but of course they could do nothing because of the storm. It wasn't until morning that we reached town, and then it was hours before we managed to get organized. Mrs. Perry had a bit of a disagreement with local law enforcement, and had to draw on some of her Pinkerton contacts before they would believe there was cause for alarm. And of course, the roads being what they were added to the difficulty.

"Around ten o'clock, Colleen came bursting in, shouting for the police, because someone was trying to kill her employer. Finally, that got things in motion from the local authorities, and we were able to go out. I was afraid we would be too late."

"No. Thankfully, you were just in time." He was still holding my hand and I gave it a squeeze.

He cupped my hand in both of his, and raised it to his lips. "I am thankful for that," he whispered hoarsely.

epilogue

June, 1866

Spring, as always, was reluctant to come to Buffalo, but at last the snow finally melted.

After such an eventful winter, I was more than happy to move my household to our summer residence, Buckingham. Agnes, Angela, Brigid and the children joined Olivia and I in the country. I still woke up at night, convinced I was trapped inside the coffin again, buried alive, but after a few weeks I could sleep alone again and Colleen was able to remove her cot and go back to her own room.

Though I continued to dream of James on and off, it was only my first night back at Clinton Street that he visited me as I slept. No longer divided by an open grave, he stood beside me, looking out on the lake. He never said a word, only handed me a white rose and kissed me tenderly on the cheek.

Mr. Richardson and Mr. Coolidge managed to avoid arrest, though Mr. Coolidge officially retired from the law. The future of the company hung in the balance as we sued and counter-sued each other, and the criminal investigation continued, peeling back more and deeper layers of depravity as one by one the employees of Talbert House began to confess the various acts they had been privy to.

With nowhere else to go, many of the patients were sent to other hospitals or back to their families. Mrs. Hurst, who had no family save the daughter and son-in-law still being investigated, flat out refused to return home. She came to Buckingham as my guest.

"They're here!" called Kevin, running down the drive towards the house, kicking up gravel beneath the heels of his good shoes.

"Well, get inside then and let everyone else know!" I laughed, shooing my nephew in the front door. I waited with my parasol for the carriage to pull up.

Two footmen jumped down and unloaded the wheeled chair from where it was hitched to the back of the carriage, and then helped Mr. Morton down into it. Julia Price followed a moment later, taking charge of her patient and fiancé.

"Welcome! At last!" I opened my arms wide to them, embracing Julia like a sister and offering a hand to Mr. Morton, who placed a kiss on my knuckles. The staff were already waiting to carry away their things. "Julia, this is Maggie. She'll be taking care of you for your stay. She'll show you where you can change. And Mr. Morton, this is Henry. He'll make sure you have absolutely everything you need." Henry was that remarkable combination of brawny broad shoulders and absolute discretion. I'd had a special lift installed—based on one of James's designs—which would allow Mr. Morton to access the second floor, where all of the bedrooms were. Henry was the only one strong enough to work it with an actual human being on board.

"Your room is this way!" Kevin said, appearing at my elbow with one of his little sisters in tow. Mr. Morton greeted her with a broad grin. She squealed happily and climbed up onto his lap. The wheeled chair was still something of a novelty to the children, and they took great pleasure in taking Mr. Morton wherever he needed to go, though Molly and Brianna were the only ones still small enough to hitch rides on Mr. Morton's lap.

Michael and Brianna burst out of the house, Brianna trailing flowers from her basket behind her. "What are you doing?" I laughed. "There won't be any left for the ceremony if you keep that up!"

Brianna giggled, spinning around in a circle and spilling the remainder of her flowers onto the gravel. Julia laughed and took her hand. "Come on. Let's go pick some more and then you can help me put on my dress. Should we put daisies or violets in my hair?"

"Violets!" Brianna shouted, pulling her towards the back garden where the tent had already been set up for the ceremony.

I retreated back into the cool shade of the entryway. While the house on Clinton Street was homey and snug, the summer house was truly palatial by comparison, inspiring Olivia to name it after the British palace. The entryway had marble floors of blue and green, and a fountain of a mermaid in an upturned shell between mirrored staircases that curved up and around. There were frescoes on the ceiling and every inch of woodwork was carved and ornamented.

It didn't feel like home, but it felt safe and comfortable. It felt like a new start, especially filled to the brim with friends and family.

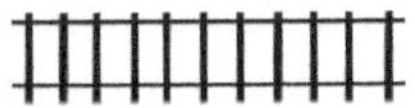

I swayed in time to the music, watching the

couples waltz across the grass under the tent.
Darkness had fallen, lanterns had been lit. Cake had
been sliced, and of course, a lovely couple had been
married. Mr. Morton, of course, could not dance;
instead, he played his violin with the other musicians,
while the new Mrs. Morton sang along in a clear,
bell-like voice I would not have credited her with.

Mary Lou and Olivia were both dancing with
relations of the bride, while Angela danced with a tall
gentleman in a crisp blue army uniform with a blush
on her cheeks that more than just the wine could be
attributed to.

I smiled, glancing up with a froth of pink lace
floated down beside me.

Olivia Baxter snapped open her fan, vigorously
waving it in front of her red face. "Oh, I do love to
dance. I'm so glad you invited me."

"I'm only happy you could come. And where is
Mr. Baxter?"

"Oh, he's around here, somewhere. I sent him to
get some punch. He's been having a very animated
conversation with your Mr. Hamilton about
investments and financing. It seems you may have a
new backer for that expansion you were discussing."
She waggled her eyebrows conspiratorially, and I
laughed.

"Well, we'll be happy for it. Whether we win the
government bid or not, the railroad will continue west
either way."

"Oh, that reminds me." Olivia put down her fan
just long enough to reach into her reticule. She
produced a folded piece of paper and handed it to me.

I opened it. It was the drawing of the Gatling gun,

the one I'd secretly mailed to her for safe keeping all those months ago.

"What is it? You never did tell me."

I studied the drawing. "It's a fire starter," I said finally. Whatever the future of R&A, it would be made by improving lives—not taking them.

Olivia snapped her fan open again. "Seems an awful lot of fuss for a fire starter." Her eyes flicked over my shoulder before I could contradict her. She smiled broadly, and hurried to vacate her seat. "We'll talk more later, dear!" she said over her shoulder, twirling away and intercepting her husband, leading him in the direction of the cake and out of earshot.

"I would ask you to dance, but I'm afraid I'm a little out of step these days," Mr. Hamilton said, helping himself to the seat beside me.

"That's all right. I've always had two left feet, anyway. James always teased that I spent so much time planning parties so I wouldn't have to dance at them. I'd likely ruin your other leg if you took me on the dancefloor."

He laughed. After a pause, he nodded to the newlyweds. "They are a lovely couple."

"Indeed. I can't think of two people more deserving of happiness."

"I can think of one that might qualify."

I tore my eyes from the dancers to look at him properly. "My goodness! Mr. Hamilton! Your beard." I'd been so busy I hadn't seen him all day.

He rubbed at his bare chin. Without the furry covering, his face looked even more boyish than usual. "Yes. I thought perhaps it was time. The beard was fine for winter, but I don't like it so well in the summer."

"Well, I approve."

"Yes, a little bird told me that you aren't fond of facial hair."

I pretended I was not blushing and wondered if it was Colleen or Olivia that had let it slip. James had once toyed with the idea of mutton chops or even a full beard, which I heartily discouraged.

"If I want to kiss something with that much hair on it, I'll get a dog," I'd told him.

His only response was to laugh and an attempt to lick my cheek, but the mention of facial hair was never made again.

"It's good to see you in something other than black."

Technically, I was still in mourning, but white was acceptable for the summer months. My light muslin gown was striped with black, with beaded lace trim of ebony. I had, however, taken a page from Mrs. Hurst's book in honor of the occasion and added three small red rosebuds to the crown of my straw hat, which had a black silk band, and replaced the jet buttons on my gloves with red ones. It was the only color I'd worn in months, and was likely to wear until at least the end of the year.

"I hope...I hope it is not seen as improper for me to bring a gift?"

I jumped at the change of subject. "Oh, of course not. We have been placing the gifts on that table there," I said, nodding in the direction of the heaping table in the corner.

"I meant for the hostess."

I turned to look at him again. He offered me a

white rose, tied with a red satin ribbon.

It was not until I took the stem in my hand that I realized it was not truly a rose at all, but a mere carving of one. I leaned closer to the candle on our table to get a better look. "Did you make this?" I asked in wonder. It was so lifelike, from the irregularity of the stem to the perfect curve of every delicate petal. It could have been picked straight from the garden.

"I did."

"It's magnificent." I turned it over in my hands. The paint was so smooth I could not find a single brush stroke.

"Thank you."

"A white rose. A peace rose." I held it up again. It was a strange color to choose for a gift for a friend.

The smile that had once been hidden behind his beard pulled at the corners of his mouth. "Yellow did not seem right, though we are, I hope, everlasting friends, and red…red seemed too forward."

I glanced at him over the petals. I half expected them to have a fragrance. "And white…?"

"I hope, after the trials you have suffered, that if I do nothing else, I might bring you some peace."

I twirled the flower between my fingertips, remembering a dream I'd had after my return from Talbert House.

A white rose. A peace rose. *Síomha Róisín.*

I wondered if James had told him, or if it was something he had uncovered during the course of his work for me. Or if he even knew at all.

I thanked him and set the flower down between us, turning back to the dancers.

"If there is one thing I can say you have done for me, Mr. Hamilton, it is that."

about sine peril

Sìne (pronounced SHEE-nah) is the author of historical fantasy and horror for adult and YA audiences. Growing up isolated in rural Ohio, her childhood would not have been out of place as the plot for a Gothic novel, and provided the perfect backdrop for a developing author.

With a degree in fine art and art conservation, Sìne has a slight obsession with history, costumes, and historical fiction. In her spare time, she volunteers as a living history interpreter, where she specializes in women's rights in the late 1800s and accidentally terrifying small children with ghost stories.

Her favorite thing about writing historical fiction—and alternate history—is examining the way attitudes and people don't really change over the course of centuries, even if technology does.

Sìne lives with her partner in crime and five little beasties that *might* be cats, or maybe just very fluffy genetic experiments gone wrong. She also writes urban fantasy and YA contemporary fiction under the name Sophia Beaumont.

Find Sìne/Sophia online:
Socials: @Knotmagick
Website: http://www.knotmagickknitter.com
Ko-Fi: Ko-Fi.com/KnotMagick
Youtube: Youtube.com/@SinePeril

If you enjoyed *Off the Rails*, please consider telling others and writing a review.

Other books by Sìne Peril
By the Grace
Colors in the Dark

Books by Sophia Beaumont
The Evie Cappelli series:
The Spider's Web
The Ferrymen
Moreau House
The Night Wars Collection (with Missouri Dalton)
Bind Off: The Evie Cappelli Bind Up Omnibus

Other books by Sophia Beaumont:
All for One
Dru Faust and the Devil's Due